# DIAL

# M

# FOR

# MERLOT

Howard K

Interior format by The Killion Group
http://thekilliongroupinc.com

*Dedicated to the memory of my dear friend and mentor Franz Bartzsch; talented composer, musical brother, French wine and food lover. I miss you.*

# ACKNOWLEDGEMENTS

Extra special thanks to writer and friend Marilyn Baron, without whom this book would most likely never have been completed. Her guidance, enthusiasm and constant hand-holding provided me with all of the support this first-time author needed to turn the glimmer of an idea into a coherent, flowing story.

Thanks to Sharon and Maya Goldman for their creative, eye-catching cover design. I'm still wondering what the wine in that bottle tastes like!

Cudos to Scott Oliver at PagesOnly.com for his outstanding website design, internet wizardry, video savvy and his 'hollow leg' in helping me empty many bottles of outstanding Bordeaux.

Thank you to Ally Robertson for her long hours and wonderful work in editing the book and massaging it into its final form— and for her patience in "taking me to school."

And finally, thank you to my lovely wife Patricia and my wonderful sons Aaron and Alex, and to all of my family and dear friends, for being my eternal fountain of love and happiness.

# A SPECIAL THANK YOU TO MY
# KICKSTARTER SUPPORTERS

This book was self published with the help of the many generous souls that participated in my Kickstarter Fundraising drive and made it a success. Your outpouring of support, backing and enthusiasm has left me completely humbled and speechless. That's a first! Thanks to all of you once again for helping me to reach my goal and realize a dream, and especially to my "heavy hitters":

Andy de Ganahl

Anita Kleinfeld

Jill Lonstein

Gloria Litwin and Norman Wemhoener

Cynthia and Gary Lubben

Marc I. Sachs

Ingrid and Michael Moynihan

Barb and Jeff Browder

Karen and Brad Trumbull

Andrew Jacobson

Sherry and Scott Mittleman

Belinda Wicksteed and Eduardo Iborra Vicente

Janet and Scott Oliver, PagesOnly.com

Nadia and Bertrand Ollier, Tampa Bay Grand Prix

Diane and Mark Daley

Coleen and Garry Brady, The Wine Shops

Mike Kwasin, Fine Wine and Spirits Warehouse

John Larkin

Patrick Montlary

Dr. Ronald Walsh

Priscilla Hechler

Phyllis Eig

Lori and Bryan Hughes

Stuart Dornfield

Bill Carter, Carter and Company

Linzi and Mike Matthews

Phyllis and Barry Eagle

# CHAPTER ONE

Justin James felt the pounding in his head even before he fully regained consciousness. When he finally succeeded in prying open his hangover-heavy eyelids, the room slowly came into a blurred, topsy-turvy view of unreality.

The soft light filtering through the yellowed linen curtains suggested a peaceful post-dawn morning, but the foul taste in his mouth and the fire bubbling up in the back of his throat screamed midnight in Hell.

He slowly propped himself up on one shaky elbow and tried to rub the pain out of his brain. That wasn't working too well. He resumed crash position and massaged his throbbing temples, struggling to remember just how he had gotten back to the house after what must have been a very long night of wine-fueled debauchery.

Yesterday evening had started on a remarkably high note; attending an invitation-only wine tasting and dinner at one of the most renowned châteaus in all of France. The gigantic, but elegant, gala was co-sponsored by the largest, most powerful wine distributor in North America—the Richard Fox Company, along with its French counterpart, Beverage DeBussey.

It was the *Célébration de Vin*, an event held only once every ten years, and yet, Justin and his traveling companions managed to wrangle admission. They weren't a particularly well-connected group of important movers and shakers in the wine industry, just a small band of vino tourists on-the-loose in France for a little fine living and some excessive wine drinking, during the week of the Vin Expo trade show in Bordeaux. Their names were nowhere on the guest list. But no matter.

Right place, right time, a little language barrier misunderstanding, and *voila*—admittance into the wine party of the decade. In some corners of the world that would be called *chutzpah*, but as some pissed-off Frenchman would later remark, "Those American bastards had some big balls." Big balls, indeed.

So there they were—rubbing elbows with some of the most well-known figures in the world of wine, all of whom Justin had never even heard of until a few months back. He watched as the guys spread out into the main tasting room, standing side-by-side with some of the rich, famous, and beautiful people he had read about here and there, but never dreamed of actually seeing in person, let alone tasting outrageously expensive wines with and then discussing their marvelous attributes. Mind blowing. Really. Mind blowing.

Yes, it had started out as a wine enthusiast's night-of-a-lifetime, but something had gone awry. Between the pounding, the bubbling, and a fair amount of spinning, he couldn't remember much of what had happened after those first few minutes at the Grand Tasting. How had he wound up back in his bed, wearing clothing he didn't recognize, with a half-empty to-go box of some sort of disgusting French version of KFC planted next to his head on the pillow?

And where were the guys? He should have at least heard them snoring their brains out in the adjacent bedrooms of their rental house, but strangely, he heard … nothing. If he hadn't been in France on a vino-expedition, he might have vowed never to drink again.

Being a novice wino was hard work.

# CHAPTER TWO

*Six Months Earlier, Orlando, USA*

It had been another long week in cubicle-land and Justin James was looking forward to this evening. Tonight was going to be date number two with a woman he had met only a few weeks before, and he had a really good feeling about this one. He always had a good feeling about date number two. The problem was getting to date number three and beyond, something that had last happened, well…never.

On that late Friday afternoon, as he left the FedEx building where he had worked as a shipping manifest controller for the past seven years, he caught a glimpse of his reflection in the double-paned glass of the entryway doors. He was just shy of six feet tall, clean shaven, thin and trim, with a full head of longish, almost wild coal black hair that framed his intensely bright, blue eyes.

*Looking good. This time, I just might get to date number three.* Based on past performance, a less positive or more realistic person might have thought otherwise, but in his heart, Justin believed it.

His natural assets and good-natured—but naïve—self-confidence notwithstanding, most of the time he looked like the conservative number-crunching nerd he was. Perhaps it was his mix and match collection of well-worn, wash-faded T-shirts with the oddly paraphrased *Star Trek* quotations emblazoned across the front of each: "Kiss me, I'm Vulcan," "I Like Big Photons," "I am Klingon, Hear me Roar," etc. Outside of his blue FedEx work outfit, his everyday attire T-collection paired perfectly with his high-water Khaki pants and odd-colored shoes.

Or maybe it was the fact that he actually bought those shirts at a "Trekkie" convention, one of a handful of Sci-Fi Comic Con events he had attended. All by his lonesome. Outside of work, he didn't have many—any?—friends, and none of his coworkers shared his passion for what one of them had termed "total geek-i-tude."

But he was actually a highly valued member of his team, THE go-to-guy for resolving any problems and discrepancies with his office inventory schedules. As the resident math wizard—and he *really* liked that term—he had an uncanny ability to look at a mind-numbing spreadsheet, see past the numbers and find errors on the fly.

His superiors noticed him and let him know that he was in line for bigger things. His colleagues respected and liked him, and he had an open invitation to the weekly Wednesday beer and darts night at a nearby Irish pub, which he never attended.

But his general likeability and skills didn't stop any of them from constantly ribbing him about the assortment of Star Wars, Harry Potter, and Spiderman action figures lining one of the shelves of his workspace. "Dude, how many Yodas do you NEED?" Last year, for his birthday, his coworkers chipped in and bought him a Day-Glo green "The Geek Shall Inherit the Earth" T-shirt.

And, at some point during the recent season's office Christmas party, someone had rearranged his toy menagerie so that when he showed up for work the following Monday, he was treated to a plastic action-figure orgy scene, complete with Harry getting Pottered by Chewbacca the Wookie and Princess Leia performing magic on Dumbledore's wand.

"Yeah, yeah, okay you guys," Justin said, brushing it off as a harmless, drunken prank. But the sad reality was that his encounter with the perverted plastic porno parade was the only remotely sexual activity he had been involved with in...forever.

All kidding and self-pity about the fact that C3PO was getting more than he was aside, it had gotten his thoughts going down a path he seldom followed. At thirty years old, it seemed he was devolving into a solitary little mouse stuck in a drab, grey maze, repeating the same actions over and over again for a tiny morsel of cheese as the only reward for his troubles. And, he didn't even like cheese.

While he drove the short distance from the FedEx office to the small cottage-like house he'd inherited from his aunt, his thoughts drifted to his current state of affairs, or lack there-of. It wasn't as if he was completely unhappy. Things were going exactly as planned, and life was generally good.

Once home and inside the cozy living room, he took a minute to check the water level in the bubbling fish tank. Its former residents, his aunt's pet fish Skipper and Gilligan, named for her favorite characters from one of the many old sitcoms they had watched together through the years, were long gone, but he couldn't bring himself to shut it down. The house still looked exactly as it had when he was growing up, and although his Aunt Annette had passed away more than two years ago, he had no plans to change a thing. He just wasn't ready.

He still slept in the same room, leaving the much larger master bedroom, his aunt's room, untouched and intact. All of her clothing, her books and pictures, all of her life's artifacts remained. Somehow, it made him feel as though she was still with him, watching over him, helping him to make the important decisions and plans that had shaped his life into the future he was now living. His aunt. Mother and father rolled into one. Love squared. Subtracted from his world by one of life's most simple and cruel equations.

He entered his closet-sized bedroom, rifled through his very orderly wardrobe and found what he was looking for. He quickly changed into his favorite and most formal shirt—a sporty, black, Ralph Lauren Polo, the only designer label item of apparel he owned. He remembered a few years back, when Aunt Annette had given it to him for his birthday. She had told him that it made him look "dashing and sexy," and he might have been, too…as long as you ignored the off-pink deck shoes and brown corduroy pants he chose to wear with it for his big night out. He splashed on a little Old Spice, and was out the door.

# CHAPTER THREE

As usual at eight o'clock on a Friday night, The Bonefish Grill was packed with patrons welcoming in the weekend, and the air was thick with loud, post happy-hour conversation, laughter, and the delicious aroma of wood-fire grilled seafood. It was a good ambience. The perfect backdrop for a fun second date.

But there was something else swirling in the air. Anticipation. Who knew where tonight would lead? Always the optimist, Justin was positive things would go well and that he might finally have met someone that would "get him." He usually managed to say or do the wrong thing at the wrong time, but he promised himself he would be extra vigilant this evening, and keep his "anti fuck-up filter" on alert.

After he collected his seating pager, he sat watching the door for Karen. Two weeks ago, they had gone to see the latest big budget blockbuster remake of *Superman*, and while the film had been well done and enjoyable, a stop afterwards at a small bistro had been the highlight.

Karen ordered a glass of white wine and, because he never drank, Justin went for a café macchiato. The bistro was crowded and a bit understaffed, so they had to wait a while for the drinks to arrive. But he was glad to have a few extra minutes of face time with her. She was cute, funny, and easy to talk to. And she seemed to have a healthy interest in Sci-Fi. Perfect.

Best of all, he found that he wasn't feeling any of his normal self-conscious nervousness around the opposite sex. When the server finally returned with their order, they toasted to Gene

Roddenberry, George Lucas, and J.K. Rowling. His coffee was sweet, warm and fragrant—like her.

When he got back home that night, he felt he had really made a connection with a kindred spirit, and over the last ten days or so, they had exchanged texts and made their plans for this evening. He was beyond pumped.

When the pager went off and stirred him out of his reverie, he realized he had been waiting for almost forty- five minutes and Karen had still not arrived. He approached the host at the stand and asked him to hold the table for a few minutes while he sent a quick text. *Hi Karen. At the Bonefish. Table ready. What's your ETA? Hope you didn't forget!! lol! J*

Five minutes later, as he walked out of the Bonefish Grill, he read the response for the third time: *Hi Justin. Sorry, I did forget... just got back together with my boyfriend and we're in line to see the final Harry Potter. Hope U have a nice life. K.*

Shoulda seen that one coming...

# CHAPTER FOUR

He wasn't exactly sure why he always crashed on romantic take-off, but for whatever reason, he always did. At least he was consistent. Aunt Annette had always said that consistency was one of the building blocks of a good character. How nice...the award for Mr. Congeniality goes to Justin James... also voted most likely to never-get-laid. The emergency condom he carried in his wallet was so old it had partially fossilized. At this rate, he would never need to replace it.

He walked through the well-lit parking lot that the restaurant shared with a small shopping plaza, searching for his aunt's old beater. It was hard to miss; the ancient, metallic burnt-orange Buick Electra's fading and pock-marked paint-job looked like a five-day-old slice of pepperoni pizza with most of the meat plucked off.

When he reached for the door handle, a wave of anxiety crashed into him like a blast from a Romulan disruptor. Suddenly, he was the sorry, solitary mouse trapped in a gigantic maze of his own making, with walls as thick and high as a Medieval castle. And he was never, ever going to get out. He could even feel his little, pink mouse nose twitching and his tiny whiskers tickling his cheeks. The sound of his mini mouse heart was pounding in his ears like a bass drum beating double-time in a heavy metal song.

It took him a moment to snap out of it and realize that what he felt on his face were the first raindrops of a potentially torrential downpour and the thundering in his ears was actually...thunder. Since the windshield wipers didn't work and the driver's side window was stuck halfway down, instead of getting soaked and possibly driving into a telephone pole, he decided he'd be better off waiting out the storm at the shopping plaza. He barely made it to the covered walkway in front of the shops as the deluge began.

He really didn't want to take a trip to negative Never-never Land, but he'd just had his ticket punched. Again. Where was all of the real fun and excitement he thought he'd be having at this point in his life? And what the hell was real fun and excitement, anyway? How about some up close and personal examination of the female anatomy? He was definitely going to the Honda dealer tomorrow morning and start looking for that new ride. Maybe that would help get things started. Maybe.

Back in high school, he had been interested in traveling and seeing the world. He had even studied a foreign language in preparation for the senior trip to Europe. It had been exciting, looking forward to visiting those faraway places with the strange sounding names. And, he had never thought he would do well in a subject other than math. That had been a revelation! But the trip had never happened, at least for Justin. One month before graduation, the sponsors had backed out of their co-funding commitments, and his aunt just didn't have the cash to make up the difference.

So he had never gone there, or anywhere else that he could recall, either. One of these days, maybe he'd go on a trip that would take him beyond some tacky hotel ballroom filled with a motley collection of fellow geeks dressed up in ridiculous fantasy costumes. Someplace in the real world, full of average, everyday souls experiencing life as it was and not viewing it through the eye-holes of an old, tired Klingon mask.

He walked past the small, closed–for–the night shops, and they all seemed as dead and empty as his love life. With the wind kicking up, the downpour played staccato sixteenth notes on the pavement. He loved that sound. And he loved the smell of the rain. There was always something special about the simplicity and goodness of that all-natural scent. It was comforting, calming, reassuring. Like his Aunt Annette— forever urging him to look to the future and ignore the disturbing past. He'd always trusted and closely followed her advice, and taking that thought to heart, he instantly felt better about his prospects. And maybe, just maybe, it was time for a new car. Perhaps something exciting, like a Prius or a Civic.

Lost in his thoughts, Justin slowly walked toward the end of the row of shops. The night had grown fully dark by now, so he couldn't look up for a break in the clouds or tell how much longer his wait would be. Shouldn't be too long. And in any case, he would still get soaked because of the jammed-open driver's side window. He'd give it another five minutes and then head home. It would have to be yet another in his never ending series of early weekend nights. At least he was consistent.

Turning the corner and approaching the last shop, unlike all the others it was alive, brightly lit and full of smiling, vibrant people. He looked through the non-descript storefront window. The crowd stood in small, close-knit groups, or waited in front of three or four low tables that were set up between rows of display racks.

A small sign posted in the window next to the entry read, *"Tasting Tonight! 8 p.m.-10 p.m. $10. Featuring the wines of the Rhone Valley."* The wine shop was named "In Vino Veritas," and with its dusty and ancient-looking décor, it looked like it must have been there for a very long time. Not being at all interested in any kind of alcoholic beverages, or in collecting anything other than kitschy Sci-Fi figurines, Justin had never noticed it before.

He turned around to head back to the car, but something on the wall inside caught his eye and made him stop; a large relief map of France, very much like one that had hung on the wall in his high school French class. He also remembered the pretty Asian exchange student that had sat next to him and had been his conversation-drill partner.

*Liberté, Egalité, Fraternité...*that was one of their first language drills, and one they repeated every class period. She was beautiful, delicate and already fluent in French and was probably the only reason he had done so well in the class. The memory made him smile. But that was ancient history, and now, he couldn't even recall her name.

Inside, a man in a purple Polo shirt noticed him looking in and pulled the door open.

"Hey you," he said in a friendly, but emphatic way. "Why not come in out of the rain and have a glass of wine?"

Surprised, Justin quickly explained he didn't really drink, wine wasn't his thing, etc., etc. But the man wouldn't be denied and, with a knowing grin, pressed on.

"Well, let me ask you a question, and I don't mean to get too personal here, but have you ever tasted a great or even good wine? Would you be able to tell the difference?"

Justin had to admit that the answer to these direct, disarming and challenging questions was a definitive *No*. And as he said it, he also had to admit to himself that there was way too much *No* in his life already. On an almost spiritual level, Life had said *No* to him far too often; taking his aunt from him much too soon, preventing him from ever knowing his parents, cursing him with his social ineptitude and inherent "nerdliness." There were so many things he might never try or experience if he didn't personally say *Yes* to some of those variables in life that were actually within his power to control.

"Then you don't know what you're missing, do you?" said the man, his smile revealing a purplish tint on his teeth.

"I guess I really don't." *And I might never know.*

"Well here's a life-changing offer for you young man; this is my shop, so come in, grab a glass, and I'll waive the tasting fee. Whaddya say? And by the way—tell me your name so I can introduce you to your new best friends!"

"My name is Justin James...and I say *Yes*."

# CHAPTER FIVE

The proprietor, Brad Garrison, was a well maintained fifty–something with an air of good-natured mischief about him. His sandy brown hair and fair green eyes accented an open, friendly face that was remarkably free of wrinkles, crow's feet or any other major signs of aging. He walked Justin past a number of wine racks filled with dozens of bottles and back to the counter where a few unused glasses remained.

He slid behind the counter, typed something into the computer/cash register and said, "The only price of admission for you tonight is your e-mail address and contact info for our mailing list."

Justin complied and was handed an elegant, long-stemmed wine glass.

Brad pointed to the bottom right quadrant of the map behind the counter that Justin had been eyeing from outside the shop and explained that they were tasting wines from the Rhone valley, where wine making dated back to Roman times.

"Are you ready to go to France?" he said excitedly, as is if they were actually getting ready to board the plane.

*This might be the closest I ever get,* Justin thought, as he followed Brad to the first table.

"This is Justin and tonight is his first time at a tasting," Brad said, as he introduced him to a few of the participants and the wine rep pouring at table number one. There were six bottles of white wine opened and lined up in a neat row on a white tablecloth, bracketed on each end by what looked like ice buckets. No ice, though.

"Those are for expectorating," the vendor said. Justin's expression must have shown he didn't have a clue as to what he was talking about.

"At a wine tasting," he explained, "you don't have to drink every drop that we pour for you. After sipping a bit, if you want you can empty your glass into one of these, and you can also, carefully, spit out what you haven't swallowed. It's all good and a smart way to keep from getting too tipsy, especially if you try all twenty-five wines that are open this evening."

Justin looked around the shop and didn't see anyone spitting their wine into a bucket. What he did notice was one tall, rather rotund, red-faced guy at another table swirling his glass around in the air, stuffing his nose into it and then loudly inhaling the aroma like an alcoholic asthmatic trying to get every last bit of juice out of his spent puffer. Justin thought it looked totally ridiculous.

"Pay no attention to the large man in the corner," said Brad in a *Wizard of Oz* voice. "That's just Frank *the Tank* doing his thing, in his own inimitable way." They both watched as Frank then took a taste of his red and began to violently swish it around in his mouth, his facial expression morphing between a look of exquisitely painful torture and orgasmic delight. He didn't spit, either.

"Is he sane?" Justin asked nervously.

"Not completely, but you'll get used to it." Brad had the wine-rep pour Justin his first sample of a Côtes du Rhone *blanc*.

"OK, young Mr. J, this is how we do it. Frank's method, like everything about him, is a bit extreme, but it is correct. First, we swirl the wine around in the glass to mix it with the air, noting its color and viscosity. Then we check the wine's "nose"– its bouquet and aroma and what that might tell us about its pedigree and potential. Then we slowly taste a bit, letting it fill our mouths with the essence of its *terroir* and palate-coating goodness. Cheers!"

That seemed like a lot of technique just to taste a simple beverage, and he didn't have a clue about the meaning of *terroir,* but Justin followed Brad's instructions, very carefully swirling, gently sniffing and slowly sipping. Then he did it all again. And again. He could taste the natural fruit flavors in the wine, but it really wasn't "grapey" or even sweet. *Interesting.* He methodically made his way through the next few wines thinking, *This actually tastes pretty good,* and *that's nice,* or *this one might be missing something* and even put some into one of the buckets here and there, to show good form.

After the vendor poured some of last white, Justin swirled his glass and inhaled "the nose." He instantly experienced heavenly aromas of thick, unctuous, peach, apricot and candied tropical fruits, all wrapped together by a divine, honeysuckle thread. It was unexpected. And unbelievable. Almost unconsciously, his head cocked to one side like a dog hearing an ultra-high-pitched whistle. And then, he howled.

"Whoa...what *IS THAT?*" he nearly shouted.

Brad had been chatting with some of the tasters at an adjacent table. He turned toward Justin, lifting his eyebrows as Justin stuck his nose back into his glass and then took a long, slow, almost sensuous sample of the wine's bouquet, finishing off with an animated sip. *It's beyond delicious.* He felt transported to some mystical, far-away place as an invisible five-hundred-watt light bulb flashed brilliantly over his head. Somewhere, a little kid hit a G on his toy xylophone...*ding.*

"Well, well," Brad remarked, returning to the white wine table, "I might have been wrong about you, Justin. It seems that you *can* tell the difference between a good and a great wine."

"I can?"

"You just did! The last white is called Condrieu, and it can be one of the most interesting and exotic-tasting wines in the world. As a matter of fact, this particular bottle is rated a "classic" by all of the most well-known wine gurus and reviewers. So, based on your excitement and enthusiasm, I would say that, yes, you definitely "get it." Well done, newbie, well done!"

Justin simply smiled and held out his glass. "Please sir, may I have some more?"

Brad shook his head. "We're moving onward and upward to the reds, and you, my friend, have an appointment with Destiny."

*Destiny? If I don't get something to eat, I might have an appointment with a major headache.*

Walking across the shop, Justin honed in on his surroundings and the tasting attendees. It was an older, well-heeled crowd, and the shop was humming with the happy sound of relaxed people engaging in and toasting to their passion. He was probably the youngest person there. Except for the wine rep pouring at the next table.

She was dressed in a short black skirt and a tight-fitting deep purple top made of some kind of soft, clingy, fabric. Justin's gaze was first drawn to the soft olive skin revealed by a major plunging neckline. That quickly led him into a deep valley surrounded by soaring mountain peaks. *Heavenly!*

After he caught his breath and made it past her Greek-Goddess-on-steroids body, he saw that her real beauty was revealed by dark, almost violet eyes, a perfectly proportioned aquiline nose, and rich, full lips that looked like they should be smiling up at the Mediterranean sun from beneath a stylish cabana umbrella on an exclusive island retreat. Her thick hair was a mass of impossibly curly black ringlets even more wild-looking than his own. *Breath-taking*! But how could this Mediterranean bombshell stand there for hours on those sexy little stiletto heels?

Lined up in front of Ms. Amazing at table two were six more bottles of wine, all reds this time, with one of the "overflow receptacles" standing alongside a carafe of water. Brad picked up the water and poured a bit into each of their glasses. "Swirl the water to clean your glass, and we'll start on the reds," he announced.

"Do we have a beginner in our midst?" asked the young Sofia Loren as she flashed a radiant smile.

"We do." Brad made the introduction. "Justin, this is Destiny Verrano, and she works for a big distributor. She knows a lot about wine, so if you have any questions, don't be afraid to ask her—she'll definitely have the answers. I'll be back soon to check on your progress."

While Brad walked to another table, he turned and discreetly shot Justin a sly, double raised-eyebrow Groucho Marx look. *Hunh? Oh.* Justin made a quick mental note to try and pretend to be someone else for the next few minutes and avoid any "geek speak" or potentially embarrassing comments about…anything.

# CHAPTER SIX

"So, you're a real blank slate, an unformed lump of clay that I can take in my hands and mold into whatever I'd like you to be?" Destiny said in a playful, teasing voice.

Normally, he would have melted into a quivering puddle of goo and oozed away, but somehow, he just managed to get out a response. "Yes," Justin droned in a zombie monotone. "I am a lump of clay." *This is going downhill way too fast...snap out of it!*

"All right then, Mr. Clay, try this wine first. It's a nice little Côtes du Rhone *rouge* from a producer named *Perrin.*"

Moving closer to the table and presenting his glass, he caught a hint of Destiny's perfume. It was a hot mix of spicy, musky sensuality. Far more irresistible and intoxicating than that last, *uber*-delicious white wine. After she poured an ounce or two for him, he repeated Brad's three-point tasting ritual: Swirl, Sniff, Taste.

"Wow, this is so surprising," he remarked. "This wine doesn't really taste like grapes at all. I mean, it's so different than I expected it to be. It *is* made from grapes, isn't it?"

After giving him a quizzical *"you're kidding me, right?"* look, she offered him a sample from the next bottle.

"This next wine is a Côtes du Rhone *Village* and it's a step up in quality. Tell me, since you're not getting "grapes," what do you taste in each wine? I'm always interested in knowing how people experience the different flavors in wine, especially someone with a virgin palate, like you."

A virgin *palate...if she only, really knew...*

He took another sip and slowly rolled it around in his mouth, trying to discern all of the competing flavors bouncing off of his teeth and tongue.

"This probably sounds really strange, but at first, I tasted a deep, peppery, almost raspberry flavor, and then, after I swallowed the wine, I got this earthy, rich black cherry fruit. How is that possible with something made entirely out of grapes?"

"Oh, you'd be *surprised* at the possibilities," Destiny replied in a soft, smoky voice. She reached for his glass, and her fingers brushed lightly against his hand. A hot flash coursed through his body and turned into small beads of sweat that left a prickling sensation all over his skin.

"Uh, possibilities?" he croaked.

"Of course, it really depends on the weather."

"Right," he said, as she poured a sample of wine number three.

*The weather. Where would I be tonight without the weather?*

Each of the following wines at Destiny's table were full of even more flavor variations. One was a deep ruby color and tasted of earth and minerals. The next had an astringent, drying bitterness that she told him was something called "tannin," but it still had an interesting, dark fruity bouquet and contained an almost leathery, tobacco note. But the star of the line-up was, once again, wine number six.

"What do you think about this one?" Destiny poured a bit for both of them. "It's from a part of the Rhone valley called Châteauneuf du Pape. "

Justin swirled the inky purple, almost black elixir in his glass and marveled as it coated the interior like just-poured maple syrup dripping down the side of a stack of Aunt Annette's world-class, buttermilk pancakes.

And smelling the wine provided Justin with another blast from the past. "Please don't think I'm weird, but I could swear that the nose of this wine smells eerily like my Aunt's Christmas Fruitcake."

"Weird? Now why would I think that you're weird just because you think a stunning Châteauneuf du Pape smells like fruitcake? As a matter of fact, I think I totally agree with you. It certainly does have something like that going on." Her voice trailed off as she took a small taste of the dark nectar.

*Score a BIG point for me!* He swirled again and then lifted the glass to his lips.

"But, I *would* say that your pink shoes with brown pants and a black shirt does qualify as weird. Or at least... offbeat."

*OUCH!* That stinging zinger dropped his pulse down a few beats per minute, blew his Italian mountain-climbing fantasy apart like a clay pigeon at a skeet shooting range, and brought him brusquely back to his reality of schlubby sexual solitude.

*I am who I am.* What else could he do or say? He took his taste of wine number six, heard a high-C chiming on that little kid's toy xylophone and then forgot what day it was.

This wine was different from the others. Although it started off with a similar hint of deep, dark cherry fruit, it had quickly morphed into a mouthful of intense black licorice, with a pinch of white pepper and some kind of Asian spice. As he set his glass down on the table and tried his best to focus on the flavor collage exploding in his mouth, the fruitcake he had gotten from the nose washed over him in a wave of tongue-coating sweetness and then disappeared down his throat. But he could still taste it. All of it. For, like, a full thirty seconds!

Destiny smiled as she watched him profoundly enjoying his first experience with a stellar red wine. She took his empty hand in hers and said in a throaty whisper, "I'm so glad that we could share this moment together," and added with a coy giggle, "You're not a virgin anymore!"

That stunned Justin even more than the abso-friggin-lutely unbelievable wine he just drank. She asked for his thoughts on the Châteauneuf, and he recounted his impressions, complete with the bit about the "exploding collage." She nodded approvingly.

"I am so impressed with your palate, Justin. You seem to have the ability to really focus in on the many diverse flavor aspects in such a complex wine, and give a surprisingly informed description about your experience. That's highly unusual for a newcomer to vino and even more than that, I find it very refreshing."

"Well, thanks…I…ah…" He didn't know what else to say.

She looked at him with an almost affectionate smile. "I hope you enjoyed my table…you *will* come back and see me next time? By the way, I *like* your offbeat pink shoes. They're the color of a nice rosé. Maybe we'll drink one together sometime!"

After promising her—and himself—that he would definitely attend the next tasting, he floated off to the next table.

There he found Brad talking with an older couple and kibitzing with another wine rep. They were all laughing at some sort of insider-humor wine pun. Justin didn't get it, but he *was* getting the wines, and that was cool!

"So, are you glad you accepted my offer to come in from out of the rain?" Brad asked, as he looked back in the direction of Destiny's table. "I've been keeping my eye on you." he quipped, with a Spock-like raised eyebrow.

Justin also looked in her direction. "Ohhhh yeah, I am very glad to be here. That is the most beautiful woman I have ever met!"

"Hey, forget the girl. I'm talking wine here. This is a wine shop, not a singles bar!"

Justin immediately apologized, naturally having said the wrong thing. "Oh, I mean, ah…sorry…yes… ah…the wines."

Brad cut him off with a hearty laugh, a nudge in the ribs and a sound clap on the back.

"It's all good, kid. Let's try this next group of reds."

They made their way through table three's line-up, with Brad explaining what village, town or sub-region each wine was from and then asking Justin for his "tasting notes."

He was really getting into it now, and he swirled and tasted his way through the six or seven bottles on the table, holding forth with his impressions of each: from *"seems simple and pleasant"* and *"really nice dark fruit with a touch of smoke and leather,"* to *"I'm puckering…is that tannin?"* and finally *"this is unbelievable… it's like some kind of black road tar flavor with a dark coffee chaser."*

Again and again, Brad mentioned that he couldn't believe Justin had zero experience with wine before this evening.

"It's uncanny," he said. "I have a very good to excellent palate. That's the ability to deeply and analytically taste a glass of wine and discern very specific characteristics about it, like its origin, what sort of grapes it contains, how long it's been aged in oak casks, if at all...things like that. I might even be able to make an educated guess about its pedigree and vintage, but it took me years to develop the kind of faculty that I think you may possess right now...on your first day in Wine 101."

"Really? I'm the man with the golden tongue?"

Brad shook his head and chuckled, "No, putz, you're the man with the pink shoes! Now, go and explore the last table. I've got to ring up some orders."

# CHAPTER SEVEN

As Justin tasted his way through the last group of wines, he again saw the almost larger-than-life Frank *the Tank*, this time on his way out the door. *Where have I seen that guy before?* He was followed by Brad, who was wheeling an overloaded hand truck stacked high with three or four cases of wine.

He finished up at the last table, tasting all, but pouring out most of the juice. He didn't want to get too buzzed. Feeling a small but pleasant glow from the alcohol, he realized he'd had a genuinely good time tonight, especially considering how things had started out at the Bonefish Grill.

Brad was cool, Destiny was hot, and while the whole experience of coming in out of the rain and embracing the unknown was totally out of character for him, for once, he felt comfortable with this group of strangers and, with himself.

And participating in a social event without having to wear a Klingon mask or talk to people dressed in ill-fitting Darth Vader or Borg Queen costumes was a big plus.

He glanced out of the front windows just in time to see one of the largest, most tasteless-looking passenger vehicles he had ever seen pull up in front of the shop. It was a radically oversized, bright yellow Hummer sporting all kinds of extra-large chrome piping and bumpers, along with a double rack of roof lights, all of which were on full-blast on and flashing. On the passenger-side panel was an almost mural-sized caricature of a large man dressed in a tuxedo, wearing a top hat and waving what looked to be a magic wand spewing fairy dust.

*Of course I've seen that guy before. Frank the Tank is Magic Murphy of Magic Murphy Auto Sales!*

When the rear hatch popped open and Brad began to load the cases into the Hummer, Frank Murphy appeared next to him and hoisted the last case into the car, slamming the hatch closed and giving Brad a quick back-patting man-hug as they said their goodbyes. Lights still flashing, the Hummer drove off into the night.

"Wow, Frank is Magic Murphy, and he's your customer!" Justin exclaimed, as Brad reentered the shop with the hand truck. "I've watched his wacky car commercials on TV for years."

"Oh yeah...he's one of my *best* customers, as well as being a longtime friend." Brad positioned himself behind the counter, ready to rake in some more cash from the now thinned-out crowd of wine enthusiasts. "So, what are *you* going to buy?"

Justin looked over the list of the wines he had tasted. His favorites of the night were almost all in excess of fifty dollars per bottle, with the incredible Châteauneuf du Pape commanding a price of just under one hundred dollars per bottle.

"I don't think I'm ready to spend that kind of money at my first wine tasting."

"Justin," Brad said with a smile. "Of course you don't have to buy anything, but because you seem to be so tuned-in to what to we all love about wine, I'd like to give you some things to take home with you tonight."

Brad got an empty wine box from behind the counter, walked over to one of the tasting tables and grabbed a couple of the unopened bottles that had been left there by the now departed Destiny.

"These two very good, but inexpensive Rhone reds are on me, and this, lucky boy, is from Destiny." He reached down to another open box and retrieved an interesting looking bottle that sported a warm pink hue. "It's a delicious rosé from Provence, and Destiny said for you to drink it while you're wearing those shoes, and nothing else but the shoes!"

"*Really?*" That left Justin completely speechless.

Brad dropped all three freebies into the box, along with a few rolled-up back issues of *The Wine Spectator* magazine.

"Read-up, drink-up and make sure to come back for the next tasting ...I'll email the details soon."

Justin could only smile and nod as he walked out of In Vino Veritas and into the parking lot.

He wasn't exactly sure how or why, but as he walked toward his car, he knew that, in some small but significant way, something in his life had changed. A corner had been turned, a wall had been scaled, a boundary breached. An obstacle overcome.

Saying *Yes* was good. Very good.

He hoped that the driver's seat of Aunt Annette's old Buick wouldn't be too wet and splash cold water all over his warm glow.

# CHAPTER EIGHT

*St Émilion, France*

"Slam the door in their faces, kick them off the property, run them over with a tractor, whatever... *I don't care!*" Guy DeBussey raged into the phone and forcefully slammed it down into its cradle. *Those God damned nuns. Why do they torment me so? Let them keep coming and begging for my money...*

He took a deep breath, a long taste, and a loving gaze into his expensive crystal Bordeaux glass, now only half full of a beautiful red wine from this year's astonishingly great vintage. He was going to be rich. Again.

Sinking down into the comfort of his favorite wing chair in the quiet, richly-appointed tasting room of his flagship estate, Château la Tour Noir, in the heart of the St. Émilion appellation, he took a moment to reflect on how good it was going to feel to finally be able to really stick it to everyone who had ridiculed and insulted him or belittled and discounted his intelligence and abilities.

Especially that American asshole, Cosmo Koulouris, whose company, Cosmo Brands, had always stood in the way of his achieving total, unequivocal success. Anyone who had called him, by turns, "The Dwarf in Dior" and "The Gorilla in Gaultier" deserved to be crushed like so many grapes in a harvest hopper.

He had been an outsider with no business or viticulture background, but over the last twenty years and from its lowest rung, he had worked his way up the wine trade's long and formidable ladder: from truck driver to vineyard worker, then to a stint as a grape picker and winemaking assistant. Soon after, he graduated to the front office and became an inexorable force in sales, marketing, planning, and eventually, management.

After a few successful years in the business he had come to the realization that he would never acquire the wealth he truly desired by merely selling wine. It seemed that in Bordeaux, and probably everywhere else in the world, the really big fish swam in a different pond: Real estate. So he hungrily plunged in.

Driven by a growing and insatiable need to conquer, manipulate and control, he built his empire step by step and deal by shady deal. Employing plenty of arm-twisting, threat making and some bone breaking, he overcame obstacles and objections and acquired property, people and their souls.

Vineyards. Wineries. Châteaux. Literally dozens of estates of all sizes and descriptions. Now it was all vertically integrated with his interests in trucking, shipping and delivery companies. And along the way he had become, arguably, the most despised figure in the French wine business. And he was good with that.

Very soon now, every lie he had told, every back he had stabbed, every friendly acquaintance he had turned into an enemy, each and every single thing he had stolen, robbed, fleeced or bamboozled would be made all-the-more worthwhile. Just after this coming summer's gigantic Vin Expo International trade show in Bordeaux, he would drop the hammer on his competitors, and his company, Beverage DeBussey, would become the largest and most important distributor of fine wine and spirits in France.

At forty-nine years old, he looked much as he had his entire adult life: short, squat, and swarthy. He knew most women considered him unattractive, with a bulbous balding head, a wide flat nose, thick lips and dark, cold, humorless eyes. If he had lived fifty thousand years ago and dressed in animal skins, he would have looked right at home sitting by the side of a Neanderthal campfire or making cave paintings in the famous prehistoric grotto at Lascaux.

And although he was fashionably dressed and reasonably well-groomed, his overall demeanor and coarse mannerisms never failed to project an almost peasant-like air of ignorance. Many had ridiculed him or mistaken his appearance for a lack of intelligence and savvy. This they did at their peril.

In truth, he had come to relish all of the negative notoriety he had received and actually got a deeply perverse sense of personal satisfaction and accomplishment in seeing his picture on the covers of various domestic and international trade magazines with captions like, "The Villain of *Vin*," or "The Megalomaniac of Merlot." Bruno, his factotum and head henchman, was tasked with keeping a large, leather-bound scrapbook full of press clippings, photos, Internet posts and all manner of "Guy fucks-over-the-world" stories.

In the very few sentimental moments that he allowed himself to enjoy, he would sit by the fire in this very room, paging through his well-worn book of golden memories, reliving his triumphs while sighing in contented bliss and sipping on a snifter of ancient cognac.

His favorite example of negative press was, by far, the scandalous episode that involved his recent purchase of fifty hectares of real estate in nearby Côtes de Castillon. It had made the front page of newspapers throughout France and earned him the title of "The St. Émilion Scrooge."

DeBussey possessed an almost supernatural, golden sixth sense for identifying prime investment opportunities where others saw nothing but a desolate, empty field with poor soil, a derelict vineyard in need of a multimillion Euro restoration or a worthless, used-up estate from long ago, and he almost always acquired his latest conquest for mere cents on the Euro.

And so it had been with this particular parcel. In fact, the land had never been used for any sort of farming at all. It was, however, occupied. For the last one hundred years or so it had played host to a small, ramshackle compound of buildings collectively known as Our Lady of Mercy Orphanage. Now an almost iconic institution in Southwest France, through the years it had housed, fed and clothed literally thousands of needy orphaned and underprivileged kids.

But Guy DeBussey, with his total lack of compassion for the kids or anyone else, smelled money in the air and had to possess this particular plot, at any cost. After a few months of unsuccessful wrangling and cajoling, he turned up the heat on the eighty-year-old scion of the family that had owned the property for generations and forced the old gentleman to sell. No one knew the exact details, but rumors of intimidation, duplicity and blackmail abounded. It was all standard operating procedure for the Bastard of Bordeaux.

This past Christmas Eve, while the newly homeless kids and their equally dispossessed attendant nuns watched from slowly departing buses, along with a media circus and a handful of poster-wielding, effigy burning protesters on-hand to bear witness, the wrecking ball fell on the old, idyllic country home while a pack of hungry bulldozers blasted through the out buildings in a carefully choreographed dance of destruction.

The country was outraged. DeBussey was ecstatic. The animosity and vitriol his actions produced in print and other media were pure bonus material and served as fuel for the malicious fire that burned in his twisted, avaricious soul.

He was looking forward to viewing Bruno's multipage layout in the scrapbook. It had been his most gratifying victory and would remain so—until just after the Vin Expo in late June.

The most well-respected and influential châteaus in Bordeaux notwithstanding, his Beverage DeBussey presently had a controlling interest in more properties in the region than any other business entity. With the demand for this year's vintage going through the roof, he was in perfect position to selectively slow distribution and export, squeeze the supply and cause his rivals intense pain, suffering, and loss. And with a little extra luck and timing, he could double or even triple his profit margin.

But it wasn't really about the money. It was about payback. And it would taste sweeter and more delicious in his mouth than any wine ever could.

Life was so good.

# CHAPTER NINE

*Orlando, Florida*

Justin checked his email. Over the past two weeks, he had received three messages from Brad at the wine shop. But the FedEx front office had kept him hopping with a promotion to management. Between studying the information about his new responsibilities, boxing up all of his action figures and memorabilia and moving into a new, larger cubicle and working many hours of overtime, he hadn't had a minute to follow up on his big night of excitement at In Vino Veritas. But he had thought about Destiny Verrano, the scrumptious wine babe more than a few times.

With a little more free time on his hands, he finally got around to reading Brad's messages. Besides two e-mails about events that had already taken place, he immediately noticed that something was up for tonight at a locale called, The Twisted Cork. He read the invitation. *7 p.m., $15 per person, featuring a selection of wines from Spain and a Tapas buffet courtesy of Restaurante El Gordo.*

Justin had heard of tapas before but wasn't exactly sure what they actually were. In any case, it would certainly be better than his usual home-cooking repertoire of bologna, beefaroni, or a microwave pizza.

*Ole! I'm going, and she might be there, too!*

He added his name to the guest list, clicked submit, and left work half an hour early to chill.

At home, he repeated his daily ritual of checking the fish tank, plant watering, mail reading and light cleaning. In truth, there wasn't much to straighten up. There was never much going on at the homestead. No parties, no guests, no anything.

As he headed into his closet-sized bedroom to survey his choices for tonight's attire, he made a mental note to try to keep things understated and tasteful. That immediately ruled out ninety percent of his wardrobe. Destiny had made easy fun of his pink shoes, so he chose to wear his other favorites, the forest-green Converse Hi-Tops with black laces. Very cool. And a decent match with blue jeans and a very non-descript, striped V-neck tee.

He had a few extra minutes, so he sat at the small, early 1960s vintage kitchenette table, complete with its vinyl orange-tree motif seat cushions, matching salt and pepper shakers and placemats, and reached for the small stack of wine magazines Brad had given him.

The pages were packed full of colorful information and stories about people and places all devoted to the pursuit of the finer things in life: upscale living, dining, cooking, travel, fashion and schmoozing. Justin just couldn't believe the depth and breadth of the wine subculture.

There were recipes for dishes he had never heard of and suggestions for pairing the correct wines with each course. In every issue, there seemed to be hundreds of wine reviews based on growing regions from around the world. *Do they really make wine in Alaska?* Interviews with famous and not so famous wine collectors. *Holy crap! The actor that plays Harry Potter has a wine cellar with 1,000 bottles! Is he even old enough to drink?* Recommendations for the perfect crystal glasses, gas grills, coffee grinders, espresso makers, nitrogen gas wine preservation systems, mail-order steaks and seafood, stemware cleaning products, and even wine stain removal agents.

Of course, the central thesis and main mantra of nearly every page—including the nonstop advertisements—was that enjoying fine wine was the key to experiencing life to the fullest. It was all fascinating, eye-opening and more than a just little obsessive.

*Hmmm...my new hobby could become expensive.*

But as he considered his "fun and fine living quotient," which was currently at zero, Justin thought it just might be a worthwhile investment of time and money.

Before he headed out for the evening, he checked in on Aunt Annette's room, smoothed her covers, fluffed her pillows and bid her a good night.

The Twisted Cork was a twenty minute drive, located in an older part of town that had lately gotten a little seedy. The neighborhood didn't seem unsafe or dangerous; it just had a certain kind of funky, used-up ambience that seemed to inhabit the area like the ghost of economic good times past.

A block from his destination, with the old Electra's springs and shocks roughly protesting every bump and imperfection in the road and the stuck driver's window allowing the cool night air to blow in and continually readjust his already eccentric hairstyle, Justin drove past the very sparklingly-lit Magic Murphy Auto Sales car lot. It was famously sandwiched between two very old-school strip clubs: The Booby Trap and Popatopolis.

They, too, were well-lit, but instead of employing daytime-bright lights, the clubs' signs and parking lots were illuminated by a brash, colorfully loud array—pink flashing tubes of light twisted into the form of a very buxom female, yellow flashing neon lights shaped into what appeared to be a giant martini glass, a huge neon-green champagne bottle popping its cork every few seconds and releasing a geyser of effervescent white-yellow light bubbles.

The marquees of both locations promised "The Biggest and Best in Town" "No Viagra Needed" "Happy Hour all Day" and more. Justin had never been inside a "gentleman's club" before, but if things didn't pick up in the romance department very soon, he thought he might have to investigate.

Across the street, just beyond the glow of a pair of blinking, giant-sized Marilyn Monroe-esque lips that were shooting ruby-red kisses into the night sky, the Twisted Cork sat in stark, quiet contrast to its garish neighbors.

The location and building seemed vaguely familiar. After parking and making a half-hearted effort to wrestle the window shut—he never gave up on trying to get it closed—he realized this had been the location of the old Sambo's restaurant that Aunt Annette used to take him to on Sunday mornings when he was a little kid. He didn't know how long ago it had changed hands or closed, but he could still taste the special Cinnamon French Toast covered in buttery syrup that he had ordered almost every weekend.

The vintage 1950s restaurant building had been stuccoed over, white washed and with a few darkly colored, strategically placed wooden planks tacked up here and there, made to resemble an Old English Tudor-style roadhouse. Somehow, they had even gotten the pitched roof to look like it was thatched by using some kind of broom-like, spindly material. Justin had to admit that, all in all, and despite that fact that it sat on a sea of asphalt, the Twisted Cork looked like it actually belonged on a winding, tree-lined lane somewhere in the English countryside.

The interior, however, was another story. After he swung open one of the heavy oak doors, with a handle that was made to look like a gold-plated wine bottle, he entered a world of chrome, glass block, granite countertops, multicolored tables and chairs in a variety of shapes and sizes, none of which really matched, a bank of dark leather booths across the back wall, and an assortment of wine kitsch, memorabilia, paraphernalia, and wine-related artwork. Each interior wall was painted a slightly different shade of purple and the entire ceiling was bordered by some kind of grape arbor motif stick-on appliqué.

It was a total mash-up that seemed to have been put together by an interior decorator with multiple personality disorder. But surprisingly, it all came together into a slightly off-key harmony that gave the Twisted Cork a fun, festive, Disney World-of-adult-beverages atmosphere. And best of all, it was full of people having a good time, a number of whom appeared to be female. But, he did not see the lovely Destiny pouring wine or sitting at any of the tables.

Walking across the main room toward the bar, which ran the length of one of the side walls, he could see that almost half of it was taken up by an assortment of platters, bowls, and covered serving trays, each with a card identifying the kind of tapas contained within. As he got closer, he could smell the alluring aroma of the combined contents. The cards had names like *Croquetas, Bombas, Spanish Tortillas, Albonigas,* and *Patatas Bravas.* This was definitely going to be better than a meal made by Kraft, Franco American or Chef Boyardee.

A long slab of colorfully-flecked, beige granite sat atop a glass block pedestal that was back-lit in soft-hued purple, violet and rose tones. Hanging from the ceiling and running the length of the bar were a series of miniature wine bottle lamps with not-too-bright halogen bulbs casting a soft glow on the patrons indulging below.

Behind the bar were what looked to be three double-wide, chrome and glass-doored refrigerators. Justin could see that they were each filled with dozens of wine bottles. A bartender opened up the closest one, pulling out two already open bottles of red wine, pouring a glass of each before returning them to the fridge.

Sitting at the far end of the bar, just past a line-up of what Justin assumed must be tonight's Spanish wine specials, was the larger-than-life Frank *the Tank* Murphy. The man he was talking with could be another bartender, because he was standing behind the counter and pouring wine, but Justin had his doubts. He was deeply tanned and wearing an ensemble that consisted of a Hawaiian shirt, board shorts, flip-flops and sunglasses, all in the middle of February. At night! Justin was impressed with the man's fashion sense.

When he reached them at the end of the bar, the laid-back beach-bum said, in a voice that sounded like two sheets of coarse sandpaper being enthusiastically rubbed together, "I already know who you are. You are Justin James."

Justin was surprised. He'd never seen Beach Bum Guy before.

"How could you possibly know that?" he asked.

"Simple," the man rasped. "I'm psychic."

Frank *the Tank*, sitting next to him at the bar, his nose deeply buried in a glass of red wine, looked up and slowly said, "Oh no, he's not psych-*ic*, he's psych-*o.*" Both men then burst into a fit of laughter.

*Frank looks insane when he laughs,* thought Justin.

After they regained their composure, Surfer Dude explained. "Yours is the last name to be checked-off from tonight's reservations list. Everyone else has already shown up. Simple as that. By the way, this is my place. I'm Mike Lazarus. The Hysterical Hulk sitting across from me is Frank, aka Magic Murphy. I don't think I've seen you in here before, so welcome to the Twisted Cork." Mike reached over the bar as he and Justin shook hands, and Frank lifted his glass in greeting.

# CHAPTER TEN

Justin was really happy he had decided to come. After paying the tasting fee and receiving his glass, he walked to the back of the short line for tapas and immediately struck up a conversation with a very well-dressed, stylishly coiffured and bearded man.

With his salt and pepper beard and hair, in his perfectly tailored ultra-swank suit, he looked like a middle-aged fashion model straight out of the pages of *GQ* or *Esquire* magazines, both of which Justin had once been given, anonymously, as a prank at work. At the time he'd thought that the attached Post-it® Note saying *Get a Clue!* was a bit much and that, in general, expensive clothing and fashion were a complete waste of time and money. But he had to admit, this guy's attire and appearance were top-shelf. Very classy.

*GQ* Guy watched as Justin lifted the lids of each tray, read each name card and tried to decide where to start.

"I usually choose which wine to taste first and then try to pair it with the most appropriate food," *GQ* Guy suggested.

"Good idea. That's what I'll do," Justin replied, hoping he didn't appear too ignorant and uninformed. Quickly remembering his first tasting at Brad's shop, he asked "What goes well with white wine?"

They both filled their small plates with a few pieces of heavy, crusty bread and a dish called *Gambas*, which were delicious-looking shrimp sautéed in garlic, olive oil, brandy and a little red pepper. To accompany the shrimp, the other bartender poured them each a small glass of white wine number one: a Godello—a very light, dry wine with a pleasant peach and honey aroma that tasted perfect with the shrimp.

"Not too bad for a Wednesday night, is it?" the bearded man said as he took a seat across from Justin.

"I would say it's outstanding, especially for fifteen bucks!" Justin enthusiastically replied. "I might have to become a regular here."

After finishing the shrimp, they quickly returned to refill their plates. This time, Justin stocked-up on *Jamon Croquetas* –deep fried ham and cheese fingers –*Tortillas de patata*–a very interesting-looking Spanish omelet stuffed with all kinds of veggies, and *Pan con tomate*, which were pieces of the crusty bread rubbed with fresh tomatoes, olive oil and garlic.

To complement round two, the bartender poured them each a small taste of the other white wine of the evening, something called Garnacha Blanca. After a swirl, a sniff and a small taste, Justin immediately thought of the incredible French white that he had experienced at Brad's shop. Like the French wine, whose name he couldn't remember, this one was tongue-coatingly rich and had an insistent note of tropical fruit. But, it was far less sweet and more citrusy in tone. It was certainly a lot more interesting than the first wine of the night. He really liked Garnacha Blanca.

Justin took a bite of each tapas, another taste of the wine and, shaking his head and broadly smiling, said, "How on earth can this all be so extremely delicious?"

After savoring another bite or two of each item and emptying his glass, he lamented, "I really, really, *really* wish I had discovered the world of wine earlier than just two weeks ago."

The bearded man finished up, and with an inquiringly raised eyebrow, pointed back towards the bar. *Round three?*

As they made their way through a few rounds of different red wines and assorted tapas, Justin learned that his tablemate's name was Steve St. Clair, a regular "Twisted" customer and the owner of The Oasis Center for Serenity and Wellness. Justin had never heard of it, and the reason became clear after Steve explained that it was located in the very tony, upscale, far-west side of town. Justin had never been anywhere in the vicinity.

"Besides the usual features of a day spa, The Oasis also offers a plastic surgery practice, a state-of-the-art gym, an indoor lap pool, and a health food shop and juice bar," said Steve. "From boobs, botox and body wraps to tits, tush and toenails, we've got you covered...or uncovered...as the case may be."

"Is that your advertising slogan?" Justin joked as he finished red wine number three.

"You're a funny kid, aren't you? Somehow, I don't think that would work on billboards, but it might fly on the Internet. Why don't we try the last red?"

Hoping he hadn't said anything dumb or offensive, he followed Steve to the other end of the bar where Frank was still sitting in his nose-stuck-in-glass position, and Mike was pouring some red wine for a small group of somewhat older, but still very attractive women. As soon as one of the women saw him, she let out a giddy laugh and exclaimed, "There's Steve!"

They quickly abandoned Mike and surrounded Steve like a kaleidoscope of colorful butterflies.

"Oh, that St. Clair, he's a smooth one." Mike chuckled. He reached for Justin's glass and gave him a small pour of the last wine of the tasting.

Looking over his shoulder, Justin watched in amazement as the women collectively ooh-ed and ahh-ed, laughing at whatever Steve had to say. And one or two of them, for some reason, seemed to be compelled to reach out and touch him. Repeatedly.

"It's like he's a rock star," Justin exclaimed. "It's awesome."

"Well," Mike said with a knowing smile. "You've heard the expression *clothes make the man*? In Steve's case, while that's certainly true, I think the girls are more interested in what's *under* those clothes, if you catch my meaning."

Justin was expecting another wave of laughter from Mike and Frank, but Mike just gave a nod and Magic Murphy half-smiled, with a wistful, far-away look in his eyes.

He took his glass from Mike and was about to have a final small taste and call it a night when he saw Brad Garrison walk into the room with a bulky, padded bag slung over his shoulder. Trailing Brad was a stout, fireplug of a man in Desert Storm-era combat fatigues, his long, wispy white hair pulled back into a ponytail that flowed out from under his decoratively pinned, black beret.

He had a bushy, white Fu-Manchu-style moustache, *à la* Hulk Hogan, and an accompanying bad-ass scowl. He looked a little dangerous, and Justin thought that if he'd had a few machine gun belts draped across his torso, he could have attended any Comic Con as Rambo. He, too, had a black bag slung over his shoulder. *Loaded with C-4?*

# CHAPTER ELEVEN

"Lord above, it's Barry Love!" Mike Lazarus croaked as he came out from behind the bar to give Rambo a big, back-slapping hug. "And my evil nemesis from across town, Mr. Bradley G. Come in boys and let's get the *real* tasting started."

Each carrying similar shoulder bags, Frank and Steve made their way through the small maze of tables and joined the others in the middle of the room. Greetings out of the way, Mike disappeared behind the bar as a few of the guys pushed two of the tables together.

From their black bags, Brad, the guy from Seal Team Six, and the others produced at least half a dozen bottles of red wine and Brad began to open them, one after the other. The bartender arrived with a tray of decanters, set them down on the table, and before returning behind the bar, handed Brad a Sharpie marking pen.

Looking up to take the pen, Brad's eyes momentarily locked with Justin's, and smiling, he called out, "Hey, young Mr. J, we meet again!" Pointing to the bottles and decanters, he added, "Give me a minute to take care of this and I'll tell you what's going on."

Using the Sharpie, Brad wrote the name and vintage of each bottle onto its corresponding decanter and then slowly poured out each wine. Mike reappeared with fresh glasses and distributed them among the men, now all settled in around the long table,

Brad finished up with the decanting, said something to Mike, and then made his way over to Justin, who by now had started talking with one of Steve's female fans. Her name was

Phyllis Braunstein, and she was tan, toned, and decked out in an expensive-looking, but casual, outfit. She seemed nice and looked very sexy for a woman her age.

He remembered Steve's catch-phrase for The Oasis–*tits and tush, et al.*, and thought s*he's definitely a satisfied customer.*

"You have *great* hair," Phyllis cooed as she tried to run her fingers through Justin's tangled mop. "It's so thick and wild. Where do you get it done?"

Justin, enjoying the attention and feeling a pleasant tingle, until he imagined what a tummy-tuck scar looks like up close and personal, tentatively replied "I usually go to Salon Electra."

At that moment Brad approached them at the bar. "Hi, Phyllis. You're looking wonderful, as usual. I hope you won't mind if I borrow this guy for a few minutes."

She might have been trying to pout, but with her botoxed lips it was hard to tell. She stopped massaging Justin's scalp and extricated her fingers from his wavy mane.

"That's okay Brad, but you can't keep him out of this cougar's clutches forever," she joked. Justin thought he detected a slight smile. Still hard to tell, though. They touched glasses as he got up.

"Thanks for rescuing me," Justin said, as Brad took him by the elbow and led him back to the table where the guys had now all convened. They were examining the decanters and passing them around, and Justin noticed that there were two empty chairs. "Fifty-year-old women aren't really my thing."

"Fifty! Are you kidding me?" Brad exclaimed. "I think she's closer to sixty, and she *might* be eligible for Medicare, but I'm not really sure." With eyes wide open, Justin took a quick, over-the-shoulder glance at the surprising Phyllis and her cougar-pack friends.

"And, by the way, I've heard through the grapevine that she is *absolutely amazing* in bed. Son, you might learn a thing or two." He laughed and delivered a playful punch to the bicep. "You look like you could probably use it."

Back at the table, Brad took one of the vacant seats and directed Justin to take the other, between him and Steve St.

Clair. He reached for one of the decanters and poured an inky, purple red wine into each of their glasses.

"Hey, you winos," he said, getting the attention of the group. "This is Justin. He came into my shop a few weeks back for his very first tasting and became an instant convert. He also showed excellent palate potential, so I thought that, if it's okay with everyone, he could sit in with the group tonight and take a little trip to *España* with us."

"Really? I mean, ah, wow, that would be great," Justin said, stumbling over his words like Woody Allen negotiating for a discounted lap dance with a stripper.

With his arm firmly around Justin's shoulders, Brad went clockwise around the table and introduced each group member. "This is Steve, Mike and Frank, whom I think you've already talked with, and next to me is Barry Love, who works with a big distribution company. Juice Brothers, say hello to my little friend."

Justin was greeted by nods, raised glasses, and smiles. Except for the scowling Barry, who looked like he was still suffering from post-traumatic stress disorder from his last Black Ops mission to the Belgian Congo or some other far-flung destination. Above his cammo shirt-pocket flap, his last name was stenciled in large black letters. L-O-V- E. Justin looked across the table at him and felt vaguely uncomfortable. He was *not* feeling the love.

"We get together almost every month or so and have a themed tasting," Brad continued. "And we each kick in a few bottles of, what we hope will be, great stuff."

The bartender reappeared with a rolling sideboard full of various types of cheese, more of the tasty, crusty bread and a few plates full of the remaining assorted tapas.

"Okay dudes, before we get started, everybody pony-up five bucks for the food," Mike said, holding out an open palm.

"The kid's gotta' pay, too, right?" asked Barry Love, looking across at Justin and turning up his glare to "eleven." But he said it in a thin, reedy, voice that was about an octave too high–somewhere between Mike Tyson and Barney Fife–and delivered it with a comic flair that was as disarming as it was unexpected. The scowl quickly turned into a wry grin, and shrugging in mock surrender, he pointed at Justin, offering a very loud "Gotcha!"

Hearing that voice and watching Barry's frown turn upside down, any possible feelings of intimidation Justin felt quickly evaporated. "No worries, I'm in," he replied, and along with everyone else, placed his five in Mike's hand. "But I do have to work tomorrow morning, so I can't stay too late."

"We'll tell you when you can leave," the bug-eyed Frank said with mock seriousness. Then, he exploded into a diabolical laugh that got the night rolling and kept the wine flowing.

# CHAPTER TWELVE

Justin was having the dream again. He'd been having it as far back as he could remember, and it felt as familiar as a comfortable, worn pair of shoes. Always starting the same and ending the same, it was as predictable as the rising and falling of the tides. And despite the fact that he was aware he was asleep and dreaming, he was completely powerless to alter the sequence of events or influence the outcome.

There he was, riding along in the backseat of the open convertible, with the force of the air rushing over his ears creating a familiar windblown soundtrack. The air felt cool and damp on his skin as they drove down the mountain road back toward the highway. He couldn't tell if it was night or day: there was a silvery disk hovering lazily in the sky, but he wasn't sure if it was the sun or the moon.

And then he remembered. It was daytime, but the sea fog along the coast was so thick it had swallowed everything up. While there appeared to be shadow-like objects in the distance or flying by the car as they drove downward, they were too indistinct and far away to have any real form, color or shape. They were all floating together on a giant, milky-white cloud.

He could barely see into the front seat, where the driver and passenger, a man and a woman, were holding hands. Did they know he was there? He wanted to get their attention and ask if everything was all right, but strangely, he couldn't move or talk. The woman—the passenger—turned around and reached out to take his hand. She smiled and said something, but the sound of the rushing air, now growing louder, was all he could hear. His hand felt good in hers. It was full of warmth and reassurance, tenderness and love. He wished that he could live forever in that moment.

Suddenly, the woman turned away, screamed and instinctively held up her hands in front of her face. Time slowed down as he saw the silhouette of a large object blocking their path, the flashing lights and a man in a uniform frantically waving his arms over his head in warning. But all he could hear, after the loud screech of tires and a thudding impact, was the familiar deafening rush of air against his ears. All he could see was the fog, and all he could feel was the deep sadness that followed him like a shadow into his every waking moment.

# CHAPTER THIRTEEN

The theme from *Star Wars* called Justin out of the cloud and out of his dream. It took him a moment to realize the tune was coming from the alarm clock he had purchased at last year's Sci-Fi convention. Even through the heavy, sleepy haze, it sounded unusually distant, and it seemed to take a long time for his fingers to find the off button. With eyes still closed, he groped for the nightstand, but it wasn't where it was supposed to be, and he came up with a handful of nothing. Then just as R2D2 joined in with the orchestra, the alarm stopped.

Justin opened his eyes to find himself sprawled on his back, totally naked, sideways on Aunt Annette's bed. When he got over his initial shock at lying nude in his aunt's bedroom, he noticed that most of the blankets and pillows were strewn around the room like they had been blown-off by a gale force wind. On the dresser just across from the bed, he saw a half empty bottle of wine and a couple of glasses, along with a can of Reddi-Whip and a tall pump-topped container with some kind of clear liquid inside. He got out bed, picked it up and read the label: *Love You Longtime Lube and Moisturizer. WTF?*

He almost jumped out of his skin when he heard a woman's voice from behind him say, "Good morning, sexy pants." He grabbed a pillow from the floor and, trying to cover himself, whirled around to see who was behind him. This was no dream.

Phyllis Braunstein stood in the doorway wearing his aunt's purple felt bathrobe and matching slippers. The robe was hanging open, and as he caught a glimpse of her perfect breasts and shapely, tanned torso, the mental blanks in his brain started slowly filling in.

"I hope you don't mind," she said. "I made us some coffee." She handed him a mug, held out her hand and gestured for him to drop the pillow. "And there's no need to be shy, *especially* after all of the wonderful things you did to me last night." Then, she put her cup on the dresser, kneeled down, and took him into her mouth. Her hands were warm. Her tongue was hot. Justin nearly passed out.

# CHAPTER FOURTEEN

After disengaging himself from the very willing and enthusiastic Phyllis, he made his way into the bathroom to start getting ready for the day ahead. He nudged the shower's ancient temperature control as far into the "blue" as he dared and hesitantly stepped into the cascading cold.

The nearly frigid water blasted him back in time a few hours earlier to the previous evening at the Twisted Cork, and his mind's eye mind played back the events like a stuttering, low-resolution *You Tube* video.

They were all sitting around the table tasting wines and eating tapas. Brad was telling the guys about the wine that they were currently savoring, something from Rioja, in Spain. Then Steve passed around a decanter with one of the wines he had brought and they all sipped on something fresh and elegant from a region called Ribera del Duero.

And on it went, with each member of the group taking their turn and giving a small recitation about each of the wines they had brought until they had all sampled each one. Then they mixed and matched, compared and contrasted, and discussed their findings.

All the while, Brad had asked Justin to provide the group with his impression of each wine, and he did his best to describe what kind of flavors he detected and make a good impression on the table of attentive wine enthusiasts.

The wines were fabulous: all so different and delicious and not totally dissimilar from what he remembered about the Rhone tasting at Brad's shop. Justin was so taken with the flavors and fragrances, he found it easy to put into words.

He tasted smoke here, vanilla there. A touch of leather and minerals in one of the drier wines and a super concentrated nose of licorice and spice in a wine from a region called Priorat. Frank had brought a few bottles from a region called Montsant, and like Frank *the Tank*, they were big, brawny and powerful.

Barry's thin, piccolo voice had piped up in agreement. "I'm getting exactly the same thing in spades—it smells like Chinese five spice powder, and with that deep licorice flavor... Ooh that is just so fine." He was starting to sound like he'd been inhaling helium.

And then Frank added "Justin, I have to say that your palate is damn good! Your hair looks ridiculous, but there's nothing wrong with your taste buds, bud!"

That got all the guys laughing long and hard, and their quiet, controlled tasting quickly devolved into a decanter-emptying free-for-all.

Steve waved to Phyllis and the cougar pack and motioned for them to come on over and join in. They pulled up a few chairs and squeezed around the table, now nearly overloaded with a dozen glasses, numerous decanters and a handful of plates filled with leftover tapas.

Justin and Brad scooted down as Steve was immediately flanked by the same two touchy-feely women from earlier. They still couldn't keep their hands off of him. He didn't seem to mind. Two of the other ladies slid in between Mike and Frank, and Phyllis, who was looking even better than she had an hour or so ago, took a seat next to Justin. He hoped she wouldn't start fondling his hair again, but when she did, he actually started to enjoy it.

Mike got up and disappeared behind the bar for a minute, returning with his contribution and the last bottle of the night. It was a super sweet wine made from a grape called Pedro Jimenez that had the unctuous consistency and color of maple syrup. They all toasted and tasted. Ironic that, here in the old Sambo's building where Justin had eaten countless platefuls of syrup-drenched French toast as a kid, he was enjoying this smooth, confectionary beverage as a man.

He tried to recall more details beyond that point, but things were starting to get a little fuzzy. He dialed the water temperature back into reasonable territory, hoping that a little warmth would stimulate and refocus his memory.

He did remember having a difficult time getting to his feet to go to the men's room, and it was at that instant he realized that he was actually drunk for the first time in his life, and he was really enjoying the moment—the camaraderie, the laughter, the wines, and the buzz. But the more he drank, the more difficult it became for him to be objective and think clearly. About the wines. And about the potentially dangerous ride home in the old Electra. But here he was, out and about, part of a fun group of people, just living it up. And no one was wearing a cheesy costume. Except, perhaps, Barry.

When he returned from the restroom and came back to the table, he tripped, possibly over an unseen outcropping of table leg, and stumbled into Phyllis's chair, nearly knocking her out of it.

Barry helped Justin to his feet, checked to see what condition his condition was in, and asked him where he lived.

While the guys were in the middle of trying to figure out who would have the shortest drive to take him home, Phyllis volunteered. And although she didn't live anywhere near his neighborhood, she insisted. Mike and Brad exchanged a look and Mike said, in his sandpaper rasp, "I'm making all of us an espresso before the ride home. Justin gets a double." And with a Cheshire cat smile, he added "I think he's gonna' need it!"

# CHAPTER FIFTEEN

*St. Émilion, France*

The view from Lala Chang's bedroom window, high in northeast turret of the main building of Château La Tour Noir, afforded a majestic view of the rolling limestone and clay hills of St. Émilion.

Under a canopy of heavy clouds, dozens of vineyards with thousands of perfectly straight rows of vines, now bare in the chill of winter, stretched as far as her eyes could see into the surrounding countryside, disturbed only by the occasional hillside farmhouse or some other charmingly picturesque wine-producing estate.

It was all so beautiful. And so boring. She lit a candle, closed the window, drew the curtains and sat alone in the near darkness to brood.

Lala had arrived in France, her mother's homeland, three years earlier with high hopes and expectations of a grand life full of fashion, high society, travel and, above all, money. Lots of money. Money to pay for all of those shopping trips she would take to Paris and the lavish dinner parties she would throw at the château. Funding for all of the first-class trips she would take back home and the holiday vacations in the Caribbean. It had all been promised to her. For her entire life, it had all been promised to her.

And she had gotten some of the money, but only whatever her husband allowed her to have. In truth, her lifestyle was one that most people would consider affluent or wealthy: she had a domestic staff and a chauffeur, a quiet country life in an extraordinary, quintessentially French late eighteenth century estate home and never a care about having to pay for the expensive wardrobe that looked so very fine on her attractive, graceful frame.

But for Lala, all the money in the world could never assuage the isolation she felt or fill the growing emptiness in her soul. *I've wasted three years of my life*. she thought grimly. How had she ever agreed to an arranged marriage with such a God-awful control-freak and tyrannical asshole?

But did she really ever have a choice? Her mother was happy that her only daughter was going to live in France and she promised to visit often, especially after the grandchildren were born. Her totally old-school father, owner of Chang and Sons Limited, a large and influential wine and spirits importer based in Hong Kong, insisted that it was her familial duty to marry his main supplier from France, one of the most successful wine merchants in the world.

Without a second thought as to her happiness and spiritual well-being, he wanted to simply marry her off to ensure an even more profitable long-term business relationship. How typical. She had been born female and groomed to be a lovely, porcelain-skinned bargaining chip for her family's benefit. Nothing more, nothing less. The old school way.

At an early age she had been sent away, first to an exclusive boarding school and then later to various exchange-student programs in different countries, all so that one day, she could become a small part of an important business deal over which she had no control.

So she married the man she had only met once, at the annual French Wine and Dine Festival held in Hong Kong each spring. He wasn't attractive or particularly interesting, but he did dress well and possessed a certain rough charm that Lala thought she could at least tolerate, especially if it made her rich! What a mistake.

Sitting in her room accompanied only by the shadows cast on the darkly paneled walls by the dim candle light, she understood all of it. He had married Lala for the same reasons that her family had offered her to him: The deal.

After the first few months, he was no longer interested in sex, at least not with her. The rough charm she thought that she had seen in him disappeared and was replaced by indifference. There was never any discussion about starting a family, or doing anything else together. And he never really conversed with her, either. He gave orders. And if she refused to follow those orders, his indifference quickly turned into hostility.

So there were never any trips back home or to the islands, no grandchildren for her mother to visit, no lavish parties to plan and enjoy, and only infrequent jaunts into the nearby Bordeaux city to spend a few hours shopping or having a coffee or a meal.

There were social functions to attend here and there, but she felt that she existed as nothing more than her husband's sophisticated, elegant arm-candy. She was seething with anger and frustration. But what could she do? She couldn't go back to Hong Kong.

When the deal had been made three long years ago, her fate had been preordained. Her lucky brothers, heirs to the family business and fortune, got wild, vibrant Hong Kong as their kingdom, an unending supply of French wine and total control over their own lives with Chang and Sons. Lala got an exquisitely gilded cage in St. Émilion, a prescription for Prozac, and a self-absorbed, dangerously volatile dictator of a husband—Guy DeBussey.

# CHAPTER SIXTEEN

*Orlando, Florida*

After getting out of the shower and putting on in his FedEx blues, Justin was surprised to see that Phyllis had totally straightened up Aunt Annette's room, removing all traces of last night's very physical activities, including her tube of lube. He found her fully clothed, sitting at the orange tree dinette table in the kitchen and drinking the last of the coffee.

"I was going to make some breakfast for you, but bologna and diet coke isn't a recommended combination for the first meal of the day, my dear."

"I, uh, usually grab something on the way to work," he replied, and added, "Thanks for tidying up the bedroom. It doesn't even look like anything happened in there last night."

"Oh, but something did happen, didn't it?" She was smiling so broadly that even the botox in her lips couldn't prevent the corners of her mouth from turning up.

"And I really didn't mean to take advantage of you when you invited me in, but I couldn't help myself." She laughed, stood up and put her arms around him in a very warm embrace. "I could tell that you didn't have a lot of experience, but you, Justin, are really something very special. You're just... a natural. *And*, you take direction *so* well. I don't think I've ever had quite that many orgasms in one night. Now, I'm not sure if I should introduce you to some of my friends, or keep you all to myself."

With that, she gave him a light peck on the cheek and headed out the door. He could only follow in stunned silence, trying to digest what he had just heard.

With Phyllis at the wheel of her sexy little black Infiniti G37, Justin directed her on the short drive to the FedEx office, where, he hoped, none of his coworkers would spy him getting out of her car. Not that he was embarrassed by the fact that he had just spent the night with a woman at least twenty years his senior.

On the contrary, he was feeling good. No, great! And Phyllis looked wonderful this morning, even beautiful. He just didn't need to be the butt of any more office jokes or the target of any ribbing, no matter how good-natured the intent. That was getting way too old.

After she programmed her number into his cell phone and made him promise to call soon, he got out of the car and waved as she drove away. The air was cool and fresh, and the sun was just starting to peek through the clouds in the misty morning sky. He knew that it was going to be a good day; a different kind of day, and he smiled as he walked into the building.

Throughout the morning, he kept having little flashbacks— Phyllis stripping down to her G-string and slowly removing all of his clothes, pushing him down on Aunt Annette's bed, covering his face and chest with hot, wet kisses, climbing on top and slowly gyrating her hips and riding him, telling him to turn her over and kiss his way down from one set of lips to the other, and then turning herself over again, propping-up her amazingly shaped ass on his aunt's fluffy, frilly pillows and commanding him to literally pound her from behind.

And she was loud. And so was he. Their bodies and voices made beautiful music together, again and again. *Wow!* The memories were having an effect on him...he'd never been aroused at work before. This was indeed a different kind of day.

But between the wine, the lack of sleep and an amount of expended energy that must have been equivalent to competing in an Olympic decathlon, his ass was seriously dragging. By noon, he was having trouble focusing on his work.

He decided to take himself out for a big lunch and was already out the door into the parking lot when he realized that his car was still at the Twisted Cork. *Shit!* He went back inside to the break room and made do with stale vending machine fare and two cans of Red Bull. Not such a different kind of day, after all.

Just before returning to his cubicle, his cell rang. It was Brad Garrison. Justin must have given him the number with his contact info at the wine shop.

"Justin, I'm just checking in on you. Did you make it home safe and sound last night?"

"Hi Brad. Yeah, I'm still in one piece, but my head hurts a little."

"Really? Which one?"

"What do you mean?"

"Come on, you *know* what I mean! Tell me, my young friend, are you suffering from post-traumatic stress disorder this morning or did Phyllis screw you so long and hard last night that you've developed amnesia?"

"Well," Justin admitted sheepishly. "I think it's a little bit of both."

"What did I tell you! Good to know that you survived and all is well. Is your car still at Mike's place?"

"Yeah, Phyllis drove me to work this morning. I guess I'll take a taxi after I get off."

"Forget the taxi. I'll take you. After all, it's my fault that you got drunk and laid, so I feel responsible for getting you back to your car...plus, I want to hear all of the juicy details. But, I'm alone in the shop today and can't get out until after seven. Does that work for you?"

Justin thanked Brad for his offer, but explained that he was off at five and just wanted to get it done and go home. Muscles in his legs and lower back that he never knew existed were starting to feel sore and stretched, so much so that he had to ask around the office and get a couple of Advil from a coworker. He hoped two would be enough.

But he still felt great. Bit by bit, as the day wore on, he recovered his strength and focus and just after five he found himself sitting in the back seat of a taxi, headed across town to pick up the old Electra at the Twisted Cork.

Chilling in the cab, his thoughts drifted to the unlikely chain of events that had led to the all-night acrobatic sex marathon with a stunning, if not one hundred percent natural, tigress.

Being a math wiz, his brain naturally began to try to put it all into a quantifiable formula, or some sort of empirical theorem.

Wine. Food. Sex. Could it really be that simple? They were all, undeniably, key variables in his newly devised equation for a gratifying and happy life. But, of course, there was also romantic love to consider; searching for and finding that special significant other with whom to build a future. That was an absolute, a given. But there was something else beyond those four main elements. At the moment, he couldn't put his finger on it.

The taxi turned onto the main highway that ran through the old center of town, and his thoughts turned to the guys last night at the Twisted Cork. Brad, Steve, Mike, crazy Frank *the Tank* Murphy and Barry Love.

While introducing him to the group, Brad had referred to them as my "Juice Brothers." He didn't really know much about any of them, but he knew there was a strong bond between them all. He smiled. He'd been doing that a lot today.

And then, there was the lunch-time call he had gotten from Brad. Since Aunt Annette had passed, the only time Justin's cell phone rang was either because a woman was canceling their next date or he was receiving a work related text from his boss or a coworker. But Brad had been concerned enough about his well-being to actually call in and check on him. That was a first, and it was huge. Maybe today really was a different kind of day.

Passing the strip clubs and Frank's Magic Murphy Auto Sales lot on the left, it all clicked into place for him, and his agile mind found the last variable to complete his new formula for life. Friendship was the missing fifth element in his equation. The discovery put another warm smile on his face and a shined a bright, new light on his life.

# CHAPTER SEVENTEEN

Arriving at the Twisted Cork, Justin instructed the cabbie to pull around back to where he had parked last night, when the lot had been nearly full. Rounding the corner, an ear-splitting *"What the Fuck!"* escaped from Justin's mouth before he'd realized he'd shouted it. There was the old Electra, sitting there in all its pock-marked, burnt orange glory, minus all four of its tires and teetering precariously on four cinder blocks of slightly differing heights.

The trunk and hood were wide open and three of the doors had been removed and, presumably, carted away with the rest of whatever some enterprising thieves deemed to be "salvageable" parts. Broken glass, engine hoses and other debris were scattered around the car in a wide arc, and the sad, old hulk was listing heavily to port, like a sinking battleship right before the final torpedo strike.

"Is that your car?" the cabbie asked with a poorly disguised snicker. "I can't believe anybody would even bother stripping a piece of junk like that."

"Thanks dude, you just blew your tip." Still stunned, Justin paid the exact amount on the meter and got out of the taxi, shaking his head in disbelief. As the cab and the disgruntled driver exited the lot, a police cruiser pulled in and Mike Lazarus appeared out of the wine bar's back door.

Once again wearing sunglasses and shorts, today he was sporting an impossibly multi-colored, pastel Hawaiian shirt, his tan skin even darker against the vibrant colors of the bright sun shining down on the foaming aqua, turquoise, and azure waves that were breaking over his chest and stomach. He was flagging down the cop car when he noticed Justin standing next to the Buick's cleaned-out carcass.

"Holy shit! Justin, is that your car? I can't believe it!" His excited voice sounded like compressed hot steam escaping from a pinhole in a pipe. He came up to Justin and clapped him on the back. "Well, my friend, I'd say this calls for some champagne."

"Sorry Mike, I don't get what you mean."

Justin couldn't take his eyes off of the wasted hulk that used to be his sole mode of transportation. The police officer was out of his car, clipboard in hand, making a 360 degree inspection of Aunt Annette's now terminal Buick Electra with 196,000 miles.

"What I mean is that you're getting a new car, dude!" Mike said. "It looks like you probably needed one anyway. And now, you might get some insurance money out of it, to boot. So, I'd say *that* calls for some champagne…and I'm buying! Plus, we have a mutual friend right across the street with literally hundreds of cars for sale. Some of them actually run," he said, barely suppressing a laugh. "I'll call Frank right now, and have no fear. He'll take care of you. Just come see me inside when you're finished out here." Mike turned and disappeared through the back door.

Craning his neck and leaning over the driver's side windshield trying to make out the VIN number on the dashboard, the investigating officer ever-so-slightly brushed against the mirror on the car's only remaining door. It was enough.

One and then another of the cinder blocks abruptly popped out from underneath the car, and the Electra made one final voyage, toppling over and rolling onto its side, coming to a stop ninety degrees to the horizon. After the dust settled, the officer made his way over.

"You're the owner?"

Justin nodded.

"I need your driver's license and registration."

Justin fished both out of his wallet, and the officer finished filling in the forms, handing the clipboard to Justin when he was through.

"Sign here, here and here." He pointed to the three circled X's on the page.

Justin signed, the officer gave him his copy and then was immediately on the radio to HQ calling for the wrecker.

Since Justin didn't keep anything in the car, there was really nothing to retrieve and nothing else to do or say. He took one last look and with a long sigh, turned and went through the back door to hold Mike to his offer.

Inside the nearly empty "Cork" Mike stood behind the bar with the phone in one hand and a silver ice bucket in the other. When Justin took a seat directly opposite, Mike hung up, placed the ice bucket on the bar and retrieved a bottle of champagne from under the counter.

The label read *Krug Grande Cuvee 1998*. He set two elegant-looking champagne flutes on the bar and then quickly popped the cork, pouring each of them a glass of the bubbling, pale-gold libation.

"I think you're going to like this." He handed Justin a glass.

"I've never had champagne before." Justin checked the wine's effervescent nose. It smelled toasty, lemony and vivacious.

"Of course you haven't," Mike replied. "And until about twenty four hours ago, you'd never had Tapas, Spanish wine, sex with a fifty-nine year old woman, or had your old beater stripped for parts, totaled, and hauled away." He held up his glass, touched it to Justin's offered his Zen-like toast. "A journey of a thousand miles begins with just one small step, and you have just taken a few big ones. So here's to all of the steps you will take, large and small, on your journey through life."

Justin was genuinely touched…but....*Phyllis was fifty-nine?* He sipped the champagne and the wine's sparkling acidity and rich, almost buttery flavor danced across his tongue.

"Now, let's enjoy this 95 point Krug and send you over to see Frank. He's waiting for you." Mike refilled their glasses and they toasted once again.

# CHAPTER EIGHTEEN

Frank *the Tank,* aka Magic Murphy, owner of the hugely successful, humongous used   car dealership Magic Murphy Auto Sales, was sitting at his desk working out today's crossword puzzle in the *Orlando Sentinel.*

From his office perch high on the third floor, he took a moment to look out through a semi-circle of panoramic picture windows like a commodore on the bridge of his flagship, and he surveyed the thriving business he had built from scratch.

Directly to the front sat his fleet of late model "pampered and pre-owned" cars and trucks that were selling almost faster than he could replace them. And to his left and right he gazed out on a nice pair of *real* money-makers, The Booby Trap and Popatopolis, which he had never intended to buy, but was so very glad he had.

The two sleazy old strip bars had more or less fallen into his lap after the previous owner, who was rumored to have had a serious gambling problem, disappeared and was then found, piece by piece, in various dumpsters throughout the city.

His car business had been doing fairly well before, but the cash flow from the dueling  "gentleman's clubs" had become a growth engine for the dealership, and it had enabled him to increase the quantity and quality of his inventory, build a new state of the art show room, service facility and the luxurious office space that housed the sales and management staff. He'd even put some money back into the clubs to spruce them up a bit.

But most importantly, the tsunami of money from the clubs had allowed him to buy television advertising time. Mega amounts of it.

His self-invented, on-air pitchman persona, Magic Murphy, had become a local legend, and he was infamous for the late night, low-budget used car commercials that were both poorly conceived and tackily executed.

And because he was so seemingly oblivious to the high cheese factor, his TV spots were, more often than not, unintentionally hysterical. And endearing. There was just something authentic and sincere about his gap-toothed smile and almost boy-like enthusiasm for the cars and the deals.

Over a music bed of carnival-like calliope music, with his fat, florid face even redder under the harsh TV lights and his wavy, sandy hair blowing in the breeze, he delivered the 411 on this week's assortment of limited time offers, once in a lifetime deals and everyone qualifies financing scams with the wide-eyed, awe-struck conviction of a true believing, Southern Baptist tent revival preacher.

And people ate it up. There was a Magic Murphy fan club website. There were Magic Murphy bobble-head dolls for sale, mini magic wands for the kids, drink cozies, and dashboard protectors. A Magic Murph-air hanging air freshener was included with every car.

Each commercial had the same ending, and late night TV viewers always waited for the tag of each spot. There was a shot of Frank, decked out in his tux and top hat, holding his magic wand while standing in front of the lot and enthusiastically delivering his now-iconic closing line: *Let me make some magic...for YOU!* That was usually followed, time permitting, by a last wave of the wand, a flash of smoke and light, and a *POOF* sound effect.

Yes, Frank Murphy, the large man with the large appetite for the finer things in life was riding high and loving it. He was making so much money now that the big, well-publicized payouts he'd had to make to both of his ex-wives didn't seem to slow him down for a minute.

He loved driving his gas-guzzling toys, like his big yellow Hummer or his triple engine speedboat. And he loved over-indulging with the boys and keeping his nearly full, personal 5,000 bottle wine cellar stocked with the biggest and best names from France, Italy and California. And every now and then he got "friendly" with one of the girls from his nightclubs.

But his real passion in life, his secret guilty pleasure, was playing all manner of word games: crossword, Sudoku, online Scrabble, Hangman, or Scribbage. And it was a guilty pleasure that he kept secret from everyone except for his closest friends: his Juice Brothers.

So when Justin James was shown into his office by Frank's personal assistant, he didn't feel the need to hide the puzzle page of the *Sentinel*.

"Hi Justin. Long time, no see."

"Hello Frank. I guess Mike called and filled you in on my problem." Justin said, leaning across the oversized desk, shaking Frank's extra-large hand before taking a seat.

"Problem? Are you talking about the severe case of rug-burn that Phyllis gave you last night or the fact that your old car is headed to the big junk yard in the sky?" He clapped his hands together and, throwing his head back, unleashed a deep, room-filling belly laugh.

Justin looked around the room and took note of all the Magic Murphy posters, pictures and paraphernalia that adorned the back wall and the dark walnut shelving units. *This guy is a one-man industry...maybe Frank isn't so nutty after all.* Finally, the silly seizure subsided and Frank continued.

"I'm sorry, kid. I don't mean to have fun at your expense, but I couldn't resist the set-up...hope you'll forgive me." With that he did a little of his Magic Murphy routine, rolling his eyes and bouncing his bushy brows up and down.

That gave Justin a good laugh, and he couldn't resist being the fan boy that he was, as he nearly gushed, "You know, I've been watching your TV spots for years, and I can't believe that I'm actually going to buy a car from you, like, right now."

"Yes...yes you are!" Frank grabbed either arm of his chair and roughly propelled himself upward. It was a little like watching a slow-motion space shuttle lift off. "Let's talk about what you're interested in on the way down to the lot."

Frank whisked Justin around the expansive lot in a luxurious little golf cart that featured leather seats, GPS Navigation, Dolby surround sound, a minibar, cup-holders and, even though it had no doors or windows, air conditioning! It was total overkill, and it was totally Frank *the Tank*.

"Nice, hunh?" And pointing at no one in particular, he added, with mock gravity "Nothing's too good for my customers! Hey, why not take a look in the minibar and get us a drink?"

Justin got them each a small bottle of water as Frank started down the next row.

"Okay, so you told me that you want something small that gets good mileage and you want to stay under 15K - that about sum it up?"

"Exactly," Justin replied "You know, I had actually been considering getting a Civic or a Prius."

"What?" Frank barked, stomping on the brake and bringing the cart to an abrupt halt. "Trust me. You don't want a little pussy-car like that." He spat out the "P" in pussy with unmistakable disgust.

Turning towards Justin and wagging his finger, he said, emphatically "You, my friend, need a babe-magnet. A car with class, flash and sass." That was one his of standard TV ad lines. "*And,* one that's guaranteed to help get you some *ass!*" Justin hadn't heard *that* line on TV.

Frank paused for a quiet moment and focused on the Magic Murph-air freshener that dangled from the small rearview mirror mounted to the cart's tinted windshield. Then, he suddenly looked up and shot Justin a quick sideways glance. "I think I've got *just* what you need." He gunned the little cart down the row, across the lot, and into the cavernous service center.

Sitting by itself in the center of the garage area was lust on wheels. At least that was the phrase that popped into Justin's head when Frank brought the golf cart to a stop next to one of the most beautiful things Justin had ever seen, the vision of

Phyllis's nearly perfect ass rocking up and down in energetic reverse cowgirl position notwithstanding.

The big man jumped out of the driver's seat, took his sales-pitch stance, and went directly into his Magic Murphy shtick. "This little creampuff came in earlier this week and was just completely serviced and detailed. She's all ready to go!" He stood in front of a sparkling, metallic champagne-colored sports coupe that looked like it was already flying 100 mph around a tight corner on a steeply-banked racetrack.

Justin could almost feel the wind in his hair and the G-Forces pushing him back in his seat. Taking a closer look, he saw that the car's nameplate said it was a Hyundai Genesis coupe. *Hyundai?* It looked more like a sexy, high end European sport machine.

"Less than a year old and driven only five thousand miles by a frigid, nervous librarian that never took it over forty five miles per hour and....ah...just kidding, Justin. I've always wanted to say that on-camera. This hot little number's got every option—leather, navigation, Bluetooth, Dolby surround sound with XM radio and IPod hook-up, a back-up cam, anti-theft alarm, nineteen inch low profile custom wheels, and a powerful turbo-engine."

With Frank winding-up for the final pitch, Justin could barely contain his excitement. He walked over and ran his hand over the freshly waxed, smoothly contoured body.

Taking a look through the window, he was treated to an inviting view of so much soft creamy beige leather upholstery and richly elegant wood trim that, for a moment, he thought he was looking through a display window at a chic furniture store.

This was a car that he would have NEVER, up until this moment, considered buying under any circumstances. All he had ever needed was cheap, dependable transportation that would get him from "A" to "B". But this was different—this was lust on wheels!

He was reaching into his pocket to make sure that he had his FedEx MasterCard on hand when Frank cranked up his voice a few decibels and said, "The Kelly Blue Book says this car is valued at over twenty-five thousand dollars."

Justin's heart sank. Way out of his price range *and* his comfort zone. Sure, he could probably afford to pay that much for the car, but he knew in his heart that he could never impulsively spend that kind of money on anything. Aunt Annette had always told him to make important decisions based on logic and planning, both of which were, at the moment, in very short supply.

He left his wallet in his pocket and started to walk back to the golf cart but stopped when he saw that Frank had, seemingly out of thin air, donned his TV top hat and had his magic wand firmly in hand. Striking his famous manic-magician pose, he delivered his signature sales line with even more gusto than usual.

"And now...Magic Murphy says *...Let me make some magic for YOU!* Fourteen Nine Ninety-Nine!" Frank stabbed at the air with his wand for extra emphasis. Justin half expected to see a flash of light and smoke and hear the *POOF* effect.

They both laughed all the way to the finance office, where Justin couldn't stop thanking Frank or smiling.

*My new car!* Having friends was sweet.

# CHAPTER NINETEEN

*St. Émilion, France*

Spring was an early arrival in St. Émilion, and Guy DeBussey would have been quite happy to throw open the windows in his front offices at Château La Tour Noir and let the cool, refreshing mid-March air surround and invigorate him as he sat at his desk and continued planning his upcoming master stroke of deception.

And he *would* have enjoyed it. Except the damned nuns were back again, along with at least a dozen or so protesters armed with posters, signs and megaphones. *Why can't these idiots just let it go already?*

He opened the only set of windows that didn't offer the hostiles a direct view into his personal office space. Almost every week since the nuns and children had been evicted from the Our Lady of Mercy orphanage, groups like this had been showing up at the gates of his château and making a scene.

When they weren't beheading him in effigy or calling for a divine lightning strike straight to his private parts, they were demanding that he beg God's forgiveness and atone for his legion of sins. That involved, naturally, paying for the construction of a new orphanage on land donated by none other than...him. "What fucking planet do these morons come from?" He turned to Bruno, who had just entered the room bearing a tray of coffee, croissants and fresh fruit. "At least when I die and go to hell, I'll never have to see another one of these fucking nuns again." DeBussey was about to stuff one of the croissants into his mouth when he was interrupted by excited shouts from outside.

"Look. There he is. The Bastard of Bordeaux!" *Merde...how do they always spot me?* Both men watched out the window as the nuns and the platoon of protesters ran to a spot on the gravelly sidewalk just in front of his window, queuing up like a column of seventeenth century soldiers on a battlefield firing line. Bruno laughed as he pointed at the two nuns standing in the center.

"Boss, look...Laurel and Hardy are with them again!" While the odd couple in black habits might have borne a distant resemblance to the old comedy team, Guy DeBussey didn't find anything humorous about their presence at his office this morning.

Over the last few months, he had learned that the tall skinny one with the long, craggy face was named Sister Marie Agnes, and she had been in charge of "Our Lady" before they had all been given the boot by the "St. Émilion Scrooge." He shuddered. That face could give a blind man nightmares!

The other nun was even taller and at least three times as wide, and although he wasn't sure of her real name, he had overheard some of the others call her Sister "Ralph." Maybe because she appeared to be trying to grow a moustache under her unattractive pug nose.

Today, over her rumpled, ill-fitting black habit, she was wearing some sort of a marching band percussion harness with a small brass snare drum attached. When Sister Marie Agnes raised her ever-present megaphone and gave the sign, Sister Ralph began her cadence and the protesters all joined in with one of their irritating, mindless chants:

Rat tat tat. Rat tat tat.
*Guy DeBussey repent*
*Guy DeBussey repent*
*Help the sisters pay the rent*
Rat tat tat. Rat tat tat.

On and on it went, with the chant growing louder and more exuberant with each passing round. Normally after a few verses, he'd shake his head, flip them the finger, close the curtains and walk away. But on this beautiful, sunny morning, the Bastard of Bordeaux had arranged for a little light entertainment for himself and his staff.

"Bruno," he barked, "assemble the men outside. Chop chop!" As Bruno bolted out of the room, DeBussey opened one of the doors of the old, ornately carved armoire that ran half the length of the back wall and took out a nondescript white box. From it he removed a very large, gold-plated bull horn that was adorned with the La Tour Noir crest. He'd had it custom-made and enhanced, and it was guaranteed to be deafeningly loud. He couldn't wait to try it out.

His cell phone vibrated. It was a one word text from Bruno: *READY.* When he reappeared at the window, the crowd became even more agitated, and he had to duck to avoid being pelted by the volley of tomatoes and eggs launched at him by the now unruly protesters.

He flipped the bullhorn "on", pointed it at the center of the group and gave it a few "crowd-control" test blasts. *HOOG HOOOG!* It was even louder than advertised, and the result was immediate. Nearly in unison, the stunned protesters dropped their signs and posters and covered their ears. Sister Ralph even dropped her drumsticks.

DeBussey was completely thrilled with his new toy. "You don't like it, yes?" he yelled, his metallic-sounding voice thundering harshly out of the bullhorn's large, elongated golden speaker cone. He gave them another double shot of eardrum splitting pain.

*HOOOG HOOOOG! Why didn't I think of this before?*

"You people disgust me!" he bellowed through the bullhorn "Why don't you call the fucking pope in Rome. He's got *much* more money than I do." Totally caught up in the glory of the moment, DeBussey waxed poetic and composed his own spontaneous chant:

*I will NEVER pay*
*I Will NEVER pay*
*Piss-off and go away*

While he was making his bold, artistic statement, a few members of the crowd recovered just enough to launch one last coordinated fusillade of mixed vegetables and protein. One of the eggs caught him right on the top of his nearly hairless head and caused the startled DeBussey to cease his chanting and momentarily retire from the battlefield.

A cheer went up through the small crowd of protestors, and even the usually stone-faced Sister Marie Agnes smiled and raised her hands in victory. She high-fived with Sister Ralph, who then picked up her sticks and started drumming another cadence for a new chant.

Moments later an irate DeBussey reappeared at the window with a towel draped over his balding skull. Into the gleaming bullhorn, he yelled "BRUNO, NOW!" Running from around the corner of the building, Bruno and three accomplices arrived on the scene, collectively lugging a large gauge fire hose between them. They took up a position a few meters from the mob and waited the boss' next order.

The drumming and chanting ceased, and in that brief moment, as the two groups warily eyed one another, a calm silence hung over the courtyard. Then, with Bruno aiming directly at the sisters in the middle, the Bastard of Bordeaux loudly issued his next command: "BRUNO, CLEAN-UP THIS RIFF RAFF. LET THEM HAVE IT!"

His head thug got a firm grip on the nozzle of the high pressure hose, ripped open the valve and unleashed a powerful torrent of liquid chaos onto the annoying nuns and their supporters. As the water plowed into the crowd, its force knocked them, one by one, off of their feet and onto the rapidly muddying ground. Still at the window, DeBussey laughed maniacally into his golden bullhorn and harangued the floundering protesters with insults.

"Is someone thirsty? Well, my friends, drink this!" *HOOOOG! HOOOOOG!* Even the squarely built, jumbo-sized sister Ralph couldn't withstand the pressure from the hose. She crashed down with such force that when she fell on her little snare drum. it was crushed flatter than a folded crepe.

"HA, HA, HA, HA," DeBussey hooted "No more drumming for you, Sister Mustachio!" As some of the people tried to regain their feet, he called for his strike force to give them each another blast. "There's one on the left...don't let that woman up...Bruno, you idiot, you are too slow...faster...FASTER!"

The protestors were all slipping and flopping down like so many drunks on ice skates. The next burst caught Sister Marie

Agnes directly in the face, knocking off her head covering and revealing that she had a balder, shinier pate than even DeBussey himself.

"HA, HA, HA—look—it's my twin sister!" DeBussey cackled into the bullhorn. He was laughing so hard now that tears streamed down his cheeks and he could barely catch his breath. He flashed his men the cut-off sign, and when he regained his composure, he addressed the mud-soaked, water-logged crowd for the last time.

"Thank you sisters and friends. That was more fun than I've had in a very, very long time. I hope that we will have the chance to do it again soon! Adieu." *HOOG. HOOOG*! He flipped them the finger, closed the window, and sat down to enjoy his coffee and croissants. *MMMM...delicious!*

# CHAPTER TWENTY

*Orlando, Florida*

Buzzing around town behind the wheel of his hot little car gave everything a new and different feel for Justin. In the weeks since he'd gotten his new ride, it seemed he might have actually started living someone else's life.

Instead of being viewed as the picture of pathos in a battered old Buick, the new attention showered on him by his coworkers at FedEx and the approving looks he got from strangers at stoplights told him he did have a new image— Hunk in a Hyundai!

He knew that attributing his new-found confidence solely to his car purchase was shallow, superficial thinking at its finest, but what the hell—he couldn't deny that his perception of reality had changed for the better.

He had joined the lunch carpool and started enjoying his midday break with his colleagues away from the vending machines and had shown up, *sans* Star Trek T-shirt, at last week's FedEx beer and darts night at Clancy's Irish Pub. And he was pleasantly surprised to find a decent Côtes du Rhône on the menu, which he enjoyed all evening while chatting up Alyssa, a cute office new-hire. And he'd tried his hand at a few games of darts, too.

His Juice Brothers had added him to their group e-mail list, and most days he received all sorts of wine news, entertainment and dining info, jokes, political commentary, recipes and soft core porn from one or more of the guys.

Steve St. Clair liked to send cartoons from *The New Yorker* magazine and links to provocative articles from similar, stylish periodicals. He also sent a daily picture of his "set of the day"—women with perfect breasts. Justin always opened Steve's e-mails first.

Brad was all about wine news from around the world, new wines in stock and the specials of the week. In one of his e-mails, he had also mentioned something about a trip to France later in the year. *What was that about?*

Mike Lazarus was into humor and kept up a nonstop flow of comedy links, funny stories, news of the weird, one liners and strange quotations from invented "before and after" historical figures, like Marcus Aurelius Twain, Benjamin Franklin Roosevelt, and Clarence Thomas Jefferson.

Frank didn't correspond very often, but when he did, he was usually looking for word game assistance; "Guys, help— what's an eight letter word starting with the letter *E,* for *erection*—other than *erection*? Thanks."

And then there was Barry Love, with his practical jokes and totally off-center thoughts and obsessions. Justin learned Barry had served in Afghanistan and that he had, in some capacity, seen real life-threatening action. Perhaps that explained all of his strange and sometimes cryptic emails.

But no amount of depleted uranium ordnance poisoning or stress-induced psychosis could explain his fascination with a website called "Afghan Amateurs: Bodacious Burka Booty." Against the repeated protests of all recipients, almost every day he continued to send the guys disturbing split image JPEGs.

The first half of each picture showed the image of a woman covered head to toe in the dark robes and veils of a traditional Burka. The second half of the photo showed the robe lifted to expose different body parts, or it was removed entirely and the woman was left wearing only her face-covering head scarf or hijab. In Justin's opinion, ninety-nine percent of them should have remained covered, for the good of all mankind. He always opened Barry's e-mails last.

But no matter what the content, Justin was happy with all of the chatter, which heretofore had been nonexistent in his life. He gladly clicked on the links and learned about all sorts of wine related topics, or laughed his ass off at a funny story, read a thought-provoking piece on the mayor's attempts at intrusive Nanny-state control over the lives of the citizens of Manhattan, sent Frank some suggestions for his crossword clues, or looked for the hot one percent of the girls of Afghanistan.

And when he thought about sending the Juice Brothers links to things that he found interesting, he realized that he hadn't gone to any Sci Fi/geek websites in weeks and had even let his subscription to *Wired* magazine expire. Surprisingly, he hadn't missed any of it. Instead of *Wired,* he now subscribed to *The Wine Spectator* and Robert Parker's *Wine Advocate.*

With Brad's advice and guidance, out of the back of the *Spectator* he ordered a self-contained one hundred bottle capacity wine cellar to house his small but growing collection. It hadn't arrived yet, but when it did he was finally going to drain aunt Annette's fish tank in the living room and replace it with the vino-fridge.

And all the while, he and Phyllis had been texting back and forth but couldn't seem to find a convenient time to get together. He had learned she was a high-end real estate agent in the middle of a busy season of listing appointments, showings, and closings, and because of the demanding work schedule, her time was at a premium.

Finally, they had agreed to meet at a Starbucks to say hello and so Justin could show off his new wheels. When he walked in, she was already sitting at a table drinking her latte, looking like sex on a stick. She got up and gave him a hug and a deep, long kiss that tasted like sweet cream and sugar. The effect on him was instantaneous, and she knew it.

They spent the next half hour chatting intently while he peered over his Vente café macchiato at her wonderful cleavage, and as they walked out the door to say their goodbyes, Phyllis announced her intention to "christen" his new car in her own special way. When they got in, Justin tried to stay cool as she told him to put his seat all the way back. Then, right there in the parking lot directly in front of the coffee shop and a Five Guys Burgers & Fries restaurant, with her head bobbing up and down over his exposed lap, Phyllis christened both Justin and his new car "The Love Machine."

# CHAPTER TWENTY-ONE

*St Émilion, France*

Bruno Bastian had been working for Guy DeBussey for so long he almost couldn't remember his life before they'd met. The two bad seeds relationship had taken root not far from where he now stood, at the side of the Château La Tour Noir helipad, watching his boss ascend in his private, luxury chopper. DeBussey was heading out for a weeklong business trip to Burgundy and the Rhône valley, and Bruno watched as the helicopter disappeared into a bank of low clouds. There would be more conquests and land for his boss and more broken dreams and ruin for someone else. And without a doubt, more entries for Bruno to file in the DeBussey family scrapbook.

Working side by side during a harvest all those years ago, they had become fast friends and then willing enablers of one another's distinct talents. Bruno had a knack for breaking things—windows, locks, thick, heavy chains, warehouse doors and, when necessary, human bones. His new best friend Guy was a dreamer and a schemer, and his gift was devising ever more creative and lucrative ways for Bruno's true talents to be employed.

First, they boosted cases of expensive top name wines from warehouses all over the Bordeaux region. Then they moved up to entire loads of product and the vehicles that carried them. Bruno did the dirty work and Guy made the merchandise disappear quickly and quietly. And once or twice, they had even made people disappear, too. Together they made quite a dynamic duo, and for a few years, as the black cash poured in,

Bruno thought it would never end. They kept their jobs, and they kept quiet about their successful partnership and profits.

But then little Guy's star had begun to rise and he moved up the ranks into the front office. He started wearing nice clothes and hanging out with the stiffs in sales and management. And, as he climbed ever-higher in the hierarchy of the wine business, he had less and less time for their extra-curricular activities. And then, it was over.

Bruno's career, or rather his job at the winery was a dead-end position in motor pool maintenance. He tried to continue on his own, but without Guy's brain power, his felonious after-hours forays became much more dangerous and far less profitable. Bored and frustrated, he considered moving on, but his ex-partner in crime had come to him and asked him to stay.

"You trust me, yes Bruno?" he asked, his dark eyes darting around the garage to see if there were any potential listeners close by.

"Of course I trust you. Why do you ask me this?" Bruno replied as he slid out from under the vineyard tractor he had been working on. His hands were covered in black and his coveralls were liberally smeared with grease, oil, and whatever else one found on the floor of an engine repair shop.

"Because, my friend, I have a plan for the future and I want you to be a part of it. All I ask is that you be patient, and be ready to help me when I need you."

Bruno liked what he was hearing—a chance to get back into the easy money and out of the grease pit. He smiled as he gave a Gallic grunt and said "So then, partners again?" He extended his filthy hand to shake on the deal, but pulled it back when he realized that DeBussey had made no effort to take it.

"Partners?" DeBussey asked in a haughty tone. "No, Bruno, not partners. I want you to work *for* me, just like before. Sure, we used to split fifty-fifty, but we both know who ran the show, yes?"

Bruno's smile fell and his mouth narrowed into a slit. He was trying to quickly think of something to say in protest, but thinking quickly wasn't exactly his strong suit.

DeBussey pressed on. "Before you get mad and walk away, please hear me out, old friend. I have big plans to do things that are going surprise a lot of people in the wine business, and most of them are not going to be very happy. But so what? Fuck them all!" His cold eyes flashed with the hot anger he worked so hard to conceal from his business associates and clients. "And some of these things I am going to accomplish might require the services of a...hmmm...of a *specialist* to bring some of these idiots around to my way of thinking, if you know what I mean."

Bruno knew exactly what he meant.

"Someone I know and can trust. Someone who will be paid extremely well and never have to get his hands dirty again, at least not with oil and grease," he said, raising a thick eyebrow.

Bruno knew exactly who he meant. His smile returned as Guy DeBussey extended his stubby little hand and they shook on their new deal.

"Now," DeBussey ordered, "get me something to clean this *merde* off of my hand!"

As the sound of the helicopter faded into the distance, Bruno walked toward the main house and thought about that first command his new boss and ex-partner had given him. The first of many, it had been delivered with an authority and edge that he'd never heard in the short man's voice before.

Over the years that authority had grown more assertive and the edge had become much harder and intimidating. But it never had bothered him. He was paid extremely well and never had to get his hands too dirty. And he liked being the right hand to such a successful tyrant. It just felt...well...*right*. As Beverage DeBussey grew in stature and success, so grew his own fortunes, and he began to make the kind of money that he had never thought possible. It was even better than the old days, and for many years he felt as though he was living in a dream so perfect and fulfilling he never wanted it to end.

But then something changed, Bruno remembered the exact day and time he awoke from his perfect dream and into a world that tormented and conflicted his newly found soul. It was the day he fell in love with Lala Chang, the newly minted Mrs. Guy DeBussey.

# CHAPTER TWENTY-TWO

The grand dining hall was long and fairly wide and decorated with a number of old, darkly colored tapestries that were hung vaulted-ceiling to floor on three out of its four soaring walls Suspended over the expansive oak table with seating for twenty four was an immense antique chandelier, its eighty-four candelabra lights supported by gilded fixtures sitting atop a hanging menagerie of the finest crystal money could buy.

On those extremely rare occasions when the hall was full and guests were seated beneath the fully lit fixture, the effect was said to be like gazing up at brilliant sunlight filtering through a frozen waterfall. Today however, the lights were off, the table was empty, and the grand dining room played host to but one solitary guest.

The great room's remaining side wall consisted of a bank of large, heavy, wood and etched glass doors. They, too, stretched from ceiling to floor and offered a panoramic view of the winery, a few of the other buildings on the property, and the rolling, vine covered hills beyond.

The morning was relatively warm, and before breakfast, Lala had asked that the doors be opened to allow the sweet spring air into the château, hoping it would blow away the last, stale remnants of another dull, emotionally desolate winter in St. Émilion.

Sitting alone at the head of the grand table and finishing her tea, she also hoped that the fresh air and the change of seasons would bring her renewed energy and the courage to follow through and do what must be done. Today.

As the thump of the now departed helicopter's rotors receded into the spring sky, she became aware of the rhythmic crunch of distant footfalls making their way up the gravel path towards the back of the château and the grand hall. *Here he comes. Right on time.*

After breakfast had been served, she had given the domestics the rest of the week off as a paid holiday. With the staff gone, there would be no prying eyes or ears, and she would have total freedom to put her ambitious plan into action. It was time to regain control of her own destiny. There was only one obstacle to overcome and it was a big one. But a woman's intuition is almost always right, and she had a feeling things would go as she hoped. The footfalls were getting closer. She didn't have much time.

As Bruno made his way up the path towards the rear of Château La Tour Noir, he considered his boss' last, brusque order before he bundled himself into the chopper: "Don't fuck anything up while I'm away. OK?" *So typical.*

Ever since he'd fallen in love with the lovely, mysterious Lala, his perception of his employer had been slowly evolving. Before, he had thought himself immune to the little prick's crass comments and demeaning attitude towards his staff, himself included, his wife, his rivals, his few friends— basically everyone.

Now, the sound of the man's voice was wearing on him and the shouted orders and commands that used to bounce off his back were getting under his skin. Deeply under his skin. Day by day, it was becoming more and more difficult to put up with the mordant little midget's nonstop bullshit and swallow his pride and his feelings, although he knew that regarding Lala, those feelings were strictly one way.

At least his bastard boss was away for the next few days, so there wouldn't be much for him to do. And truthfully, a five day break from Guy DeBussey would be like a month-long stress-free vacation for the average person. He was looking forward to an uneventful week of total peace and quiet.

When he reached the covered deck at the back of the château, he noticed that the tall doors to the grand dining hall were all open, so he headed for the closest one. As he crossed the threshold and entered the great room, the sight that awaited him made short work of his uneventful week, and his peaceful quiet was disturbed by the sound of a sharp intake of his own breath.

In the center of the table directly under the massive chandelier was Lala. His Lala. Lying seductively on her side on top of a plush black and silver chinchilla blanket, her head delicately resting on one hand. The dark shimmering hair cascading over her bare shoulders and partially covering her naked breasts provided a stunning contrast to her creamy alabaster skin. If that sight caused Bruno's heartbeat to accelerate into overdrive, the rest of the picture almost caused him to lose consciousness.

With her thick, full lips pursed into a round little *ooooo*, her eyes locked onto to his and then swept down the fine line of her delectable torso to the smooth, tender fold between her legs, where her other hand was pressed erotically against her flesh and making slow, sensuous circles over her clitoris. And then, she smiled.

Bruno stood in the doorway with his mouth agape and his jaw dangling in midair. It was the only part of his anatomy that was dangling. He didn't know exactly what to make of the situation or what he had stumbled on to, but when Lala disengaged her hand, raised it to her lips and suggestively licked the tip of each moist finger, he knew exactly what to do.

# CHAPTER TWENTY-THREE

*Orlando, Florida*

After he had read the e-mail invitation, Justin was pretty sure that he would RSVP with a *no, cannot attend.* Steve had sent the guys the announcement/invitation and had urged them all to come:

*The Oasis Center for Serenity and Wellness presents our tenth annual Bordeaux Grand Tasting for charity. Please join us as we celebrate the fabulous world famous wines of Bordeaux at a gala evening featuring live music, a Summer fashion show, and all of your favorite French hors d'oeuvres. All for a great cause. Next Friday evening. 6:30 p.m.- 9 p.m. $75 per person. Black Tie Optional.*

His first thought was that the seventy-five dollar fee was more than he was willing to spend. His second thought was that he had nothing to wear. But his third thought was of the wine rep he met at his first tasting at Brad's shop, back in early February. *Destiny. Would she be there?* And then he read Steve's additional note: *Guys – P.S.: this will be a good launch party and an opportune time for a planning session for our upcoming trip to Vin Expo in June. Late dinner at my place after the event. Girlfriends spouses/wives optional. Be there! P.P.S.: Justin, this includes you, too.*

Justin had seen other e-mails about a planned Juice Brothers trip to France, and since he knew that *vin* meant *wine* in French, his astute mind immediately postulated that Vin Expo was some sort of a wine fair or event. *It's probably no big deal.* He turned his attention back to Destiny and the charity tasting, trying to decide if it would be worth the money and a trip to the Men's Wearhouse or Macy's for something to wear other than his one nice polo shirt and a pair of blue jeans.

*But what is Bordeaux all about, anyway?* He definitely wanted to know more. In addition to various wine magazines, he had also recently subscribed to eRobertParker.com, wine guru Robert Parker's online offering of articles, blogs and reviews, so he quickly logged-on and searched for anything related to *Bordeaux.* After clicking on a few different links, he wound up at *Bordeaux.com,* and settled in for a lazy Sunday afternoon in front of the fish tank with his IPad.

Like most people in the western world, he knew the name Bordeaux and associated it with fine wine, but beyond that, he had no idea. So far, he had experienced wines from the Rhône valley in France and wines from all over Spain, but he had yet to taste a wine from Bordeaux. As he read through the wealth of information on the website, he learned that the region was located in Southwest France and consisted of the large, bustling Bordeaux city and all of the surrounding wine growing areas, called appellations.

The most important and well known of these appellations were Margaux, Paulliac, St. Julien and St. Estephe to the north, St. Émilion and Pomerol to the east, Pessac-Leognan and Graves to the southwest and Sauternes to the south. The red wines from each appellation were all made from the same types of grapes in varying amounts or blends. And while these grape *varietals*—cabernet sauvignon, merlot, cabernet franc, petit verdot and malbec—were universal throughout the Bordeaux region, in addition to the type of grapes used in a wine, the specific growing conditions in each appellation, or the *terroir*, ultimately determined a wine's characteristics and flavor. *There's that word again...terroir...it's all about the micro-climate, the soil, the elevation and exposure to the sun. Fascinating!*

Justin was surprised to learn that, for example, the wines from Margaux were different from the wines of St Estephe, and wines from Pessac-Leognan had different characteristics from those grown and bottled in Pomerol. The wines from Paulliac were dominated by the cabernet grape whereas in St Émilion, merlot was king. The dry white wines of the entire region were made from sauvignon blanc and semillon grapes, as well as the sweet dessert wine from the appellation of Sauternes. Who knew?

There was also a classification system that dated from the mid-nineteenth century, and it divided the wines estates or *Châteaux* into a multi-tiered hierarchy made up of first growths, second, third, fourth and fifth growths and a few other designations for wines of lesser pedigree or quality. He saw names that he recognized from looking through his recent wine mags: Lafite, Mouton Rothschild, La Tour, Pétrus and Haut Brion, but there were many more Châteaux and so many other sub regions to learn about.

But what really grabbed his attention and gently tugged at his soul were the pictures of the French countryside and the old buildings and architecture. The images of lush, green rolling hills surrounding acre after acre of perfectly manicured vineyards, and the grand châteaus, with their steeply pitched roofs and medieval-looking towers and turrets left him with a nostalgic feeling that brought him back to the end of his senior year in high school.

He had been disappointed when, at the last minute, the local business sponsors of his class trip to France had hastily withdrawn their financial support, but Aunt Annette had been truly heartbroken that she couldn't afford to pay the difference or make other arrangements for him to go with the rest of the class. They had sat on this same sofa reading the old travel guides and brochures and imagining just how wonderfully unforgettable the whole experience of his trip to France would be. The senior trip that never was.

Clicking through dozens of images of country lanes winding through verdant forests and vineyards, fields covered with sunflowers in full bloom, distant farmhouses with their characteristic slate roofs, or an eleventh century hill-top cathedral with its spire jutting into a cloudless, blue summer sky gave him a sentimental longing for the romance and mystery of the trip abroad that he had never taken. *Maybe Vin Expo is a big deal.*

He RSVP'd *will attend* to Steve's charity tasting invite, clicked-off the IPad, and set out for the mall to find something decent to wear to a "Black Tie Optional" affair.

# CHAPTER TWENTY-FOUR

The week passed by in a flash, and late Friday afternoon, Justin was entering the address of The Oasis into his Hyundai's on-board navigator when his phone rang. The car's Blue Tooth system, which he had chosen to be voiced by Leonard Nimoy, announced, with its halting, robotic delivery: *call from… Steve….Saint…Claire…totally…illogical!* Even though he wasn't quite as into the Sci-Fi thing anymore, he just couldn't say no to having Mr. Spock announce his incoming calls.

"Hi Steve, I'm just getting ready for the big event. What's up?"

"Justin, can you hear me?" The background noise was over-powering and it sounded like Steve was standing in the middle of a tornado.

"Yes, just barely. Is everything okay for tonight?"

"Absolutely. I just wanted to make sure you have the directions to my place for the late dinner after the event. I'm probably going to be too busy to do much socializing during the tasting and—" Steve was cut-off by a long, loud squeal of feedback that was immediately followed by a pounding drum beat and what sounded like a DJ yelling *YEAH BAABBY.* "Justin, still there?"

"I'm here…sounds like you're in the middle of a rave party, not that I've actually ever been to one."

"Oh yeah, that. Towards the end of the tasting we're having a little summer fashion show featuring some of our female members, and they're testing-out the system for the catwalk music. I think you'll be surprised at how much you're going to enjoy it."

*Catwalk?* Steve gave him the directions and rang-off, and Justin headed out of his humble neighborhood and into unfamiliar territory—the west side of town.

Closing in on six-thirty, he was well on his way to the Oasis for the Bordeaux charity tasting and driving through the heart of the very upscale Westside.

*Must be nice.* That was the recurring thought he had every time he passed by a different, gated community. Lined up one after the other on both sides of the road and perfectly positioned amongst the area's dense greenery, they sported names like The Preserve, Sapphire Trace, Portofino Bay, and Cypress Creek and were each packed full of enormous McMansions with megabuck landscaping and professional outdoor lighting.

Even the neighborhood streets were impressive, with their extra-wide median islands featuring covered gazebos, fountains, flower beds and sculpture. Ornate signs pointed in different directions to the country club, the golf course, the tennis courts, and the equestrian park.

*Must REALLY be nice.*

Rounding the next corner, the Nav System, also voiced by Leonard Nimoy, informed him that his destination was less than one mile away and gave its final instructions: *fascinating....turn left in .5 miles...illogical human.* He still loved that dry, Mr. Spock humor.

After he made the last turn, he drove by one final community. It was called The Grand Bayou, and its doublewide wrought iron gates embellished with golden eagles and Fleur de Lis designs, uniformed guards at the gatehouse and imposing eight foot perimeter wall gave one the unmistakable impression that anyone living within those walls had truly achieved elite status in life. *Sooo... THAT's where Steve lives.* Justin hoped he would be able to convince the burly gate guard with the communications head gear and the stun gun to let him in for the dinner later in the evening.

Arriving at the Oasis made an equally grand impression on Justin. As he cleared the trees, he came to a large circular drive with a reflecting pool in the center, but his attention was drawn to the elegant three story structure laid out in a lazy "U" shape: a center building flanked by two slightly smaller wings placed at gently sloping angles. The façade was done in pink stucco with white trim and featured a variety of arched openings and windows. Each building had a multi-tiered central structure that was crowned by a domed cupola and topped with colorful flags flying in the evening breeze.

It made Justin think of a giant, pink, art-deco wedding cake. He hoped tonight's events would be as sweet. He pulled under the portico and hesitantly turned the keys for his Genesis Coupe over to the valet. He would have bounded up the staircase by twos, but his new dress shoes felt a bit stiff and unnatural on his feet, and the last thing he wanted to do was fall flat on his ass before the festivities even began. *Later, no problem. Now, not so good.*

Standing at the top of the stairs in front of the arched double doorway and looking, once again, like he had just stepped out of the pages of *GQ* magazine, Steve St. Clair was busy glad-handing or air kissing the arriving attendees for this evening's soirée. They, like Steve, were turned out in their formal best and wearing almost excessive amounts of shiny, high class bling. *I don't even wear a watch,* Justin thought, glancing at his bare wrist and fingers.

When Steve noticed Justin, he did a double-take and then lit-up with the best thousand watt smile money could buy. "*Well, Well.* What, or rather *whom,* do we have here?" he said, just loudly enough for only Justin to hear. As they shook hands, Steve continued "You clean up very nicely, my friend. A few of us had a bet on whether or not you'd show up in corduroys with pink or green shoes tonight, but I'm happy to say that you have proven us all wrong—and in a big, *big* way!"

"Really?" Justin returned the high wattage smile with one of his own. He was glad and gratified that he had spent the time and money, more money than he should have, shopping for the right ensemble for this evening's event. From Steve's reaction, he could tell he had done well.

Standing with Steve under the portico at the entry to the Oasis, in his classic black, slim-fit Hugo Boss suit and matching Italian leather loafers, and sporting his new, layered, swept-back almost down-to-his-shoulders hair style, it was with good humored confidence that he happily honored Steve's request: "Do a 360…Let's get the full effect!"

With hands raised, Justin obliged and did a slow, graceful turn before entering the building to check-in and receive his tasting glass for a night with the wines of Bordeaux.

# CHAPTER TWENTY-FIVE

It wasn't quite six-thirty and the Oasis' reception area was packed full of people standing and talking in small groups, waiting for the doors to the tasting room to open. Justin slowly made his way through the maze of bodies towards the reception desk, where he presented his ticket and was given a list of the evening's wines and their tasting-table numbers, as well as a glass.

A *Bordeaux* glass!

The interior of the building was just as striking as the façade. The overall color scheme was vaguely tropical, but done in a muted, tasteful style. The overall effect was one of relaxing, understated elegance, and Justin marveled at the impressive collection of art that adorned the atrium's sweeping, two-story walls.

A large banner above the reception desk read "Welcome to Paradise" and just beneath it was a large, well-lit sign that resembled the menu in a fast food restaurant. It listed the multitude of services on offer at the Oasis, with names like the "Maximum Indulgence" Day Spa package, the "Coconut Sea Salt Body Scrub," a "White Caviar Illuminating Pedicure," and the "Advanced Marine Biology Facial."

There were body wraps and Swedish deep tissue massages. Aroma therapy and hot stone rubs. Manis, pedis and Brazilian waxing. Tennis lessons, swimming pool memberships and cabana rentals. But there were no prices posted. Anywhere! *If you have to ask, you probably can't afford it.* Why would anyone want a "full-body pomegranate polish?" *What the hell is that, anyway?*

He took a step back and scanned the room for familiar
faces, but not seeing anyone he knew, worked his way back
through the crowd of at least one hundred and fifty people
towards the south wing of the facility. There, sitting on a large,
artistically paint-spattered antique easel, he found a detailed
site map of the entire property.

*Wow, Steve!* This place had everything, just like Steve had
said when they first met at the Twisted Cork. In addition to the
Day Spa and the separate plastic surgery practice, which was
located on the second floor of the main building, the Oasis
offered its members two tennis courts, an Olympic-sized pool
with a cabana relaxation area, a sauna, thermal pools, a private
hedge-enclosed Japanese meditation garden, and a state of the
art gym. *Maybe this IS paradise...*

Walking past the sign, he came to the juice bar and health
food shop, two side-by-side Kiosks made of shining glass and
stainless steel, both shuttered for this evening's activities. Just
beyond, he looked through wide glass windows and doors into
the pool area, where a jazz band was set up on the deck under a
striped pink and white awning and just beginning their first set
of the night. Near the stage, half a dozen tables were awaiting
the attendees, and a cadre of white-coated servers was busily
setting out trays of what Justin assumed were the promised
selection of *hors d'oeuvres* and finishing their last second
preparations. As the first notes from the band drifted through
the evening air, a small smattering of applause broke out in the
atrium as the doors to the tasting room were opened. Justin
turned and hurriedly made his way back. *Bordeaux, here I
come!*

The tasting itself was being held in the north wing of the
property, in the Oasis's café-restaurant named "The Paradise
Bistro." As Justin entered, he immediately spotted Brad, Frank,
and Mike gathered in front of one of the tables at the far end of
the room. Glasses in hand, they were already sipping on the
first pours of the evening.

Like the south wing section near the juice bar and health food kiosks, through its own series of large windows, the "Bistro" also over-looked the pool, cabanas and deck, and its doors were opened wide to allow the live music in and the guests out. The dining area had been cleared and all of its tables placed in a "horseshoe" around the perimeter of the room. Each tasting table had a number hung overhead, and the guys were standing by table seven. Justin looked on his list and saw that this was the "Richard Fox Company" table, and it featured about a dozen wines with names he didn't recognize. As he made his way through the center of the room and the throng of tasters, the band launched into their next song, "I've Got You Under My Skin."

*Grape skins, perhaps?*

Negotiating his way through the crowded room, he brushed past a distinguished-looking gentleman who was arm-in-arm with two provocatively dressed femme fatales, one of whom was a tall blond with striking features. The other happened to be Phyllis Braunstein. The missing-in-action Phyllis Braunstein, and what was she doing with this skinny old dude? Ever since he had decided to attend the charity tasting, he'd been trying to contact her about tonight, but she'd never responded. And here she was. He tried a little wave to get her attention and say hello, but instead of smiling or even waving back, she looked directly at him, or rather through him, immediately turning her attention back to her silver-haired escort.

*Hmm...not even a flicker of recognition.* It was a little shocking and even disheartening, but Justin thought of a phrase he learned back in French class—*C'est la vie*—and with a shrug, decided to make it his theme of the night.

As he approached his friends at table seven, it appeared that both Frank and Brad were wearing stylish, formal attire. For such a big guy, Frank looked almost svelte in his nicely tailored tux. Mike's getup, however, was another story entirely. From a distance, he also seemed to be dressed for the occasion, but as Justin joined them and took a closer look, he thought something about his "tuxedo" was a little "off." He was wearing long dark pants, but instead of a real suit, he was actually sporting a white T-shirt emblazoned with a tacky-looking iron-on tux design, complete with a faux bowtie. Further inspection revealed that Mike's trousers were really super-casual, loose-fitting cargo pants, and that, along with the requisite number of superfluous pockets, there were horizontal zippers on each of the pant legs, just above the knee. *What a character...at least he's not wearing his sunglasses and flip-flops!*

The guys all greeted him with looks of wide-eyed surprise that quickly gave way to broad smiles, as they, like Steve, complimented Justin on his transformation from second rate to fashion plate.

"That is an outstanding look for you, Mr. J," Brad said as they fist-bumped. "I guess I owe St. Clair ten bucks on losing our bet."

"It took me a second to recognize you," Frank added, along with a quick Magic Murphy eyebrow-bounce and a light back slap. "I'm going to have to pay up, too."

"What are you guys talking about" Mike quipped with mock sarcasm. "True...his hair looks great, but his duds can't hold a candle to mine!" He laughed, as he held his arms wide open for their approval and then took Justin by the shoulders for a man-hug.

"Thanks guys!" Justin said gratefully, as they turned their attention back to the table to resume sampling the wines. He could see that they had already worked their way through most of the bottles on the table. "How did you three manage to taste so many of these wines already? I mean, the doors have only been open for like ninety seconds."

"That's true," Brad answered, his lips and teeth already bearing a slight purplish tint. "We came with Barry and got in early. He's pouring over at table fifteen."

Justin scanned the room and spotted the number fifteen hanging from the ceiling, but the room was so jam-packed with tasters that he really couldn't see beyond them. He looked on his list and saw that table fifteen was sponsored by "Cosmo Brands," and he actually recognized a few of the wines that they were pouring this evening.

"Wow, Barry's table has got some big names. Shouldn't we start there?"

"Ah, impatient, impulsive youth," Mike rasped in his desert-dry tenor. "We'll get there, but we always save the best for last. Meanwhile, why don't you try some these *fine* wines imported by our *dear friend* Richard Fox," he added in a caustic tone.

"Mike obviously doesn't like Richard Fox," Brad offered.

"He's a fucking dickhead!" Mike spat, albeit quietly, with real contempt.

"I wouldn't go *that* far," Brad replied "You're just pissed that his "WineMax" stores have negatively affected our businesses."

"Well, aren't you?" Mike asked. "Aww, fuck it! Let's sample the rest of his swill and move on." He and Frank moved back closer to the table to resume tasting.

"I've seen the WineMax across from the mall," Justin said to Brad. "It's like a giant warehouse superstore."

"It *is* a giant warehouse superstore." Brad shook his head. "It's even got a wine bar and a beer tasting room. Mike is angry at the Fox Company because of how much market share WineMax has gobbled up."

"Wow, I had no idea," Justin answered and added, "So, do you think that for my first experience tasting Bordeaux, I should just skip this table all-together?"

"Well, there is one Richard Fox wine that you could try." Brad led Justin to the final bottle on table seven. It was from St. Émilion, and its label featured a curious-looking oval-shaped coat-of-arms with a tall black tower in the center. Brad and Justin presented their glasses, and the server poured each of them a small taste of the Château La Tour Noir. Justin swirled the garnet-hued wine in his glass and was immediately surprised and impressed by the rich, seductive aromas of roasted coffee mixed with a slight hint of menthol, black cherries, and notes of sweet herbs. The sensational, enchanting bouquet rose out from the top of his glass like a soft whisper saying "drink me, drink me." He could only obey.

As he took a small sip, his first taste of Bordeaux, and rolled it around in his mouth, he was quickly and completely swept away by the rush of smoky, earthy flavors that poured over his palate like a mighty river roaring downstream at flood stage. The cedar, crème de cassis and deep, dark blue and black berry flavors that followed were like the thick, delectable icing on a substantially rich and complex layer cake. He took a long moment to savor the wine's lengthy finish and reflect on its impact—this was a different kind of wine experience, and it was truly profound and almost transcendent in its intensity.

He glanced over at Brad, whose eyes were closed as if he were in deep thought, no doubt savoring the fabulous flavors for himself. He then looked to Mike, who nodded and silently mouthed the word *wow,* and then to Frank, whose nose, as usual, was buried as deeply into his glass as it could go. His face had gone a bright red and he was hyperventilating. Loudly. *I hope he doesn't start snorting it!*

Brad opened his eyes and looked directly at Justin. "Now, *that's* an outstanding Bordeaux! It's young, but it's got amazing structure and the sweet tannins are already well integrated. My, my, my...this has to be the best wine *ever* made by La Tour Noir!" Frank, who had now cooled down to a shade of hot-pink, just looked-up, grunted and kept inhaling.

"It *is* an amazing young wine" Mike agreed, "...and a great one at that. But Richard Fox is *still* a dick! Let's move on, gentlemen."

Justin followed as the guys trekked across the crowded room to table one. Over the next hour and a half or so, they sequentially tasted their way through most of the tables, with Brad attentively checking in with Justin to see how he was enjoying his first experience with the wines of Bordeaux. And although he kept an eye out for Phyllis and her friends, he hadn't seen them again. *Oh well...C'est la vie!*

Each table was set up in the same left-to-right formation, with the wines ranging from the lightest to the heaviest in body and quality. After tasting through the first two tables, Justin thought that although many of the "starter" bottles at each table were merely pleasant and nondescript, each of them still gave one a sense of place and origin—something about them just said *Bordeaux.* And he wasn't sure exactly what it was or how he could tell, but he could. And with the fuller bodied, better-made wines, that sense of place was even more notable and striking.

*Terroir...I think I'm beginning to understand.*

So far, they had sampled wines from all the major appellations, plus others from Medoc, Côtes de Castillon, Fronsac, Lalande de Pomerol and Bordeaux Superieur, and while he still couldn't concisely define the basic essence of Bordeaux, he was able to begin differentiating between the wines based on region and style, especially the ones that were better made and more substantial on the palate.

There seemed to be more wines from St. Émilion than any of the other appellations, and Justin found these wines to be softer and easier on the palate, with more accessible round fruit. But maybe that was just an "age thing." Brad had explained that at an event like this, the distributors always showcased the latest vintages, but that the best of the wines were really meant to age in the bottle for years before they were actually ready to drink. But sometimes, even a very youthful wine could reach the hedonistic heights they had all experienced earlier in the evening with the Château La Tour Noir at table seven.

Could it be that a wine from St. Émilion was easier to enjoy when young because, in that appellation, they tended to use more merlot in the blend? When he suggested this to the guys, Mike immediately shot his theory down.

"That's way too much of a generalization, J," Mike said, his usually scratchy voice somewhat mellowed by the nonstop intake of delicious red fluids. "Sure, merlot is less tannic and acidic than the other varietals used in Bordeaux and can reach maturity at a younger age, but there are plenty of châteaux throughout the region that use fairly high percentages of merlot in their final blends. But, there are too many other factors involved, and there are scads of merlot-based wines that need time in the bottle to age so they can really shine."

*Factors, variables...hmm...* That brought Justin back to his colorful, 3D mental graphs and to a new, budding equation. But he knew he couldn't properly construct the problem and search for a solution because he lacked both the information and experience necessary to even begin to define the question:

*what is the true essence of Bordeaux?* As he sipped on a small taste of a spicy, tightly knit wine from Château Beau-Sejour Becot, also from St. Émilion, he realized that he needed much, much more information. And experience. And that meant much more wine!

# CHAPTER TWENTY-SIX

After almost two hours, the crowd was thinning a bit as many of the attendees had migrated outside to the deck where they were enjoying the *hors d'oeuvres*, the soft evening air and the jazz band. But Justin and his Juice Brothers were having none of that. With one final table to go—Barry's table—they stood in the now less crowded center of the room and compared notes.

Justin declared, and they all agreed that, so far, nothing could top the sensational wine from Château La Tour Noir. But, there were quite a number of wines that stood out from the pack, and Justin had highlighted his favorites on the list he had received when he checked in. He wanted to fill the racks of his new vino-fridge when it arrived, and he hoped that his Bordeaux faves wouldn't be too expensive.

"Okay boys, let's go get a little *love* at Barry's table!" the crimson-faced Frank suggested eagerly, and he quickly led the gang of four through the dwindling crowd. *That Frank can REALLY move when he's motivated!*

Justin and the guys greeted Barry Love, who was wearing the definition of an ill-fitting, cheap suit. Like his clothing, he looked a little rumpled and frayed-around-the-edges, and he appeared to be stooped to one side. Underneath his black beret, his long yellowish-white hair was pulled back into a ponytail that was hanging listlessly halfway down his back, and even his bushy Fu Manchu was drooping. Tonight, it looked much more Wilford Brimley than Hulk Hogan, and Justin could instantly see the growing concern on the faces of his friends.

"Barry, what happened?" Brad asked urgently. "You were fine when we came in with you. Is it the leg or the shoulder?"

"Hey, it's nothing that major." His high pitched-voice sounded strained and much thinner than Justin remembered. "I just threw my back out grabbing a case of wine...as soon as the *Oxy* I just popped kicks-in, I'll be feeling *better* than good...so...no worries my friends."

Justin could see and feel the guys relax as they digested Barry's report.

Barry then shot Justin a glance and gave him a quick up and down appraisal. Nodding his approval, he laughed and said, "The kid looks good...no pink or green shoes!" His voice was already sounding a bit stronger and it seemed to have regained some of the lilt and good humor Justin remembered from the big night at The Twisted Cork. "I guess I owe St. Clair ten bucks! Anyway, my back's not an issue because I've got plenty of help this evening." Glancing towards the entryway, he added, "I believe you all know my lovely Cosmo Brands comrade, Ms. Destiny Verrano..."

As their heads slowly turned in unison, time seemed to stand still, and Justin took a silent moment to appreciate the stunning vision of smoldering sensuality that approached him from the arched double doorway.

"Oh...My...God!" he said in a hushed half-whisper, breaking the spell. "*It's her!*" That comment earned him a light nudge in the ribs from Brad and a look that said *down boy* from Barry.

Although her arms were heavily-laden with half a dozen bottles of wine, she moved with a catlike fluidity and grace and with a knowing confidence that said she knew every male eye in the room was on her. Her beauty was that natural and radiant. With a bright smile and a slight shake of her thick, dark tresses, she set the bottles down on table fifteen and greeted the guys with a quick, cursory hello.

"Barry, are these the wines you wanted for the dinner at Steve's house?" she asked, as she carefully turned each bottle so Barry could view the labels.

"Yeah, perfect! Thanks, my dear and thanks for all of your help. Fellas, check out the partial line-up for later tonight."

While Barry and the others chatted excitedly about the vintages and pedigrees of the six soon-to-be-emptied bottles and about which wines Steve might be pulling from his own cellar, Justin watched as Destiny quietly resumed her duties pouring for the other tasters at the table.

Tonight, wearing a sheer, low cut, caviar-colored liquid satin blouse, and black, form-hugging lambskin leather pants, she was even more desirable than Justin remembered. A long, solo strand of opaque natural pearls hung invitingly around her neck and onto her chest, the diaphanous quality of the satin blouse leaving little doubt as to what awaited beneath. And just like when he had met her at his first tasting at In Vino Veritas, she was once again balancing ever-so-elegantly on a pair of sexy, spiky stilettos. *She looks divine!*

At the moment, Destiny was busy pouring for three or four other attendees, so he took a minute to check his list. There were no "starter bottles" at the Cosmo Brands table. Most of the wines were classified growths, and they were all from very well-known and highly respected châteaux. Justin even recognized some of the big names from his research and reading on Bordeaux— Cos d'Estournel, Pichon Baron, Leoville-Las-Cases and Clinet.

As Justin edged closer to her in the short line, he started to feel the familiar but almost forgotten thump in his chest and lump in his throat—the anxiety and insecurity around the opposite sex that had hounded him throughout most of his adult life...*I thought I was over that BS*... But instead of reverting to the socially inept, *Star-Trek*-shirt-wearing-nerd version of himself, he flashed back over the all of the improbable and almost unbelievable events of the last few months and thought about everything that had transpired since the last time he had actually felt this way; after getting stood-up for a date at The Bonefish Grill. Feeling emboldened, and with a growing self-confidence, he quietly told himself...*no...things have changed...I have changed...and I'm good!* He took a long, slow breath to further calm his now-under-control nerves and stepped up to Destiny's table to present his glass.

"Hi. I'd like to try the Haut-Bergey, please," Justin said, as he placed his glass in front of the first bottle, hoping for a warm response. Without looking up, Destiny poured a very small amount of the opaque ruby-colored wine into his glass.

"This is a fifty-fifty blend of cabernet and merlot from a small estate in Pessac-Leognan, and it's a great value, especially in the current vintage. Parker rated it a ninety-two," she said, as she continued pouring for the others in the line. Justin slid down to his right to accommodate those behind him, but he kept his position tableside. When she did look up and met Justin's gaze, she simply gave him a small, friendly smile and turned her attention elsewhere. *Crap! She doesn't remember me.*

Disappointed, Justin swirled the wine in his glass and sampled its nose, where he discovered notes of soft, smoky minerality and sweet cedar. When he tasted it, he found that the wine possessed a combination of earthy, tobacco-like flavors balanced by a ripe cherry fruit, followed by an enjoyable, medium-length finish.

"I like that a lot," he said, as Destiny returned with the next bottle. "It's bit lighter in color than some of the other wines I've tried tonight, but it still delivers the goods!" He offered his glass for a taste of the next wine. As she reached across the table to take it, he was just able to catch a fleeting hint of the same musky, intoxicating perfume that she had been wearing the night when he had been introduced to her at Brad's shop.

"Well, I'm sure you'll like this one, too. It's Malescot St. Exupéry from Margaux and Robert Parker has also given it a big score, although at the moment, I can't remember the exact number. Anyway, enjoy!" She poured, smiled, and again turned to offer a small taste to the others at the table. *Why doesn't she remember me? Oh well, C'est la vie...again.*

But when he swirled, sniffed and tasted, any thoughts of disappointment or frustration he might have been having instantly evaporated into a sensuous cloud of ethereal crème de cassis and dark berry perfume. *"OH WOW!"* he exclaimed a bit too loudly, and then quickly looked from side-to-side in feigned embarrassment. "I wasn't ready for *that,*" he said, as he took another sip and savored the almost other-worldly combination of complex and intense flavors.

After his slightly over-the-top reaction, Destiny turned back around and once again faced him while he was comparing notes with the other tasters, all of whom were equally impressed with the stellar Malescot. Her deep, almost violet eyes drifted slightly skyward and seemed to search her memory.

"I get this intensely extracted black raspberry fruit and a smidgeon of...and I mean this in a good way...tar...or charcoal...if that's even possible in a wine... with a little touch of cedar and oak flavors," he said. "It's outstanding, and for me, one of the best wines of the night." The others nodded in agreement and quickly re-tasted to verify Justin's opinion. When he turned back to the table and looked up from his glass, his eyes met hers. *She is SO amazing.*

But her expression was still free of any trace of recognition, and with that realization, he felt his heart sink just a little. Actually, it was drooping lower than Barry's moustache before the oxycodone kicked in.

"You don't remember me, do you?" he said, surrendering to the inevitable. "We met back in February at a Rhône tasting at Brad's shop."

With that, her entire demeanor changed as she snapped her fingers and nearly shouted "Yes, *that's it!* You're Justin the wine virgin, he of the pink shoes and the overactive taste buds!" With a broad, effervescent smile she continued, "I *do* remember you, I just didn't *recognize* you! It looks like you've had a Hollywood makeover."

And after she had poured him a taste of the deeply purple, unctuously textured Clinet, she leaned across the table, took his free hand warmly in hers and in a hot, breathy whisper said, "I like the new look. I like it *a lot.*" Justin's heart shot into space when she added "I hope you're going to be at Steve's for dinner later tonight...let's talk more then."

At that moment, just as the band finished playing the smooth jazz classic "Masquerade," Steve St. Clair's voice came piping over the PA system as he thanked everyone for coming. He also asked for all of tonight's models to report backstage to get ready for the fashion show. "The band's going to play one or two more songs, and then it'll be time for our second annual catwalk," he announced to light applause and a few hoots from the crowd.

Justin was pretty sure that he wouldn't be too interested in watching a fashion show for older women's summer clothing, so he planned to stay inside and continue exploring the wonders of *Bordeaux*. But when the band launched into their penultimate song, the funky classic "Who's That Lady?" by the Isley Brothers, Destiny suddenly handed the pouring duties back over to Barry.

Grabbing her little black purse, she quickly came out from behind the table, gave Justin a quick peck on the cheek and said "I've gotta' go get ready. You *are* going to cheer for me, aren't you?" As he watched her walk out the back doors and through the pool area, he remembered his phone call with Steve earlier in the day, while he was programming the Hyundai's Nav system, and he recalled what the DJ was yelling in the background over the pounding disco beat, *OH YEAH BAABY!*

With Barry pouring, Justin joined the other guys as they finished the tasting with the amazing line-up at the Cosmo Brands table. Frank, Mike and Brad all kept a close eye on Justin's reactions as they worked their way through the remaining wines from Clinet, Cos d'Estournel, Pichon Baron, and Leoville-Las-Case, and Justin even got an extra taste of the magnificent Malescot St. Exupéry, which he then proclaimed to be his favorite of the night.

Frank loved the tannic, massive Leoville-Las-Case from St. Julien, although he admitted it needed a few years to really come together. Brad was partial to the inky-purple, silky smooth Clinet from Pomerol, and Mike was mad for the Pichon Baron from Paulliac. He put his arm around Justin's shoulder as they re-tasted it and offered, "For me, this is the type of wine that most people think of when they hear the name *Bordeaux:* incredibly structured and complex, with hints of coffee, chocolate, rich, dark berry fruit and a touch of smoky, cedar. It's way too young to drink now, but it's still outstanding."

Justin wasn't sure about the Pichon Baron, or any other wine, being described as the *essence of Bordeaux*. He had way too much to learn and experience. What he could say with certainty was that he had really enjoyed all of them and couldn't wait to get to Steve's house to check out some of the older siblings of these young beauties.

"It's eight-forty-five," Barry announced as he poured the last remaining drops of the Clinet into his own glass. "That means I'm all done here...I'll see you guys at St. Clair's in about half an hour. And, Justin," he added with a wine and oxy induced glaze in his eyes, "try to keep your pecker in your pants during the show!"

*WTF?* Justin looked to the other guys for an explanation. Brad and Mike just grinned as Frank gave him his eyebrow dance and slapped him on the back. As they went out into the night air, the jazz band finished their final song and a DJ pumped up the volume with a thumping dance groove.

# CHAPTER TWENTY-SEVEN

The deck area was lit by strands of festive white lights that were strung throughout the branches and around the bases of the many palm and oak trees that populated the perfectly landscaped garden paradise. The pool was nicely lit and the reflection from its still, crystal clear water cast a cool aquamarine glow over the deck and cabana area. The food tables had been taken away and replaced by a narrow runway that now extended from the small stage out into the crowd. It was also lined with party lights, but at the moment, they were dark.

Standing right in the middle of the runway and illuminated by a solo spotlight, Steve was busy shuffling through a series of index cards. As the DJ brought the music down, he was handed a microphone and began his announcements. Even though Justin was looking forward to watching Destiny parade around in some sort of summer wear, he hadn't had any of the food and was getting really hungry...*hope this is over soon...*

Steve tested the mic and began with, "Once again, thanks to all of you for participating in our annual Bordeaux grand tasting, tonight benefitting the Wounded Warrior Project." The crowd offered some light applause and he continued, "Last year we added a little summer fashion show to the festivities, and it was so well received, we decided to do it again. So tonight, I would like to thank *Monsieur René's House of Couture* for supplying this season's fashions to our lovely models, gratis. Monsieur René, would you please join me on the stage and take a bow?"

There was a bit more polite applause, and as Steve worked his way back onto the stage from the runway, the crowd pushed in a little closer, lining either side of the runway. He was met onstage by Monsieur René, who also happened to be the same distinguished looking gentleman Justin had seen escorting Phyllis and her hot friend. After taking a quick bow, Monsieur René and Steve shook hands, posed for a few photos and exited stage left. As the spotlight dimmed and the stage lights began changing colors, the DJ started the show with a rumbling, low drone that was punctuated by distant sounding kettle drums... *dumm...dumm dumm...*

"Yeah, baby!" a voice boomed out of the PA speakers. "This is MC St. Clair and we are ready to get this party started!" Mike and Brad were now both clapping and Frank had his fingers stuffed into his mouth in a vain attempt at a wolf whistle. As the low drone got louder, the drums increased in tempo and intensity... *dumm dumm...dumm dumm...dumm dumm...*

"Ladies and gentleman," Steve continued over the PA, "tonight the Oasis Center for Serenity and Wellness presents ten of our most devoted, most hardworking members, all wearing the sexiest styles of the season...it's going to be... A LONG...HOT...SUMMER!"

All the lights turned a shade of deep red and hidden fog machines flooded the stage, the runway, and the spectators with a thick, rolling blanket of wine-colored mist. As the music erupted with an ear-splitting snare drum fill, a white-hot spotlight blazed on, and the first model appeared on stage.

"Our first visitor to the catwalk is twelve-year Oasis member Cynthia Schmidt. And doesn't she look wonderful?"

*Soo...THAT'S what Steve was talking about.* The entire crowd, including Justin, was now bouncing in time to the old hit, "I'm Too Sexy," as Cynthia made her way to the platform wearing a tulip-yellow beach maxi wrap that went all the way from her shoulders to her ankles. Justin judged her to be in her mid-sixties. The lights ringing the narrow walkway were also pulsating in time to the beat.

"Cynthia does fifty laps each day in our pool and teaches our yoga class twice a week. And can you believe it? She's seventy-four years old?...she's truly amazing." The crowd cheered. Justin couldn't believe it. He also couldn't believe it when she pulled off the maxi beach wrap and revealed a matching, one piece swimsuit with sexy lace-up straps crisscrossing her lightly muscled and toned back. She looked good!

Frank was especially interested as she turned at the point of the catwalk and walked back to the stage, his head moving in sync with her ass as it swung left to right in time with the music. "No woman *that* old should look *that* good," he yelled in Justin's ear.

The crowd continued bouncing to the pounding music and the flashing lights as the next model appeared on stage. "Please say hello to Mrs. Miriam Weiss, also an Oasis member for twelve years. Miriam is a big fan of aroma therapy, Brazilian waxing, and the full-body pomegranate polish."

Miriam was fairly attractive in her striped, off-the-shoulder beach dress, but she was a little chunky and didn't look like she worked out in the gym too often. Justin was thankful when she finished her walk and joined the first model back on the side of the stage, without revealing any more skin.

"I'm Too Sexy" kept the crowd pumped-up as a succession of women took to the stage in colorful, sexy beachwear. Some displayed a bit more in their swim suits, some didn't. One of the oldest women even appeared with her three French poodles all wearing matching outfits. Cute!

All of the ladies were attractive in their own way, but none of them except for Cynthia Schmidt really had what it took to rock the crowd. He was getting hungrier by the second and couldn't wait for Destiny to make her appearance so he could check her out and head to Steve's—Brad had mentioned something earlier about French bread and cheese waiting for them upon their arrival—but the other guys didn't look like they had any intention of leaving just yet. He almost winced as another slamming percussion fill blasted out of the PA, as the DJ picked-up the pace and began playing the English girl-group Bananarama's 80s disco hit "Venus."

"Yeah Baby, she's got it! Please welcome Ms. Chloe Stevens, who just joined us here at the Oasis in January."

Justin did a double-take as the statuesque knock-out blond he had seen earlier with Phyllis appeared. As the lights flashed bright white and the fog machines went into overdrive, she moved across the stage and onto the catwalk like a seasoned pro, her every move timed to the beat and designed to illicit the maximum response from the crowd: total awe.

"Chloe participates in our Zumba dance workouts and enjoys the sauna and thermal pools here at the Oasis."

Framed by the flashing lights of the runway, Chloe twisted and twirled in her hot pink, knee-length mesh cover-up. The outfit was totally see-through and all were treated to a view of her gorgeous, figure, clad only in a minimalist, hot pink bikini. Then she stopped right in front of Justin and slowly peeled-off her mesh covering, depositing it gingerly on top of Frank's wildly gyrating head. The crowd went crazy.

"Her name is really Amber, and she works for me at Popatopolis," the grinning Frank yelled into Justin's ear. *Who?...What?...Frank owns Popatopolis?* With wide-eyed glee, Frank took her discarded wrap and held it just under Justin's nose, shaking it gently. "Smell that?" he asked, again bellowing into Justin's ear, "that's stripper perfume, my boy!" They both turned their attention back to Chloe/Amber just in time to watch as she reached down and ripped her pink bikini bottoms away, leaving nothing more than a teeny, tiny G-string that covered...almost nothing.

The crowd continued to cheer wildly as she sashayed her way back down the catwalk to the stage, her bare, firm buttocks forming a nearly perfect, classic heart shape as she took her place with the others. Frank finally managed to pull off a deafening wolf whistle.

"Now, that's what I'm talkin' about," exclaimed Mike, as he high-fived all around.

Justin couldn't agree more.

"Got your money's worth yet?" a laughing Brad shouted as the music cranked-up another notch.

"Next up, please welcome Ms. Destiny Verrano!"

Justin held his breath as Destiny appeared on stage in a white, hooded, crochet beach cover-up. It hung just to her thighs, and what thighs they were! The taut, dark olive skin of her upper legs rippled as she slowly negotiated her way across the stage and onto the catwalk for her run.

"Destiny, a seven-year member of the Oasis, also attends our Zumba dance workouts, enjoys kick boxing and hits the gym three times a week with one of our personal trainers."

As her feet touched the catwalk, she pulled the hood from her head and shook her wild black curls free while moving seductively to the surging beat. Then in one fluid, effortless motion, she lifted the white cover-up over her shoulders and let it fall to her side, revealing her stunning goddess-like body covered by a zebra-patterned monokini bottom and matching wrap-around top. Descending from either side of her lithe, graceful neck, the top's fabric was stretched ever-so-tightly around her voluptuous, gravity-defying breasts and tied in back by one single, straining clasp.

She moved down the catwalk towards Justin in an intense, hypnotic halftime, and his heart rate shot into the stratosphere as he caught her eye and she gyrated her heavenly hips in a suggestive, slow grind. *Down boy!* He quickly came back to earth and realized that, along with Mike, Brad and Frank he was clapping his hands and cheering her name in time with the thumping groove; *Des Tin Eee ...Des Tin Eee...* And he was loving it!

As she turned and danced her way back to the stage and joined with the other women, Justin leaned towards Brad shouting, "*Now*, I've gotten my money's worth!" He was about to suggest that they all cut out and head over to Steve's when the music stopped and the lights abruptly dimmed. After three seconds of silence, the DJ reprised the low drone intro with the echoing kettle drums, as the fog machines clicked back on and the lights glowed a devilish red. "Ladies and gentlemen, thanks once again for attending this evening's festivities here at the Oasis for Serenity and Wellness. And now, please welcome our final model of the night, the one...the only...Ms...Phyllis...Braunstein!"

As the DJ blasted the Tubes hit song, "She's A Beauty," Phyllis appeared on stage as the last summer fashion model of the evening, but she was wearing something other than a beach cover-up or swimwear. If the blond Chloe had been the classic, statuesque beauty of the night, and Destiny the Mediterranean bombshell, Phyllis was the rock solid, fifty-nine-year-old firecracker, and in her ruby red, flyaway baby doll lingerie, she looked like the sexiest, most explosive stick of dynamite the world had ever seen.

As she bounced down the catwalk like a manic majorette performing at the fifty-yard line of the Super Bowl halftime show, she literally ripped the delicate lace top from her torso and revealed her perfectly amazing tits, in all their surgically-enhanced glory. Many in the crowd, including Justin, were shocked as she bumped and jiggled her way to the edge of the runway almost totally nude, wearing only the smallest gauge angel hair G-string ever made.

Chloe suddenly appeared at her side, removed her own bikini top, and threw it into the crowd to a chorus of cheers and catcalls. She then produced what Justin instantly recognized as the tube of Phyllis' *Love You Long Time* lube, and both women began squirting it onto one another and then vigorously rubbing it into each other's breasts.

"Now *that's* entertainment!" Frank roared, as he hoisted his considerable bulk up onto the catwalk and attempted to squeeze in between the two women, who were now locked in a slow, grinding embrace and oblivious to his presence.

It was difficult to look away, but somehow, Justin managed to tear his eyes from the salacious spectacle directly in front of him and glance back to the rear of the stage, where an alarmed-looking Steve was giving the DJ the cut-off sign. The music and light show faded out and dimmed. Destiny and all of the other models had already disappeared from the stage and most of the crowd was rapidly departing the pool deck area, some shaking their heads in disbelief.

"Thanks again for coming," Steve said sheepishly into the microphone. "That concludes our program."

In the quiet after the storm, Brad and Mike struggled to help Frank climb down from the runway as Monsieur René walked from behind the stage and handed each of his nearly naked escorts a fluffy, terrycloth robe. He looked at Justin with a sad half smile on his face, and with a Gallic shrug opined, "*C'est la vie, mon ami!*" Justin could only laugh.

# CHAPTER TWENTY-EIGHT

Justin followed the guys caravan-style for the short drive to Steve's house, and as he cleared The Grand Bayou's guardhouse and drove through the impressively gilded double wrought iron gates, he thought he had entered an episode of the old *Lifestyles of the Rich and Famous* TV show.

It was long after dark, but because the neighborhood was so well illuminated by the combination of unusually bright nineteen century style streetlamps and the mega-buck lighting utilized by most of the individual properties, it was easy to view the ostentatious parade of exquisite homes lining either side of the winding street.

Although he was following the others, had he been on his own, he would have had absolutely no trouble recognizing the sumptuous home of Mr. Steve St. Clair—it looked exactly like a smaller version of the Oasis, complete with the picture-perfect landscaping, but instead of a pink and white color scheme, the palatial home's façade was finished in deep, rich earth tones and eye catching decorative stone. There were already a few cars out front, and in order to find a space, Justin had to cruise to the far end of the vast property's semicircular drive. Walking back towards the house, he found Mike, still in his tacky tuxedo tee, leaning up against his vintage Porsche Carrera and removing his shoes.

"Slipping into something more comfortable?"

"You betcha...watch this." Mike undid each of his pant legs with the horizontal zipper located just above each knee of his black cargos. He threw the detached legs and his shoes into the front seat of the Porsche and produced his standard pair of leather flip flops, which he unceremoniously popped onto his tanned feet. "That's how we do it in my world" he said with a hoarse laugh and pointed towards the house. "Onward and upward..." They met up with the guys in the garage of the grandiose house, and took Steve's private elevator to the main floor.

The doors opened on a world of more decorative stone, Italian tile floors, a high, darkly beamed ceiling and two-story tall walls faux painted in a combination of burnt sienna, beige and cream tones. Justin followed the others around a slowly curving corner and into an industrial-size kitchen impressively appointed with granite counter tops, hard wood cabinetry and many of the sleek, modern, ultra expensive stainless steel appliances he had seen in ads in *The Wine Spectator*. There they were met by Barry, sans rumpled sport coat, hard at work preparing side dishes with one of the chefs from the Paradise Bistro.

"Welcome, boys!" he said in greeting "Why don't you pull up a chair and set awhile?" he added, looking and sounding as though he was feeling no pain whatsoever.

"How's the standing rib roast doing?" Steve asked. He made his way past the two cooks and peered into one of the twin convection ovens, cracking the door open an inch or so and immediately flooding the kitchen with the savory aroma of twenty pounds of prime rib slow cooking to perfection.

"Just checked it," Barry replied. "We're looking good and about forty-five minutes out. And by the way, how was the show? The guests out on the verandah didn't have much to say about it."

"And the less said the better," Steve replied tersely, still seeming to be a little on edge after the events at the fashion show turned flesh fest. "I'm going to pop upstairs to change, and then we'll start decanting for dinner." He disappeared down a short hallway as Barry looked to the others with raised eyebrows.

"Well?" Barry chirped in his hummingbird-high voice. Seemingly unimpressed after listening to Frank's vivid and heavily detailed account of all the bumps, grinds and boobs, he replied with, "So, what's St. Clair's major problem? If you've seen two, you've seen 'em all."

"I think he's concerned that some of the more straight-laced members at the Oasis might give him some grief or even quit," Brad offered, while sticking a spoon into the large mixing bowl his walrus-moustached Juice Brother was working on. "Nice job Barry. Mashed potatoes with truffle butter!"

As Frank and Mike loudly rifled through a drawer looking for tasting spoons of their own, Justin's attention was drawn outside to the verandah overlooking the pool and grounds. There, sitting at a grouping of comfortable-looking outdoor lounge furniture and sipping on champagne, he found Phyllis, Chloe, and Monsieur René, along with a few others he recognized from earlier in the evening. He once again gave a smile and a little wave to say hello, and while the others all responded in kind, Phyllis remained a complete and total blank. He wasn't really disturbed by her behavior; he was more *perturbed*. But he quickly forgot all about Phyllis when he turned to take in the grand view of the Steve's over-the-top, outdoor entertainment area.

Like the Oasis, Steve's backyard had a luxurious covered cabana and strands of festive white lights strung throughout the trees and around the manicured hedges. But the main attraction and the centerpiece of *Chez* St. Clair's back garden paradise was a custom designed swimming pool lit in a luminous jade green and the nearly one story tall natural stone waterfall that took up its entire far side. The pool was shaped to resemble a small natural lake with a small side-pool that was probably a Jacuzzi or hot tub, and the stone structure was built and landscaped like a mini-mountain, with the waterfall, also lit in a glowing green, cascading over a living room sized grotto area beneath. Behind the transparent, flowing turquoise mist, Destiny sat in the grotto and beckoned to him with a pair of wine glasses in hand. *Could life possibly get ANY better than this?*

# CHAPTER TWENTY-NINE

Justin headed down the stairs, across the deck and followed the path around the side of the stone mini mountain and into the grotto underneath the waterfall. There he found Destiny waiting for him, once again dressed in her clinging satin top and skin-tight leather pants, with a half-bottle of wine already opened and ready to be poured. Before he could say a word, she jumped up, threw her arms around him and gave him a kiss that was so deep and so passionate, he felt sure that his long black hair would stand straight on end and wind up looking worse than it had when he used to drive in the beat-up old Electra with the window stuck halfway down.

"I've been wanting to do that ever since we talked earlier tonight," she said, as she pulled him even closer and kissed him again. The fragrant smell of her hair and perfume nearly overwhelmed his senses, and her magnificent breasts forcefully pressed into his chest.

"Really?" he asked incredulously. He couldn't believe his luck. And while he certainly didn't want to revert to the Justin of old and say something wrong or off-putting, he couldn't help following his true nature. "Destiny, please don't take this the wrong way...I mean...at the very least, you're an 'eleven.' You're articulate and intelligent and way beyond beautiful...I'm pretty sure you could have any guy you wanted...so...why me?"

Gazing into her dark violet eyes, he was encouraged by the fact that she hadn't backed-off an inch and was still holding him tightly. Very tightly. "And don't get me wrong...if you kiss me like that again my hair may spontaneously curl into a giant afro... but really...*me*?"

Destiny stepped back, and, with a mysterious smile, took Justin by the hand and led him over to the cushioned rock bench that lined the back wall of the grotto. She poured them each a glass of the wine from the small bottle and said, "Tell me how you like this." She took a taste from her own glass and watched as he swirled, sniffed and tasted.

"It's refreshing and clean," he said and took another small taste, "...lightly citrus with a lemony touch on the finish...mmm... I like it —it's like summertime in a glass! A Rosé, right?"

"Well done, once again!" She took his glass from him and set it down on a side table. Then, she straddled him on the bench. "Now, tell me how you like this."

She gently took his face in her soft, warm hands and covered his mouth with hot kiss after hot kiss. Justin put his arms around her, closed his eyes and kissed her back with an emotional intensity he had never before experienced. In that moment, with the sound of the rushing waterfall filling his ears, he felt like they were both suspended weightless in their own universe, their bodies, minds and souls intertwined in an erotic slow-dance of desire. It was intimate, electric and explosive.

"Well...?" she whispered.

"At first, your lips tasted like the Rosé," he answered breathlessly "But then, Destiny, you hit me with a bolt of lightning and sent me to another world." *Where did* that *come from?* He instantly regretted saying something that would probably make her wince.

But instead, she held him even tighter and softly murmured, "I was hoping you'd say that, 'cause it was the same for me, too." Justin couldn't believe his ears. She kissed him softly on the lips and continued. "You know, in some way, you might have been right before when you said that I could probably have any guy I wanted...but Justin, all the men I meet are like hungry sharks circling, just waiting to move in for the kill, and I don't like that feeling. I've been chased after by so many men for so long that I've lost count!  And it's always the same. They try to impress me with their money, bling, swagger, you know, every line of BS and every cliché in the book. But you are something else; something warm, real and unpretentious. You have a good soul, you love wine as much as I do, and I can just tell that you're not after me for all the wrong reasons." She sat back and coyly added, "If you're after me at all!"

Justin could only respond by taking her hands in his and lightly kissing each one of her beautiful fingers.

They spent the next twenty minutes or so quietly talking, with Destiny still on Justin's lap, face to face, up close and very personal. She explained that even though she hadn't immediately recognized him that night at the grand tasting, she had often thought of when they had first met at Brad's shop and had hoped that their paths would cross again soon.

"You really got my attention that night with your cute, quirky personality, and your extremely sensitive palate." Grabbing his lapels and then playfully tousling his long hair, she said, "And the fact that you now look like a million bucks is a pure bonus!"

She wanted to know all about his life and he gave her the quick tour through his past: being raised by his beloved and now departed aunt, attending the university here in town, working for Fed Ex and his recent promotion, and the fact that he lived on his own in Aunt Annette's 1950s style cottage. And he told her that ever since the night they had briefly met at Brad's Rhône tasting, his life had been changing and evolving in ways he had never dreamed possible.

Of course, he left out any mention of his escapades with Phyllis, but filled her in on the details of his growing friendship and association with the Juice Brothers and her colleague, Barry Love.

He asked about her life and family, but before she got the chance to answer, Steve's voice wafted in above the sound of the rushing waterfall as he called everyone in for dinner. And more wine!

As they ascended the stairs from the deck to the main level, she told him, in a confidential tone, that Barry was really like an uncle to her, a very ornery, protective uncle. He had hired her right out of college and mentored her throughout her years at Cosmo Brands and was always on the lookout for the circling sharks. Justin got the message, said he understood, and gave her one last, quick kiss on the cheek as they reached the verandah and the now glaring Phyllis Braunstein, whom he realized must have been watching them the entire time through the crystal-clear waterfall.

# CHAPTER THIRTY

All the guests wound up in the kitchen where Steve and the boys were finishing decanting the wines for dinner. Destiny had gone to freshen up, and Justin was checking out the labeled decanters. He read through the names, a *Who's Who* in the Pantheon of Bordeaux wines: 2000 Cos d'Estournel, 1990 Lafite Rothschild, 2000 Lynch Bages, 1996 Pavie, 2000 La Mission Haut Brion, 1999 Vieux Château Certan, 2000 Angelus, 1996 Gruaud Larose, 1989 Pichon Lalande and a 2000 Château Margaux,

He glanced up to find Barry opening one of the double-tall cabinets and handing out beautiful Riedel Vinum series glasses to anyone that needed one, and as he put one in Justin's hand, he whispered, "You've got Destiny's lipstick smeared all over your face."

Justin quickly reacted by ripping a paper towel off of a nearby roll and furiously rubbing his lips and cheeks. Upon seeing that no lipstick appeared on the towel, he looked back to Barry who was convulsing with laughter. He pointed back at Justin and simply said, "Gotcha!" He then came over, put his arm around his shoulder and said "Just be nice to her Justin. She's a great kid, just like you, and I think you two could be good for each other. But you must never, and I mean NEVER, tell her about the Bodacious Burka Booty website! Deal?"

"What Bodacious Burka Booty website?" Justin replied.

"Good boy," Barry said, gently patting Justin's cheek before walking back to the cabinet to hand out the remaining glasses.

By the time Destiny reappeared, they were all moving into the long, expansive dining room and taking their places at the simply-laid, double wide table. Steve and Barry took their places at the head, and after the other Juice Brothers took what Justin assumed were their usual seats by Barry and Steve, he sat next to Brad, and Destiny took the chair to his immediate left. Chloe and Monsieur René sat directly across, and the other guests took the remaining seats around the table. Phyllis, however, was nowhere to be seen.

The remaining bread and cheese had been brought in and placed directly in front of him, and although he didn't normally like cheese, Justin was so hungry that not even the toenail-curling aromas of a runny *Epoissess* and an extra funky *Pont L'Eveque* could put him off. He poured a little wine from one of the decanters, took a few bites of crunchy baguette slathered with a rich, reeking *Roquefort,* and was transported to epicurean Nirvana. Destiny was enjoying her share of baguette and cheese as well, and the crowd was buzzing as the decanters passed clockwise from the head of the table.

"Steve, Phyllis sends her regrets," Monsieur René said over the chatter at the table, his last cigarette before dinner dangling from his lips. "She said she wasn't feeling so great at the moment and went home for the evening."

"Bet she caught a cold from dancing around naked in the night air," Frank suggested as he and Mike cracked-up and fist bumped. Justin felt like he had just dodged a major bullet.

"Boys, boys, boys…," Steve scolded. "Thank you, René, I understand. But  Phyllis *did* have quite an interesting evening, didn't she?"

Chloe giggled, Monsieur René exhaled a cloud of smoke and shrugged, and then all was forgiven and forgotten and as the next decanter made its way around the table.

After he poured them each a small taste of the Gruaud Larose, Justin turned to Destiny and ever so softly asked her what she thought about the turn of events at the fashion show.

"Well, everyone knows that Phyllis, Chloe and Monsieur René are a *couple,"* she replied.

"A couple? A couple of what?" Justin wasn't sure what she meant.

"You know...they're...together," she said quietly, but raising her eyebrows in emphasis. "They knocked back a few of bottles of Heidsieck Monople champagne backstage before and during the fashion show, and I smelled someone smoking a joint, too. I think they were probably trashed, got carried away and then gave us a sneak preview of what goes on behind closed doors." Justin began to lightly perspire. "I've heard a lot of crazy, kinky stories about Ms. Phyllis...she's into *all* kinds of things."

"Really?" Justin said weakly, about an octave too high. He was trying to think of something to say to change the subject when Brad stood up and broke into the growing din loudly tapping on his wine glass with a fork.

"Alright you winos," he said, getting the attention of the Juice Brothers. Casting his eyes towards the other guests at the table he politely added, "and all ships at sea. Before we get too deeply into tonight's incredible line-up of knockout wines and the awesome deliciousness of Steve and Barry's culinary efforts, we need to have a quick headcount for our trip to Vin Expo week in late June. All right...who's in?"

All the guys *and* Destiny and Monsieur René raised their hands, and Brad made a list.

"Alrighty then," he said as he wrote each name. "So it's all of us...but what about you, Justin? You *are* coming with us, aren't you?"

"I...ah...," he mumbled and then watched as the guys, one after the other, grinned, nodded, gave him the thumbs-up or the Magic Murphy eyebrow bounce, all encouraging him to answer in the positive. Even Monsieur René gave him a smile in between drags on his foul-smelling *Gitane*. But he wasn't sure how he was going to respond until Destiny grabbed his leg under the table and whispered "Come with us, Justin...you won't be sorry," hotly into his ear.

"Well, how can I say no to you all of you guys!" he said with a wide smile, instantly feeling an electric wave of excitement and anticipation wash over him. He had never felt so free or so alive, and he thought of his Aunt Annette and how happy she would be to know that her long-ago dream of a trip to France for her nephew was finally going to come to fruition.

*And,* he was going to be there with the incredible woman sitting to his left. "I am honored and humbled to be among you all!" he toasted.

"Don't get too carried away with the honor and humility, young Mr. J," Brad said with a sly grin on his face and the ever-present mischievous spark in his eye flashing a bit more brightly than usual. "You're the freshman here, so you'll need to go through the standard Vin Expo rite of passage to qualify for the trip."

"A rite of passage?" Justin responded. "Like what...an initiation to a fraternity?" He had a momentary glimpse into a horrendous "hell night" scenario where he would be tormented by the brothers, whacked on the ass with large paddles, and forced to drink some unimaginably disgusting concoction, in this case most likely the combined contents of tonight's wine tasting spit buckets.

"Yes, that's it exactly!" Mike rasped. "You've got to pay your dues, if you want to sing the blues!"

Frank removed his nose from his glass long enough to add, with his bug-eyed Magic Murphy pitchman delivery, "If you're man enough to take it, then you're man enough to join us!"

Justin started getting a little nervous as the guys all high-fived and laughed it up.

Brad quieted the group down and continued. "Over the years, we've all been to Vin Expo numerous times, so to earn your keep on your first trip, you will be tasked with certain duties that will start tomorrow morning, if not sooner."

"Duties?" Justin asked skeptically. He could almost taste the "chum bucket" swill he was certain they were going to make him drink.

"First," Brad said, holding up a thumb to count French-style, "you will need to get on the Internet and find us all a place to stay; a hotel, a B&B, a house rental...something like that. It should be somewhere near the expo hall, but at this late date, you're probably not going to find  anything too close." Justin was instantly relieved as the prospect of a total gross-out began to fade away. "We'll need accommodations for at least five of us," Brad continued "Destiny and Barry will be staying somewhere near the hall with the group from Cosmo Brands and Monsieur René usually stays with family in Bordeaux City. Is that your plan this year, René?"

"*Oui,*" replied the enigmatic Frenchman, a trail of blue smoke curling around his head.

"Second," Brad said, as his lifted index finger joined his thumb, "you will need to secure the rental for a vehicle or van large enough to carry eight or nine. We've tried doing multi-car rentals in the past, but we all want to try the one vehicle approach this time, right?"

The guys all nodded in agreement. "And third, and this is the big one, you will be our designated driver. That means that while we are all drinking and tasting with wild abandon, you Justin, at least when we're out at parties and lavish dinners every night, will need to keep yourself in relative check."

"That's it? I can absolutely do that," Justin said, comfortable with his assigned tasks and not missing for a second the potential ass-paddling and other torture-like aspects of a real frat hazing.

"Whoa, not so fast." Steve wagged a finger. "Let me state for the record that being the designated driver on a no-holds-barred wine tour is not as easy as it sounds. I know from past experience. And France can be full of surprises, especially on a first trip. And so, young man," he said with blustery mock gravity, "you, must be vigilant, alert and aware. Are you prepared to assume these responsibilities and thereby become a full-fledged Brother of the Grape?"

"Oh yeah, baby!" Justin nearly yelled.

"Well then, welcome aboard." Steve raised his glass and signaled the chef to bring on the main course.

# CHAPTER THIRTY-ONE

*St. Émilion, France*

Lala collapsed in a sweat-soaked heap on top of Bruno's chest and tried to catch her breath. She had been riding him hard for the last forty-five minutes and he had finally reached his climax, exploding into her with such force it made her shudder and scream. "Do you love me, my Big French Oak tree?" she asked in a wanton, throaty voice.

"Oh, Lala...my Lala. You are a dream," Bruno said, still tightly gripping her ass. "My dear, I love everything about you, but especially that you are always so hungry for love." Then he aggressively rolled them onto their sides, suddenly on top of her for round two. Or was it round three...or four? He had totally lost count.

Since Lala had pulled her heart-stopping stunt in the center of the table in the grand dining hall at the beginning of the week, they had managed to have sex in every possible position they could think of and in nearly every room of the château. They had copulated in the kitchen and fucked in the foyer. They did anal in the atrium and had oral in DeBussey's private office. And the most surprising thing was that all of different locations and gymnastic positions had been Lala's idea. She was highly creative. And insatiable.

"Bruno, when you walk into any room in the château," she had said while kneeling in the subterranean wine cellar, cupping his balls, about to inhale his "Big French Oak," as she called it. "I want you to remember what we have done in that room. And, then I want you to think of my pussy, waiting for you, wanting you; ready for you," she said lustily, just before taking him all the way down to his thick "tree trunk." He simply couldn't believe that the sweet, delicate Asian flower of his three-year fantasy had turned into a wanton animal; a man-eating Venus Flytrap. Thank God for huge miracles.

But tomorrow was Saturday, and the boss was due back from his business trip. That meant Bruno's own trip, deep into Lala land, would have to come to an end. Or would it? How would they be able to keep their affair secret, especially the way she screamed in Chinese whenever he entered her? He didn't know exactly what she was saying, but he was sure it was something hot and dirty, and it drove him mad with desire. He didn't know what to do, but maybe she had a plan to keep their love alive...

Lala had finally caught her breath and pushed herself up from Bruno's heavily muscled torso. The man was an unstoppable sex machine, and after five days and nights of his relentless but very skilled pounding, she was having trouble walking straight. Her lower back was beginning to ache, her throat was raw from yelling Chinese curses while faking half of her orgasms, and she was almost out of *Love You Longtime Lube and Moisturizer*. Good thing her troll-husband was due back tomorrow so Bruno would have to stop and she could recuperate. And though she had an ulterior motive and desperately hoped all of this hard work would be worth all of the effort and the serious case of rug-burn she was developing, she had to admit that Bruno was a tireless lover and as large and hard as the grand oaks that lined the lane leading onto the property at Château La Tour Noir. And, he gave her pleasure, too. So much so that she had surprised herself with the creative lengths to which she was willing to go in order to seduce Bruno into being her obediently blind love slave.

She had especially enjoyed the episode in the underground wine cellar, where Bruno had answered her hellacious deep-throating blow job by laying her spread-eagle over a 225 liter barrique full of her husband's precious wine and making her squeal and squirt all over the wooden barrel, using only his lips, tongue, and a well lubricated fist.

Things had gone even better than she had hoped, but now with her hated husband returning home, she had to figure a way to keep things going so that Bruno could give her the ultimate pleasure: the removal of Guy DeBussey. She was more than ready and willing when her Big French Oak suddenly rolled her on to her back .

Bruno was always ready. But was he ready for *anything*? Was he ready *to do* anything?

# CHAPTER THIRTY-TWO

A dull smudge of light shone overhead, and as Justin looked up into the milky sky in hopes of determining his whereabouts and situation, his face was buffeted by the swirling crosswinds created by the car cutting through the dense fog at a high rate of speed. Way too fast. Dangerously fast.

The thick mist was cool and damp, but tearing down the mountain road, their increasing velocity turned the wind pouring into the open car ice cold, stinging his eyes and making it almost impossible to keep them open. But so what? He was in the middle of the dream again, and it always ended the same. Why fight against the forces of nature when you already knew what the outcome would be? He'd seen this film before, and he didn't like it.

But something was different this time. They seemed to be driving much faster than usual, and the voyage through the dense roiling fog was more like a noisy roller coaster ride than the usual, tranquil, almost soundless glide through a cloud.

He forced his eyes open against the biting chill wind and gazed into the front seat, just able to make out the forms of driver and passenger. The passenger moved closer and took his hand, and he was surprised to see that it wasn't the same woman he was used to finding there. She was a little younger, beautiful, and as she looked into his eyes, he could sense all of the love and warmth she felt for him, but it was love of a different sort than he usually felt emanating from the passenger seat in his foggy fantasy. But when he tried to focus on the person in the driver's seat, events veered sharply off of their normal course.

The driver was usually a youngish man with bright blue eyes and jet black hair, but not this time. This time, a woman turned to look back at him, and Justin was instantly familiar with the profile, the brow-lifted forehead and the heavily botoxed lips. When their eyes locked, he realized just who was recklessly driving the speeding convertible screaming down the fog-bound mountain road: It was Phyllis Braunstein, and she was pissed-off. Her extra plumped-out lips were impossibly twisted into an angry snarl and her heavily made-up eyes were shooting deadly white hot daggers through the mist at both him and the woman in the passenger seat. Holy shit!

Suddenly, the passenger turned away, screamed, and defensively raised her arms in front of her face. Time seemed to speed-up as the silhouette of a large metallic object appeared through the silvery haze, an eighteen-wheeled gas tanker truck, blocking their path amid flashing yellow emergency lights. Phyllis screeched like a psychotic she-devil as she spun the wheel and aimed straight for the uniformed man on the side of the road frantically waving his arms in futile warning.

And then, all Justin could hear, after the loud squeal of tires on pavement and a crunching impact, was the familiar, deafening rush of white noise and wind against his ears. And all he could feel was a hollow emptiness in the pit of his stomach as his body hurtled helplessly through space.

# CHAPTER THIRTY-THREE

*Orlando, USA*

R2D2 was singing along with the orchestra as it blasted the *Star Wars* theme, and his alarm clock jolted him out of a deep sleep and into a late Saturday morning, alone in his tiny bedroom. Or was it afternoon?

For Justin, it didn't matter. All that mattered was that today was the day he was going to begin planning his trip to France, and he had to get started on the logistics *ASAP*. After getting the coffee maker going and hitting the shower to get refreshed, he fired-up the IPad, sent a good morning text to Destiny and started searching the net for B&B's in Bordeaux.

After last night's dinner had ended, he'd walked Destiny to her car, a sleek, black Acura TL, and they talked about spending some quality time together and getting to really know one another. He was still tingling from their last, steamy goodnight kisses outside of Steve's house, and he really hoped she wouldn't come to her senses in the light of day and blow him off like every woman had done before.

His fears were instantly allayed when she texted back: *Good morning, handsome! I can't begin to tell you how happy I am about last night, and I'm not just talking about drinking the Château Margaux, lol! Don't mean to intrude, but would you like some help finding a place to stay in Bordeaux? I've been a few times and my knowledge of the area might be useful. I could pop over in about an hour. Plus, I'll bring lunch! Let me know, D. P.S: I won't be wearing any makeup... you've been warned!!*

Justin nearly set a speed record typing his reply. He sent her his address, a link to a map, a set of directions and a virtual bouquet of roses. Now all he needed to do was get rid of the *I Like Big Photons* T-shirt he was wearing and brush his teeth.

But before he made a move, his email inbox pinged and he opened it to find a message from Brad with a link to the *Vin Expo* website and date info. The trade show started on the last Monday in June and lasted for four full days, and the guys all wanted him to secure accommodations for seven nights, beginning the preceding Friday before the show started. Brad closed his email with two very important tidbits of travel info: *J, the flights to France arrive the next day Euro time, so make sure to book your flight to depart on Thursday evening, arriving Friday AM in France. PS- better fast track your application for a passport.*

Justin had plenty of vacation time available. Over the last seven years, he had only taken time off when Aunt Annette had gotten seriously ill and needed his attention around the clock. After she had passed, his supervisor told him that whenever he wanted to take some time for a *real* vacation, all he had to do was ask. He submitted his request for the two weeks starting the Thursday before *Vin Expo* and received a positive response within ten minutes.

He logged on to his FedEx MasterCard rewards account, which he had opened seven years ago and never used, and saw that with the triple points bonus he'd received on the purchase of his car from Magic Murphy Auto Sales, he had accrued over 100,000 points. That had to be worth something, and as he zipped through the list of rewards airline partners, he saw that he qualified for a free ticket to Europe or an upgrade to business class with a paid fare. Awesome!

After sending out an email to the guys for advice on what he should do, the answers came back fast and furious—with the exception of Barry, whose mantra was "cheap is sweet"—everyone agreed that business class would be the way to go. And Steve pointed out that with a business ticket, he would have access to the airline's luxury airport flight clubs, which offered a quiet, stress-free environment, free drinks and food, very comfortable seating, clean private restrooms and even shower facilities. *Hmm…a totally free ticket or $1,750 and perks, bells, comfort and whistles out the wazoo…?*

He heard Destiny pulling into the driveway thirty seconds after he had hung-up with Air France and finished writing down the confirmation number for his roundtrip business class ticket to Bordeaux. He jumped up from the kitchenette and bolted into his room to lose the *Star Trek* nerd shirt and clean his teeth for what he hoped would be another lip-locking kiss-a-thon.

When he opened the front door, the woman he found standing there was the girl of his dreams, even more so than the sex bomb from last night in the skin tight leather pants and the spiky stiletto heels. Today, Destiny was dressed down in skimpy blue jean cutoffs, a baggy T-shirt and flat sandals, and for the first time he realized that she was probably only about 5'3" tall. Her wild black curls were pulled straight back and tied behind her head and her lips, cheeks and eyes were one hundred percent make-up free. Justin found her radiant, natural beauty breathtaking to behold.

Smiling, she held out a large bag full of goodies from Einstein's Bagels, and as Justin took it from her, he was surprised to read the lettering on her shirt, which had been obscured by the oversized bag. It read: *Kiss me, I'm Vulcan.* *WHAT?* No way!

He welcomed her into his little cottage home, and after a quick kiss, they unpacked the Einstein's bag in the kitchen, laying out the turkey wraps and side salads and chips on the retro orange motif kitchenette table. Justin poured coffee for both of them and having made a brave decision, momentarily excused himself.

"I'll be back in flash. Start without me." When he returned seconds later, Destiny burst out laughing when she saw that he had changed into his *Photons* tee. "You like it?" he asked.

"I *love* it!" she exclaimed. "My dad has the exact same one, except his shirt is neon green."

Over the next hour she talked, and he listened. She had grown up in Miami and had been raised by her widowed father, now a retired Colonel in the Army Reserve. Her mother had passed when she was very young, and she had no memory of her whatsoever.

Her dad was a sci-fi nut, and over the years he made her attend all sorts of *Star Trek* conventions and similar related fan events with him, usually dressed in costumes. She had loved it as a kid and still enjoyed the genre, if not the conventions and the dressing up. Justin couldn't believe it.

Her father was also into wine, had a small cellar of his own, and had brought Destiny along with him on a few trips to Italy to explore the bucolic Tuscan countryside and the wines of Chianti and Montalcino. They also searched for family history and roots, and while on their second trip, when she was eighteen, they had discovered a distant branch of the Verrano family, making wine and running a quaint *Agri-Tourismo* B&B on their property in a small village just outside of the scenic hilltop town of Sienna.

Their long-lost cousins once removed had been so happy to meet their American relatives that they had invited them back the next summer to stay with them and work in their vineyards and small winery.

She returned with her father the next year and spent most June and July with the Tuscan branch of the *Famiglia Verrano,* learning how the Italians tended their vines, made their wine, and enjoyed their rustic country lives among the rolling Tuscan hills. Her dad had been back several times and had even learned to speak Italian, but she had other plans.

Two years later, when she finished school, her father put her in touch with an old army buddy from the Orlando area who was the district manager for one of the bigger wine distributors in the USA, Cosmo Brands.

Barry Love hired her sight unseen and became her teacher and mentor as she learned about the sales side of the business, from the ground up. In just three short years she had risen to become one of the company's top reps and had gone on to travel to some of the top wine producing regions of the world to meet with Cosmo's partners, learning first-hand about what went into making a top-class wine.

Justin sat spellbound, munching on his turkey wrap and chips, never for a minute imagining that the beautiful girl he had met pouring wine in a small, local shop had such a worldly wine background.

"And I thought you were just a hot wine-babe!" he said, as he tried without success to dodge the love tap she delivered in the form of a nudge to the ribs. "I mean, who knew?" he said, and delivered his own love tap; a tender caress on her soft cheek and a gentle kiss on her lips. He couldn't get over how comfortable they were together. It was so effortless and so...normal.

"Destiny, I..." She cut him off by putting a finger to his lips.

"You don't need to say anything, Justin. I feel it, too. Let's just take things slowly and see where they lead us. Okay?" She took him by the hand. "I love your house. How about showing me the sights?"

After giving her the forty-five second grand tour, they wound up on the old sofa in the comfy living room and each used their IPads to go online and look for a place for Justin and the boys to stay in Bordeaux.

# CHAPTER THIRTY-FOUR

*St. Émilion, France*

Guy DeBussey was fuming. It was early Saturday evening and the house was empty. Other than Bruno, no one on the staff was standing by to attend to his every whim. There was no dinner ready to be eaten, and not even his cellar-master was available to bring up a few choice bottles from his collection for a celebratory toast to his successful arm-twisting business deals in Rhône and Beaune.

After Bruno had picked him up at the helipad and driven him back to the main house in the official Château La Tour Noir golf cart, his boss had spent the rest of the late afternoon in his office going through a stack of mail and writing checks, totally immersed. He had a bit of catching up to do because he never delegated anything that had to do with his business affairs or his money to anyone else. It wasn't until that moment he must have realized there was absolutely no activity in the château, and it was unnaturally quiet.

"BRUNO!" he bellowed into the empty hallway outside his private office. "Where the hell is everyone?" He had an unusually loud voice for such a small, squat man, and as the sound waves bounced and reflected off stone walls and floors, they reached Bruno on the other side of the château

He was standing alone in the dark in the atrium, remembering the last few days and specifically, what had happened in this exact location. His thoughts made him smile, but it was bittersweet. How could he face dealing with this arrogant little prick when all he had been doing and all he wanted to do was fuck the man's wife? Again. And again and again. Life was hard, but not as hard as the Big French Oak! He and his Lala would have to find a way. After a few more minutes of private reflection, he heard DeBussey loudly rummaging around in the kitchen and met him there to be greeted by the expected barrage of abuse.

"What the fuck were you thinking, Bruno? Why isn't the chef here, or the cellar master, or anyone else for that matter, except *you?* What the hell are *you* going to do for me, make *Nutella* sandwiches?" he spat, while violently opening and closing drawers and cabinet doors. The man was going into megalomaniacal overdrive.

*Maybe I can have a little fun.* "Boss, I haven't been here since you left on Monday. No one has. Madame Lala told us that she wanted to be alone and gave all of us the week off." And to really push him over the edge, he added, "with pay."

"What?" DeBussey exploded. With his swarthy face turning a bright crimson, he ripped open a dinnerware cabinet and started launching expensive designer plates through the air and ultimately, down onto the hard, marble kitchen floor. "You don't take orders from her, you idiot!"

"But boss, she is the mistress of the château. We must *always* respect her wishes," Bruno said loudly over the crash of porcelain breaking into a million and one shards. *And you wouldn't believe what she wished me to do to her, asshole.* He smiled inwardly while dodging a Royal Copenhagen cup and saucer set aimed directly at his head.

Sitting in the adjacent grand dining room, sipping her tea in the darkness and listening to the blithering bastard in the kitchen throwing a fit, Lala smiled contentedly. Things were moving along quite well...it wouldn't be long, now.

# CHAPTER THIRTY-FIVE

*Orlando, USA*

It had taken most of the week, but Brad, Steve, Frank and Mike finally agreed on one of the three available lodging choices Justin had submitted to them last Sunday. Justin sat back in his chair in his small office at FedEx, printed out the payment confirmation from the owners of the house in a little town called St. Quentin de Baron, e-mailed a copy to each of the guys, and tried to keep his growing excitement under control.

He and Destiny had spent all of last Saturday afternoon and half of the evening clicking on links, looking at sites and taking notes about all of the possibilities for hotels, B&B's, apartments and something Destiny had told him about called a *Gite*—the French term for a self-catering house rental. She explained that it was like living with a French family, without the family being at home.

There were plenty of properties throughout the region, but nothing was available within at least a forty-five minute drive from the Expo hall. The first possibility they found was a B&B in St Estephe, all the way at the north end of the Haut Medoc region. Destiny estimated it was an hour drive each way, but it was a scenic route through the heart of some of Bordeaux's finest vineyards and wine producing châteaux. There was a dumpy-looking hotel with two rooms available in the city of Libourne to the northeast, but that was even farther away and involved all *autoroute* or highway driving.

And then, after searching for another hour, they found the perfect candidate—a private, modern property midway between Bordeaux city and St. Émilion in a small, quiet town. It was walled and gated, had a full kitchen, six bedrooms, a swimming pool with a covered deck and a BBQ grill, wireless internet connections, and flat screen TVs, and the house itself it sat in the middle of its own small vineyard planted with one-hundred percent merlot. As far as Justin was concerned, it was perfect.

Of course, it was more than the guys wanted to pay, but not *too* much more. And after they realized it was the only good choice, they ponied up the funds via PayPal and booked it.

Even Destiny had been thrilled about it and promised Justin that, if they booked it, she would come for a dip in the pool if her Vin Expo schedule allowed.

After Justin sent the guys the initial information on their choices, he also found a reasonable deal on a nine-passenger Mercedes van from a French rental company called *Sixt*. They were located right in the terminal at the airport. So, they were set for the moment, and he and Destiny had ordered in some Thai food to celebrate, topped off with the bottle of crisp, refreshing Rosé she had left for him at that first tasting at Brad's shop.

After dinner, she'd given him a series of long, spicy, Thai-basil-flavored kisses and said goodnight. Then, he hadn't seen her all week because she'd been travelling on Cosmo Brands business and wouldn't be back until Sunday afternoon. Every day since, today included, he had to fight the urge to obsessively and repeatedly call her, Skype with her, e-mail her, text her or send smoke signals. He quickly responded to her evening texts, but remembering that she wanted to "take things slowly and see where they led," he made a point of keeping it light and keeping his emotions under control.

But it was difficult. He'd never had a girlfriend before, if he dared call her that, and he just couldn't wait until the next time they could be together. At least they had plans for dinner on Sunday night. Checking the clock in his office for the one hundredth time today, he smiled when he realized he only had another forty-nine hours, twelve minutes and sixteen seconds left to go.

# CHAPTER THIRTY-SIX

*Castillon-la-Bataille, France*

As the rickety old Citroën "duck" made its way out of the clinic parking lot, Sister Ralph was glad to be moving. It was an early June afternoon and the entire southwest of France, especially the province of Aquitaine, was suffering through a pre-summer heat wave the likes of which hadn't been seen in years. And Sister Ralph was feeling every degree of it, in Celsius. Wearing her short-sleeved, lightweight summer habit gave her no relief from the nearly unbearable temperature, and even her patchy moustache was sweating.

Driving out of town across the ancient, arched stone bridge over the calm, clear waters of the canoe and kayak packed Dordogne river, she was grateful for the relatively cool breeze that rose off the water and wafted through the open windows of the rusty old car. She looked across the shabby cabin of her small vehicle at her passenger and hoped that, she too, was getting some relief from this God-awful heat.

Sister Marie Agnes, the normally independent, no nonsense leader of the Our Lady of Mercy orphanage, always stone-faced and strong, was today slumped in the passenger seat of the Citroën, her frail, bony hands shaking and her pallid face the color of chalk. Minus her habit and headpiece, she looked exactly like what she was—a dying old woman.

She was muttering what might have been a prayer, and Sister Ralph would have joined in except she wasn't quite sure which chapter and verse in the New Testament included the terms "fucking bastard" and "blood-sucking vampire." She reached across and gently patted the old sister's deeply wrinkled forehead with one of the cool compresses the nurse had given her after the chemo treatment back at the clinic.

Today, the oncologist had taken her aside and confided how sorry he was to inform her that Sister Marie Agnes' prognosis was not good. The news didn't come as a surprise. Her friend's cancer, while slow-growing and controllable at first, was now in aggressive full bloom and had outrun all of the radiation and chemo treatments the poor woman had endured.

This was it. All they could do for her now was to prescribe ever-increasing dosages of painkillers. And pray. There would be good days and bad days ahead, but today was a particularly bad one.

Behind the wheel, Sister Ralph was almost in tears. As they approached the roundabout with the cutoff to the route that would take them back to the orphanage and her beloved children, Marie Agnes had a moment of lucidity. She lifted a spotted, blue-veined hand and lightly touched Sister Ralph on the arm.

"Don't worry, my friend. God is with me. I will be all right," she said, her old strength momentarily returning. "But the Lord has one last mission of salvation for me to perform. You must take me to see Guy DeBussey. Immediately!" Sister Ralph bypassed the cutoff and instead took the route to St. Émilion.

Twenty-five minutes later, Lala was just emerging from Château La Tour Noir and in the process of opening a multi-colored parasol to protect her delicate skin from the blazing sun, when her attention was drawn to a creaking, rusted-colored Citroën driving slowly into the courtyard.

"Shit! What now?" her husband said as he passed her and quickly descended the steps from the towering manor to the large, chauffeur-driven Mercedes waiting for them below. The driver of the lumbering old car reacted to DeBussey's appearance by stepping on the gas and whipping the vehicle directly in front of the big Mercedes, blocking its path. Two Catholic Sisters got out and waited.

"Why are these nuns here?" Lala nervously asked her smirking husband. She'd heard talk of nuns and an orphanage, and something about an eviction and protestors, but beyond that she had little knowledge or interest. "What do you think they want?"

"Shut up and get in the car!" DeBussey strode defiantly onto the dusty gravel driveway to confront the two women. Lala didn't move.

"Ah, sisters. So nice to see you again. Would you like me to get out the fire hose so you can cool-off on this hot afternoon?" He laughed, taunting them. "Oh, you don't look so good," he said to the nuns. "Can I get you something to drink? Perhaps a hot coffee or a bottle of red wine?"

"Monsieur DeBussey," the older, sickly-looking nun said with great effort, her voice a dry, strained whisper that already sounded as if it was coming from beyond the grave. "The Lord has told me to come here today and once again beg you to help the poor orphans of Our Lady of Mercy."

"But of course!" DeBussey replied. "What else could it possibly be?"

"Don't you see, Monsieur? You must do something to atone for all of your many sins and save your soul from eternal damnation!" the old nun cried, her hoarse voice quivering with emotion and wildly oscillating like she was trying to talk while being driven over an extremely bumpy, potholed road at a high rate of speed. "You *must* help the children you have thrown out of their quiet, peaceful home in Côtes de Castillon. God has told me to tell you that you *must make restitution*!" When her vehement outburst was over and whatever reserve of energy she possessed expended, she collapsed into the waiting arms of the very large, much younger nun standing at her side.

"Oh, *really*?" DeBussey replied with an exaggerated, condescending sneer. "Wait…*what's that*?" he said, cupping a hand to his ear and making a show of looking around the courtyard. His black eyes darted back and forth like a frog tracking a fat, juicy fly for its next meal. "Guess what, Sisters? *I* have just received a message! God has just told *me* to tell *you…*to *fuck-off*! How do you like that, *hunh?*" With a wave of his stubby, hairy-knuckled hand he dismissed them and made his way back to the Mercedes, where Lala was still standing beneath her parasol, shaking her head in disapproval.

"Guy, why don't you give these poor nuns some money and help them? You have enough," she snapped.

"I thought I told you to shut up and get in the car…now…*shut up and get in the car!"* the diminutive dictator shouted at his wife as he climbed into the air-conditioned comfort of the backseat of the large car. Lala folded her pretty parasol and followed, but before she got in, she overheard the labored, wheezing voice of the old nun, praying.

"And don't worry, Sister Ralph." the fragile woman said, " I promise you…God will give me the strength to make that evil little bastard see the light before my time on this earth is done. And his."

# CHAPTER THIRTY-SEVEN

*Orlando, USA*

Late Wednesday afternoon, while Justin hurried home from work, he reviewed his mental checklist to make sure he hadn't forgotten anything. *Passport? Check. A few new extras from Macy's? Check. Touch-up on the cool hair style? Check. New suitcase? Check. Hot sex with Destiny?*

Everything seemed in order, and in any case, he still had plenty of time until his flight left tomorrow afternoon at one. Tonight, it was off to the Twisted Cork to meet the guys for a last toast before they all boarded their various flights and rendezvoused in Bordeaux on Friday. Barry and Destiny had left earlier in the week, but everyone else would be there, and Justin was looking forward to an early, easy evening. *Nothing too crazy tonight. I've got to get a good night's sleep and be ready for the big day!*

He still couldn't believe how quickly the time had flown by since he decided to go to *Vin Expo* with the guys, whom he'd hardly seen in the past six weeks or so. Brad had dropped by a few weeks back to help him put his new vino-fridge together, and then they had gone out to dinner a few days later after Justin had stopped by his shop to buy a few cases of affordable wine to start getting the cellar stocked.

Destiny had come by a few nights after that so that he could show off his new mini wine cellar, and she had brought him a wonderful gift: a mixed six-pack of top name red Bordeaux from the Cosmo Brands line-up, all classified growths and costing much more per bottle than he was currently prepared to spend on wine. He suggested they celebrate by opening one of them, but she opted for something more forward and ready to drink, telling him to forget these bottles of age-worthy Bordeaux for a while and "lay them down for a few years."

They had seen each other on and off over the last six weeks, but she was on the road a lot in preparation for the Vin Expo trip, and he had to be happy with whatever time she could squeeze in for them here and there. But they did spend some quality time together and were becoming real friends. Close friends.

Slowly, as he gained her trust, she began to really open up to him about some of her past relationships, the most recent of which had ended suddenly and painfully at five minutes to midnight on last New Year's Eve. At a friend's party, with midnight approaching, she had lost track of her date and went looking for him in anticipation of the traditional New Year's midnight kiss. With no luck after looking through the house, she went out to the driveway, where she found her boyfriend of almost a year with his head firmly planted between the spread and raised legs of her now ex-best friend, who was lying with her dress up over her head in the cargo area of his SUV. The hatch was wide open and they were being watched by a small cheering section, loudly urging them on.

It had been humiliating and devastating, and Destiny had gotten misty as she told Justin her story. He had felt terrible for her, and after that, her advice that they should "take things slow and see where they lead us" took on a new meaning for him. So, they would go slowly and surely. They did a dinner here, a movie there, and he had even gone with her to the Oasis for a tennis lesson and a swim in the pool.

The highlight had been the night she had invited him for dinner to her cozy home on a small lake in Winter Park, and cooked him a deliciously authentic meal that she promised he could only find at her house or in Sienna, Italy. She chose the wines from her own cellar, a nearly five-hundred bottle collection housed in a converted kitchen pantry, now climate controlled and  lined with sweet-smelling cedar wine racks, and they feasted on *Insalata Caprese, Bistecca Alla Fiorentina* and *Misto Griglia,* while enjoying earthy, deep cherry and berry-infused Sangiovese-based wines from Chianti Classico.

After dinner, holding hands, they sat and talked for hours outside on the moonlit deck and sipped on another one of Destiny's choices, a Tuscan dessert wine called Vin Santo. It was a sweet end to another wonderful, but chaste, evening with Ms. Destiny Verrano, and Justin had been too tired and tipsy to drive home. When she offered her guest room to him, he gratefully accepted, secretly hoping for a late night visit from his alluring host.

Sometime before dawn, he was awakened by the touch of warm hands on his arm and a soft voice calling his name in the dark, thanking him for being so understanding and patient. *I'm not ready yet...* she said, *but I will be soon.* As Justin drifted back off to sleep, he wasn't quite sure if it had been real or a dream. One thing that was real, however, was the ache in his loins and the intense and growing desire he felt for her.

They had said a quick good-bye last Sunday night, when he had taken her to the airport and seen her off on her flight to France. Barry was also on the same flight, and Justin waved to both of them as they went through security. With Destiny's last kiss still hot on his lips, his mind kept replaying her last, promise-filled words: "Hope you're ready for Bordeaux...and *me!*"

# CHAPTER THIRTY-EIGHT

As he pulled into the parking lot of the Twisted Cork, Justin made sure to find a well-lit spot in front of the building. He certainly didn't want a repeat of his last visit here and wouldn't park his beautiful Genesis Coupe around back.

He entered to find the mood quiet and low key; there were only a handful of people at the bar and scattered about at the tables and booths. The only real action was taking place in the center of the room, where Frank, Mike, Steve, Brad, and Monsieur René were sitting at a large round table. There were already five decanters being passed around between them and Brad waved Justin over, pulling out the chair between himself and the perpetually puffing Monsieur René.

"Hope you're not going to be this late for your flight to France tomorrow, Mr. J," Brad said, pointing at his watch, a sarcastic note in his voice.

"Oh…hey, sorry guys," Justin answered. "I got tied up with my neighbor, Mrs. Lippincott, who's going to be collecting my mail. She's known me since I was a little kid, and I think she's even more excited about this trip than I am, if that's even remotely possible."

In the center of the table Justin spotted a platter full of French bread and cheese, and after filling his glass with a lovely, straw-colored white Burgundy from Meursault, Justin loaded up his small plate with a liberal helping of crunchy baguette and creamy, room temperature *Morbiere.*

"That'll be five dollars for the food, young man," Mike croaked, sounding way too much like Mr. Haney from the old *Green Acres* TV show. "And by the way…we know you're just starting to fill your cellar with wine, but in the future, you'll need to start bringing a bottle or two to our boys' nights."

"And *only* the good shit!" Frank quickly added, his face turning hot pink.

"Come on, cut the kid some slack." Brad put his arm around Justin and trapped him in a mock headlock. "Between my shop and Mike's inventory, we'll get him stocked and ready for the next hundred or so boys' nights."

"Here, here!" Steve exclaimed, raising his glass in toast. Monsieur René said nothing and kept silently smoking. After Brad released him from the wrestling hold, Justin joined in the toast and forked over a five. He was just glad that Brad didn't apply any "noogies" along with the headlock.

Working their way through the wines, which included another white Burg from Montrachet, a red Burg from Beaune, an impressive Oregon pinot from Joseph Drouhin and a stellar bottle of 2000 La Mission Haut Brion, they compared itineraries and planned their arrival strategy for Friday in Bordeaux. Justin was flying with Delta and Air France and would arrive in Bordeaux first, at nine-fifteen a.m. He would pick-up the Mercedes van and hang around the airport waiting for the others to arrive.

Frank and Mike were flying together with British Airways and were due in next at eleven, with Brad and Steve arriving separately shortly thereafter, so Justin wouldn't have to wait too long. Hopefully, there wouldn't be any delays and things would go smoothly. In any case, on the advice of Brad, Justin and a few of the others had rented Euro cell phones, so they had the ability to remain in close contact. All that was left to do now was wake up in the morning and get to the airport on time. *That should be easy enough*, Justin thought.

As the decanters were emptied and the bread and cheese platter cleared away, Monsieur René got up, wished them a *bon voyage* and said he looked forward to seeing them all on Saturday in St. Émilion. He turned and walked out of the Cork, followed by an unpleasantly aromatic trail of blue smoke from his ever-present, stinky French cigarette.

"What's Mr. René all about, anyway?" Justin asked, after the silver-haired Frenchman had cleared the room. "He really doesn't say much, does he?"

"That's *Monsieur* René to you, bub. Show a little respect." Frank's face glowed the color of a red hot coal, and he seemed a little agitated tonight; his googly eyes kept darting around the room and he constantly checked his watch. *Maybe he's always nervous before he flies.*

"The truth is, we don't know a whole lot about him, at least nothing too personal." Steve emptied his glass of the last precious drops of the La Mission Haut Brion. "He appeared on the scene about eight or nine years ago and has been a member of the Oasis ever since. He runs his high-end women's shop and does very well, buys a lot of wine from these two yahoos sitting across the table from me and has almost always had Phyllis Braunstein as his part time girlfriend, along with a never-ending succession of attractive younger women that they seem to share between them."

"He's a man of few words, but he's gotten more pussy than all of us at this table put together!" Frank *the Tank* added, his face now the color of smoking, molten lava. Justin thought the top of his head might erupt at any moment.

"Barry knows more about him," Brad interjected, "and I think he knew him before he came here from France. But beyond the fact that his family in Bordeaux used to be in the wine business, we don't know much. In any case, and despite the fact he's a very economical conversationalist, he's been a good customer and is a *great* friend to have along with us on our trip to Vin Expo."

"No doubt!" Mike agreed. "This will be his third time with us, and over the years he's turned us on to some amazing restaurants and little-known *petite-château* producers that have blown our minds with their high quality juice. This time, he's getting us into the St. Émilion Growers Association dinner on Saturday night, and he's always got some surprises and cool suggestions for us while we're there."

"Do you think he knows about me and Phyllis?" Justin asked. It hadn't bothered him before, but now he was suddenly nervous about the prospect of spending a week in close proximity to the boyfriend of a woman he had recently screwed the hell-out-of.

"He knows," Brad said as the last of the decanters and glasses were taken away by one of the staff, "but I wouldn't worry about it."

"You *wouldn't?*" Justin hoped that Monsieur René wasn't a trained martial artist and prone to violent outbursts and fits of rage.

"No, not at all. As a matter of fact, he told me he likes you and was glad to have a night off from Phyllis," Brad said, adding with a shrug, "What can I tell you? He's French!"

As they all stood and Justin was preparing to say *au revoir*, Frank fished around in his pockets and pulled out a tarnished, old silver dollar, which he handed to Justin saying, "Okay, kid, you do the honors this year. What's it going to be, heads or tails?" If Frank's face looked like if it got any redder, his head would spontaneously combust. "Flip it, son!"

Justin took the old coin, gave it a flip, and watched as it spun on the table. *What's this all about?* When the coin stopped, he announced "Tails."

"Tails it is," Frank shouted with unmolested glee. "Popatopolis, here we come!" Whipping-out his cell phone, he made a call to let his staff at the strip club know "Magic Murphy One" was en route. And then he grabbed Justin tightly by the arm.

After the coin toss and the announcement of their destination, Justin had protested and tried to beg-off for the night, but Frank *the Tank* and the other guys wouldn't hear of it.

"This is a Juice Brothers tradition, newbie!" Frank said loudly as they escorted Justin out of the Twisted Cork and into the parking lot. "We're all in, and that means you are too, my young friend. And, not to worry, it's all on the house and I do mean *all!*" He laughed with devilish intent.

His Juice Brothers quickly surrounded him like a cordon of armed guards, marched him to his car as if he were a condemned man on his way to "the chair" and extracted his solemn promise that he would follow them down the street without delay.

"Don't worry, Justin," Mike shouted hoarsely through Justin's closed door "The girls don't bite...too hard!"

With Frank in the lead car, they caravanned across and down the street, passing The Booby Trap and Magic Murphy Auto Sales and pulling into the lot at the garishly-lit Popatopolis

# CHAPTER THIRTY-NINE

*Somewhere over the Atlantic*

When Justin awoke after being jostled by some in-flight turbulence, the business class cabin of the Air France Air Bus A330 was quiet, and the lights were low. He stretched his nearly six-foot frame out across the fully reclined flat bed of his sleeper-seat and once again thanked himself for listening to the guys. Spending the cash on a business class ticket upgrade instead of going for the freebie econo-class torture device, also known as a standard airline seat, was certainly money well-spent, especially at this moment and *especially* considering the kind of *bon voyage* party he had been given last night at Popatopolis. Or was it this morning?

He brought the seat up with the automatic controls on the side panel, flipped on his personal video screen and saw that they were somewhere over the Atlantic Ocean. It was 3:55 a.m. Euro-time, and that meant it was 9:55 p.m. back in Orlando. He smiled thinking that, last night at just about this time, he'd been blind-folded with his hands tied behind his back, sitting in his underwear on a chair on the main stage at Frank's strip club. Unbelievable!

When they'd arrived at Popatoplis, the guys had all filed into the dark, smoky club and were quickly escorted to the private VIP room, where they found half a dozen sexy, nearly naked young women sipping on vintage Roederer rosé champagne. The dancers were very friendly, especially to Frank, but even more so to Justin, and he suddenly found two of the lithe, seductive women sitting on his lap.

After popping a few more corks and making a number of toasts to the kickoff of their trip, Frank asked the girls to give Justin the full "bachelor party" treatment. The next thing he knew, the ladies had taken him by the hands—one of them actually had her hand on a *third* appendage—and led him out of the VIP room to the main stage

As the DJ started blasting the old Motley Crue song "Girls, Girls, Girls" through the megawatt sound system, he announced that this was Justin's first time at Popatopolis and to please "give it up" for him. The dancers brought him to center stage, where they slowly stripped him down to his Jockey shorts and made him sit on a folding chair, surrounding him in a sea of undulating skin.

One dancer pulled his hands behind his back and tied them to the chair, and just before another placed a sleep mask blindfold over his eyes, one just like Aunt Annette used to wear to bed, he looked out into the crowd to see Frank, Mike and Brad laughing their asses off and pumping their fists to the thumping rock track. The next thing he knew, he was being bumped and grinded by boobs and butts, while some of the girls took turns straddling and dry-humping him as he sat helplessly tied to the chair amid the flashing lights and ear-splitting music. It was F-ing awesome, and the blindfold made it even better!

He knew he should have been totally embarrassed to be out in public in his underwear, but he was having way too much fun to care. And the best was yet to come: when they removed the eye shade blindfold, his hungry eyes were treated to the sight of two absolutely enormous, beautifully shaped breasts being juggled in his face by a tall red head wearing freaky green-glitter eye make-up. She then took each one of her quadruple D-cup knockers, encircled Justin's head in a tight halo of hooters, and bounced it back and forth between them like a ping pong ball being swatted by two huge pink paddles.

When the song ended, the girls paraded him back through the half full club, still in his shorts, and into the VIP room, where the redhead poured a little of the champagne onto her tits and encouraged Justin to lick it off. He'd never had a rosé champagne before, and after sampling a bit from column A and a little more from column B, he decided the bubbly was really delicious, but probably a little warmer than it should have been.

Another round of turbulence rocked him back to reality at 35,000 feet, and as he once again lowered the seat into its comfortable, flat position, he put on the Air France sleepy-time eyeshade one the flight attendants had given out earlier and tried not to laugh too loud.

# CHAPTER FORTY

*St .Émilion, France*

It was four in the morning and Lala was tired, and not just because Bruno was going at it again for the third time in the past hour. In the weeks since she had enticed him into their affair with her brazenly lurid offer of hot sex in Château La Tour Noir's grand dining room, they had been meeting as often as possible in secret, in the middle of the night, at various locations on the grounds of the château.

Tonight's tryst was in the winery among the huge stainless steel tanks used for fermenting and filtering her husband's precious wine. The twelve large, almost two-story containers were arranged in two rows on the basement floor of the winery building. She and Bruno were lying on her lush silver and black chinchilla blanket in the secluded, open second level loft area created by the series of walkways and narrow platforms used for maintenance and cleaning at the top of the tanks. It was dark and almost cozy, and this seemed to be Bruno's favorite location to make love to his "delicate flower."

"So, my lovely Asian orchid," he said as he increased the depth and speed of his stroke, "what do you like more, your husband's juice in these tanks, or this?" He gasped breathlessly into her ear as he pulled his considerable member from deep within her and spilled his own hot effluent all over her belly. Lala came instantly, spouting a geyser of Cantonese curses that Bruno still thought were declarations of her love and affection. Her orgasm was more explosive than a crate of Chinese fireworks!

After Bruno rolled off, she reached for her glass of champagne and took a long slow drink. The cool bubbles helped to soothe her throat, now raw and burning after the many long, forceful climaxes she'd experienced tonight, events that always triggered her loud, nonstop stream-of-consciousness appeals to the gods for the demise of her husband and a bit less stamina for her tireless lover.

But in truth, after almost two months, some of her Chinese tirades had actually started to include terms of endearment directed at her Big French Oak. Lala was surprised, but there was no denying the fact that doing the horizontal mambo with Bruno had turned into something special and unforeseen. But, she couldn't let any new and unexpected feelings stand in the way of achieving her ultimate goal.

She was tired of France, tired of waking up in the middle of the night to keep Bruno's allegiance and devotion intact, and sick and tired of her maniac husband's bullshit and total control over her life. Soon, though, with Bruno's help, she would find a way to take her life back. But how? And just how far would she and her Big French Oak be willing take things?

Lala knew DeBussey would never let her go quietly—his narcissistic personality and towering ego couldn't and wouldn't allow it. In case of a divorce, he would make sure she'd find herself penniless. Without money, she would then be shunned by her father with his ridiculous, archaic, old-school Hong Kong values. She would find herself homeless and adrift. And moving in with Bruno around the corner from Château La Tour Noir was *never* going to be an option. There weren't a lot of choices...

*But there must be a way... I will find a way!* she told herself as Bruno began to stir again.

# CHAPTER FORTY-ONE

*Merignac Airport, Bordeaux*

It was early afternoon, and Justin, along with Mike and Frank, were camped out in the waiting area of the next in-bound flight from Paris. Hopefully, Steve and Brad would be aboard *this* one, both having missed their connections at Charles de Gaulle airport.

Other than that slight glitch, everything had gone perfectly—Justin had arrived on time earlier in the day, picked-up the over-sized Mercedes rental van and then caught some extra shuteye in the quiet Air France Business Class lounge. It was just as Steve had described. There were lush leather chairs to relax in. He enjoyed some of the plentiful, freshly baked croissants and hot, strong French coffee for a late morning snack, and was even able to use their elegant, private facilities to take a quick shower. He was wide awake, refreshed, and bursting with exuberant vitality, ecstatic to finally have made it to France after more than a decade of delay. Better late than never.

When passengers Murphy and Lazarus arrived, he helped them to the Mercedes with their bags, and then they ventured up to the airport's rooftop observation deck where they each had a glass of crisp, white wine at the small garden bar overlooking the runways and nearby cityscape. The temperature was perfect. The sky was a cloudless deep blue, and the jet exhaust-tinged breeze blowing through the rooftop gardens could only add to the sweetness of his first moments under French skies. Finishing his glass of tasty white Bordeaux, he made a silent toast to his aunt Annette and a

promise—he would have the trip of a lifetime –one that he
would never forget.

After realizing that Steve and Brad had missed their Paris
connecting flights, the three had taken up positions in the
arrival lounge, where Mike and Frank immediately lapsed into
jet lag-induced comas.

Justin must have dozed-off too, because when he opened
his eyes, the waiting area was filled with passengers filing off a
just-arrived flight from Paris. He watched as the missing Juice
Brothers walked out from the jet way and greeted their friends
with tired smiles, waves, and man-hugs.

After they loaded the last of the bags into the big van,
Justin handed his pre-printed MapQuest info and the extra
Mercedes key to Brad Garrison, self-appointed navigator and
co-pilot for their journey, and they were off, east-bound into
Bordeaux city and beyond.

Today, Marie Agnes was having a good day. She was fully
dressed in her nun's habit and her wrinkled, gaunt face had
regained some, though not all, of its color. With Sister Ralph
once again at the wheel of the little rust-colored Citroën, they
were approaching the exit for 'Air Cargo' at Merignac airport.
The old Sister was once again in full control of her mental and
physical faculties and ready to take care of business. Long
overdue business.

When they parked in front of the FedEx cargo office, the
ancient nun withdrew from the glove box the hang-tag delivery
notice FedEx had left on the doorknob back at their makeshift
orphanage, when they had all been out on a field trip with the
children yesterday afternoon.

"My special medicine has arrived," she announced to Sister
Ralph. "Tomorrow we must pick it up at the airport before they
close for the weekend."

Sister Ralph wasn't sure what kind of special medicine her
friend had ordered, but if it could help the old girl and bring her

some peace and comfort in her waning days, it would be a great blessing.

And she was still very worried about her dear friend. After the terrible heat wave had subsided, Sister Marie Agnes had spent almost three entire weeks in bed suffering from the effects of the weather and her final chemo and radiation treatments. For days on end, she had been in and out a fevered delirium so severe that, on more than one occasion, Sister Ralph had prayed for the Lord to end her suffering and give her peace. And her incoherent ramblings had been frightening, full of hellfire, brimstone, and God's retribution for evil deeds done. She had no doubt as to who and what was so tormenting the old nun's soul.

On a relatively cool morning a few Sundays past, Sister Ralph was relieved and overjoyed when two of the children had awakened her and led her into the old sister's room. There, propped-up in her bed with a smile on her face and a strange, almost beatific light in her eyes, the reinvigorated Sister Marie Agnes greeted the other nuns and her faithful congregation by saying, "Praise God! He has shown me the way!"

Now on their way back towards Côtes de Castillon, Sister Ralph watched her passenger out of the corner of her eye, lovingly cradling the FedEx box containing her special medicine as if it were the baby Jesus himself. She was amazed by, and grateful for, the woman's resilience and strength and really hoped that whatever was in the box would give her friend some comfort and joy.

"How about some music?" the old nun said as she reached for the radio dial and searched the stations for an uplifting tune. She surfed the dial for a few moments before deciding on a just the right song. Patting Sister Ralph's pudgy knee and smiling broadly she said, "This one is good, very good! You will see…"

It's was Manfred Mann and the Earthband's hit from the '70s "Blinded by The Light." Sister Ralph hoped her friend wasn't starting to lose it again.

# CHAPTER FORTY-TWO

*St. Quentin de Baron, France*

After Justin punched in the code the rental agent had emailed him with his payment receipt, the gate slowly swung open and the guys *ooh-ed* and *ahh-ed* as the van cruised through the narrow lane leading up to the house. They were surrounded on either side by short rows of fruit-laden grape vines, and just where the little vineyard ended, the beautifully landscaped grounds spread out before them like a verdant paradise.

"Holy crap, Justin!" Brad said excitedly as he delivered a whack on the shoulder and tousled his hair. "The Internet pictures don't *begin* to do this place justice!"

"Dude, you done good." Mike laughed from the backseat, reaching around and also giving him a nudge. The modern, two story home sat in the shade of a stand of old oak trees, and more of the lush, green vines snaked their way up and around an arched grape arbor that led to the home's front door. Justin thought back to the sign he had seen at The Oasis— *Welcome to Paradise.* That sign would certainly be appropriate here.

They were met at the front door by the owner's rental agent, a Brit ex-pat named Suzi Brighton, and she gave them the full upstairs-downstairs tour, walked them around the back garden area, and showed them where the pool and BBQ grill supplies were located.

"Well, gents, happy with the accommodations?" she asked, as she stuffed the five hundred Euro damage deposit into her purse. There were smiles all around. Before leaving, she gave

Brad directions, in English, to the nearest supermarkets and the names of the best local shops for fresh bread, meats, and of course, wine.

The guys all agreed that since Justin had done such an outstanding job of finding and securing this unbelievable gem-of-a-property, he should have his choice of the six bedrooms. There were four upstairs and two downstairs, and thinking ahead to a possible visit by Destiny, he chose the most private—the downstairs master suite with its own bathroom and double sliding glass doors that overlooked the pool and back garden. It also had the biggest bed.

After unpacking and freshening-up, the guys headed to the *Geant Casino* to do a little grocery shopping. Following Brad's directions, Justin drove them two towns over and pulled into a stadium-sized parking lot filled with what looked thousands of cars.

"This must be the biggest supermarket on earth," he said in wonder.

"And you ain't seen nothin' yet," Mike quipped, "Just wait until you see the friggin' Vin Expo hall. It's so astronomically huge, that I've heard the building generates its own indoor weather systems."

"What about this place?" Justin asked.

Steve explained that the building they were now looking at, the *Geant Casino,* in reality only fractionally as large as the Expo Hall, was what the Europeans call a *hyper market*: one humongous retail outlet that sold almost everything under the sun. "I think the closest thing we've got to this in the states is Costco or Sam's Club."

"Yeah," Frank grunted as he hauled his ass out of the fourth row seat, "but Costco and Sam's Club don't sell *foie gras...* by the kilo!" The moment his feet hit the parking lot pavement, he clapped his hands together, gave the boys a Magic Murphy eyebrow bounce and then went full speed ahead towards the entry doors.

"Don't *ever* get between that man and his foie gras," Mike laughed as they all followed in the big guy's wake. Justin wasn't sure if that was meant to be taken as a joke.

Just before entering the superstore, Steve got a text from Barry Love. He wanted to know if he, along with Destiny and two or three other members of the Cosmo Brands crew, could come by around eight for a "look-see" and some dinner, and, if so, what could they bring? All were in favor, especially Justin, so Steve composed a short reply and hit send: *"C U then & bring wine…lots of wine!"*

# CHAPTER FORTY-THREE

*Bordeaux City, France*

Madame Gascogne was so happy to have her son sitting
with her at her dinner table that she was able to overlook the
fact that, once again, he had returned to France unmarried and
without any grandchildren for her to make a fuss over. But then
again, her tiny and modest apartment was already packed full
of family, with her two daughters, their husbands and her
existing grandchildren, and there was simply nowhere else to
sit. No, things shouldn't have worked out this way. They
should all be sitting around the large table in the grand dining
hall of their former home, prosperous and happy, laughing,
loving and celebrating underneath the old antique chandelier,
basking in the warmth of its fully lit, eighty-four candelabras
and drinking the best bottles their underground wine cellar
could provide.

But nine years ago, everything changed, and five
generations of work building the family's name and brand had
come to a sudden end. Her husband had died bitter and nearly
broke after his business was destroyed by an upstart rival, and
her eldest child abruptly left France to start a new life, in a new
country.

Her silver-haired son hadn't said much during dinner; he
never did. He was a man of action, not words. In the early
evening, after dessert, and the others had left, she found him in
her small study, smoking another cigarette and drinking what
remained of the family's last, prized bottle of a fine hundred-
year-old cognac. He was looking through the old photo albums,
snapshots full of moments and memories from better times:

posing with his father and sisters in one of their vineyards; mother and children picnicking under the grand oaks that lined the lane near their old home; father and son standing atop one of the large stainless steel tanks in the winery like a pair of triumphant mountain climbers after reaching the summit of a fabled peak: the son in full battle gear, standing arm in arm with his special forces comrades around an attack helicopter somewhere in Afghanistan.

As he reached for the last volume on the shelf, his mother held his arm and asked him to stop. "Please, don't look in there," she begged him, "It's too painful... put it down...let it go."

"Mother, I have put it down and let it go for almost a decade, but now, I think, it's time to remember. I need to remember."

As his mother left the room, Monsieur René Gascogne lit another Gitane and pulled the last photo album from the shelf. On the cover was an unusual oval coat of arms that featured a tall dark structure towering over the turrets and pitched roof of a quintessentially eighteenth century St. Émilion château.

The inscription read *Château La Tour de Gascogne.* René knew it very well. It used to be his home. Perhaps, with a little luck and time, it would be his home once more.

# CHAPTER FORTY-FOUR

It had taken almost half an hour, but they finally got all of their groceries and supplies unpacked and put away. Justin had been amazed that five grown men could spend close to two hours shopping for food, but he had to admit, the *Geant Casino* was unlike any supermarket he'd ever seen. The depth and breadth of the items on offer was jaw-dropping, and the presentation of the fresh produce, fish, meats, baked goods and cheese in each of their respective departments was both artistic and inspiring. The French *really* knew what they were doing.

There were mountains of fresh shrimp, prawns and langoustines, schools of fish of all types laid out on wide, thick beds of ice, and buckets full of ocean fresh mussels and oysters. There were delicious looking, crusty rounds of country-style French breads, long thin baguettes, and chunky, rectangular loaves of whole grain goodness studded with all manner of sunflower, flax, poppy, and sesame seeds. In the next department, Justin guessed there was more cheese in the hundred-foot refrigerated display case than in the entire state of Wisconsin. And it smelled incredible! He was really beginning to like cheese, as long as it was paired with a glass of wine.

When they entered the *charcuterie* department, they found Frank standing speechless and spellbound in front of a case containing nearly every conceivable type of duck and goose pâté, mousse, terrine and confit. There were hundreds upon hundreds of all shapes and sizes of sausages made from lamb, pork and beef, smoked and cured meats and specialty hams from all over France and Spain, veal chops, pork chops, racks of lamb, hills of beef and some peculiar looking prepared mash-up loaves of unidentifiable proteins suspended in a coagulated, gelatinous aspic. Justin passed on the free sample offered by the friendly woman behind the counter, but the other guys seemed to enjoy it. Maybe later… much later.

In the end, everyone made their selections, and Frank picked up his precious kilogram container full of foie gras. They also snagged a few mixed cases of locally produced red and white wine and some French *Kronenbourg 1664* beer, which they were now enjoying by the pool as they watched Frank splash around in an impromptu water ballet like a hairy, drunken manatee.

"Just another day in paradise," said Brad, as he tapped beer bottles with Justin.

After Frank had fallen asleep face down in one of the lounges by the pool, the others made it back to their rooms for a round of short naps and showers. When Justin showed up in the small but adequate kitchen shortly before eight, he found Steve had taken on the role of head chef and was working out the details of their evening menu. Since his own expertise in the kitchen was limited to can opening, Steve made him the official prep-cook. His first task: peel, slice, and boil enough potatoes for ten people!

"Bet you didn't think you were signing up for this," Steve laughed, as he pointed to an open drawer full of knives and kitchen utensils.

"It's all good," Justin replied. "Maybe I'll learn something."

"Just stick by Barry, when he gets here. He's the king of side dishes and garnish." Steve pulled a large platter out of one of the cabinets and started filling it with sausages and small lamb chops. On a second, he laid out two medium pork tenderloins and a handful of filet steaks, which he sprinkled with liberal amounts of salt, pepper, and whatever else their absent hosts had on hand in the spice rack.

After a few minutes, a door chime sounded and a high-pitched voice came squeaking over the front gate intercom, "I hope this is the right station, because the Love Train has arrived!"

"I'll let them in," Justin said excitedly. He couldn't wait to see Destiny, but before he could even lay down his knife on the cutting board, he was beaten to the button in the foyer by Frank, dressed only in his size 4XXL Fruit-of the Looms.

"Go away...we don't want any.... you *sheet Americains!*" he bellowed into the intercom.

"Yup, this is the right place," Barry said to his passengers and shot back, "Open up, or it's no *Lafite* for you!" Frank's fingers quickly found the buzzer and let them in.

"Monsieur Murphy, will you be dressing for dinner tonight?" Steve asked as the big man brushed by him on his way upstairs to, presumably, put on something a little less revealing.

Moments later, the guys, minus Frank, made their way outside and stood under the grape arbor to greet their guests. Justin was treated to the sight of his dream girl, looking like a drop-dead-gorgeous movie star, exiting from the backseat of a stylish Audi hatchback, wearing an outfit that included typically skin tight leather pants and a breast-hugging top. The front seat passenger was an older fellow with crazy Einstein hair and a black, bushy moustache that reminded Justin of the former *Today Show* movie critic Gene Shalit.

"Whoa!" Brad said enthusiastically. "Barry brought the "old man" himself." The other passengers were an attractive, well-dressed woman in her forties and a young, chunky guy in a T-shirt and jeans. Handshakes and hugs were exchanged, but Destiny didn't give Justin the big hello he'd been hoping for. Barry brought the older gentleman over and introduced him around.

"Justin James, please meet my boss, Mr. Koulouris," he said, beaming proudly.

"Please, please, call me Cosmo," he said in a voice that still had a hint of his Greek island heritage. "And everyone, please say hello to my West Coast manager Dorinda Hope, and my son, Klitos. Of course, you already know Destiny."

Justin and the other guys waved to Dorinda and then turned to see the wine icon's bushy-haired son fumbling around in the hatchback trying to pick-up a heavy, full case of wine.

*Klitos?* Justin thought, *Klitos Koulouris? Nah...I must've heard it wrong...*

"He's learning the business, and this is his first trip to Vin Expo," Cosmo said, a bit too apologetically.

"*COSMOOOOOO!*" a voice sounding like a deep Alpine hunting horn boomed loudly from behind them.

"Oh, no!" Cosmo exclaimed in mock terror, "It's Frank *the Tank*. Hide the women...and the wine!" They were all laughing as they entered the house and split off into groups. Barry, Steve and Justin headed for the kitchen, Mike went out to the pool house to start the grill, and Brad and Frank gave their very impressed guests the grand tour.

Justin looked on as Steve went to work making a *Bordelaise* wine reduction mushroom sauce and Barry drained the now softened potatoes and started melting sticks of butter in two large skillets.

"Watch and learn," Barry said, "This is how we do it!" In no time at all, Barry had diced three or four onions and had them sizzling in the melted butter. After he put a little color on the onions, he added the sliced potatoes to each pan, a little salt and pepper, and a touch of freshly chopped garlic. And more butter! "We're making classic *Potatoes Lyonnaise,* my friend." He handed a wooden spoon and a spatula to Justin. "Now, you cook, and I'll open some wine."

Barry pulled out a bottle of white from the fridge, one of the local Entre deux Mers sauvignon blancs the guys had just bought at the *Giganto SuperMarche,* and poured for himself and the other two chefs. He saluted them with, "Livin' la Vida Loca, gentlemen!" and took a long sip. "*That...* is surprisingly good," he opined, and Steve and Justin followed suit. "Start turning those 'taters, Justin!"

"How am I doing?" Justin asked, trying not to make too much of a mess.

"Just fine, and right on time," Barry answered. He and Steve had already finished their wine and were pouring more, so Justin did a hurry-up chug and held out his glass. Barry shot him a frowning, skeptical look.

"Hey, I'm not driving tonight, right?"

"That's right," Steve agreed. "*Barrissimo*, pour the man another glass." Frank and Brad popped in to carry a few bottles and glasses out to the table they had set up poolside and then returned to bring the meat platters out to Mike, who, by the smell of it, had a roaring fire going on the BBQ and was ready to start grilling.

"So Barry, what's the story on Monsieur René?" Justin asked as they were transferring the deliciously browned and fragrant potatoes onto two large plates.

"Why, do you have a problem with him?" Barry responded through a test-mouthful of buttery potatoes.

"No...not at all," Justin assured him, "It's just that, you know, I had my little escapade with Phyllis, and he's so quiet and mysterious...I don't know how he really feels about it or if he has a problem with it...or me. Brad said not to worry, but you know him a lot better, I guess."

"Let me tell you something about our friend," Barry replied in his reedy, high pitch as he added a bit more pepper and thyme to Steve's sauce. "René Gascogne is one certified bad-ass dude. I know it's hard to believe, with his silvery hair, his slight physique and the fact that he runs a chichi women's clothing shop. But it's true."

Justin tried but couldn't hide his surprise, or his alarm.

"Years ago, we served together in Afghanistan, in a joint US-French operation," Barry continued as he sprinkled some freshly chopped parsley over the now perfect and ready-to-be-served potatoes. "He was the sub commander of a top French Special Forces unit attached to my chopper squad, and we did a quite a few *very* hairy missions together that I really can't talk about, even now."

"No way!" Justin said, pulling his jaw off the floor.

"Way!" Barry chirped, "All I can say is that, if he wanted to, the man could kill you with a sheet of paper, a bottle cap, his bare hands, you know, whatever's available. He was the best!" He chuckled, looking skyward, remembering the good times.

Justin instantly blanched three shades lighter, and Barry could see that his young friend was breaking a sweat.

"Gotcha!" Barry laughed loudly, pointing at Justin and then slapping him on the back. "Look kid," he continued as he handed Justin one of the large plates of the potatoes and pointed him towards the waiting diners outside, "I'm not saying anything I just told you is true or not, but what is true is that René Gascogne is my friend, and now he's your friend, too. So, relax!"

And Justin did relax. For the next few hours he sat next to Destiny, under the stars on a picture perfect night, his first night in France, while the guys traded stories with Cosmo, and Mike served platter after platter of the various meats he had grilled over a fire made from the stack of grapevine kindling the rental agent had shown them earlier in the day.

Everything from the lamb sausages and the pork tenderloins to Barry's potatoes and Steve's sauce was amazing, and the wines were pure magic; all from producers within an hour's drive of their party house here in St. Quentin de Baron, and each one a revelation! Justin's evolving take on *terroir* hit a new level of understanding and appreciation, and he discussed the wines at length with Cosmo, Dorinda, Destiny and the guys. Klitos, however, didn't say too much and seemed to be more interested in playing a video game on his IPad. And the wine icon's son drank only water. Justin couldn't figure that out.

For dessert, Dorinda went into the kitchen and came back with a fifteen-year-old 750 ml bottle of Château d'Yquem, the gold standard in Sauternes. But before Justin could even get a taste, he was hijacked by Destiny, who said she wanted a private tour of the house and vineyard. Full glasses in hand, they excused themselves and made for the vineyard, now lit only by a waxing three quarter moon and starlight.

"Is everything all right?' he asked in between tastes of the heady, powerful sauternes and a few light kisses, "I missed you this week."

"Justin, it's so wonderful that you're here in France." She pulled him closer and nuzzled his neck, "I missed you, too. But, I couldn't go crazy and throw myself at you in front of Cosmo, my boss. He's a very by-the-book guy, and for him, this was a business dinner, although it's turned into a fun social event. And by the way, I could tell he was very impressed with you and your golden palate. Now, show me your room so I'll know if I'll like the bed I'm going to be sleeping in for a few nights on this trip."

He took her by the hand and walked as quickly as he could, without spilling the wine, back towards the house and into his private, first floor master suite.

# CHAPTER FORTY-FIVE

It was just after midnight when the stylish Audi pulled out of the walled mini estate and headed back toward Bordeaux City. As the gate closed and the guys went back inside to cleanup, Justin was smiling uncontrollably as he looked up at the stars and thanked them for allowing him to be right here, right now.

After showing Destiny to his room, she had pushed him over onto the bed and pounced on him, grinding her body into his as he held her as tightly as he dared. Before they grudgingly pried themselves apart, she promised to return on her own tomorrow evening and spend the night with him, after the dinner they would all be attending in St. Émilion.

Justin really wanted to soak up and enjoy every single moment of his time in France, but as he walked into the kitchen to help Steve with the dishes, he found himself wishing he had a hand-held temporal device just like one of the aliens used in a *Star Trek Enterprise* episode to move back and forth in time. He'd only have to hit fast forward and *voila*, Destiny would be naked in his bed and fulfilling all of the erotic promises she had made tonight while fully clothed in his room.

But, in lieu of sophisticated alien time travel technology, he'd have to wait. But that was all right with him. He could wait, and dream about heaven on earth.

At about the same time, twenty-five miles to the northeast in Côtes de Castillon, all was quiet in the small grouping of shabby buildings that served as the makeshift home for the nuns and children of Our Lady of Mercy. And all was dark, except for one bulb burning dimly in the bedchamber of the destitute orphanage's director and guiding light.

Ever since she and Sister Ralph had returned from the airport earlier in the day, Sister Marie Agnes had been waiting in anticipation of this moment. She couldn't risk opening the FedEx box containing her "special medicine" until she was quite certain that everyone was asleep and she wouldn't be disturbed by one of the children or any of the other nuns. No one else could know. No one except, of course, the Lord himself, who had put this bold plan of action into her head in the first place.

Now the moment had arrived. Quietly, she used her cherished, Vatican-issued plastic Jesus-on-a-crucifix letter opener to cut through the tape securing the package, and opening the box, she slowly removed its tightly bubble-wrapped contents, carefully unwinding the noisy packing so as not to wake a sleeping soul.

And there it was, just like the unit she had seen and ordered on the Website: The Rattle Snake Terminator XXX stun gun—ten million volts of dual-pronged, agonizing and incapacitating power, disguised as an ordinary-looking flashlight! It was devilishly ingenious, and she couldn't wait to give it a test run. She hadn't been this excited since she'd won the Mother Teresa look-alike contest back at the convent thirty years ago.

She unwrapped the charger, plugged it into the wall, and snapped the unit into its base. The charger's small LED glowed red in the dim light of her room, and while she waited for her Rattlesnake to power up, she took a quick look through the owner's manual.

The unit had a simple on-off switch, a large white button, and a smaller red button. The manual said the switch activated the flashlight and also sent power to the stun gun's prongs. Pressing the white button sent a single powerful charge to the prongs and it could be depressed numerous times to defend against and shock an attacker. The red button was even more dangerous. When it was pressed, the unit sent out a constant, elephant-dropping ten million volt charge until the button was either pressed again, or the unit ran out of power, whichever happened first.

These brief instructions were followed by a few pages of disclaimers, caveats, and limits of manufacturer liability. Marie Agnes read on, *Under no circumstances should unit be discharged while operator is standing in or surrounded by any liquid substance,* was no-no number one. *Do not operate unit barefoot.* That made sense. *For full power, discharge, and duration, unit must be plugged into base and charged for a minimum of three hours.* She would have read the others, but with a small chime, the unit's LED switched to green. She got up from the bed and silently opened her door, looking both ways and listening for anyone stirring or waking up to use the toilet. All clear. She quietly closed the door.

Marie Agnes then snapped the stun gun out if its base and with a trembling hand flipped the switch on. The flashlight instantly sent a beam of intense bright light that nearly blinded the poor woman, and the quiet calm of the night was pierced by a malevolent hum and an evil electric crackling that scared her half to death. The potent charge it emitted into the room would have made her hair stand on end, had she had any.

She paused for a moment to again listen for anyone stirring, catch her breath, and say a quick prayer for strength. Then, holding the unit out in front of her and pointing it towards the window, she gave the white button one short press.

Instantly, with a sound resembling a small thunderclap, a spindly, white hot bolt of lightning shot out of the two prongs at the end of the gun and filled the room with an eerie blue glow before it dissipated as quickly as it had appeared, and the unit went dead.

*"Mon Dieu...Holy Shit!"* the old nun shouted as she dropped the now powerless device on the floor and stumbled back, falling onto her bed. There was commotion in the hall and the sound of footsteps running up to her door.

"Sister Marie Agnes!" one of the nuns yelled as she knocked nervously on her door," is everything all right?"

The old nun picked herself up, made her way to the door, and cracking it open a few centimeters answered, "It's nothing, Sister. I had a bad dream, but now everything is fine. Please, don't worry. God is with me." Making the sign of the cross, she closed the door, picked up the stun gun, and snapped it back into its base.

She wanted to put her plan, the Lord's plan, into action at once, but understood that she would have to bide her time and wait for the perfect opportunity to present itself. But that was all right. She could wait. And dream of heaven and of bringing an evil sinner to salvation. Just as long as her Rattle Snake Terminator XXX was charged for at least three hours, God would be with her. And, she knew He wouldn't make her wait long.

# CHAPTER FORTY-SIX

Saturday morning in St. Quentin de Baron was glorious. Mug full of French press coffee in hand, Justin was walking alone through the small vineyard in front of the house, deeply breathing in the ethereal fruited-scent of the cool morning air as bright sunlight glinted off the still dew-covered grapes. The old world was a new and completely different world for him. And it was wonderful.

Taking an extra moment of quiet introspection to review the path he had taken in the last six months, the path that had led him here to this beautiful property in Southwest France and its gravelly little vineyard filled with the goodness of the earth and the sound of a hundred birds singing their sweet, melodic song of life, he was nearly overcome with emotion; so supremely happy and grateful to be here with this group of wine-crazy guys, friends he hadn't even known half a year ago.

*Funny how quickly things can change*, he thought as he walked back under the grape arbor and into the house.

An hour or so later, after a breakfast of freshly baked breads, locally made all natural jams, cheese and *Bayonne* ham, the guys set out for a day of sightseeing in the vineyards of the Haut-Medoc, north of Bordeaux city. With Justin at the wheel and Brad navigating, they headed west and then north, towards the famous *D2 Wine Route des Châteaux.*

After traveling on the ring road around the large city and across an impressively tall bridge towering over the Garonne River, things started to get interesting. As they descended onto the river's left bank, Brad pointed out the Exposition Parc, home to the Vin Expo, just north of the highway to their right.

Justin could immediately see that Mike's earlier description of the gargantuan size of the main exhibition hall had been no exaggeration whatsoever. Even at a distance, the five-story structure appeared gigantic, stretching for what Brad said was just over half a mile. Although it was built in the shape of a rectangle, Justin told the guys that its sheer landscape-dominating size and form reminded him of pictures he had seen of The Pentagon in Washington, DC.

"I can see that," Frank replied from his rear seat and added, "but this baby isn't going to be filled with military brass or pencil-pushing bureaucrats—it's going to be filled to the rafters with more wine than we could possibly hope to taste in a year! Are you man enough, Justin? Are you wine-fan enough?" Justin looked into the rearview mirror and saw two buggy eyes blinking at him under wiggling, bushy eyebrows.

"Oh, I think he can handle it," Steve said, "We've all seen him in action enough to know he has no qualms about tasting all sorts of wine under the most adverse conditions."

"That's right!" Mike chimed in, his sandpaper rasp full of paint-removing grit this morning. "We've seen him fending-off the advances of a wild cougar, taming a supermodel-hot wine-babe, tasting rosé champagne off of the heaving bosom of a very zaftig stripper, and heroically whipping through an obstacle course of spit-buckets in a single bound." The guys were all laughing now, and Justin had to admit, he was impressed with his record.

"And," Brad added, "the *most* amazing thing of all is he never spilled a drop." The volume of the laughter and conversation in the big van increased at least ten decibels as the highway led them across a large, wide lake, and Brad pointed Justin to the exit for the *Avenue du Medoc*. After a few minutes of stop and go driving on a congested two-lane road through the heart of suburban, small-town France, they emerged into a more rustic setting of small country houses, dense greenery and stone fence-enclosed vineyards.

When they passed a street sign that read *Margaux 9 km*, Brad announced, "Margaux five miles gentlemen, welcome to the Haut Medoc!" Driving farther north, it was obvious to Justin that they were now in the heart of the Bordeaux wine country, comfortably ensconced in greenery, bucolic scenery and row upon row of grape vines as far as the eye could see.

Some of the vineyards were surrounded by stone walls or low stone fences, quintessential examples of what the French call a *clos,* as Steve pointed out—while others were simply cordoned off by either basic wire and post fencing, or nothing at all. It was all very low-key and not exactly what Justin had expected, until just before the entering the small town of Margaux, when they passed by the very impressive edifice of Château Palmer, sitting regally off to the right behind a light bluish wrought iron fence, complete with its colorful manicured front garden, dual-turreted towers, and a steeply pitched tile roof crowned by the flags of France and England blowing in the summer breeze.

"Awesome! My first château!" Justin whooped enthusiastically

With the D2 twisting and turning through the quiet town, the Mercedes van full of vino tourists meandered through a small, nondescript locale made up of tightly packed single or two story stone buildings all in need of a good coat of paint. The sidewalks on either side of road were full of cars haphazardly parked at odd angles, and they drove by a collection of small shops and businesses, including a video shop, a Laundromat, a gyro stand, and a very greasy-looking car repair garage.

Every block or so there were banners hanging from sign posts emblazoned with the names of some of the better-known area châteaux, but it was all a bit mundane. But it was still charming in its way, and it *was* France. Before he knew it, they had left the close streets of Margaux behind and were back into wide open vineyard country.

As they headed towards the next appellation, St Julien, the topography changed ever-so-slightly and the vineyards spread out on either side of the D2 seemed to roll gently into the distance. Sign posts pointed to turn-offs for destinations like Listrac, Poujeaux, Lamarque, and Moulis, all names Justin recognized from his reading and from the Grand Bordeaux tasting he'd attended at the Oasis. That had been a wonderful evening, but Justin had a feeling that, excluding his hot make-out session with Destiny, it would pale in comparison to today, tonight, and the rest of the week here in France.

Entering the slightly larger town of St. Julien, the guys pointed out each famous name as they drove by the properties one after another, but these structures looked more like white-washed warehouses than grand manors. It seemed to Justin that for every opulent, castle-like château they had seen, there were at least half a dozen wineries that, other than the fact that they were located on the world-famous *Wine Route des Châteaux,* looked ordinary and unremarkable.

After a few more minutes on the D2, a waist-high wall of stone and mortar lined the roadway, and looking to his right, Justin was treated to a majestic view of the famous, monolithic tower of Château Latour, a few hundred yards in the distance, nestled among hundreds of hectares of first-growth grapes. Next up on the right and directly adjacent to La Tour was the estate of Pichon Lalande, elegant and stately behind white wrought iron gates, a stand of tall trees shading it from the bright, early afternoon sun.

"Justin, slow down and get ready to make a left turn," Brad instructed as they neared the next major attraction, the awe-inspiring façade of Pichon Baron, just across the street from Pichon Lalande, and a few notches higher on the scale of grandiosity.

As the Mercedes pulled into a small parking lot, Justin was, in fact, awestruck by the property's extravagant mix of traditional and modern design, from the flamboyant towers and turrets of the tall eighteenth century main house to the angular lines of the ground-level side buildings that stood on either side of a large rectangular reflecting pool. It was picture perfect and looked exactly like the label adorning each bottle of the famous wine, including the one that Destiny had given him, now quietly aging in his vino-fridge in Orlando.

After the guys piled out of the van and posed for a few photos in front of the château, it was back on the road through the relatively large, prosperous town of Paulliac, past the expansive property of Mouton Rothschild just north of the city limits, and onto the last major appellation of the Haut Medoc,

St. Estephe, where they once again posed in front of a château for a few quick pics.

This time, after cresting a small hill guarded by a small circular tower that resembled something straight out of the Middle Ages, they pulled over in front Cos d'Estournel, with its pagoda-like spires rising behind stark, sandstone walls. As the guys posed in front of Cos's impressive entry arch, topped by powerful dueling lions arrayed on either side of its coat of arms, Justin crossed the narrow street and stood at the edge of a vast vineyard to take the photo. After he clicked off a couple of shots, he took a minute to look down and touch the tiny grapes that hung in small clusters from each of the vines.

On the back of his tongue, he thought he caught a fleeting note of vanillin and crème de cassis, very reminiscent of the outstanding 2000 Cos d'Estournel he'd had at Steve's house a few months back. He smacked his lips as he savored the memory and then suddenly thought about what he might be doing today back in Orlando, had he not taken a chance and gone into Brad's wine shop last winter.

A year ago at this time, he would have probably been locked in his cubicle at FedEx, getting ready for another solo Saturday night, or dusting off his Klingon mask and planning his next trip to a Comic-Con convention. But here he was, under the sun and sky of Bordeaux, standing amidst its fabled terrior and holding in his hand the grapes of what might potentially become a classic bottle of wine. It was almost magical.

From across the road, the voices of his Juice Brothers brought him back to reality and they resumed their sightseeing pilgrimage, driving through the one-horse hamlet of St. Estephe and looping back to the south, down the D2. The guys all agreed to stop somewhere for a late lunch, and Mike suggested an alternate route back towards Bordeaux, one that would take them by a property he had visited more than twenty-five years ago.

"You mean back when you were young?" Justin quipped.

"Shut up and drive, Justin," Mike hoarsely chuckled in response. "I'll tell you where to stop."

Somewhere after passing back through Margaux, they took a side road that led them southeast through even smaller, sleepier villages, and as they drove on, from time to time they caught a glimpse of the Gironde River through the dense forest greenery that cropped up at the beginning and end of each tiny town. Just like on the D2, there were signs everywhere offering *degustations,* wine tastings, but it wasn't until they were nearing a town called Macau that Mike perked up.

"It's right around here, somewhere," he croaked,

"That must be it," Justin said as they rounded a bend and a fairly large, rustic farm house came into view. It sat behind a nicely trimmed hedge fence and a large sign welcoming all to Château Beau Rivage de Medoc.

"Nah, that's not it. Keep going around the next bend, and we'll all be in for a real treat!" Just around the next twist in the road, a crudely hand-painted sign for *Château Maison Mobile Degustation* directed them to turn right on to a very narrow, unpaved rutted trail, and as the big Mercedes van bounced along the one lane road, Justin hoped that no one was driving in the opposite direction.

"Mike, where the hell are we going here, the movie set of the French version of *Deliverance*? Is someone going to start playing "Dueling Accordions?" Brad asked as they drove into a clearing filled with nearly a dozen cars and two rusting 1950s style mobile homes that looked like they had spent their formers lives on the road with a now-defunct two bit carnival. Each of the trailers had a faded, discolored canvas awning pulled out over a service counter and small seating areas, and there were people sitting here and there on rickety chairs and picnic tables, drinking wine, eating lunch, and generally having a good time.

"Yeah, that's pretty much where we are," he rasped in reply. "After all these years, I can't believe I actually found this place again! I hope the same family's still running it."

"Running *it*? Running *what?*" Steve asked incredulously as they exited the van and stretched their legs.

"I happened upon this place on almost thirty years ago, on my first trip to Bordeaux," Mike said and stepped out of the van. "There was only one trailer then, so I guess business has been good."

"*Business*?" Brad asked. "What *business*?"

"I guess you could say that this is a kind of Bordeaux equivalent of a fruit or produce stand back home," Mike said as he pointed to the first trailer. "This place was run by a family that owned a small vineyard just beyond this clearing. On weekends during spring and summer, they sold their wines along with sandwiches, cheese and even foie gras. "

"Did someone say *foie gras*? I'm in," Frank said and hauled himself out of the backseat. As he got to his feet and quickly made his way toward the trailers, their collective attention was drawn back to the bumpy lane where a World War Two-era motorcycle with a sidecar was noisily driving into the clearing. It sported an earth-tone camouflage paint job and was being driven by a chrome-domed older man dressed in biker leathers and wearing oversized goggles. His passenger in the sidecar was the largest dog Justin had ever seen, a huge chocolate-brown Great Dane. The dog was also wearing a pair of oversized goggles and a T-shirt that read *Securité.*

"Yep," Mike said with a smile, "Same motorcycle...definitely the same family!" The man parked next to the first trailer, unhooked the dog's seatbelt after removing its goggles, and pulled a bag full of baguettes out of the cargo carrier in the back. He handed the baguettes over the counter to a slim dark-haired woman in her thirties who was in the process of putting out a tray of sandwiches and fruit, and then walked over to the service counter at the second trailer where another slim dark-haired woman handed him a glass of white wine.

"Hey, it looks like those women are twins." Steve said as the dog ran over to Justin and nearly knocked him down.

"Lucy, no!" the biker shouted as the dog started humping the now embarrassed Justin's leg. He grabbed a towel from the counter and ran over to shoo the Great Dane away by flicking the towel at her rear end while apologizing to Justin in French. When he realized he was dealing with a group of American tourists, he promptly switched to heavily accented English. "I am so sorry. My Lucy, she is a bad girl, but I guess she really like you! She is a good judge of character, so please join me. I invite you all for a glass of wine." Lucy kept her distance as they walked over to trailer number two, where glasses of white wine were waiting for each of them on the service counter.

While they tasted the crisp, refreshing Château Maison Mobile blanc, Mike introduced the group and recounted his visit all those years ago.

"Welcome back," the biker said, and explained that his twin daughters now worked with him in the vineyard, making and selling the wine, carrying on the tradition started by his family a long time ago.

Within a few minutes, the guys were all sitting around one of the picnic tables as the twins, Nicole and Nadia, brought out plates with delicious-looking baguette sandwiches, cheese, and foie gras, and Jean opened bottles of his two Bordeaux Superieur red wines.

The first, the Maison Mobile rouge, was made from one hundred percent Merlot, and was priced at the equivalent of only $14 per bottle. The second red was the Cuvée de Maison Mobile, and Jean explained that it was an equal blend of Cabernet, Cabernet Franc and Merlot. It was priced at just $19. The guys all thought it was a steal.

Justin found the wines to be very palate pleasing: simple and fresh, with nice, dark cherry fruit, a hint of smoky oak and just enough structure and sweet tannin to make them really interesting; much more so than their humble price points would suggest. After pouring and tasting, Jean excused himself as the guys relaxed and Frank devoured his foie gras.

"Well, Mike," Brad said raising his glass, "I've got to hand it to you! We would *never* see red Bordeaux this good for under twenty bucks in the states." Steve and Justin followed suit and saluted both Mike and Château Maison Mobile. Frank was too busy wolfing down his lunch to be bothered with any small talk.

"And," Steve added, "the loony ambience of this whole set-up just has to be seen and felt to be believed. This experience is the antithesis of what the big châteaus that we saw today are all about, but it's just as valid and memorable. Great call, Mike...great call!"

At that moment, Justin felt something nuzzling his leg and looked down to find Lucy staring at him, holding a very large plastic doggie dish in her mouth, her long tail wagging vociferously and smacking into Frank's leg.

"She likes the Merlot!" Jean called out from behind the counter. Lucy laid her dish at Justin's feet, and he obliged by pouring a small taste into the battered and bitten old bowl. She made the wine disappear in an instant and then, the dog was off—rolling on her back in the grass, snorting and growling. "She says it need another year in the bottle," Jean translated, as he came out to collect the empty glasses and plates. Frank laughed so hard that he momentarily had to stop shoveling the duck liver paté into his mouth. But only momentarily.

After they'd finished their tasty lunch and most of the wine, they settled the meager bill and bought a mixed case of the reds. The guys then posed in front of the trailers for pictures with Jean and the twin sisters, and Steve got a shot of Justin sitting on the motorcycle with Lucy in the sidecar. Both of them were wearing goggles and smiling broadly. As they pulled back onto the road and headed for St. Quentin de Baron, Justin was laughing and shaking his head, still grinning ear to ear. *Did I really just share a glass of wine with a Great Dane in the boondocks of Bordeaux?* It had been funny, funky and unforgettable. The guys had told him that France could be full of surprises.

*Hmm…I wonder what's coming next?*

# CHAPTER FORTY-SEVEN

After the security gate swung open, they drove through and emerged on the other side of the mini-vineyard to find a small car, *sans* driver, parked in front of the house.

"How did anybody get in here without the access code?" Justin asked.

"Maybe it's the rental agent or the owner," Brad answered as they pulled to a stop and exited the big van.

Justin unlocked the front door and the others followed him into the warm, stuffy rental house, opening windows as they went to their respective rooms to let the late afternoon's cooling breeze do its work.

When he entered his own room and opened the double French doors to the pool deck to let in some fresh air, Justin thought he smelled something smoky and familiar. There, lying on one of the lounges, puffing away on his ever-present cigarette, was Monsieur René, the mystery car's driver, his slight, sinewy form on display in a tight, taut neon-green Speedo.

He was in the middle of a heated discussion with someone on the other end of his cell phone, but he looked up and gave Justin a wave and an enigmatic smile. Within moments, he was joined by Mike, who handed him a cold beer, and by Frank who soaked the both of them by plunging into the pool while yelling "CANNONBALL" at the top of his considerable lungs.

While Brad and Steve joined the others by the pool, Justin checked his IPad for e-mail. There, he found a short, scintillating message from one Ms. Destiny Verrano: *Hi Justin. Hope you guys had a wonderful day of sightseeing...can't wait to see you tonight! I've attached a little preview of what you'll be having for dessert. Kisses! D.* He opened the attachment to find a selfie she took in the mirror of her hotel room, wearing a pair of sheer, black panties, a sexy, inviting smile, and nothing else.

When his heart started beating again, he replied *Hi. Yes, we did have a great day in Haut Medoc, but YOU are the most wondrous thing I've seen today! OMG!!!!!!! Thank you for that, my dear... going to take cold shower now, lol!* He hit send, changed into his board shorts, grabbed a bottle of water and joined the rest of the guys on the pool deck, shaking hands with René before settling into a cozy, cushioned chaise.

"Allo Joosteen," Monsieur René said in greeting. "That was Phyllis on the phone, and she sends you all her warmest regards."

"Nice...ah...thank you, Monsieur René. But, I was wondering, how did you get the gate to open without the access code?" Justin asked. "Not that we're unhappy to see you or anything like that," he quickly added.

"Oh," he replied in his dry, Gallic way, "I have—how do you say in English—I have *the knack. Santé!*" They all touched beer glasses and water bottles and relaxed for the next hour or so, as René filled them in on the evening's festivities.

Tonight, they would all be attending the *Union de Producteurs de St. Émilion* dinner at the Hotel Restaurant Palais Cardinale, adjacent to the remnants of a thirteenth century abbey in the heart of the charming, Medieval town. It was held in conjunction with the big tradeshow, and using his connections from his family's previous years in the wine business, René had gotten them all tickets and made arrangements for them to sit with Barry and the Cosmo Brands team.

"It's always a great way to start-off the Vin Expo," he said, "and you never know who will show up. It could be a very interesting evening." Justin had no doubt that it would all be *fantastique*, especially his private "dessert."

Just after six, one by one, the guys started disappearing into the house to shower and dress, and Justin, who had dozed-off, was awakened by a light nudge from his French friend.

"Time to start getting ready, I think."

"René, why don't you use the master bedroom shower and go first?" Justin replied, still wanting a few more minutes to relax. The adventures of the day and the long drive back to St. Quentin de Baron had really knocked him out. Before Monsieur René had even made it into the house, Justin was out like a light, sleeping in a contented, purple Cuvée de Maison Mobile haze, with visions of the nearly naked Destiny dancing in his head.

The first half of the forty-five minute ride to the hill-top town of St. Émilion was much like their travels earlier in the day. Once again, they drove through small, slightly dilapidated-looking villages and communities surrounded by lush green fields and vineyards, with farmhouses, silos and towering three-bladed windmills dotting the countryside for miles around.

Monsieur René, mercifully not smoking at the moment, acted as tour guide and kept them informed about points of interest along the way: a five-hundred year old *Romanesque* church here, or a *petit château* there, but it wasn't until after they had passed over the placid, slowly flowing Dordogne River on a picturesque stone bridge that Justin felt they had entered into "storybook" territory.

As they continued east, the landscape on north side of the road changed from endless flat vineyards and forest areas to one of steeply sloping hills and sheer, tree-lined promontories. René pointed to one of the bluffs in the distance and told the guys to keep an eye out for the twelfth century Priory of St. Laurent.

"It was built in the 1100's by monks and used as a collection center by the Catholic Church for all of tithes and taxes they collected. They also farmed and made wine. As a matter of fact," he continued, "the church had a whole network of these priories throughout the region to keep "God's eyes" on the people and "His hand" in their pockets."

"Is that it?" Justin asked eagerly, as they rounded a bend and a large castle-like structure came into view. It stood on the edge of a cliff, its thick limestone walls discolored and weathered by nearly a thousand of years of wind, rain and history. It was an enchanting vista; an open window directly into the past that sent a little shiver of excitement up Justin's spine. As they got closer to their destination, more and more impressive houses and buildings appeared on the surrounding hilltops and bluffs, with Monsieur René providing the play-by-play.

"René, how is it that you know so much about the churches and priories?' Justin asked after they had passed through a small town with a large church on almost every corner. He wanted to get to know more about Monsieur René, and since the normally taciturn Frenchman had just tried his hand at a little humor, he thought it might be a good opportunity to draw him out a bit.

"Well, like every good Catholic boy in St. Émilion, I went to parochial school until I graduated, and the nuns had plenty of time to fill my head full of Church history. And my parents were always very active supporters of the church's charity work for underprivileged and orphaned children. My sisters and I volunteered with them many times. You know, perhaps I should—" At that moment, René was interrupted by a resounding *whoop whoop* emanating from the rear of the van, as Frank let loose his booming baritone in, what sounded like celebration.

"Oh yeah, I finally did it," he bellowed with glee, holding up a thick, dog-eared volume of crossword puzzles.

"Did what, my large, excruciatingly loud friend?" Steve asked as he vigorously rubbed the ear into which Frank had just directly yelled.

"I finally finished the final puzzle in this damn book. It's been driving me crazy ever since the flight over. And you'll never guess the last answer to the last puzzle," he said, giving the guys his googly *Magic Murphy* eye-shtick. When no one offered a guess or expressed any interest whatsoever, he decided to tell them anyway. "You'll never believe this, but the last answer to the last puzzle is...are you ready for this... *FOIE*

*GRAS!"* The big man clapped his hands and exploded into a fit of laughter, with Mike, and then everyone else, joining in. "And now I really, *really* need some. Justin, drive faster...*mach schnell!"* he commanded.

Justin complied by hitting the gas pedal a little harder, anxious to see what awaited in St. Émilion. It was just ahead, sitting atop a steep hill, and he could see the iconic Eglise de Saint-Émilion, the old monolithic church that dominated the city's skyline, with its lofty bell tower and steeple soaring into the cloudless evening sky. Another small tremor of excitement shot through him. This trip just kept getting better and better, and it was only their second day.

# CHAPTER FORTY-EIGHT

After Justin maneuvered the lumbering Mercedes up and through the steep, narrow streets of the old town, they came to a traffic circle at the top of the hill. Following René's direction, he took the northwest turnoff, and they were all treated to the sight of the remnants of an ancient abbey, its last remaining limestone wall partially overgrown by shrubs and clinging vines. Framed against the slowly setting sun, it looked exactly like one of the beautiful pictures he and Aunt Annette had marveled at in the *France Travel Guide*, all those years ago. But this was real.

Just on the other side of the wall and standing in its shadow, the Hôtel Restaurant Palais Cardinale looked as though it had been made from the same aged stones as the old abbey. The striped blue and white awnings hanging over the arched entryway and the large, latticed casement windows on either side gave the hotel's simple façade an air of regal elegance, and the crew of smartly uniformed valets attending to the short line of cars waiting to be parked added to the overall ambience of a special occasion at a special location. But that wasn't what caught Justin's attention.

"René, look at that!" he remarked, as they pulled up to the valet stand and exited the van. At the end of the block, a small group of people holding signs and placards was chanting in a measured, almost polite way. They were being led by a stooped, elderly nun holding a megaphone, with a few other nuns in their summer habits joining in the chant or talking with people on the sidewalk. One very large Sister was carrying a wicker basket and appeared to be taking donations from onlookers. Justin couldn't make out what they were saying, but it was unmistakably some kind of protest. "I guess the Church is still pretty active in St. Émilion after all."

"I sure hope this doesn't have anything to do with the force-feeding of ducks and geese in the making of foie gras!" Frank said with a note of fear in his voice.

"No... I don't think so," René said. He had a strange look on his face as he read the signs and listened to the protestors. "I don't believe this! I know some of these Sisters. The one with the megaphone was the Mother Superior at my school when I was a boy. Guys, please go inside and get comfortable. I need a few moments to talk with her."

As René walked towards the protesters, the guys entered the hotel and were directed through the lobby toward the large banquet room at the back of the building. All except for Justin, who remained outside.

When the senior nun recognized René, she immediately handed the megaphone to one of the other protesters and greeted Monsieur René with a warm embrace and a kiss on each of his cheeks. Taking his hand, she led him a few meters down the sidewalk, away from the protestors and animatedly explained to him, Justin supposed, what was happening.

Taking a closer look at the signs and placards, he noticed that some of them were covered with pasted-on photos of some kind of a school, different groups of children flanked by some of the nuns, and construction equipment knocking down some old buildings. A few of the protestors also carried posters with photos of what looked like an extremely ugly caveman in a designer suit, flashing a jagged red circle with a slash through it freshly painted across his swarthy, malevolent mug on each and every one.

The big Sister approached him with her wicker basket and held it out for a donation, so Justin produced a 20 Euro note and laid it on top of the other bills. She smiled at him, and he thought she said something about the children thanking him, but high school French had been far too long ago for him to have any real possibility of understanding the language and engaging in any sort of rudimentary conversation. At this point, all he could really remember was the national motto of France,

the language drill they opened class with every day: *Liberté,
Egalité, Fraternité.* So, he just smiled back and nodded. The
big nun batted her brown eyes at him and smoothed her patchy
little moustache before she moved on to further work the
crowd.

He turned to find his friend bidding the old Sister good-bye,
and walking back in his direction. René's face had gone dark,
veins were bulging in his neck, and he was gritting his teeth
with such intensity that Justin thought he might break a tooth.
He surprised the rotund nun taking the donations by dropping
hundreds of Euros into her basket and then motioned to Justin
that they should head inside.

"What's up with the nuns?" he asked as the slim, trim
Frenchman brushed quickly by him.

"I will tell you later," was all he said.

As Justin turned and took one more look at the protestors,
the large nun caught his eye and gave him another smile and a
little wave. She was clearly flirting with him now, which sent
another chill up his spine, but this time for entirely different
reasons. He quickly turned back and followed René into the
hotel lobby, where he found him hungrily puffing away on a
Gitane and briskly shaking hands with a small circle of men
near the reception desk.

As Justin approached the group, the attention of everyone
in the room was suddenly drawn to a brand new and much
louder commotion in front of the hotel. Amid a chorus of angry
shouts and the sounds of a potential scuffle, Justin, René and a
few others rushed through the lobby's open doors to view the
scene unfolding on the sidewalk. The nuns and all of the
protestors had surrounded a large black Mercedes S-Class
sedan that had pulled up to the valet stand and were pelting it
with water balloons, eggs and overripe tomatoes. The car's side
windows were darkly tinted, and Justin couldn't see who was
inside, but whoever it was couldn't have been too happy.

Moments later, two police cars came screaming around the
corner with their Euro-sirens wailing and their blue lights
blazing, but before the *gendarmes* could even get out of their
vehicles, the crowd ceased its barrage and began to quickly
disperse. By the time the four officers made their way onto the

sidewalk and interposed themselves between the car, which now had the appearance of an abstract Jackson Pollock drip-painting, and the protestors, only the nuns, still led by the old Sister, remained around the Mercedes.

The driver's door opened and a large, dangerous-looking man with enormous hands emerged. He was smartly dressed in a crisply tailored suit, and with his rough-hewn, fairly good looks, one might have mistaken him for a *B-Movie* action star.

"Bruno Bastian!" René hissed under his breath. They watched as the driver, whom Justin thought exuded a kind of menace or intimidation, walked around the car to open the opposite side passenger door and assist a very attractive woman out of the backseat. She too was wearing a smart evening ensemble and was shielding her delicate alabaster skin from the setting sun's rays with a multicolored parasol and oversized wrap-around sunglasses. One might have mistaken *her* for an *A-list* movie star.

After the driver escorted the woman to the sidewalk, he then opened the other passenger door, and out stepped a short, squat man with an instantly familiar and a notoriously unforgettable face.

"It's the guy from the nun's posters!" Justin exclaimed to René, whose *visage* was now a fixed, blank stare and completely unreadable. He dropped his half-smoked Gitane on the sidewalk and slowly crushed it under his heel, while clenching both of his hands into tightly balled fists. The small balding man with beady black eyes and a haughty look on his stubbly face was also well dressed, but no one would ever mistake *him* for a movie star, unless it was, perhaps, as a Neanderthal *Munchkin* or an *Oompa Loompa.*

"That, my friend, is Mr. Guy DeBussey," René replied, "and he is the reason the nuns and protestors are here today. They all hate him... as do I."

Upon seeing the swarthy near-midget exit the car, the old Sister lunged towards Guy DeBussey yelling something in French that Justin thought sounded like the word for "light." He wasn't sure. One of the officers easily blocked her path, and DeBussey and his driver walked into the hotel, ignoring the nuns, the police, and all of the onlookers. And that was that.

But for some reason, as Justin watched the police escort the nuns off the premises, he had the strangest feeling that, behind her sunglasses, the woman with the pastel parasol had been discreetly checking him out as she walked slowly by.

They followed the rest of the late arriving attendees through the hotel, past the banquet room and out onto a wide, luxuriously detailed garden terrace, where half a dozen tables had been set up for an *al fresco* wine tasting, just in front of the scenically backlit wall of the adjacent, ancient abbey. It was an amazing view, and Justin once again thanked himself for taking a chance and saying *yes* all those months ago.

As the still-fuming René excused himself to join the same group of men he had been talking with before the ruckus, Justin scanned the throng of tasters and easily located his Juice Brothers at the far end of the terrace. It was hard to miss man-mountain Frank. He was already in full "Tank" mode: his face was blazing the color of the setting sun and his nose was deeply buried in his tasting glass. Even at fifty yards away, the sound of his hyperventilating ritual was attention-getting, and as he approached, Justin caught a few members of the crowd shooting not-so-nice sideways glances at the large American with the breathing problem.

"About time you showed up," Brad said as he handed Justin a tasting glass.

"Yeah, you've got some catching-up to do," Mike added, "but do keep in mind that you're the designated driver. We all want to live to drink another day!" With that Mike gave him a light slap on the back and walked to the next table.

"Has anyone seen Destiny or Barry?" Justin craned his neck around to take in the sight of Frank's nearly orgasmic countenance as he fairly guzzled a just-poured taste of black cherry-colored delight two tables down.

"I got a text from Brother Love a few minutes ago, and he said that they're running a little late," Steve answered as he finished whatever he had in his glass and licked his purple lips clean. "You've *really* got to try that last wine. I've never heard of the producer, but it is *outstanding!*" he exclaimed and then drifted off to explore more known and unknown quantities at the rest of the tables.

Justin spent the next few minutes with Brad, who directed him to try the selections at the first table, all of which he deemed especially good considering the fact that neither he nor any of the others had ever heard of a single one of them. Their server explained in halting English that these wines were all from smaller "satellite" appellations, like Montagne-St. Émilion, Côtes de Castillon, or Lussac-St. Émilion, and that, perhaps they weren't even available in the USA—she wasn't sure. But Justin was sure of one thing; the wines were forward and delicious, all sporting smoky, sweet cherry notes and generous amounts of dark fruit flavors. The last selection, the one Steve had recommended, was the standout, with a complex structure and a finish that wouldn't quit.

As Brad focused on the next table, Justin caught the distinct and tantalizing aromas of burning charcoal and grilling meats, and turned to discover a serving station had been set up just outside the entrance to the banquet room. A small line had already formed and the grill master was busily turning dozens of savory smelling skewers and small, plump sausages. Naturally, Frank was first in line, with plate in hand and nose in glass.

Justin made his way through the terrace of tasters and was about to join him when he noticed the lady with the parasol, now sitting at a smallish table with a few other women, once again checking him out while trying to appear not to be checking him out. She had removed her oversized sunglasses, revealing herself to be a classic beauty of Chinese descent. Justin was flattered by her seeming interest, but when he gave her a little smile, she immediately got up and disappeared into the hotel. *Hmm...*

She was quickly forgotten as a pack of white-jacketed waiters appeared with trays full of wonderful-looking gourmet snacks and appetizers. He got another taste of wine from the closest table, and after waiting in the short grill line for a few moments, Justin was rewarded with a plate full of lamb skewers dusted with kosher salt and rosemary and a pair of the little sausages. He joined Mike and Frank, who had waived him over to a small table they were sharing with a few of the other attendees.

"Just another day in paradise!" Mike said as Justin sat and sampled the melt-in-your-mouth deliciousness of the perfectly seasoned lamb and the spicy kick of a Dijon mustard-crusted grilled sausage. He took another bite, a sip of a wine from the nearby town of Côtes de Castillon and briefly closed his eyes to focus on the flavors of St. Émilion, both physical and metaphysical, swimming all around his senses.

Opening his eyes, he found himself gazing into the very deep and prominent cleavage of one Ms. Destiny Verrano. Her normally full, wild black hair was pulled back into a sleek, stylish waterfall ponytail, and she was wearing a simple low-cut black and white lace dress that was both summery and chic. She was practically glowing, and her smile was full of promise as she reached down to gently stroke his cheek and plant a tender kiss on his lips. Just another day in paradise, indeed!

# CHAPTER FORTY-NINE

Guy DeBussey could hardly contain his excitement. He was in the corridor just outside the banquet room, standing in line to use the *toilette*, when the bushy-haired Cosmo Koulouris walked by, flanked by an absolutely gorgeous woman and a man with long, wispy yellow-white hair and a ridiculous-looking Fu Manchu moustache. And the bastard didn't even notice or acknowledge his presence! But, no matter, he told himself. That Greek-American asshole was going to get his comeuppance, and it would be very, very soon. As he impatiently waited his turn, he thought about the plan he had hatched months ago and of the events that would transpire over the next few days.

Before leaving Château La Tour Noir earlier this evening, he had spent the entire day overseeing the preparations for Tuesday night's big soirée, the Célébration de Vin, a once-in-a-decade event being held this year at his flagship property and co-sponsored by the Richard Fox company, his distribution partner in North America. Many of the most important people in the wine industry would be in attendance, as well as a fair amount of celebrities from the world of sports and entertainment. And they would be coming to *his* château, paying *homage* to *him* and *his* many achievements: turning dirt into gold, water into wine and a small, festering seed of greed into a flowering multi-million Euro empire whose success and influence was about to eclipse even his own lecherous and avaricious dreams.

And none of them, not even Richard Fox, who was going to benefit greatly from DeBussey's upcoming sleight of hand had any idea of what he had up his sleeve. With his many union connections and his varied ownership interests in commercial transportation, he held all the cards in the Bordeaux wine distribution deck. At the conclusion of the Vin Expo, he was going to play his hand and deal his enemies, including that smug bastard Koulouris, a crushing blow. All he had to do was make a few phone calls and the dominoes would start to fall. He couldn't wait.

Today, there had been much to be done and many details to address. He and Bruno, whom he had noticed becoming become increasingly sullen of late and far less attentive to his needs, had spent a few hours watching over the placement and building of the big tents and the outdoor bandstand. He had also dealt with the catering company, finalizing the menu and agreeing to let them park their kitchen trucks much closer between the house and the winery than he had originally wanted; to efficiently serve over two hundred guests, the big trucks and the small army of staff employed to service them had to be positioned as closely as possible.

But, the creative director assured him, the portable hedges and landscaping they used at such events would, for the most part, conceal the trucks or at least keep them from interfering with the dazzling aesthetic of light, color and sound his design team would be creating with stage lighting and small sets, ice sculptures, fog machines and live performers.

"But, please do not worry," the director had gushed as he shook Guy's hand and got back to ordering his employees around. "It will be the party of the century!"

DeBussey had liked the sound of that: *the party of the century!* And with this year's stellar vintage, rated at one-hundred points by everyone in-the-know, he was certain the event at Château La Tour Noir would be unforgettable: a night they would all would reminisce about fondly for years to come. At least, *he* would, and that was all that really mattered anyway, no?

He stepped into the cramped but clean restroom and was glad to see that he had a choice between a normally placed urinal and one set a bit lower for those with "vertical challenges." In his experience, it was always possible to *fuck-*

up, but *pissing*-up was nearly impossible. Messy, too. He chose the lower lavatory, and as he relieved himself, he enjoyed the feeling of being in total control over all aspects of his life and future. There would be no fuck-ups here. *And piss on you, Cosmo Koulouris! It's my party, and you're not invited.*

Directly on the other side of the wall, in the lady's powder room, Lala was finishing up. As she washed her hands in the gold-plated sea shell-style sink, she checked-out the reflection of the attractive woman looking back at her in the mirror. The woman was smiling broadly as unseen wheels were rapidly turning in her mind: she had a plan! Or at least the beginnings of one.

If she was correct, this could be the perfect opportunity she had been waiting for. And the time was really ripe; Bruno was wrapped so blindly and tightly around her finger, that she was certain he would do anything she would demand of him— *anything*! If she acted quickly and discreetly, in the best case scenario, with high-powered legal counsel, of course, she could live the rest of her life in fabulous wealth and spiritual freedom, *anywhere* she wanted and with *anyone* she wanted... maybe even with her big French oak.

And even if things didn't work out exactly as she hoped, her life would still be better than it was now. If she desired, she could return to Hong Kong with her head held high. Even her rigid, stick-in-the-mud father would gladly welcome a well-to-do widow back into the family.

But she had to immediately ascertain whether or not her plan had any chance of success and act on it, quickly. Now, what to do first? An electric jolt of excitement coursed through her body—it was so good to finally be in total control of her life and future. Perhaps things were looking up.

# CHAPTER FIFTY

After his third trip to the buffet line, Justin realized that he'd better slow down. Way down. Other than yesterday's eye-opening experience at the *Giganto Supermarche,* he had never before seen such an array and presentation of delectable edibles in his entire life. But these scrumptious-looking dishes were all free for the taking! And take he had. Even Frank was impressed with his performance.

Good thing Destiny was off with Barry and Cosmo working the terrace and the banquet room, doing a meet and greet with contacts old and new. No need for her to observe his newly developed character trait—gluttony.

After entering the grand room and being shown to the table at the back reserved for Cosmo Brands, they had all been immediately impressed with the half dozen magnums, all from St. Émilion, opened and ready at the center of their table. And then they hit the buffet line. Although simply laid-out, it was totally off-the-charts in terms of color, quality and variety of items on offer.

There were little avocado and tomato canapé toasts topped with chopped basil and drizzled olive oil, followed by golden butterfly-shaped puff pastries with gooey *Gruyère* cheese oozing invitingly out of their sides.

"*Papillons,*" Steve remarked.

As Justin marveled at the breathtaking line-up, the group's resident *bon vivant* went on to describe some of the other dishes to him. A colorful mound of capers, red onion and cherry tomato-flecked salmon *tartare* had been artfully sculpted in the shape of the swimming fish. The guys each helped themselves to a bit of this and some of that, and Justin grabbed one of the imaginative-looking zucchini-tomato *verrines,* which Steve explained were multi-layered salads served in a glass. "I've had something similar to this numerous times at my favorite bistro in Paris, but these look even better," he said as he took one for himself and examined its contents. A rich, thick cloud of mascarpone crème, pine nuts and crispy bits of prosciutto sat atop the vividly hued sea of salad beneath. Justin couldn't wait to dive in.

Next up were bite-sized pieces of Camembert cheese smothered with a rich brown mushroom fricassee and chopped walnuts on top of cocktail-sized rounds of sourdough bread, mini bacon, cheese, and scallion *tartes flambées,* savory sautéed onions and fingerling potatoes with pieces of crumbly bacon and chopped parsley served in a flaky-crusted pastry shell, a classic cheese fondue with all kinds of imaginative items waiting to be dipped into a gently bubbling cauldron, a carving station for a massive pork loin and a juicy prime rib roast, and finally, a *charcuterie* that featured all of Frank's favorites; the big man arrived there first, left last, and then returned…again and again.

As Justin looked down at the bounty on his plate and in his glass, and then around the table at his Juice Brothers shoveling, slurping and otherwise reveling in this glorious moment of epicurean excess. Brad caught his eye, and smiling, touched glasses with him.

"Ain't life grand?" he exclaimed, then drained his own glass and refilled it with wine from one of the bottles in the middle of their overflowing table.

Justin followed his lead, but only took a small sip of the jammy, black Monbousquet he had just poured for himself. Truth be told, he wasn't sure exactly how many glasses of wine he'd already had, and the night was still young.

Plus, he had to be ready for dessert with Destiny! Just one more trip through the line and then time to find the men's room.

Towards the front of the banquet hall, sitting apart from the crowd at one of the tables reserved for the bigger names in attendance, Lala picked at the food Bruno had just brought her and nervously looked around to make sure her hideous little husband was still busy on the far end of the grand room. And there he was, holding-up the buffet line and arguing with one of the puffy-hatted chefs about something or other.

Sitting directly to her right, Bruno had just dug into a rare piece of thick prime rib and was about to wash it down with some of this year's incredible Château La Tour Noir, when Lala reached underneath the tablecloth and into his lap, quickly pulling down his zipper and thrusting her petite hand into his trousers. Eyes wide open, he instantly froze in place and scanned the room until he located his lover's husband: his boss. Satisfied that he wasn't in immediate danger of being discovered and losing his job, he slowly turned his head towards his Asian dream-girl and quietly and calmly asked her just what the fuck she thought she was doing.

"Oh Bruno," she looked down at her plate with a pretty pout, "You brought me such a small portion... I need a *much bigger* piece," she purred as she tried to wrap her fingers all the way around him. He swallowed hard. "Now, quickly, listen to me before the troll comes back and ruins the rest of our night." She slowly stroked him underneath the cover of the tablecloth while looking nonchalantly around the room. "I have an idea I think will help us make our dreams come true, forever!" She gripped him more intensely and slightly picked up her pace. Bruno was trying to focus on her words but was having a very difficult time, as he apprehensively kept his eyes glued on Guy DeBussey, who was now slowly picking his way through the buffet line.

"I know that you love me, don't you Bruno?"

He nodded slightly through a sharp intake of breath.

"So tonight, no matter what you hear or see, please do not react or get involved in any way. Whatever happens, you must stay out of it! Do you understand?"

As she outlined the basic details of her rapidly evolving plan and continued with her deep muscle massage, Bruno, still keenly watching DeBussey across the room, sat stiffly at attention and listened, until suddenly, his body jerked forward and his eyes momentarily and almost imperceptibly rolled up into his head.

Lala had just withdrawn her hand and excused herself to go and tidy up as her husband arrived back at the table, his plates piled high. He glanced at his right-hand-man, who at the moment, was looking just a little limp and pale.

"Bruno, what the hell's wrong with you?" he asked as his now-deflated deputy struggled to keep his composure. "You look like you've just seen a ghost!" DeBussey gave a snorting, supercilious little laugh and then attacked his food like a man with no tomorrow.

Leaving the men's *toilette,* Justin's attention was drawn to the series of maps lining the corridor back to the banquet room and terrace. Some were faded, tattered around the edges and decorated with ancient-looking symbols and difficult to decipher lettering, while others were clearly recent reproductions, nicely framed and easy to read. But what they all had in common was their subject matter: the town of St. Émilion and its surroundings.

They seemed to be placed in chronological order and looking over the sequence, Justin found it fascinating that the town's general attributes—its size and even street names—had remained constant for hundreds upon hundreds of years. One of the more detailed maps even offered a regional view of the historical network of churches, monasteries and priories that Monsieur René had spoken about on their way into town. *Go to a wine dinner and get a first-hand history lesson,* he thought and turned to head back into the banquet hall. As he did, he found himself face to face with and then bumping into the attractive Asian woman, minus her parasol, who was just exiting the lady's room.

"Oh Monsieur! *Pardon!*" the startled, but smiling woman said and then continued apologizing in rapid-fire French.

"Ah... sorry," Justin fumbled. *"No parlez Francais."* He thought that she'd been checking him out earlier, but now, up close and very personal, she touched his arm and looked at him intently, as if searching his face for the answer to a very important question. Staring intensely into his eyes and then giving him a head-to-toe once over, she suddenly stopped smiling and started to laugh while covering her mouth and shaking her head.

Justin instantly thought that the wine had really taken a toll on his senses and allowed his inner-nerd to takeover; *Shit! My zipper must be down!* A hasty check told him otherwise.

*"Vous ne parlez pas?"* she asked. "No French?" When Justin gave her the international hand gesture for "what can I say?"—two palms up and a shrug—she raised a finger as if counting to one and smiling once again, said the three words she hoped this American *would* understand, *"Liberté, Egalité, Fraternité."*

When she had recited the famous motto of France, Justin immediately answered in kind, by rote. At that point, the woman threw her arms around him, kissed him on either cheek and switched to nearly perfect English in a voice Justin thought sounded vaguely familiar.

"I knew it was you!" she burst out. "Right when I saw you outside during that terrible scene with the nuns...you're...you're Justin, from my high school in Orlando! This is unbelievable!"

Stunned, Justin was speechless and non-committal.

"Don't you remember me?" She started to look concerned with his lack of response. "I'm Lala Chang—we sat together in French class during senior year."

And then it all clicked, and he remembered the sweet, delicate girl she had been, finally recognizing that person in the bewitching woman standing before him.

"Lala...Chang...yes...yes of course...I remember," Justin stuttered, as she took both of his hands in hers. "But weren't you from Taiwan or Hong Kong or something...what are you doing here in Bordeaux?" he asked incredulously.

"What am *I* doing here? What are *you* doing here?" She laughed as she gave him another round of longer, lingering cheek-kisses. "Are you in the wine business? Are you married? Where do you live now?" She had a lot of questions.

Justin explained that he was single and still living in Orlando. He was here in Bordeaux for the Vin Expo with friends, some of whom were in the business, but he was just a very enthusiastic spectator along for the ride.

Then it was Lala's turn. She briefly filled him in on her status: married for the last three years to the man she had arrived with, one of the most successful men in Bordeaux, and they lived nearby in a beautiful château on the northeast side of the St. Émilion appellation.

When Justin inquired about what had happened in front of the hotel with the nuns and the protestors, Lala quickly dismissed the episode with a subtle wave of her elegant hand, saying something along the lines of "important men always have issues and enemies to deal with."

Then she took two steps closer and whispered in Justin's ear, "You know, I always thought you were cute, and you've turned into *such* a handsome man! It's so good to see you, Justin, *so good!*" She firmly pressed her soft cheek to his, and slowly, deliberately exhaled. Her hot breath sent an electric blast up and down his spine.

"Will you come and meet my friends?" he asked, now vividly recalling the unrequited puppy-love crush he once had on his aloof and unobtainable French drill-partner. "They'll never believe this...*I* don't believe this! Come on, I'm sitting at the Cosmo Brands table in the back the room!"

Lala shook her head, quickly explaining that her husband wasn't exactly friendly with his competitors. It probably wasn't such a good idea for her to accompany Justin back to his table, but to please bring his traveling companions by the DeBussey/ Fox pavilion in the Vin Expo Hall One on Monday, while her husband was busy elsewhere. They would all meet then and have a glass of wine. "Now," she said, energetically squeezing his hand, "come and meet my husband. I think you two are really going to hit it off!"

By the time they reached her table, Lala was sure that her hunch was going to pay off big time! A golden opportunity had presented itself, and her mind was moving at light speed, cooking up a very risky and dangerous scenario. She'd work out the details and make her proposal to Bruno later tonight, at their scheduled 3 a.m. tryst among the giant stainless steel tanks in the winery. And of course, he would have to accept: while she was riding his big French oak and shouting her declarations of love, he could never refuse her!

*But poor, innocent Justin. He has no idea what he's just gotten himself into!*

# CHAPTER FIFTY-ONE

While being led across the room in a near-daze, the math-wiz side of Justin's brain was feverishly trying to run a quick statistical analysis and work out the odds of the astronomically improbable event that had just occurred. The probability had to be incalculably small, and it absolutely boggled his mind. The other side of his brain had gone completely blank and still couldn't process what this alluring woman had just told him.

Lala led him to heavy hitters' section at the front of the dining hall, all the while smiling, holding his hand, putting her arm around him—clearly very happy to be with him. In a moment of clarity, Justin whipped his head around and caught a quick glance back at the Cosmo Brands table. They were all watching, and no one was smiling.

When Lala ebulliently introduced him to her homely husband and his menacing-looking associate Bruno, neither man so much as stood up, offered a hand, or even cracked a smile. Talk about cold! Lala then tried to steer Justin into the nonexistent conversation by switching to English and asking him to tell the obviously indifferent DeBussey all about their time together in French class in Florida.

Bad idea. His dour demeanor and arrogant attitude made Justin feel as though he were nothing more than an interloper; an insignificant little fly buzzing around the great man's head, annoying him and wasting his precious time. And during the entire introduction, DeBussey continued to sloppily gorge on multiple plates full of *charcuterie* and other buffet fare, hunching slightly forward as if warily protecting his territory.

It wasn't easy to watch, and it made Justin think of something Aunt Annette had always told him: "Never bother a hungry dog while he's eating. You'll be sorry if you do." No doubt. But he was still overwhelmed and happily surprised by the unimaginable coincidence of seeing Lala Chang, hot Chinese exchange student from high school, here in France while on his own version of the senior trip that never was. And he *absolutely* wanted to see her again!

When DeBussey dismissed him with a curt grunt, he and Lala exchanged e-mail addresses and promised one another to stay in touch. She walked with him for a few steps, and just out of earshot of her husband, apologized for his unfriendly behavior and extracted Justin's further promise to definitely come visit her on Monday.

"Guy won't be there." She gave him one last hug and another kiss, this one right on his lips! This trip was turning out to be even more spectacular than he'd dreamed. "Just come by anytime between two and five," she said, as she waved.

*But poor, sweet Lala! Why had she ever married that guy, Guy? What had she gotten herself into?*

By the time he returned to his own table, Justin was pretty sure that Guy DeBussey probably deserved whatever the nuns and protestors had been throwing at him earlier this evening. Maybe they should have used something more effective, like a *Molotov* cocktail!

All eyes were on Justin as he took a seat across from Destiny. She was flanked on either side Barry and Cosmo, and Monsieur René had also rejoined the group. The vein in his neck was bulging even more prominently than before, and whatever dinner conversation they might have been engaged in evaporated into thin air as he took his empty glass and filled it with one of the wines he had yet to try, the inky black Secret de Cardinale.

After quickly completing his standard swirl-sniff-taste routine, he looked around the table and realized the only sounds he was hearing at the moment were ambient ones: glasses and dishware clinking together, muffled conversations and laughter from other tables, or the dull buzz of crickets from outside on the terrace. From his own table…nothing but dead silence.

Each member of the group was wearing a disturbed, questioning look on their faces, and he suddenly felt as if four pairs of eyes were drilling eight separate holes directly into his forehead. It brought to mind another phrase from his French class with Lala: *faux pas!*

"*Well*," Barry said wryly, holding his hands in church steeple position and rapidly drumming his finger-tips together, "We're *waiting!*"

"Ahh…you guys are *never* going to believe this," Justin started uncertainly.

# CHAPTER FIFTY-TWO

It was after 3 a.m. when Justin was awakened by the sound of rustling curtains and the sensation of the remarkably cool night air wafting over his exposed torso. He propped himself up one arm, and after taking a long drink from the water bottle he had placed on the nightstand hours earlier, he turned to look at the exceptionally passionate, but tender woman sleeping peacefully next to him. She had hogged the entire blanket and was curled up oh-so-snuggly in it, with her arms wrapped tightly around her pillow...and his. No wonder he was cold.

But it was only a slight, superficial chill; he was still flaming on the inside after what had been, by far, the most gratifying and wonderful night of his entire life. Destiny had been everything he had hoped she would be, and more. So much more. She had unselfishly given herself to him body and soul, and their lovemaking had been a like a slow, powerful, rolling wave of deep, intense desire. And when that wave broke for the first time, it left their tightly intertwined bodies spent and slick with sweat. Then, it pulled them both back out to sea and started building all over again.

Yes, it had been fiery and physical, but also romantic and even poignant. At one point, after she had been straddling him face to face on the edge of the bed, forcefully gripping him and grinding her exquisite body into his, he suddenly felt moisture on his shoulder as she shuddered and then collapsed onto him. He took her lovely face into his hands and then kissed her tears of happiness and release away, and they had held each other for a long, tender moment.

Later, as they were falling asleep in each other's arms, he heard her softly say, for the first time, that she loved him and how grateful she was that he had been patient enough to wait until this moment to let her show him exactly how much.

And he had wanted to say things to her, too, but she was already out, already asleep. He wanted to tell her how unbelievable it was and how truly lucky he felt to have her in his life.

Yeah, he was a lucky guy, and he knew he'd been especially fortunate tonight: things could have easily gone in quite a different direction. Aside from the fact that he'd been chumming around at a despised rival's table, Destiny and the others had been watching as Lala draped herself all over him, practically groping him as she embraced, kissed, caressed and cuddled him right in front of her husband.

As the rest of the guys, had filed back to the table from the dessert line, Justin recounted the unbelievable circumstances that had precipitated his little adventure across the room, and every look of doubt, concern and skepticism quickly melted away, except for René, who seemed to visibly chafe at every mention of DeBussey's name.

"I mean, what kind of infinite sequence of random variables had to transpire for this to happen?" Justin said, still shaking his head in disbelief. And when he told Cosmo what Lala had said about her husband's disdain for competitors, he nodded in agreement.

"Yes, it's true we don't like each other" Cosmo replied, carefully avoiding smearing his bushy moustache with the whipped cream-covered tiramisu he was enjoying. "He is a little bastard, but you know, it's just business-at least for me. So, no harm no foul, Justin. It's an incredible story—let's just carry-on with the business of enjoying ourselves!"

While everyone relaxed and got busy with their respective desserts, Destiny got up, came around the table and put her arms around Justin from behind. She kissed him softly on the cheek saying, "If *my* husband looked like Guy DeBussey, *I'd* be all over you, too, Justin James."

"Yeah," Barry said between mouthfuls of luscious, velvety crème brûlée. "That guy sure puts the "ug" in ugly!" That got a laugh from the crowd, except for René, who stared blankly into space, clearly somewhere else, far, far away. Destiny suggested that she and Justin have coffee out on the terrace together, and as he got up to accompany her, he noticed that Lala's table was already vacant and being cleared off.

The ride back to St. Quentin de Baron had been quiet, and Brad had thoughtfully relinquished his co-pilot seat so Destiny could sit with Justin on the drive home. By now, it was apparent to all that these two were a hot item, or about to become one.

A hot item indeed! He took another sip of water and, not wanting to wake his sweet sleeping beauty, very quietly and carefully got up to use the bathroom. When he returned, he found her awake, on all fours, and leering at him over her shoulder, her long hair wildly cascading down her sexy, gym-sculpted back.

"We haven't done this one yet," she seductively suggested, wiggling her awesome ass and smacking one of her perfectly plump cheeks with an open palm.

Good-bye, Sweet Sleeping Beauty... hello Ravenous Rapunzel!

When the elevator doors opened on the second floor of the winery, Bruno found Lala sitting at the table in the small kitchen of the service area, instead of finding her, as he usually did here at 3 a.m., lying fully naked on her lush silver and black Chinchilla blanket in their private cozy nook between the big tanks. Normally she'd be getting herself warmed-up and applying liberal amounts of *Love You Long Time* lube to the parts of her body that he would soon be prodding, poking, and penetrating. But not tonight.

And instead of her usual glass of bubbly, she was holding a cup of hot tea in one hand and gesturing for him to take the seat next to her with the other. Bruno walked to her side, got down on one knee and wrapped his delicate flower in the protection of his big, brawny arms.

"My love, I am so sorry you had to take such abuse from that disgusting dwarf." He adoringly stroked her face and gently kissed her lips. She lightly kissed him back, and gave him a little smile. "You asked me to stay out of...whatever happened tonight...but I have to tell you that on the way back to the château, it took all of my self-control to keep from pulling the car over and choking the life out of that little prick. I promise you, I will not allow him to treat you like that ever again!" He finished his outburst and held her tightly.

This was beautiful music to Lala's ears and especially gratifying to hear; she was composing this *Magnum Opus* on-the-fly and Bruno's sincere, heartfelt rant instantly boosted her confidence, and with it, her willingness to move her plan, and him, on to the next level.

"Oh, Bruno," she whispered as she broke down, "It was terrible, wasn't it?" Surprising herself, she even managed to produce a few tears! When this was all over, maybe she could become a famous actress. God knows, she was getting a lot of experience.

But the ride home had been awful and, even though he never raised his hand to *her*, DeBussey had been so intensely brutal in his condemnation of her behavior at the Grower's Dinner—mocking and taunting her—she had finally lashed out and actually struck *him!*

"Bruno, go get the car!" he had commanded after Justin had left their table.

"But we haven't had dessert yet!"

"Fuck dessert! We're out of here." His voice dripped with disdain. He was heading out the door before she had even stood up. And as soon as Bruno had pulled the Mercedes away from the valet stand, DeBussey's verbal assault began.

"What the fuck was that all about?" His face was so close to hers she could feel little drops of his odious spittle spraying onto her cheeks. "What were you thinking, bringing that stupid American to my table?" His dark eyes flashed with anger. "Why do you try to embarrass me by flaunting your old boyfriend in my face?"

"What is your problem*?*" she had nearly shrieked in response. "I knew this guy when I was a seventeen-year-old student in Florida, and he was really nice to me. That's it! I've never seen or heard from him since. Now, suddenly, here he is in St Émilion...don't you find that incredible—and fun? *I* do! Can't I have some fun? And excuse me—it's not *my* fault that he turned out to be *so* good looking!"

"Oh-ho...yes," DeBussey exploded at her, "I saw you... we *all* saw you, touching him, putting your arms around him, kissing him... *and so good-looking,*" he added in a snide, smarmy imitation of Lala's voice.

*This is perfect. He's really getting worked up now. No one is allowed to put their hands on the property of Guy DeBussey and live to tell!*

"You hung all over that American asshole so much, I bet you can even tell me how big his cock is! Well, how big *is it*?"

She didn't answer. Instead, she laughed loudly in his face.

"That's right, go ahead and laugh. But you know what they're all saying now...*look at DeBussey's wife... mocking him...making a fool of him* ...yes...my *wife*...my little Chinese *whore*!"

She'd heard enough. Before he could get another two words out of his mouth, she slapped him across the face as hard as she could. And it felt so good, she did it again. That had shut him up.

Now, it was time to focus on shutting the ruthless runt up for good! She poured Bruno a cup of tea, and they sat holding hands while she explained exactly how they could both have everything they'd ever wanted. Each other. Money. Freedom.

At first, Bruno was hesitant. He had many questions, but Lala always had the right answers. She professed her deep feelings for him and reassured him that he was the love of her life, and that if he would only do his part, they would have a long, happy future together. He was getting close now, she could sense it.

When she felt his resolve weakening, she manufactured another tear or two, rehashed the ride home in the Mercedes, and *yes*, that finally got him. He immediately launched into another overwrought tirade about DeBussey and his delicate flower, and as his voice and emotion rose, Lala noticed something else was rising as well. Time to make sure he was in...all the way.

She stood him slowly up, coaxed his pants quickly down and kneeled to seal their deal with a deep, long kiss. *All in all, a great performance and a very good night's work!*

# CHAPTER FIFTY-THREE

Yesterday had been far too full of excitement and activity, and the strain on Sister Marie Agnes's frail constitution had resulted in a long, difficult night full of tremors, diarrhea and vomiting. But as she struggled to raise herself out of her lumpy, sagging bed, she vowed she would let nothing stand in the way of fulfilling her promise to God, and to herself.

Slowly making her way downstairs to help prepare Sunday breakfast for the children, she silently thanked the Lord for providing an opening and a miraculous opportunity. Yesterday evening, while returning from their victorious and profitable protest at the Hotel Palais Cardinale, Sister Ralph had received the wonderful text message she had been hoping for.

Once again, their friends and supporters had arranged for some of the Sisters to fill out the kitchen catering crew at yet another one of the lavish dinner parties being thrown for hundreds of guests at one of the big châteaus in the area. They had done this many times over the years, and as a donation to the orphanage, their employers always paid them double wages. And that meant more cash for the kids, Praise the Lord!

Although Marie Agnes hadn't gone along on one of these outings in years, the details of this particular assignment were simply too irresistible to pass up. This coming Tuesday evening, they were to report to the château's service entrance no later than 7 p.m. to be assigned their various kitchen duties. And yes, she would most definitely join the other Sisters this time, if it was the last thing she ever did. She would be with them, and God would be with her on Tuesday night. And oh yes, the location was one she knew all too well—Château La Tour Noir!

When René Gascogne awoke on Sunday morning, he had a seriously foul taste in his mouth that he absolutely knew wasn't the result of smoking one too many cigarettes. Last night at the Wine Maker's Guild dinner, all the way back to St. Quentin de Baron and then on to his mother's flat in Bordeaux city, he had been tormented by thoughts of what that baseborn bastard DeBussey had done to his family, the impoverished children and Sisters Our Lady of Mercy, and who knew how many others.

He had been stunned when Sister Marie Agnes, his old teacher and family friend, had taken him aside and told him all about what that little vulture had done to the orphanage last year on Christmas Eve; how he had, in one short stroke of covetous self-glorification, undone all the years of good works and service performed for the benefit of the children by his father, his family and many, many other caring souls. And how DeBussey had refused, ever since, to make amends and offer any help or restitution to her needy charges. None whatsoever.

It had set his blood boiling and been the major topic of conversation at the table with his old friends. And then to have to sit in the same room with that repulsive creature, watch him stuff his fat face with food and treat his friend Justin with rude contempt—it was all too much. But he had kept his cool as best he could and remained silent, at least for the time being.

The question was—what was he going to do about it now? He had left Bordeaux behind and made a new life for himself in the States. Years ago it had seemed like the right choice, and on the surface, his new life had turned out well—very well, in fact. He had a successful business, plenty of money, and he had his Phyllis, along with whichever new and exciting young plaything she chose to bring into their bed from time to time. What more could a man want or need?

But this time, in coming back to Bordeaux, he had been confronted with a reality he'd escaped and avoided for most of the last decade. Now, all of the hard feelings and difficult memories he'd carefully stowed away and consigned to the depths were starting to bubble up like a nauseating case of severe indigestion. And it was making him sick at heart.

In the military, he'd been trained to observe tough problems and difficult situations, analyze and evaluate all of the parameters, develop several options and plans of action and then find the best solution to make those problems, euphemistically, *disappear*. Maybe it was time to find a solution to this problem.

Perhaps a visit with Sister Marie Agnes was in order; maybe she could help him find a way to help remedy the pain afflicting his spirit and troubling his soul. *But no,* he told himself, *she has her own problems to deal with, and anyway, I'm not a schoolboy anymore.*

He would have to find his own way to fix *this* problem and make *it* disappear, for good.

When Justin finally ambled out onto the deck late Sunday morning, the guys were all lounging around the pool drinking coffee and snoozing in the sun. It was a perfectly beautiful day made even more so by the sight of the tanned, perfectly proportioned Destiny, majestically seated on a floating chaise lounge in the center of the crystal blue water. With her long black curls back in full force and wearing a chic, sheer white one-piece bathing suit, she looked every inch the goddess she was. And this morning, she was *his* goddess!

"Well, looky here," Mike said in his standard morning scratch, "…he has risen!"

Justin smiled blandly, trying to keep his expression as neutral and cool as possible and not let it reveal too much of what had happened last night. *If they only knew just how many times I had risen.* "And check-out that hair!" Brad laughed, pointing at Justin's long, poofed-out mane.

Justin caught his reflection in the placid surface of the pool: his hair was completely tangled, wildly sticking out at odd angles, and looked like he had plugged his finger into an electric socket. *Shades of Salon Electra!* Although the guys could probably guess, only he and Destiny truly knew where the real electricity had come from and exactly *what* he had plugged into *whom*...and *where*. And he wanted to keep it that way.

"What's on the agenda for today?" He stuck a toe into the water and tried to think of something other than his final memories of last night; Destiny powerfully pounding against him doggy style until he had totally run out of gas and collapsed. He was so exhausted that he hadn't moved another muscle until about five minutes ago. "I need to get Miss Destiny to the Vin Expo hall by two."

"Oh, *Miss Destiny,* is it? My, my, aren't we formal this morning." She playfully splashed at him. Addressing the others, she added, "I've got to meet Barry and Dorinda and put the final touches on the Cosmo booth for tomorrow's grand opening. It's going to be an exciting, interesting day!" She suddenly lunged off of her floating lounge and pulled the unsuspecting Justin into the pool by his ankles.

With the sound of bubbles effervescing in his ears and the sweet taste of Destiny's tongue in his mouth, the now submerged Justin couldn't imagine just how much more interesting and exciting this trip could possibly get.

# CHAPTER FIFTY-FOUR

After dropping Destiny off at the front entrance of the colossal Vin Expo hall, the Juice Brothers, with Justin at the wheel of the big Mercedes van, headed into the heart of Bordeaux city for an afternoon of sightseeing, street-food sampling, and naturally, wine tasting.

Once again their friend and part-time tour guide Monsieur René had secured a place for them at an exclusive tasting event. This time, it was at a private tennis club in a ritzy section of town west of the main square. But that wasn't for a few hours, so after finding a place to park, the guys joined the multitude of other fun-seekers on the jammed streets of the city center enjoying a gorgeous summer afternoon.

Although it was already day three of his European excursion, this was Justin's first opportunity to get a ground-level impression of big city life in France, and the ambience, sights and sounds of the old quarter didn't disappoint.

Walking down the Rue Sainte Catherine, Bordeaux's main, pedestrians-only shopping boulevard, Justin was impressed by the high volume of foot traffic and the sheer number of restaurants, wine bars, cafes, *vinotheques, boulangeries, pâtisseries, fromageries,* large high-end designer clothing and jewelry stores, small "mom and pop" style shops and stalls, and all other manner of commercial enterprise that lined main thoroughfare and the lively labyrinth of side streets, *petite rues* and alleyways. The sidewalks were dotted with awning and umbrella-covered tables and chairs, all filled to capacity with tourists and *Bordelais* enjoying snacks and libations on this perfect late June day.

While leisurely walking along the lengthy blocks of multiple story dark stone buildings, they were treated to performances by street musicians and singers, mimes painted like statutes and famous characters, a circus clown making balloon animals for the kids, vendors colorfully hawking their wares, and an old Gypsy organ-grinder with his costumed performing monkey, who was dressed as a creepy, mini Spiderman, complete with mask.

"Beware of the monkey," Frank said ominously. "I've heard the Gypsies train them as pickpockets."

"Yeah, right," Brad said, with just a touch of sarcasm. But they all checked on their belongings anyway... just to be safe. No monkey business had occurred, and they continued on their trek towards the river.

After Brad stopped at a kiosk to buy bottled water and some kitschy, mini wine bottle refrigerator magnets—only first growths, of course—they emerged onto the *Quai,* a formerly dingy working-class warehouse district, recently renovated and transformed into a series of open, clean, family-friendly riverside parks and sculpture and monument-studded promenades.

The park was packed full of people celebrating Bordeaux's wine heritage and culture, and there were tasting booths, food vendors, music stages and wine-related exhibits and decorations set up throughout the length of the Quai.

"This town's jumpin'!" Mike observed, and they walked through the crowded park and up to the river's edge to take in the magnificent view. For what seemed like miles in either direction, the *Quai* was lined with the impressive limestone edifices of eighteenth century government buildings, museums, and other official structures and cultural attractions, most of them designed in an opulent neo-classical or Napoleonic style.

Behind them, on its voyage out to the Atlantic, the wide, swiftly flowing Garonne River scenically ran under a trio of strikingly beautiful stone bridges, and Justin thought he recognized the closest one. With its low wrought iron guardrails and numerous, ornately-styled light posts, he was sure he remembered this exact bridge from pictures he and

Aunt Annette had viewed while sitting on the old living room couch, all those years ago.

"That's the Pont de Pierre," Steve said, "Ordered built by Napoleon I, it's the oldest bridge across the river in this part of France."

Justin thought a group picture with the Pont de Pierre as the backdrop was in order, but they were one Juice Brother short of a quorum.

"Where'd Frank go?" he wondered aloud and turned to scan the vicinity. The big man wasn't hard to find. He was standing in a ticket line between two giant, inflatable wine bottles that towered above the rest of the booths and displays, and he was motioning for them to come over.

"Well, in for a glass, in for a gallon,' Mike laughed as they joined Frank, who had just purchased food and drink tickets for all of them and was quickly handing them out.

"Okay boys," Brad said looking at his watch. "We've got about two hours before we meet Monsieur René, so if we get split up, we'll rendezvous right here between the giant Lafite Rothschild bottles in ninety minutes. Got it?" Everyone agreed, except for Frank who had already disappeared into the crowd.

"Where's Frank gone off to now?" Justin asked.

"I'd give you three guesses," Mike answered, "But do you *really* need more than one?"

"Yeah," Steve laughed, "Just find the foie gras, and there you will find our boy."

And an hour or so later, that's exactly where they had found him. Smack in the middle of Phillippe's Pâté Pavilion, Frank was inhabiting a small table crowded with his glass of wine, a basket of sliced baguette and dual platters of various creamed and terrine of duck, goose and pork products. A man truly in his element!

"What took you so long? I even saved a little for you!" the big man said with a Magic Murphy eyebrow bounce, as he slathered some ultra-rich goose liver pâté onto pieces of bread with a remarkably deft expertise and offered them up to the guys.

After following Brad's somewhat faulty directions and navigating the very congested streets of the city center, Justin drove them into a much more tranquil neighborhood, finally arriving at the small, private tennis club almost an hour late. Although it was surrounded on all sides by densely-built apartment blocks, the club's setting was quiet and almost pastoral. Its handful of clay courts were all empty at 6 p.m., but the limited parking lot was packed, and Justin had a difficult time squeezing the oversized van into the last available and very tight space.

René had told them that the main attraction at this event was going to be a vertical tasting of the legendary Château Pétrus, one of the most consistently great and profound wines in all of Bordeaux. Like most informed wine lovers, he'd never had the opportunity to taste the fabled wine or even see a bottle of it live and in person. But Justin was more than willing to make the difficult "designated driver" sacrifice for his Juice Brothers. Maybe he should use a thimble-sized tasting glass…that would probably help.

As they walked into the clubhouse and checked in with the concierge, they met Monsieur René, who was on his way out and seemingly in a hurry.

"Hey," he exclaimed checking his watch and then shaking hands all around, "You guys are so late…and the Pétrus is all gone!"

"Oh My God, *No!*" Frank nearly shouted. René just shrugged and exhaled a large cloud of blue smoke into their now frowning, distressed faces, letting the bad news sink in.

"Gotcha!" the normally reserved Frenchman said quickly, and laughed at their obvious relief. "I got that one from Barry. But really, you should hurry, the supply is very limited."

"Are you already leaving?" Justin asked, although it was obvious.

"Yes, my mother and sisters have rented a cottage on the coast, and I will join them tonight for some family time together. As a matter of fact, I won't be back until Wednesday or Thursday. But I will see you all then for a *bon voyage* dinner. Now," he said checking his watch once again, "I really must go." After saying his good-byes, he started out the door, but hesitated and turned back. "Justin, can you come with me for a short moment?"

While the others got their glasses and started enjoying their microscopic pours of wine, Justin followed René outside to the parking lot.

"I didn't want to say anything last night, but I thought I would give you a little information about your new *friend,* Guy DeBussey."

"That guy is *not* my friend," Justin insisted.

"I know, I know...of course he's not your friend. He is nobody's friend." With that, René gave Justin the condensed version of the Guy DeBussey saga—how he had so negatively affected his family and so many others in the wine trade, and especially what he had done to the nuns and children of Our Lady of Mercy. As he spoke, Justin was amazed by the Frenchman's command of the English language; never before had he heard so many alternate words for *bastard* and *prick* all used together so colorfully and in such a small amount of time! But it *was* a terrible tale of an extremely bad man.

"So do yourself a favor, stay away from that asshole!" René said emphatically, "and his wife, too. I mean, I don't know anything about her, Justin, but if she's together with him, her heart must be just as black as his." With that, he shook Justin's hand in farewell, lit another Gitane, and headed off for the Atlantic coast.

Walking back to the clubhouse, with the tarry smell of René's cigarette smoke still lingering in the air, Justin thought about what his French friend had just told him. No doubt, Guy DeBussey was every bit as rotten as he had said, but what about Lala? *No way.* There was simply no way sweet, delicate, Lala Chang could be anything other than what she seemed. No way in hell. And in any case, after he looked her at up tomorrow at Vin Expo and they had a quick glass of wine, they would probably never see each other again—so what did it really matter?

Now, it was time to focus on something that could have a *real* impact on his life: the Château Pétrus!

# CHAPTER FIFTY-FIVE

All the guys agreed the Pétrus tasting had been a bit of a disappointment. Not that the wines weren't impressive or dazzling, but the law of supply and demand dictated that each taster receive a tiny pour the height of a human fingernail clipping. And even though they were able to try ten different vintages of the highly-coveted wine, one for each fingernail, Justin supposed, it was next to impossible to draw any sort of conclusion about the greatness, or lack thereof, of this Bordeaux legend, currently priced at well over $1,500 per bottle.

"I have a plan," Frank loudly announced from the rear seat as they crossed over the Garonne river on the Pont de Pierre, on their way to a restaurant on the east bank. "Since there are five winos in this van, why don't we just stop at a nice shop, chip in $300 each, and pick up our own bottle of Pétrus? We could have it with dinner." That drew a chorus of derisive laughter. "What...are you guys a bunch of *wimps*?" he bellowed from the back.

"If we could find an open shop with any on hand," Steve answered, his tone pedantic, "*A*—anything ready to drink would have to be at least seven or eight years old, preferably older, and *B*—that would make the price *substantially* higher than the going rate for a more current vintage."

"Like double," Brad added.

"Or even triple!" Mike agreed.

"Oh yeah...I didn't think of that...I guess...that's right," Frank replied softly, his voice trailing off and filled with dismay. Justin glanced in the rearview and watched as Frank slipped out of full *Tank* mode, his broad face suddenly taking on the look of a sad little boy who'd just dropped his fresh stick of cotton candy on the ground at the state fair. He half-expected Frank's next words to be "I want my mommy."

"But Frank, don't you think there'll be something worth drinking inside?" Justin interjected, trying to console his brooding Juice Brother. They had just pulled into the lot of what, at first glance, appeared to be an old riverfront fishing shack. A closer look revealed a very sleek, modern-looking restaurant named *L'Estacade,* with floor-to-ceiling glass walls that offered panoramic views of the river and Bordeaux city. It stood, at least partially, on stilts directly over the Garonne, and a tasting was already in progress on the covered, outdoor, wrap-around deck. "Don't you think a dinner given by Cosmo Brands here at the Vin Expo will feature at least some their top wines?"

"Well yeah…that's right…I guess Cosmo will probably be serving Clinet and Leoville-Las-Case, " Frank answered, his voice brightening and gaining amplitude with each spoken syllable.

Justin checked the rearview mirror again: *The Tank* was back!

Justin had been right—there were plenty of wonderful wines at the Cosmo Brands dinner, but that wasn't what had made the evening so special, at least for him. It was the look on Destiny's face when he walked onto the river deck and the way she immediately dropped what she was doing to come to him, embrace him and give him a kiss that brought him right back to the edge of last night in heaven—all in front of Cosmo Koulouris, her boss!

"Are you sure this is a good idea?" he asked Destiny, while throwing nervous sideways glances towards Cosmo and Barry, both of whom were pouring for tasters at nearby tables. "I thought Cosmo was a by-the-book, buttoned-down guy, and

Barry would bite the head off anyone he deemed unsuitable for his hot "niece."

She gave him a quick peck on the cheek and took him by the hand to her tasting table, tonight featuring all whites, saying, "It doesn't matter now...everyone knows we're in love!"

That caught Justin by surprise. Last night, she'd quietly cried on his shoulder and told him that she loved him, but he had never actually replied in kind. Sure he'd had crushes, all one-way, on various lovely, unattainable girls and women throughout his life, but, love? The real deal? Justin wasn't sure exactly what that meant.

"Don't worry about Cosmo—he likes you *almost* as much as I do," she continued. "And by the way, you're sitting with us tonight." Destiny filled his glass, and as he tasted the delicious, honey-textured Châteauneuf du Pape blanc, he looked out across the river at the now spectacularly lit buildings on the opposite bank and thought about his feelings for the first woman, other than Aunt Annette, that had ever professed her love for him. After a long, quiet moment leaning against the balustrade, gazing out into the twilight sky of southwest France and enjoying the cool sunset breeze blowing across the river, he turned and watched this alluring, beautiful girl as she attended to the guests at her table, pouring, informing, laughing, and radiating.

When he first saw her tonight, dressed in a conservative blouse and skirt with her solo strand of pearls hanging invitingly around her smooth, supple neck and down across her curvaceous body, there was no doubt he felt something stir inside, something urgent and unmistakably forceful. Of course, part of him wanted to run a data analysis or plug some numbers into a formula whose product would allow him to gauge his position on life's "Love-o-meter," but he realized that human emotions and feelings were much too complex to quantify and condense into mere mathematics. No, he'd have to do what Aunt Annette had often advised: *when logic and planning fail, go with your gut.*

Had he been thinking about her all day in anticipation of seeing her tonight, and now that he was here, did he want to cover her with head-to-toe kisses and keep her close at all times? Was she the most beautiful woman he'd ever seen and perfect in almost every way? Did she give a better blow-job than even the masterfully talented Phyllis Braunstein? Was he in love with her? *Maybe...yes...maybe...*

Destiny had to turn her attention to the guests and clients at her table, so Justin spent the next hour enjoying the view and tasting some of the latest vintages distributed by Cosmo Brands. He chatted with the lady he had met on Friday night at the house, Dorinda Hope, had a few pours and a laugh or two with the rest of the guys at Barry's table and then wound up one-on-one with Cosmo, who had finished his pouring duties by filling Justin's glass with the last of a much-too-young Spanish red from Priorat and was now relaxing by the rail, looking out across the river.

"Breathtaking, isn't it?" he asked, as he touched glasses with Justin.

"Well, it might be," Justin said after he had swirled his glass in the air and taken a small taste. "Right now, though, I think this Priorat is too closed down and tannic and would probably benefit from a few years in the bottle."

"I was talking about the view, Justin," Cosmo chuckled.

"I know, I know," Justin said and then laughed as he finished the rest. "It's just that I so love and enjoy everything I've learned and discovered about wine."

"Everything?" Cosmo asked, directing his and then Justin's eyes towards Destiny, who was just finishing up at her table.

"Oh, absolutely." Justin said without hesitation, going with his gut. *"Everything."*

"Well then," Cosmo said with a smile as he put his arm around Justin and steered him into the dining room, "welcome to the family."

The dinner had been a wonderful multi-course extravaganza with Justin sitting in between Cosmo and Destiny at a table with some of their top clients, while Barry sat with the guys across the smallish dining room, raucously living it up. And even though the atmosphere was festive and a bit loud, from time to time Justin thought he could still make out the sound of Frank deeply inhaling the aromatic nose of whatever he had in his glass. Sweet music!

After coffee, Justin and Destiny stole away to the outside deck for a few private moments together. Tomorrow was opening day for Vin Expo and in just a few minutes, she would be heading back to her hotel across the street from the Expo hall.

"Are you going to miss me tonight?" she asked between coffee-flavored kisses.

"What kind of question is that? You already know the answer to that one," he answered. Then looking deeply into her almost-violet eyes and taking her tightly into his arms, he softly added, "But here's something you might *not* know, Destiny. I've never been in love before…that is…*until now.*"

# CHAPTER FIFTY-SIX

DeBussey was on top of the world. Well, not exactly the world. He was, however, standing in the crow's nest, as he called it, on the fourth level of the pavilion he shared with The Richard Fox Company, smack in the epicenter of the entire Vin Expo opening-day experience, high above the rest of the trade show booths and displays in Hall One, the Expo's enormous central exhibition venue.

Of course, he had the best location and the biggest, most extravagantly designed, over-the-top show booth. Nothing less would do. And no one else had a four-floor structure—only Guy DeBussey!

The same creative team that would help to make tomorrow night's Célébration de Vin such an unforgettable and exciting event had created an exhibition display like no other. Following his *brilliant* vision, they had constructed a virtual Château La Tour Noir right on the trade show floor, complete with faux stone walls, turrets and the signature tower in which he now stood.

The first level featured an open, *brasserie*-style bar for casual tasters passing by, dual tasting rooms for serious existing and potential clients, a small climate-controlled walk-in wine cellar, private his and hers restrooms, and a small conference room outfitted with everything one might need to hammer out and seal a deal.

Level two offered invited guests views of the trade show floor in a bistro-like setting, complete with a limited menu and a small service staff to wait on any high-rollers that might require a little extra coaxing to sign on the dotted line. The much smaller third floor featured two private and sumptuously appointed "break rooms" where a very important but weary client or buyer could stretch out his or her legs on a comfortable chaise sofa-lounge and watch a little satellite TV or listen to relaxing music in surround sound.

The whole set-up screamed success, luxury, and *in your face* to all of the doubters, detractors, and defamers that had dogged him over the years. This was going to be *his* time, *his* Vin Expo, and he wouldn't allow anyone to forget it!

He checked his watch; the doors would be opening any minute.

After waiting in one of the lengthy but fast-moving lines, Justin and the guys presented their credentials and were awarded their coveted Vin Expo badges, which allowed them access to the trade-and-press-only show for the next four days. At Brad's suggestion, Justin had recently ordered bogus business cards made using the In Vino Veritas shop logo as a template. For the rest of the show, he would be Justin James, *wine sales representative*! He thought it had a nice ring to it.

They followed hundreds of fellow opening day visitors into Hall Two, the relatively smaller entry portal into the greatest wine show on earth. Justin immediately thought that if this building housed the entire contents of the whole show, there would still be more wine available than one could possibly hope to taste in a year or more! But they didn't dawdle in Hall Two.

After passing by booths, stalls and displays representing smaller producers and distributors, trade and growers associations from all over the world, offbeat and alternative varietals, kosher and alcohol-free wines, glass makers, cork producers, wine-lifestyle knick knack providers and offerings from countries one didn't usually associate with wine production, like Iceland, Fiji or Mongolia, they exited Hall Two and found themselves outside, standing aside the gargantuan Hall One.

Between the two structures, a wide concourse stretched into the distance for over half a mile, coming to an end at another satellite building, Hall Three. They made their way down the wide path and Justin could see that its entire length was lined with dozens of food, beverage and service tents of varying sizes and configurations, all topped by puffy white, triangular sail-like canopies gently billowing in the warming late morning air. It was quite a sight. He had seen some very interesting things at the Comic Cons he had attended over the years, but nothing like this. It was like a small city whose buildings all had clouds for rooftops.

When they finally reached the mid-point of Hall One and entered the mammoth building, Justin was hit with a case of sensory overload so extreme he thought he had come down with a spontaneous instance of ADHD. He didn't know where to look first, and his head was on a swivel as he tried to take it all in.

"Whoa there, grasshopper," Mike said in his husky morning rasp. "You've got four days to explore this wine lover's fantasyland, so take it slow."

"Four days isn't nearly enough," Brad laughed as he pointed the group in the direction of a bank of nearby info kiosks.

"I don't think four *weeks* would be enough," Steve said as he walked up to the nearest vacant kiosk and accessed a site map. The halls were well laid out in an alpha numeric grid that was fairly easy to understand: the long corridors were designated by letters, and the crossing lanes were given number values. Steve keyed in the name of their first destination, Cosmo Brands, and announced that they weren't anywhere close.

"Can't we just taste our way there?" Frank asked impatiently. "I mean, we've only got until 6 p.m. before they stop pouring for the day, and seven hours just doesn't seem like enough time."

"C'mon Frank, you know we always have our first taste at Vin Expo with Barry," Brad said, wagging a finger. "It's tradition, so suck it up!" Frank hung his head and shrugged in resignation.

Before setting out for the hike across and up the hall, they all looked over Steve's shoulder as he located an agreeable end-of-day meeting point back in Hall Two. In the very likely event that they got split-up, they would all meet each day at five-thirty in the special dessert-wine pavilion, close to the main entrance.

"It's a great way to chill out and clean our palates for dinner," Mike informed the wide-eyed Justin.

"Yeah, for dinner," Frank said animatedly, giving the guys an eyebrow bounce or two. "Dinner... and *more wine*! Now, if you'll excuse me, I'm late...for a very important date!" With that, the beefy Juice Brother was off like a shot, dodging displays and nearly banging into booths as he quickly led the group through the crowded maze of people and pavilions. After all, there were only seven more hours of tasting-time remaining today, and Frank *the Tank* wasn't about to waste another minute.

After she supervised lunch preparations for the children, Sister Ralph tiptoed quietly, or as quietly as someone weighing over two-hundred-fifty pounds could, into her friend's room to check on her well-being. It had been another long, difficult night for Sister Marie Agnes, and Sister Ralph had been called on numerous times to help the old nun in and out of bed and on and off the toilet.

*Poor Marie Agnes, she had been doing so well.* The head Sister had been so full of life these last few weeks, organizing and leading the protestors in St. Émilion just a few days ago, planning this afternoon's outing with the children to canoe on the Dordogne, and volunteering to assume kitchen staff duties with some of the other nuns at tomorrow evening's big château party.

But now, perhaps, from this point forward it would all be downhill. For her, there would be no canoe trip today, and under no circumstances would Sister Ralph allow her old friend out of bed to work tomorrow night at Château la Tour

Noir. Yes, the orphanage would miss her double wages, but they would simply have to make do.

As she sat bedside for a few minutes and listened to the poor woman's labored breathing, she said a silent prayer asking the Lord to make Marie Agnes' passage to heaven as quick and painless as possible, and to please call her home and end her suffering soon.

At that moment, the old nun's wrinkled, blue-veined hand shot out like a lightning bolt and grabbed the startled Ralph's arm in a near-death-grip, squeezing it with more strength than the big Sister would have thought the frail old girl still possessed.

"Ralph," she said, with her eyes still closed and her dry, hoarse voice quivering, "is my flashlight plugged into the charger?"

The question surprised Sister Ralph and she thought she must have misunderstood. But looking around the sparsely furnished room, she noticed, for the first time, the strange-looking cylinder with the red and white buttons sitting on its base on the old nun's small dresser. Its LED was glowing a solid green.

"Yes Sister," she answered, "The flashlight is on your dresser and the little green light is on."

"Good...very good," Marie Agnes replied with relief.

"Why?" Ralph asked, as she soothingly patted her sickly and obviously hallucinating friend's hand, "Do you need it for something?"

"No...not yet," she answered with difficulty, "...not yet."

Sister Ralph said another short, silent prayer, and before leaving to round up the kids for the field trip to the river, gave Marie Agnes a compassionate kiss on her wan, translucent cheek. *Sleep, Sister, Sleep.*

# CHAPTER FIFTY-SEVEN

It should have taken them less than a quarter of an hour to reach their destination, but those fifteen minutes expanded into well over sixty as they stopped to ooh, ahh, and ogle the ever more impressive display booths they encountered on their way to the Cosmo Brands pavilion, all the way at the other end of the huge building. But no one was complaining, not even Frank.

They had stopped here and there at booths large and small as Brad and Mike said hello to this wine maker or that sales rep or other old contacts, making arrangements for sit-down tastings later in the day or the week, and the atmosphere was crackling with activity and excitement.

Justin had been especially impressed when he heard someone calling out Brad's name over the din of the crowd, and it turned out to be one of brothers from *Famille Perrin*, makers of Château de Beaucastel, the top-name Châteauneuf du Pape he had flipped out for way back at his very first tasting in January. They had been passing by the very modern *Perrin* family pavilion, but looking in a different direction, when Pierre Perrin had recognized Brad and called him over. It seemed they had met many times over the years, and Brad made an appointment to return for a visit this afternoon after four-thirty.

The Cosmo Brands pavilion occupied an entire corner space on the last row of Hall One, just before visitors could either turn around and start back the other way or make the ninety-degree turn into Hall Three. The booth was set up to resemble a Wild West saloon, with a long bar placed on a diagonal across the entire width of the pavilion. Every barstool was already filled, but the guys were able to sit at one of the large leather sectional groups that took the place of card tables and chairs in the mock bar room setup occupying the rest of the floor space.

"Popular place," Steve observed. Plenty of the stalls and booths they had seen along the way had been relatively quiet, still waiting for buyers and tasters to arrive. But not Cosmo Brands. By the time they'd taken their seats, all of the other chairs and couches had filled up, and the place was packed to capacity.

"I don't envy any of our friends for the next four days," Brad said as he caught Cosmo's eye and waved. "At least between ten and six."

Justin looked behind the bar, which was set back into and under what resembled an Old West movie set façade, but he didn't see Destiny. He did see Cosmo, Barry, Dorinda, and even Cosmo's schlubby son, Klitos, working under the hanging racks of inverted wine glasses of every shape and size, all busy pouring, chatting, and schmoozing with the tasters at the now standing-room-only bar.

Just behind the bartenders, in an imaginatively designed and lit display rack, stood the entire range of Cosmo's product offering. Justin estimated there must be close to fifty different wines arrayed across a shelving backdrop that looked like authentic rocks, boulders, cacti, and sagebrush specially flown in from the Grand Canyon. Pretty cool, and certainly unique.

"Good afternoon, gentleman," a trim, middle aged woman with a light French accent said as she came to their corner and placed an empty plastic container emblazoned with the Vin Expo logo at the center of their table. Her name tag read *Katrine Dubose, Ch. Haut Bergey*, and she handed each of them a laminated menu that listed all of the wines on display. "I am sorry, but as you can see we are very busy and so we must do a table service to accommodate all of our guests."

"That's not a problem, my dear," Frank said, smiling and turning on a little of his Magic Murphy charm. "Just bring us one bottle of everything and we'll serve ourselves." By the other guy's reaction, Justin could tell that Frank had just breached some sort of unspoken Vin Expo etiquette or protocol and committed a heinous *faux pas.* But Katrine from Haut Bergey simply brushed it off and took a short second to read all of their names from their Expo ID badges.

"Well, of course… you are Frank *the Tank*, Barry's friend from Florida. He has warned me all about you, *Mr. Murphy*," she said in a sharp tone.

That stopped Frank in his tracks. His roguish gap-toothed smile instantly disappeared and his face took on the look of a kid caught with his hand in the cookie jar while downloading internet porn.

"Gotcha!" she said, dissolving into a laugh and pointing to Barry behind the bar, who was also laughing and pointing back at Frank. "Very glad to meet you all. If you will give me two minutes, I will bring some whites for you to sample."

"Well, that went pretty well," said Frank, smiling again and anticipating a large wine delivery as Katrine headed off. "I think she likes me!" The guys chuckled and rolled their eyes. Justin stood up and approached Barry, who was filling the tray of another woman also acting as an impromptu server at the bustling Cosmo Brands booth.

"Yo J," he said in greeting, "how's it hanging? On second thought…don't answer that." They shook across the bar after Barry sent the volunteer on her way with a full tray. "I know you're looking for Destiny—she's in the back on clean-up detail, everyone's favorite duty here at Vin Expo." Barry motioned him around the bar, handed him a tray of dirty glasses, and pointed him through a small passageway to a mini-kitchen area in back.

"Where would you like me to put this?" he asked as he squeezed into the tight service area. Her face lit up when she saw him, and she flashed him an incandescent smile.

"Honey, you know you can put it *wherever* you want!" she said in a sultry purr. Even wearing ugly yellow rubber gloves and a tacky, industrial-sized apron that looked like it was designed by a Soviet-era fashion-czar, Destiny was a ravishing, walking, talking wet dream. Her hair was swept back and pulled into a "just-got-out-of-bed" up-do, and beneath the clunky apron, her black and red Cosmo Brands polo shirt was straining to contain her all-natural assets. Justin stood there for a moment, speechless, taking it all in. "What...you don't like the look?"

"To the contrary, my voluptuous vino vixen," Justin said as he found his voice and a place to set the tray. "I was just thinking about how lucky I am. And by the way...I love the outfit... and I love you, too."

As he put his arms around her from behind, kissing her cheek and nuzzling her neck, Justin closed his eyes and felt a reassuring warmth spread over his entire body. He was suddenly in a safe, comfortable place he hadn't visited for a long time, and although he was in France, thousands of miles from anywhere he'd ever been before, he felt like he was right at home; at home with her in his arms.

"*A-HEM!*" a high-pitched voice squeaked from behind them, "All right kids, keep it clean...we'll have none of that in this here establishment!" Barry was laughing as he deposited another tray of used glassware next to the small double-well sink Destiny was using to clean and rinse. But when he stopped and put a hand on each of their shoulders, his tone changed. "You know, I've got a feeling about you two...a very good feeling." As he walked back out the narrow passageway, Justin waited for him to turn and give them the punch line or a "Gotcha," but it never came.

"Come to my rescue and help me catch up, handsome prince?" Destiny said as she handed Justin a dish towel.

Bruno had told her where to look, and after rummaging through her husband's large office armoire, Lala located the box with the remaining, unsent Célébration de Vin invitations. She pulled one out, filled in a name in the space provided and stuck the now completed official invite into a gold-embossed envelope imprinted with both the Fox Company and Beverage DeBussey logos.

Today, after the driver dropped her off at the Vin Expo, she hoped she would be able to set the wheels in motion and put her future in Bruno's powerful, dangerous hands. She also hoped Bruno had stocked the pavilion's small cellar with plenty of her favorite rosé champagne.

She'd read in the gossip magazines that even the finest actresses often enjoyed a sip or two to get "in the mood" and enhance their performances, and Lala wanted to make certain that she would give a stellar "performance" later this afternoon. She sealed the envelope, placed it in her studded Saint Laurent bag, and swept down the staircase to the car waiting in the courtyard below.

# CHAPTER FIFTY-EIGHT

It was a warm, clear afternoon on the coast, and from the back garden of the small cluster of old cottages overlooking the ocean and the scenic sand dunes of nearby Cap Ferret, René Gascogne sat sipping on a cool glass of Bordeaux blanc and staring out into the deep green Atlantic waters.

"You are obsessed!" his mother had nearly yelled at him yesterday evening, as he sat in this exact spot drinking the absolute last dram of his family's stash of one-hundred-year-old cognac, smoking up a storm and staring blankly out into the dark sea towards the long shadows on the moonlight-drenched dunes.

For once, René had opened up and freely spoken his mind about past events and present conditions, but she hadn't wanted to hear any of it. "This is our life now, in this little cottage or in my tiny flat. This is our life...it's done... it's finished, and after ten years... you must get over it... as we all have!"

Last night, he had tried to fight the undeniable feeling that he would probably never get over it. Today, he had come to accept that absolute truth. Resistance had been futile, but acceptance wasn't the same as surrender, and René Gascogne never surrendered!

He realized he couldn't rewrite the history books, but if the right opportunity presented itself, could he, perhaps, rip out a page or two or make some of the bad parts simply... *disappear?* He stood, knocked back the rest of his wine, and went inside to pack a bag.

After nearly ninety minutes, the plastic bucket was almost full of expectorated or dumped wines of all colors, flavors, and qualities, and Katrine came over to switch it out with an empty one. They had tasted offerings from Provence, Priorat and Patagonia, Burgundy, Bordeaux, and Barossa, and Justin couldn't believe they still hadn't made it through the entire Cosmo Brands' lineup. And, he was especially glad that the guys had insisted on adding a very necessary fourth step to their standard operating procedure: swirl, sniff, taste... and spit! If not for that, he was sure he'd be asleep on this comfy couch instead of ready to start on the last flight Katrine had just laid out.

"It's going on one-thirty, and we've got to be across the lake for the Burgundy tasting at two," Brad informed the group, "so let's finish up and get moving."

"What Burgundy tasting?" Justin asked.

"Didn't you sign up for it?" Brad asked and then looked around their small cocktail table. "Didn't we all sign up for it from the suggested list of reserved tastings and seminars?"

Everyone nodded, except Justin. He hadn't gotten the memo or signed up for anything. Steve pulled a print-out from his shoulder bag and handed it to Justin, who looked it over and saw that the guys had made arrangements for at least one special event per day, and three on Wednesday.

"I can't believe no one told you about this." Mike shook his head.

"Hey, it's not the end of the world." Brad took out his own schedule. "I'm sure you can still sign up for some of these events, but there is no way you'll get into the one this afternoon. It was fully booked after the first day it was posted."

"I bet we could sneak him in," Frank said with a note of mischief in his voice. His face was starting to glow a light pink, and Justin was sure he'd only spit half of the wines he'd tasted.

"Guys, it's okay...I promised to look up my friend Lala at her booth today, and I thought we would all go together so you could meet her, too," Justin said. "I guess I'll just go on my own while you're across the lake and hook back up with you at the *Famille Perrin* booth or back in Hall Two later on. No worries." That raised a few eyebrows. "Hey...I'm just going to say hello, not make a distribution deal with her husband!" He took Steve's print-out and placed it in his own shoulder bag.

After walking back through Hall One and to the center doors on the lakeside of the building, Justin waved as the guys made their way over the red-carpeted pontoon bridge that lazily snaked its way over the large Exposition Parc lake and to the Congress Hall on the other side. Then, taking Steve's print-out in hand, he located an info kiosk and signed up for as many of the special seminars and tastings as he could, snagging all but one. Before getting back underway, he searched the site map and found Lala's location. He was close, very close!

She'd only been to Vin Expo once before, and at the time, she'd been thrilled with the full-throttle ambience and the colorful, creative presentation pavilions and exhibition booths that lined the congested aisles up and down the immense Hall One. But today, Lala didn't see or hear any of it. She was focused on one thing and one thing alone: steeling her resolve and willing herself and Bruno to do whatever was necessary to ensure that her vision of the future, her future, became a reality.

The Fox Company/Beverage DeBussey display was dead ahead, and it looked so much like Château La Tour Noir it sent a shudder down her spine. Even here, on the floor of the Vin Expo, she couldn't escape the dark shadow of her husband or his "black tower." Time to change all of that.

When she stepped onto the raised platform, she saw Bruno coming out of one of the tasting rooms with his brawny arms full of empty bottles. She nodded at him and lightly patted her stylish Saint Laurent purse, as if to say *I'm ready, are you?* She entered the pavilion's private center service area and made a beeline for the discreetly located ladies room. Before she could get the door closed, Bruno followed her in for a clandestine chat, locking the door behind him, and handing her a glass of her favorite champagne.

"Oh my love, you are so good to me," she said as she downed the entire glass in one gulp and gave her towering accomplice a deep kiss.

In a few minutes, Bruno would be leaving with the troll to go across the lake to a special tasting, and then on to a meeting with Richard Fox back at the château to review the final preparations for tomorrow night's big party. That would be her opportunity to make preparations of her own, but first she had to make sure Bruno wasn't getting cold feet.

"Oh Bruno, I'm getting so nervous," Lala said as she held him tightly, trembled slightly, and looked fearfully into his eyes. She'd been practicing the look in her bathroom mirror back at the château and was pretty sure she had it down. "Please, my love, I need you to reassure me," she said heatedly as she took one of the embroidered hand towels from a stack on the counter and quickly laid it over the closed-topped toilet. Then she hiked up her short skirt and sat back, guiding Bruno's head down to where she wanted it to go. "Show me how much you love me and that you are with me forever, my darling."

Bruno Bastian, love slave, quickly obeyed his mistress and went to work as Lala silently counted backwards from one hundred, preparing to start faking an orgasm at around fifty-five. Her big French oak was so very good in other departments, but not in this one. *Maybe Justin James could do better!*

# CHAPTER FIFTY-NINE

The Fox/DeBussey display was packed with guests, and both tasting rooms were filled to capacity. There wasn't one empty space at the brasserie-style bar along the main corridor at the front of the pavilion, and except for DeBussey and Bruno, who had left earlier to attend to other business, all hands were on deck to pour for the tasters and potential buyers eager to try the latest, greatest offerings from the powerhouse production and distribution team.

So far, day one of this Vin Expo had been an unqualified success, and Richard Fox and every member of the crew working in the Château La Tour Noir mock-up was smiling brightly. But not Lala.

Time was ticking away, and she was growing more nervous and impatient by the minute. For every second that passed, she saw her window of opportunity closing and the chances for putting her plan into action rapidly slipping away. Where was he?

Sitting in the second level bistro and sipping her third glass of Billecart-Salmon Brut Rosé, her favorite, she'd been searching the faces of the quickly moving pedestrian traffic below. For more than an hour, hoping to see the one that would help to keep her arcane ambitions on track.

And suddenly, there he was. Slowly walking up Hall One's main thoroughfare and taking it all in, wide-eyed and innocent, just like he'd been in high school. For a moment, she took pity on her old classmate: the gangly, awkward nerd who had turned into the nice-looking man with a lively sparkle in his bright, blue eyes. But only for a moment.

Maybe someday, while she was sitting under an umbrella on a beautiful Caribbean beach, drinking mojitos with her latest boy-toy, she would think of him fondly and shed a single tear. But not today. Or tomorrow. And certainly not tomorrow night. *Come on Justin...come to mama!*

Justin was going to double check to make sure he had come to the correct address when he spotted the lovely Lala on the partially open second level of the soaring, multi-story Fox/DeBussey pavilion. With its stone walls, turrets and tower, it looked like a mini castle and was, by far, the largest and most ambitiously designed exhibition booth he had seen at the entire Vin Expo. Very impressive.

She was sitting just behind the ramparts of one of the rounded turrets and daintily waving to him with a handkerchief. With her long dark hair, alabaster complexion and petite frame, Justin was reminded of the classic "damsel in distress." Perhaps he could come to her rescue.

As he stepped around the overflow crowd at the tasting bar and onto the display's platform, Lala descended a small staircase and greeted him with a big smile, a warm hug, and an amorous kiss. *Well, hello!*

She was dressed in a kind of haute couture naughty schoolgirl outfit with a short hot pink and black plaid skirt and sexy knee high leather boots. Over a sheer lace top, she wore a matching mixed patent leather and plaid vest, which was more like a bustier than anything else. So much for his "damsel-in-distress" fantasy. Looking at her made Justin feel as though he'd be the one in need of a rescue.

"I thought you had forgotten about me," she playfully scolded him and took his hand to show him around the first level. As they ascended the stairs, he told her about his absent friends heading across the lake for a special tasting and some of the interesting and surprising things he had seen so far at the Vin Expo.

"Well, I'm glad you like surprises," she said as she sat him down at her small bistro table and poured them each a glass of champagne, "because I've got another one for you...a big one! But first, what shall we drink to?"

Justin knew he shouldn't take more than a sip, but he did anyway. How could he say no to his school-boy crush dressed like a fantasy bad girl? He couldn't! Plus, the champagne was truly delicious and refreshing. So, they toasted to old friends, their French teacher, and to whimsical, unpredictable fate and providence, which had so serendipitously and unexpectedly brought them together after so many years.

After they shared a small plate of mixed cheese and dark, crusty bread, they took their last glasses of the bubbly with them, and Lala finished the booth tour by taking Justin up to the crow's nest, letting him soak up the unique view.

"You are one of the very few people that will get to see Vin Expo from this perspective, Justin. It's very special, and I hope you like it." She softly caressed his forearm and moved close to him.

"This *is* a big surprise. Thank you so much. But, I don't like it... I *love* it!" he said genuinely as he kissed her softly on the cheek. "I'll never forget this!"

"Oh, but the view isn't the surprise I was talking about before—this is." Lala opened her bag and presented Justin with a gold-embossed envelope. "I felt so badly about my husband's attitude and behavior towards you the other night, I thought I would do something to make it up to you. Please, open it."

"What is it?" Justin asked as he carefully opened the large envelope, noticing gold-embossed logos of The Richard Fox Company and Beverage DeBussey.

"It's an invitation to the biggest, most exclusive party held in Bordeaux for Vin Expo, and you and your friends will be my guests at our château tomorrow evening."

Justin was speechless. Lala continued to explain how special and important the Célébration de Vin was going to be and about the huge outdoor tents, the live music and the famous people who would be in attendance.

The invitation, printed in French and ghosted with an English translation, invited *Mr. Justin James plus four* to the

Célébration de Vin at Château la Tour Noir tomorrow evening at eight p.m. There were directions, a simple map, a suggested dress code—formal—and a table assignment, which had been left blank.

"We'll have to see about getting a table for all five of you when you arrive, but let's look for each other in the grand dining hall between just before nine. I'll be the lady in red, and I'll be ready to show you a night you will *never* forget!"

"But what about your husband? I don't think he likes me." Justin discreetly neglected to mention that he didn't like *him* and had learned from an unimpeachable source that Guy DeBussey was a total creep and an *A-Number One weasel.*

"Forget about him...he doesn't like anyone. But don't worry about that...there will be so many people and he'll be so busy, you two will never come face to face. I am sure of it. And if you do, what can he say? It's my home and you and your friends will be my guests," Lala said, now almost stroking his forearm, smiling suggestively and pressing her body into his.

He was going to ask if he could bring Destiny, and then realized she was committed elsewhere tomorrow night.

"It's the golden ticket, Justin. Please say you will come!"

It sounded like the crowning glory of a stellar trip and an incredible opportunity that couldn't and shouldn't be passed up. But Justin had mixed feelings. What would Destiny think about this invitation, and should he really attend a huge party thrown by Cosmo Brands' arch competitor? And maybe the guys wouldn't want to go, either. He had to consider that... if they were opposed or had something else planned, he'd have to send Lala an e-mail apology with his regrets. But for now, between the champagne, the intoxicating view, and the seductive aura of the naughty school girl enticingly pressing against him, Justin gave the only answer he possibly could.

"I'm in!"

"I say we paint his fingernails bright red, shave his legs, and give him some blue eye shadow."

Justin opened his eyes at the sound of the voice. The guys were standing around him. Seconds earlier, he'd been riding silently in the open backseat of the old convertible, slicing through the cool mountainside fog, once again in the middle of his all-too-familiar recurrent dream. But thanks to the guys, at least he didn't have to plunge through the guardrail and tumble through space this time.

It took him a few moments to remember where he was and who he was with. Good thing they were in public or this band of half-drunk, middle-aged delinquents might have actually followed through with their threatened prank.

"You didn't spit, did you?" Brad asked as Justin rubbed his eyes and adjusted to the bright sunlight. After saying good-bye to Lala, he'd gone in search of coffee at one of the outside service tents, but had been much too tired to wait in the long lines.

"No... I didn't." He yawned. After giving up on the coffee, he'd parked his butt on this partially-shaded bench directly between Halls One and Two, where he had, obviously, lapsed into a champagne-induced coma.

"Well, I hope it was worth it." Steve said and extended a hand to help their barely conscious driver up to his feet. "You missed something pretty special at the Beaucastel booth."

"But they'll still be there tomorrow," Mike rasped as he offered Justin a swig of his bottled water, "and I'm sure the brothers Perrin will give you a shot at the *Hommage a Jacques Perrin,* that is....if there's any left." All of the guys turned to give Frank—whose face was blazing the color of a homecoming week bonfire—the evil eye. He probably hadn't been spitting either.

"Hey, it's not my fault they kept pouring for me," the big man said defensively, raising both hands and showing open palms. Then he rolled his eyes around in his overheated head and blinked rapidly. "Who could ever say no to these puppy-dog peepers?" But even Justin knew it was bad form to ask a gracious host for more of such an expensive, coveted cuvée. Frank shook off whatever guilt he might have been feeling and led his cohort through a bank of doors and on to their final stop of Day One at Vin Expo: the dessert wine section of Hall Two.

Still lost somewhere in the fog, Justin had decided to pass on the sauternes, ice wines, and late harvest gewürztraminers offered at the various booths they visited, but after he was able to get a double espresso from the Portuguese proprietor of a small Madeira distributor, he accepted the man's offer to try his oldest wine, a 1920 Boal. He had no idea what that meant, but once he tasted it, he knew he would have put a few bottles of vintage Madeira on his future shopping list, price permitting.

Its light mahogany color reminded him of the syrupy Pedro Jimenez he had tried months ago at the tapas and Spanish wine tasting at the Twisted Cork, but that was where the similarity ended. The first thing that jumped out of the glass was a nutty hint of toasted almonds or hazelnuts, followed by the rich, earthy scent of figs. The wine itself had a wonderfully thick texture that coated his tongue in an almost sensual way, and its ethereal flavor was a seductive, savory-sweet combination of honey, candied orange peel, and tea-flavored tobacco smoke. It was very complex, very different, and he wanted more. But, of course, he didn't ask.

In any case, he was responsible for getting his Juice Brothers to their next destination in one piece, and he hoped it wouldn't be too much of a drive. He also wanted to keep a clear head so that, if necessary, he could do a sales pitch for the big party tomorrow night. Maybe another double espresso would help the cause.

# CHAPTER SIXTY

*Are you F-ing kidding me?...Yeah, right...Did Barry put you up to this?...Let me see that...*not exactly the kind of reaction Justin had been hoping for when he pulled the invitation out of his shoulder bag and presented it to the guys.

They were sitting at a table in a small but very popular restaurant named *La Côté Bastide,* in the quaint riverside town of St. Foy-la-Grand, and had just ordered their starters and main courses. Wine selection had been left to Cedric, the restaurant's co-owner and sommelier.

The others had visited him at least once on each of their previous trips to Vin Expo, and Cedric always played a game of "stump the winos" with them, decanting the bottles one-at-a-time in the wine cellar and serving them unlabeled or blind, challenging the "experts" to identify the type of wine, the producer, and vintage. The prize for hitting the wine *trifecta* was the enjoyment of that particular bottle with no charge. So far they'd never won, but everyone was up for the game.

Justin had waited for the appropriate moment to let the guys in on his big surprise, and after Cedric left to choose a few bottles for them, he thought the time was right. After telling his Juice Brothers about his champagne lunch and the following dessert with Lala high above Hall One, he explained how she had felt embarrassed by her husband's brusque behavior at the St. Émilion Grower's dinner and wanted to make it up to him by offering this special invitation to the Célébration de Vin tomorrow night.

After their initial comments, he tried his best to convince them, but they weren't buying it; still shaking their heads in the negative, passing the invitation around the table, re-reading it, holding it up to the light and otherwise trying to gauge its authenticity.

Justin realized that he'd have to send Lala an e-mail with his regrets and was about to ask what they were *actually* going to be doing tomorrow evening, when Cedric reappeared tableside with a decanter full of mystery and five white wine glasses.

"Well, congratulations," he said with surprise when he saw the gold-embossed envelope and invitation. "You must know or be someone very important to get invited to the Célébration de Vin."

"This is for real?" Brad asked as he handed it to Cedric, who had just finished pouring for them. "Of course we've all heard of it, but are you saying this is a genuine invitation? I'm sure none of us have actually ever seen one before."

"Oh, it's real...absolutely," the sommelier said, looking it over carefully. "It's just like the one I saw last week when a restaurant guest gave one to his client at dinner. You see this logo?" he said, pointing to the Fox Company seal, "that is his company and he is the co-sponsor of the event, so I would say yes, gentleman, have a wonderful time tomorrow evening. And to start your celebration off a day early, this first bottle, whether you guess correctly or not, is on the house!"

"You guys really didn't believe me." Justin said, surprised and just a little disappointed by the sudden smiles and high-fives all around the table.

"C'mon Justin," Mike said, trying to smooth it over, "you know Barry is always up to some crazy prank or joke, and we all thought this was another one."

"Well, I certainly believed it was some kind of left-field idea from Barrissimo, too," Steve said, "so I think we all owe Justin an apology."

"And dinner," Frank added sincerely, without a trace of his puppy-dog peepers or Magic Murphy eyebrow bounce.

They all raised their glasses and saluted Justin James, man of the hour and recipient of a wonderfully hedonistic six-course meal courtesy of his now very grateful Juice Brothers, featuring a different and more delicious wine with each course.

And, once again, no one was able to completely identify a single one.

# CHAPTER SIXTY-ONE

*Beep beep beep beep.*

Lala was awakened by a low rumbling and the sound of a large truck's back-up warning alarm, followed by the droning of another large vehicle or two, more beeping, and the shouts of workers directing the trucks into their respective parking positions on the expansive lawn below.

When she opened the curtains and looked down from her bedroom high in the northeast turret of Château la Tour Noir, the large area between the main house and the winery building was alive with activity as catering company workers surrounded the large kitchen and service trucks and began the task of getting them ready for tonight's big event.

The cavernous white tents and small bandstand that had been erected a few days earlier were also getting their final touches, and while the dozens of tables beneath the tall dining tents were being set with white linen tablecloths, expensive china, and the finest crystal, a landscaping crew was just starting to create the lattice and hedge-work that would help to conceal the bulky catering trucks from the rich and famous guests celebrating in an outdoor atmosphere of elegance and splendor.

Last night at their usual 3 a.m. carnal confab, Bruno had shown Lala the lavish conceptual drawings and detailed storyboards the catering company designers had provided her husband and Richard Fox after they had been awarded the Célébration de Vin job.

In between his typical assortment of grunts, groans, thrusts, and thumps and her predictable stream of Chinese curses and pornographic pronouncements, they worked out the final details of their game plan, creating a loose timeline and a series of signals they would use to execute their perfect crime.

This morning, comparing one of the storyboards to the actual layout of the just-parked and secured trucks on the lawn below, Lala was happy and very relieved to see that everything was exactly where the designers had said it would be. Perfect! It wouldn't be long now. In less than twelve short hours, her new life would begin with a bang.

Monday night had been far less eventful than the previous two at the makeshift Our Lady of Mercy orphanage, and Sister Ralph had actually been able to sleep all the way through. There were no panicked calls to help Marie Agnes at 2, 3, or 4 a.m., and she was grateful that the Lord had let the old Sister have a long, peaceful rest.

Good thing, too. This evening, Ralph and a few of the other nuns would be working at what was sure to be a very long-lasting, demanding château party, and she had really needed a solid night's sleep.

Because she was "big-boned," the kitchen crew always expected her to do a lot of heavy-lifting; full trays of glassware, large stacks of plates and platters, multi-liter containers of cooking oil or whatever else was needed in one of the kitchens.

But Sister Ralph never complained, because this hard work was God's way of providing for the children and for their well-being and benefit. For them, she would carry any load or bear any burden. For them, she would do anything… *anything!*

The first cigarette of the day always tasted the best, and Monsieur René savored the tarry flavor of each long drag he took as he sat at the small kitchen table in his mother's flat in

Bordeaux city and looked up a few phone numbers on his IPhone. He needed to procure a few items and was glad he still had old friends and contacts in town or nearby. Good people and battlefield brothers he could trust; individuals with short memories, tight lips, and untraceable goods to sell or loan-out.

While the coffee was brewing, he wrote down a few names and numbers. For this task, he'd be better off not calling from his mobile, and he would have to find a phone booth on the street or at a post office to make his contacts and arrange pick-up and any necessary payment. Then he would head east to thoroughly reconnoiter the enemy position and plan his strategy. After that, the only thing left to do would be to wait…and kill…time.

The mood was buoyant around the breakfast table as Frank opened his foot-long tube of foie gras and sliced off a three-inch-thick slab for his personal use and entertainment.

"Anyone else care to start their day with *one of my favorite things?*" he said, singing the last words like he was a member of the Von Trapp Family, offering a bit of his prized possession to his comrades. Mike and Steve gladly accepted his offer and eagerly allowed themselves a little good-morning-gluttony, while Brad stuck with coffee and fresh croissants.

Justin was about to bite into his own croissant when he heard the IPad pinging in his room. He ran back to answer his incoming mail and found himself stuck in the middle of a back-and-forth Instant Messenger discussion with Destiny. He'd texted her to relay the incredible news about the party tonight and fully expected her to be equally as enthusiastic. But he had misjudged her reaction, and at the moment, she wasn't too happy with him.

She couldn't understand why he had even bothered to stop by the Fox/DeBussey pavilion to see Lala yesterday and didn't think it was appropriate for him to attend the Célébration de Vin at Château La Tour Noir tonight. She simply didn't get it.

*Gotta go... talk to you later,* she had written and abruptly signed off.

"There he is, our *golden* boy!" Steve said theatrically, as Justin reappeared in the kitchen and grabbed a cup of hot French Press coffee.

"No," Mike laughed hoarsely, "He's our golden-*ticket* boy!" The others laughed along as Justin sat down heavily and sighed.

"Well, what did Destiny have to say this morning, Goldie?" Brad said, nudging him in the shoulder.

"Houston," he replied, looking morosely from face to face, "I think we have a problem."

# CHAPTER SIXTY-TWO

Day Two at the Vin Expo began on a much different note for Justin; a decidedly sour one. The vibe didn't seem as exciting, the pavilions and booths didn't look as interesting or imaginative, and even the wines didn't taste as wonderful. It was as if he was being followed around by the clichéd little dark cloud, and it left him feeling listless and dull. Not at all familiar territory for an eternal optimist.

All the way into town, they had been kicking around ideas and solutions, and there was one thing they all agreed on: the guys still wanted to go to the big show tonight, come hell or high water. They couldn't get over Destiny's negative reaction to the invitation, but they did understand, on some level, her opposition to Justin going off and drinking champagne with a beautiful, rich woman who had very recently been seen hanging all over him.

Justin had suggested he would stay at the house and the guys could go without him, but Steve was quick to point out the invitation was addressed to *Justin James plus 4.* No Justin James, no plus 4.

*And no driving us there and waiting in the van,* Mike had said adamantly.

Naturally, Frank was the one to eloquently mention that it wasn't *manly* to be pussy-whipped by a girl he'd only had sex with once, and while Justin might have agreed with him in principle, he couldn't help but feel he would severely damage his fledgling love affair with a remarkable woman by going to this party. An incredible, one-shot deal, chance-of-a-lifetime, never happen again, *are you out of your fucking mind you're not going?* party. The choice was stark; cut and dried; black and white. And he was feeling blue.

After a quick warm-up sampling of whites and rosés at the Chilean national display, they had made it just in time to a late-morning appointment with a small champagne producer that made wines of astounding quality and value. But not even the tiny, perfectly delicious bubbles of half a dozen different cuvées could raise Justin's spirits, although he really did enjoy the one hundred percent Chardonnay Blanc de Blanc, and the guys decided it was time to put together a real plan of action.

Steve suggested they contact Barry and ask his for his advice and help. The two had exchanged texts late last night, and brother Love had been just as excited as the rest of guys about the prospect of experiencing the legendary soirée, even though he wouldn't be going personally. He got it, and he was all for it.

"I believe his last comment was *"YEAH, BABY!!!!"* Steve held up his phone to show the guys the capped, italicized, bold-face phrase. "Maybe he can work a little *Love-magic* on Destiny and get her to soften her position," he said, as they headed through the jammed aisles towards their next destination. They were all signed up for a seminar and tasting called *"Women On Top...In The World Of Wine"* and while Brad led the way, Steve texted.

"What are you going to do if she digs in her heels?" Frank asked Justin as their badges were checked at the door to the seminar.

"I really don't know," was all he could come up with.

The tasting/seminar was conducted in various languages, with translations projected across an overhead screen, but Justin couldn't really focus on anything. He had read about two or three of the participants here and there, and it was kind of exciting to see famous wine dignitaries like Gina Gallo, Helen Turley or Gaia Gaja in person, talking about their remarkable experiences, but it was no good. He couldn't get comfortable, couldn't sit still, and he just needed to go see Destiny and clear the air.

*OMG...I' m in a real relationship!* It was an absolute miracle...and a total pain in the ass. Before even one drop of wine had been poured, he told the guys he'd see them at their next reserved event in a few hours and was out the door.

Justin, en route to the Cosmo pavilion, was trying to decide what he was going to say to convince Destiny his intentions in going to see Lala were purely platonic. How would he find the right words to tell her how sorry he was to have caused her pain, how she needed to trust him a little more, and that, most importantly, today he had realized he loved her even more deeply than he had known?

He decided it might be smart to leave out *by the way, no matter what you say or think...me and the boys ARE GOING to the party tonight!...*or something to that effect. He made a right turn and headed outside for a little fresh air and some coffee from one of the service tents. Maybe the combination would help him focus.

Walking down the concourse and searching for the shortest line, he was surprised to hear a familiar voice calling his name from inside one of the tents. Justin walked into the bistro/coffee shop tent and saw Cosmo Koulouris sitting alone at one of the small tables, waving him over.

"So, I hear you've got some exciting news." He took a big bite out of his ham, cucumber, and cheese baguette and dusted the crumbs from his bushy moustache.

"Destiny told you all about it?"

"That she did. I joined her for lunch and she told me of your good fortune—you just missed her by two minutes. Anyway, I hope you and the guys have an incredible time tonight," Cosmo said with a big smile.

"Well, we're not going...that's what I was on my way to tell her." Justin cast his eyes downward. "She wasn't too happy I went to see Guy DeBussey's wife Lala, and, well...we're just getting started together and I don't want to do anything else to make her uncomfortable...I know how and why her last relationship came to an end..."

"While she and I were talking, I received this." Cosmo picked up his phone and read Justin the text Barry had forwarded him, with Steve explaining their dilemma: how Justin had really intended for all of them to go to the DeBussey Pavilion together, how he had been left out of the loop about the reserved events they'd be attending and left on his own for the afternoon, and how he was now ready to pass up the big party.

"I'd say that's it in a nutshell," Justin said wistfully. "I really don't want to let my friends down after dangling this in front of them, but there are some things in life more important than...and I can't believe I'm saying this at the Vin Expo...drinking wonderful wines and having an incredibly memorable time...but there are, at least to me...and Destiny is at the top of my list."

"Well, I have some information for you, my friend." Cosmo shook Justin's hand and stood to head back to his booth. "I read that text to her, as well. We discussed it, and now you two need to talk. Soon!" Justin wasn't sure where this was going. "Have a coffee or some lunch—just give me a little head start and then come to the pavilion...I'll make sure she'll have a few minutes free." He turned to leave but added, "Oh, I think I forgot to mention...you are definitely going to the Célébration de Vin tonight!"

After working through two cups of coffee and a spectacular chocolate, pistachio and marzipan-filled croissant, Justin found himself standing in front of the Cosmo Brands Wild West display, watching his dream girl do her thing with a group of Japanese business men who were all pretending to be enthralled by what she was pouring into their glasses. But he knew it was just a ruse.

Today, Destiny was in total "goddess mode," looking very much like she had the first time he'd laid eyes on her. Her wild black curls were in full bloom, cascading invitingly onto her shoulders and framing her beautiful sun-kissed face, and every sublime curve of her stunning figure was highlighted and amplified in intensity by the tight fit of her black leather pants and extra clingy Cosmo Brands polo shirt. Justin couldn't take his eyes off of her, and neither could her guests.

They were all standing around a tall, counter-height table in the middle of the pavilion's floor space, and Justin watched for a few minutes as she poured and they tasted. He noticed that none of the men seemed to be too interested in the color or nose of their wines—that would have involved actually looking into their tasting glasses and momentarily removing their eyes from Destiny's mountainous chest. But, who could blame them?

When she looked up and noticed him, he was greeted with an adoring smile that instantly quieted the churning inner turmoil he'd been feeling all day and the little black cloud that had shadowed him all around Vin Expo Hall One suddenly evaporated into thin air...*poof!* The power of love? No doubt about it.

Cosmo appeared, and to the dismay of the Japanese tasters, took over the pouring duties so Destiny and Justin could have a few minutes alone, which they took in the cramped mini-kitchen area behind the pavilion's long bar. But the limited quarters didn't matter; two people locked in a tight embrace and kissing passionately didn't require a lot of square footage.

After their whispered declarations of mutual love and affection, they spent the next few minutes quietly talking and making sure they were both on the same page. He was sorry. She was sorry. He should have told her beforehand. She shouldn't have jumped to any conclusions. Was she really okay with everything? She was really okay with everything.

Barry briefly popped his head around the corner to wish Justin and the boys well on their big night and let Destiny know she was needed back out front. After a final, tonsil-probing smooch, the last thing she said to him as they parted company was to please "be careful and stay out of trouble."

He had to smile and laugh to himself as he headed back into Hall One to hook-up with the guys. *What kind of trouble could I possibly get into at a super-chic wine soirée?*

# CHAPTER SIXTY-THREE

After doing a few slow drive-bys of the property, his view obscured by its surrounding tall oaks and dense greenery, Monsieur René drove half a kilometer down the narrow lane that cut around and through the lush vineyards surrounding the château.

The thickly wooded grounds at the front of the property thinned as he drove into an area of rolling, wire-fenced fields and stonewall-enclosed vineyards, and he found the old half wood, half stone farmhouse exactly where he remembered it to be, right in the middle of a few dozen overgrown, unattended rows of vines.

As he pulled around the back of the deserted building to remain out of sight, he was reminded of all the times he had come to this exact spot in his youth. This had been his private "Lover's Lane," and as a young man with a pretty girl by his side and with a well-worn blanket and a bottle of wine in the trunk, René Gascogne had driven his first car to this secluded spot and learned about all the different ways a man could please a woman, how no could often mean yes, and how pleasurable results could be achieved through the application of slow, intense pressure or lightning fast strokes. So many fond memories and so many adventures under the stars.

He popped the trunk of his small sports car and got out to examine its contents. There he found a few items he had picked-up along the way this afternoon, among them a jet-black Ninja assault outfit and matching identity-concealing balaclava, black gloves and boots, a heavy, telescopic baton, night-vision goggles, light-duty cammo fatigues and a utility belt containing a few extra tools of his former trade. But no bottles of wine or old blankets. Tonight's adventure under the stars would be of a different sort.

He quickly changed into the camouflage fatigues and slipped unnoticed across the street and into the thick greenery to do a little mission-prep and recon on the grounds of his family's former generational home, Château La Tour Noir.

Sister Ralph had just put on her blue, standard-issue, kitchen-crew coveralls and found them to be unusually snug. The last time she had worn them was about one year ago, for some other château party that she and a few of the other nuns had worked to make extra cash for the children.

Between losing the old orphanage and having to move, and the advance of Sister Marie Agnes' illness and deteriorating condition, she had been under a lot of stress lately, so who could really blame her for putting on a few kilos? She'd take them off…someday.

Before leaving her dingy, unkempt room, she wrestled the last button closed, took one last mouthful and crumpled up the now empty mega pack of bacon and onion-flavored potato chips, throwing it into a bin already overflowing with a dozen similar empties, making sure to brush any tell-tale crumbs out of her patchy little moustache.

The other two Sisters working with her tonight were already downstairs waiting, so she would just say a quick good night to Sister Marie Agnes, whom she expected to find fitfully resting in her bed. Except that when she stuck her head into her room, the old nun wasn't there and the bed was neatly made.

Alarmed, she tore down the rickety staircase in a panic, through the shabby foyer and out into the front yard of the makeshift orphanage, where she found Marie Agnes, dressed in her blue, standard-issue, kitchen-crew coveralls, sitting calmly in the passenger seat of the rusty old Citroën and smiling at her, the old spark back in her rheumy eyes. Praise God—it was a miracle!

"Well Sister Ralph, let's go," the old girl said "We've all got our jobs to do tonight."

Bruno felt like he had been walking on eggshells all day and had been experiencing a persistent tingling in both of his hands that would flare up into hot pins and needles whenever he came into contact with his boss. He also felt an uncharacteristic sheen of sweat on his face that he knew wasn't in any way weather-related. And he also seemed to be much thirstier than normal, but no matter how much water or wine he drank today, his mouth and throat remained parched and bone-dry.

Nerves? Second thoughts? *No time for that now,* he thought, as he made his rounds through the château, checking in on the caterers setting up the dining hall for the grand tasting that would start in a few hours and then out through the large doors to the wide yard between the main house and the winery, to finish his preparations for this evening, both official and unofficial.

Had he not been on these grounds almost every day for the last ten years, he might not have recognized the normally vacant lawn area, now transformed into a luxurious garden playground.

Now, dual, white, multi-peaked banquet tents, each topped by flags bearing the château's oblong coat of arms, took up most of the area. Beneath their canopies, dozens of tables covered in the finest white linen, set with exquisite china and topped by custom-made crystal center pieces made in the shape of the signature tower of the host's château, gleamed brightly underneath rows of mini chandeliers suspended from the overhead support framework of each tent.

To the left of the side-by-side tents, a Gypsy band was setting up on the small covered stage, and festive bistro lights were strung overhead between the bandstand and the main tent, as well as around the perimeters of each of the three structures.

To the right, where the large kitchen and service trucks were parked, Bruno was amazed to see the kind of magic the landscaping crew had worked using lattice, portable greenery, and an elaborately painted screen hung over the wooden frame they had erected earlier today. By mixing all of the elements together, they had created the illusion of a deep, enchanted forest bordering the fantasy-world playground, and it quite effectively blocked the trucks from view.

But even better, the set-up was exactly as it had been depicted in the storyboards he and Lala had reviewed. The entrance to the winery would now be out of sight, and except for any of the kitchen workers behind the forest screen, who would all be much too busy to notice, no one would be able to bear witness to any potential visitors taking a late night tour of the grounds. Perfect!

Bruno pulled out his key ring and unlocked the door and slipped into the winery to make his final preparations.

Sitting back in his private steam room and slowly breathing in the moist, eucalyptus-scented air, Guy DeBussey was totally relaxed as one of the creative-team designers, an attractive twenty-something blond fox he'd had his eye on for the last few days, ran her fingers through the coarse, black hair that covered his body like a dirty, matted shag carpet, working her way down to the thickest, darkest part. He was waiting for her to find something buried beneath his pubic pelt, but at the moment, she was having trouble locating it.

But he really didn't care if she found it or not. This was a supreme "fuck-you" moment, and he was relishing the thought that his bitchy wife was two floors above him and fully aware that he was here with this beautiful young thing, doing whatever he pleased on this day of great honor and triumph for both him and his company.

She wanted to embarrass him the other night by flaunting that shit American in his face? Fine! He would repay the favor this afternoon by smugly parading this blond in front of their domestic staff and loudly inviting her into his private spa with him. After all, he was Guy DeBussey, king of the castle, and he was sure the girl would absolutely jump at the opportunity to "get to know him a little better."

And he'd made an important decision, too. After he'd made the calls to launch next week's surprise attack on his business rivals, he'd no longer need the relationship in Hong Kong and would start taking steps to send Lala Chang back to China, where she belonged. He might even pay for her one-way economy ticket, but she'd get nothing else from him. Not one Euro! It was going to be a sweet dessert following a delicious main course full of revenge and retribution.

He would enjoy the rest of his life as a single man, with all of *his* money, all of *his* success, and an endless supply of young women, just like the one here in the steam room that had finally found what she was searching for between his legs and was about to make him shiver and shake with delight.

When he shut his eyes to savor the moment, all he could see before him was a long, rich future, stretching out into eternity. Oh…yes…life was…so…gooooood!

He had to hand it to the little prick: he hadn't spared a cent in decorating and transforming the grounds of the Château La Tour Noir for tonight's Célébration de Vin. René was sure it was going to be quite a memorable evening, but if things went his way, it would be an unforgettable one.

From his concealed position among the oaks and dense shrubbery surrounding the side and front of the château's expansive grounds, he was able to view tonight's security and service set-ups and begin devising a plan to use them to his advantage. Of course, he would have to wait until he returned after dark to completely assess his opportunities, when the grounds were filled with guests and workers. But for now, he felt he had gathered enough intel and should return to his base camp to prepare.

While he clandestinely worked his way back through the thicket to his point of exit, he thought back on his training all those years ago and what had been drummed into his head by each of his formidable instructors: every mission had its share of unforeseen chaos-inducing mishaps that could throw even the best plans off the rails. But by the same token, there was always the possibility for a little *bon chance*— a little good luck. And René Gascogne had always found that advice to be true.

As he came to the end of his cover, directly across from the main entrance to the winery, its door opened and Bruno Bastian came slinking out, casting quick, furtive glances in all directions. René hunkered down low and watched as Bruno posted a "Winery Out of Service" sign on the now closed door. He did not, however, lock the door and even double-checked to ensure that it had been left open.

René thought it was very curious behavior for the head of security for tonight's big event. And perhaps, it was a little *bon chance,* too.

# CHAPTER SIXTY-FOUR

They had finished the second day of Vin Expo in the dessert wine section of Hall Two, excessively indulging themselves by taking advantage of a tasting at the booth of an Australian distribution company that specialized in all things sweet. The proprietor was an affable chap named Joe Terry, and he had recognized the guys from years past. And naturally, he remembered the unforgettable Frank *the Tank* by name.

Joe had pulled out all the stops by offering them a platter full of sliced baguette and foie gras and an unbelievable selection of every top name Sauternes, Barsac, and other Bordeaux sweet wine in existence. No one had spit a drop of the "nectar of the Gods," as Frank colorfully called it, and now Justin was paying the price.

After a nearly hour-long drive back to Saint Quentin de Baron, through traffic backed and stacked for what seemed like miles, he found himself under a powerful, almost icy stream of water in the shower of his master bathroom, rubbing his temples and massaging the cobwebs out of his head.

The cold plunge blasted him almost all the way back to reality, and after laying out his Hugo Boss suit, he adjourned to the kitchen and joined the others for some extra-strong coffee. Everyone wanted to be wide awake. It was going to be a long night.

Justin grabbed cup number two as the guys all went back to their respective rooms to suit-up for the big event. He just hoped Mike would wear something other than his tuxedo T-shirt and the zip-off-legged cargo pants. My, wouldn't that be nice for a change!

While the sounds of the Gypsy band tuning-up wafted in from below, Lala sat naked at her vanity and put the finishing touches on her makeup. Then, she slowly and almost erotically rubbed creamy, fragrant lotion all over her smooth, inviting body to keep her skin velvety soft and irresistible to the touch.

Usually, she enjoyed the sensuous feeling of her fingers on the more delicate areas of her anatomy and gave those parts a little extra attention, but she really didn't have the focus to indulge herself just now.

This would be her last quiet moment of the evening, and she took a few deep breaths in a vain attempt to relax and make the tension in her neck and shoulders disappear. Maybe she should take one of the capsules Bruno had given her. That would probably help, but she knew she needed to resist the temptation.

There was too much that could go wrong, and she'd need a clear head to make it all happen as planned. So, she passed on the self-induced orgasm and was even willing to forego a glass or two of the rose champagne sitting on ice in her changing room.

Tonight, the fledgling actress would be playing two distinctly different roles in the crescendoing drama of her life. She knew she would have no trouble acting out her first part, the gracious, dutiful party-hostess she'd been trained her whole life to actually be. It was the second role that was starting to give her a case of butterflies.

Opening the envelope Bruno had discreetly passed her this afternoon, she let its contents tumble out and examined the three little pale green and yellow capsules that had fallen into the palm of her hand.

He had said it was something called Narcozep, the "I can't remember what happened" pill used by dirt bags worldwide to tranquilize various unsuspecting and most likely unwilling parties into sexual submission. He hadn't mentioned what *he* was doing with a small supply of the date-rape drug, also known as *roofies,* and Lala hadn't bothered to ask.

All that mattered now was that she follow his directions and let the little capsules work their dark magic on whomever might ingest one or two of them. Then, she and Bruno would have to follow-through and do the rest. What could possibly go wrong? Nothing...*everything!* Her mouth suddenly went dry.

That foregone glass of champagne was starting to sound like a good idea after all...and perhaps a little more of the fragrant lotion, too, delicately applied to the right places. The combination just might soothe her jitters away. She poured a glass, took a long taste, squeezed out a few more creamy, skin-softening drops from the nearly empty tube and leaned back to enjoy.

The big kitchen trucks were already in full swing when the Sisters from Our Lady of Mercy arrived and were assigned their various duties by the service manager, the same friend that had been responsible for getting them hired in the first place.

Tonight, they would be tasked with the washing, drying, and stacking of dishes and glass-ware, and that meant they would be kept well out-of-sight of the festivities and party-goers. Which was just fine with Sister Ralph. The last thing she wanted was to have Marie Agnes come face to face with Guy DeBussey and create an ugly, stressful scene that might end her current miraculous recovery and send her right back into her sickbed, or worse.

But here in the very last service truck, behind a few, tall portable hedges and some sort of large partition, Ralph was sure they would be left alone to do their work and that Monsieur Guy DeBussey wouldn't set foot anywhere near. She had already found a chair for the old Sister and positioned it just outside the service truck directly in sight of her clean-up station, right at the edge of a thicket of trees and underbrush.

Whenever Marie Agnes needed to, she could excuse herself and take a rest in her chair. She could even sit there all night if she wanted. Sister Ralph would pick up the slack and cover for her, and the children would receive double wages times four. Thank the Lord, it was perfect!

Although it wasn't all that bright on the service side of the partition, Ralph figured there would still be enough ambient light from the party and the adjacent winery building for her to keep a close eye on her old friend.

And if Sister Marie Agnes needed more light...well...she could always use the odd-looking flashlight she'd been clutching tightly ever since they left the orphanage. Its little LED indicator was glowing a bright green. Green for go.

# CHAPTER SIXTY-FIVE

In the end, they really hadn't needed to use the directions on the invitation, a GPS device, or the MapQuest Navigation App on Steve's phone. After arriving in the general vicinity, all they had to do was follow the searchlights and drive toward their origin, just to the northeast of the town of St. Émilion.

The instant Justin turned the big Mercedes into the narrow gravel entry lane and pulled underneath the thick canopy provided by the parallel rows of ancient oak trees, the small group of vino-tourists inside grew suddenly quiet. The only sound to be heard in the van's normally boisterous passenger cabin was the crackling and crunching of the tires as they slowly rolled over the stones and pebbles of the driveway and joined the queue of cars and limos waiting to gain admittance to the wine party of the century. The view was that awe-inspiring.

Rows and rows of colorfully festive Japanese lanterns hung from the intertwined branches of the old oaks that formed a natural archway over the lane, and each side of the drive was lined with large decorative paper luminary lanterns, their candles casting a warm glow onto the surroundings and into the rapidly approaching dusk.

"Somebody please tell me you're getting a picture of this!" Justin said, breaking the silence, and three flashes went off almost simultaneously, nearly blinding him in the process.

"And let's all make sure that we're not shy about taking a few more shots this evening," suggested Steve as he opened the sliding side door and hopped out to get a better photo-op of the magically-lit lane.

The queue moved rapidly forward, and in a few short minutes they'd cleared the tree line and emerged into the wide, open, and very busy courtyard of Château La Tour Noir, its brightly-lit façade, turrets, and tower rising majestically into the twilight sky. Justin presented his invitation to one of the attendants at the dual concierge stands while Brad hung out his window and snapped a few more pics.

"I am sorry, Mr. James," the man said as he scrolled down the computer's touch screen . "Your name is not on the list, so I must ask you to pull around and leave the grounds of the château."

"Hey buddy, what's the problem?" Mike rasped as he leaned forward from the second row. "We're close personal friends of Richard Fox, the guy who's putting on this shindig."

"Shindig? I'm sorry, I do not understand *shindig,*" the concierge replied curtly. Justin waved Mike off and took his invitation back from the attendant.

"I was given this invitation only yesterday by my good friend, so I understand why my name isn't on your list," Justin said, surprising himself with his confident tone and delivery. "And I know you're just doing your job, but Lala DeBussey, my good friend, told me that if there was any question or problem about us coming in tonight, you must immediately call and talk to the man at this mobile number. I believe he's the head of security." Justin handed the attendant the business card Lala had given him just-in-case, and the concierge blanched as he read the name—Bruno Bastian.

"What did you say to him?" Frank asked from the back row as they slowly drove by the big searchlights and stopped in front of the marble staircase leading up to the main entrance of the château.

"I just told him about all of my friends in high places," Justin replied. They exited the Mercedes and the valet handed him his ticket.

"Way to go, J," Frank said and fist-bumped with Justin while they all ascended the stairs and entered the castle-like building.

Before entering the grand dining hall, they were asked to pose for a commemorative group picture in the soaring atrium, directly in front of a marble bust the of the château's owner, Guy DeBussey. The depiction looked cold, hollow, and unfriendly, and Justin thought it was a remarkably true likeness. For the photo, he wound up standing just under the gargoyle-like bust and found he didn't like the feeling of the ugly, hostile little man looking over his shoulder. He sincerely hoped that this would be his closest encounter of the evening with their disagreeable host!

They were then directed to the grand dining hall, tonight fully lit by its immense crystal chandelier and strands of gala bistro lights strung around the ornate grand dining table. All of the chairs had been removed and the grand table's surface was covered by hundreds of glasses already filled with champagne.

After snapping a few photos of the impressive, tapestry-decorated room and exchanging looks of approval and appreciation for their sumptuous surroundings, the guys each picked up a glass of the bubbly—Frank took two—and followed the rest of the revelers through large floor-to-ceiling doors to the covered esplanade and then out into the sensational, dazzling Célébration de Vin fantasy land.

"Holy shit!" Mike erupted. "I think we've all died and gone to vino heaven."

"Roger that," Frank agreed and downed his entire first glass of champagne.

In addition to the glowing tents, the resplendent bandstand and the luminous enchanted forest screen, half a dozen large abstract-art ice sculptures illuminated from the inside-out with pastel neon lights had been positioned along the walkways, each shrouded in a thin, colorful veil of wispy dry-ice vapor, magically evaporating into the night air.

Brad put his arm around Justin saying, "I know this is an over worn cliché, but it doesn't get *any* better than this, my friend."

Frank had already gone back into the grand dining hall for another champagne twofer, but Steve and Mike also voiced their enthusiastic thanks to Justin, who was totally feeling the love and completely in awe of the epic party scene unfolding before them.

All of the footpaths were designated and bordered by small paper luminaries, and the guys followed the one leading to the bandstand, where the musicians were just picking up their instruments and preparing to entertain the growing crowd.

As they approached the stage, Justin looked around but didn't see Lala anywhere. He did, however, notice Guy DeBussey and Richard Fox, whom Lala had pointed out to him during his Vin Expo visit, each take the stage with microphones in their hands.

"Good evening, ladies and gentlemen," DeBussey announced in French, with Richard Fox following each of his lines with the English translation. Justin couldn't believe it—the man was actually smiling and appeared to be happy!

"Beverage DeBussey and the Richard Fox Company welcome you to the once-in-a-decade Célébration de Vin. We are so very honored and privileged to be your hosts this evening for what we hope will be the greatest party on record. So, please raise your glasses and join us as. *Santé!"* With that, the crowd toasted in unison and there was a ripple of light applause.

Coming out of the mouth of Richard Fox, the words were eloquent, engaging, and heartfelt. Listening to the sound of DeBussey's stiff, plodding read, however, brought to mind the character "Mongo" in the old Mel Brooks comedy, *Blazing Saddles,* except Mongo probably sounded a tad more intelligent.

"Dinner service will commence in about ninety minutes, and until that time," the hosts continued, "we invite you to enjoy a very special tasting in the grand dining hall featuring multiple vintages of Vieux Château-Certan, Château Lafite Rothschild, Château Haut Brion, Château Palmer and our own, humble Château La Tour Noir. Very special thanks to our friends at these noble châteaux for providing their excellent vintages for the Célébration de Vin tonight, and we wish you all a wonderful, unforgettable *soirée.*"

With that, the Gypsy band launched into their first song, and the guys headed into the grand dining hall for what was sure to be the tasting opportunity of a lifetime.

# CHAPTER SIXTY-SIX

Now that the first grand toast of the night had taken place and many of the guests were heading back into the main building for the big wine tasting, the used glassware was starting to stream in to the service truck, and the nuns, including Marie Agnes, were all busy hand-washing and drying the champagne glasses and racking them up.

Sister Ralph was keeping a watchful eye on her old friend and was happy to see that the wrinkled, ancient nun was standing nearly straight up, smiling, and humming a happy tune while she dried and polished the glasses before putting them into the service racks for reuse. It was a remarkable turnaround, and she said a silent prayer to thank God for another one of His many unexplainable miracles.

*What is it that keeps her going?* Sister Ralph thought as she carried two of the replenished racks outside the service truck and placed them on a table to be taken back to the main house by a runner.

After hearing the echoes of the band starting up, René left the solitude and safety of the old farmhouse, crossed the deserted narrow street, and disappeared into the tall trees and dark underbrush surrounding the Château La Tour Noir property.

Dressed head to toe in black and wearing the identity-concealing balaclava and a set of borrowed night vision goggles, he would be able to remain completely invisible and anonymous as he worked his way towards the edge of his cover, at the end of the line of service and kitchen trucks and just across from the entrance to the winery.

As he approached his intermediate destination, he was glad to hear the music growing appreciably louder. Masking noise was always useful for covering up and drowning out unwanted collateral mission sounds that could give away one's position to opposition forces, witnesses, search parties and the like...sounds like screams, loud pleas for mercy or automatic weapons fire... yes, loud music would definitely be beneficial and aid in this mission's success.

Coming to the end of his crawl at the edge of the trees and the beginning of the line of service and kitchen trucks, René removed the goggles and realized that he would have to proceed with an extra measure of caution: the immediate area was a bit brighter than he had anticipated it would be, and someone had placed a chair exactly at the point he had chosen for his entry and egress.

There was nothing he could do about the light, but he could get rid of the chair. Just as he was about to roll out from the brush and remove it, someone carrying two large dishware racks appeared at the doorway of the last truck and placed them on a table, just a few paces from his position. *Merde!* His skills must be much rustier than he thought. As the service worker turned back into the light, he caught a glimpse of his ...er...her face. *No...it couldn't be!*

After Sister Ralph returned to the truck, he was able to execute his roll-out, move the chair a meter or so to the side and creep into a position that gave him a view directly into the doorway and directly into the eyes of... Sister Marie Agnes. *Shit!*

René instantly understood what the nuns were doing here and why, and decided that their presence wouldn't be a hindrance or create any sort mission-jeopardizing chaos. After all, he was doing this as much for them as he was for himself and his family, and they would never even know he had been here.

As soon as the large sister turned her back and he was certain no one else was looking or about, he silently bolted from his hidden position and stealthily entered the winery building.

Bruno hung back and carefully watched as his boss worked the small crowd of wine-world dignitaries on either side of the bandstand. His first task tonight was to keep him occupied and away from the grand dining hall tasting for as long as possible. Each time DeBussey appeared ready to make a move back to the main building of the château, Bruno interceded and pointed out another celebrity or steered him towards a well-known guest that he just had to personally meet and greet out here amid the revelers under the gala lights.

It wasn't easy work: Guy DeBussey wasn't exactly a voluble, charming conversationalist, and Bruno did what he could to keep the chat going and his boss' attention directed away from the tasting in the dining hall and on the party guests at hand.

Luckily, there was an ample and growing crowd enjoying the free-flowing champagne, the delicious *hors d'oeuvres* being served by the wait staff and the music of energetic Gypsy band, and the al fresco fantasyland was full of time-consuming opportunities for meaningless conversation and diversion. That was all to the good.

While he was talking and admiring his magnificent, magical venue with this wine mogul, or that sports star, DeBussey made a point of snagging each waiter as they passed by and sloppily sampling one of everything that was offered on their trays. And each time his champagne glass was empty, he signaled to Bruno, who made sure that it was instantly refilled. Even more to the good.

When this bottle was gone, Bruno would get another, and then it would be time for his second task of the night. Just the thought of it was bringing back the burning pins and needles in his hands and feet again. He filled his own glass and drank it down in one gulp. *Relax, Bruno...relax!!*

The dining hall was large, loud, and densely packed, but Justin had no trouble locating his Juice Brothers. When he looked to his left, there was the deeply tanned and pony-tailed Mike Lazarus, decked out in an honest-to-goodness business-formal suit and looking rather classy, comparing tasting notes on the 1986 Château Haut Brion with famed French oenologist and internationally known consultant Michel Rolland.

To his right, he watched Frank, dapper in his tux, sampling the nose of the 1989 Château Palmer, along with an equally large man that Justin knew he had seen somewhere before, but just couldn't place. The other man's face was even redder than Frank's, and it looked like they were having a contest to see who could get their nose farthest into their glass. They were laughing, slapping one another on the back, and carrying on like old friends.

Behind him, just beyond the large doors and out on the esplanade, Steve and Brad, also in slick, formal attire, had the 2003 Vieux-Château-Certan in their glasses and were chatting up Gaia Gaja, beautiful daughter of esteemed Italian wine-giant Angelo and one of the speakers at the seminar he had bugged out of this afternoon.

Throughout the room, he recognized other wine "rock-stars" he had read about and seen in magazines or in online articles, but there were also some real rock and movie stars in the crowd, looking glamorous, tasting the wines, shooting the breeze. The mood so was jubilant, so joyous and so relaxed Justin was sure it would be perfectly all right to walk up to Penelope Cruz or Johnny Depp and simply say *"so, how do you feel about the 2000 Haut Brion?"* What a scene!

Lala had been right; she had given him the golden ticket. As he stepped up to receive his taste of the very young Château La Tour Noir, the same wine and vintage he had tried and loved at the big tasting at The Oasis a few months back, he picked out a few other familiar or famous faces dotting the room. And then, walking in from the atrium through the tall arched doorway, he saw the most captivating, compelling person he had glimpsed thus far tonight.

She was wearing a stunning, full-length, off-the-shoulder gown, its red sequins glimmering in the soft light reflected from the amazing chandelier and the bistro lights. Her beautiful long hair was parted on the side and swept over, cascading down her one bare shoulder and sexy, exposed back. As she walked slowly towards him, her left leg was tantalizingly revealed by the gown's provocative thigh-high slit.

With her eyes locked on his, she moved seductively and almost cat-like towards him, and Justin felt himself suddenly come to attention as she embraced him and pulled him closely to her while subtly, and almost imperceptibly, grinding her crotch into his.

"Hi Justin," Lala cooed softly, and then shot a quick glance down below. "My, my…aren't *you* happy to see me!"

# CHAPTER SIXTY-SEVEN

It felt strange to be back in this old, windowless building. As René Gascogne walked the perimeter of the bottom level of the dimly-lit winery, his footsteps echoed lightly off of its bare, concrete floor, and the sound brought him momentarily back into the distant past, to the first time he could remember walking this exact path with his father, just starting to learn about his family's business.

After he passed the rear stairs and doubled back around, he looked up at the tall tanks and scaffolding and thought how little everything had changed. Then, while riding in the service elevator up to the tank-top level, thought just how much everything *had* changed. Although that awareness gave him pause, it didn't weaken his resolve: this was no time for brooding, dwelling, or pondering. This was the time for action.

All that mattered was the now, and right now he had to get himself set up on the roof to keep watch on DeBussey and wait for an opportunity to present itself. It would probably take all night, but he knew every nook and cranny of the château and its grounds, and if he had to make a three a.m. visit to the little bastard's bedroom, so be it.

Making his way around the narrow walkways and platforms at the top of the stainless steel tanks, he noted that each control panel was lit and all of the tanks he passed were in service. As he entered the small loft area, he reached into one of the compartments of his utility belt and extracted one of his most important tools for success, a Gitane. But before he could light up, he tripped, lost his footing, and fell onto a soft, cushy blanket that was laid out in the small alcove between tanks seven and eight.

*What the hell is that doing here?* He removed one of his gloves and ran his hand over the luxuriously plush fur. *Hmm...chinchilla.* Next to the blanket, he found a bottle of Billecart-Salmon Brut Rosé on ice in a stylish bucket and two champagne flutes. Luckily, he hadn't knocked the glasses over or broken anything, but what was this all about? Did this have something to do with Bruno's strange behavior earlier in the day and the "out of service" sign he'd tacked up on the winery's door?

After he smoothed the blanket and regained his feet, he lit his cigarette and more closely examined his surroundings. It was then he spotted something well out of the ordinary, especially for this time of year. He moved closer and to the edge of the dark, unobstructed opening and used his small, intensely bright penlight to investigate.

Tank seven's power had been switched off, and its controls had been set for "cleaning mode." This mode allowed the winery workers to slide the top open and gave them full body access to the tank's empty interior for a thorough inter-vintage cleaning. Except this tank was more than half full, and at this time of year, the wine inside would still require months of aging to reach its potential.

Why would anyone, especially a notoriously hard-nosed business man like Guy DeBussey, ruin this wine by exposing it to the air, and in the process, flush thousands and thousands of Euros down the drain? It didn't make sense...unless he was missing something.

Looking from the blanket to the champagne to the dark tank, and then considering Bruno Bastian's odd behavior in purposefully leaving the door unlocked, René decided he was definitely missing something, and whatever was going to take place here tonight would either be a stroke of good luck or a bolt of chaos-producing lightning. In either case, he needed to be ready and fully prepared.

He took a few short moments to remove his newly purchased Security-Man wireless MiniCam from his belt and set it on top of the adjacent tank eight. Then, he switched it to 'record' and checked the signal and picture feed into his IPhone. Thank God for technology…there was an App for everything these days! The picture wasn't good, but it would do.

René lit one more Gitane before heading up to the roof; there would be no smoking out in the open. He crossed over the loft and through the small kitchen and directly behind a rack filled with white coats and coveralls, he found the door to the stairwell to the roof. It was double locked and covered with cobwebs, but that wouldn't present a problem for an old, seasoned pro like René Gascogne.

He let the last drag of smoke fill his lungs and slowly exhaled before forcing the door open and stepping through. No obstacle could stand in his way now.

The runners were picking up their pace, and more and more dishes were making their way back to the service truck for the nuns to wash and stack. After well over an hour on her feet, Sister Marie Agnes was really starting to feel the strain on her frail body and decided she needed to take a break to conserve her strength.

She was overjoyed that the Lord had allowed her to participate tonight and help provide extra funds for the children. But God also had another, more important reason for her being here this evening, and she must find a way to make His will be done.

Dear Sister Ralph had found a chair for her so she could rest her old bones, and as she sat listening to the sounds of the Gypsy band and the party-goers beyond the enchanted forest screen, she thought about how much she would miss this world, the children, and her fellow nuns. She prayed her actions tonight wouldn't damn her soul to Hell for all eternity, but if that was the price for making this one last sinner see the light, she would gladly pay it.

Tentatively lifting herself out of the chair and then slowly walking around the side of the big service truck, she peered around the partition and took a good look at the beautiful lights, tents, and the well-dressed people, all eating, drinking, and enjoying their special night.

And then she spotted him, walking along a lantern-lit path back towards the château, with that big brute who was almost always at his side. Her hand instantly reached for her security flashlight, now hanging benignly around her neck, and she stroked it, almost lovingly.

As she hobbled slowly back to her chair, Sister Marie Agnes thought how special this night would be for her, too. She and the Lord, along with a little ten million volt assist from the Rattle Snake Terminator XXX, would finally make the *Bastard of Bordeaux* see the light—she was sure of it! No obstacle could stand in her way now.

# CHAPTER SIXTY-EIGHT

Bruno's phone vibrated in his jacket pocket, and he pulled it out to read the text message: *Go* was all it said. Excusing himself, Bruno went to get another bottle of champagne, which he had on ice nearby. Unceremoniously, he popped its cork and grabbed two fresh glasses, but on his way back, he took a detour to the darkened area behind the bandstand and removed one of the little pale green and yellow pills from his other pocket.

Carefully, he pulled the capsule apart and made sure to carefully sprinkle less than half of its powdered contents into one of the glasses, letting the rest fall to the ground. After all, they didn't want him totally incapacitated, just a little "out of it" and a touch more malleable.

When he returned to his boss' side, Bruno was glad to find DeBussey deeply involved in a heated discussion with a fat, bald German sporting a waxed handlebar moustache. It was something about France illegally re-annexing Alsace-Lorraine from the Weimar Empire after World War One, and the troll was so distracted that when Bruno delivered the doctored glass into his hairy-knuckled hand and filled it with champagne, DeBussey knocked it back in one gulp without missing a beat.

Bruno breathed a long sigh of relief, drank down the contents of his own glass, and pulled out his phone to send his own one word text message: *done.*

After recovering from Lala's shocking grand entry and settling down a bit, Justin had proudly introduced her to the guys, and they were all now quizzing her for funny stories and tidbits about Justin's nerdy high school days. Surprisingly, she didn't have a lot to say on the subject and mostly laughed politely in between sips of champagne and bites of the *hors d'oeuvres* that were being served to the crowd by a cadre of waiters.

She didn't need to say much; the guys were all mesmerized by her exquisite beauty and radiant skin, and Frank couldn't take his eyes off of her for a moment. His face was shining a shade of red that was even more brilliant than Lala's glittering sequined gown, and Justin hoped he wasn't about to launch into full "Tank" mode any time soon. When she excused herself for a few minutes to greet some of the other guests, the guys had nothing but admiration and praise for their lady-killer friend.

"What a beauty," Steve said as he watched her walk away.

"When did you become such a babe-magnet, J?" Brad said with a playful nudge.

Frank was starting to follow Lala like a lost, lonesome puppy, but Mike grabbed him by the sleeve of his tux and pulled him back.

'Whoa...back, Simba, back," he chuckled.

"You know," Frank said as, he stared in her direction, "I think we need more Asian dancers at Popatopolis and The Booby Trap."

They all lined up to try some of the Lafite, and by the time they'd each received a healthy pour of the 1996 vintage, which Steve reminded them had been rated a perfect one hundred points by Robert Parker, Lala had returned, this time leaning snuggly against Justin, her arm tightly wrapped around his waist.

"One thing I *will* tell you about this guy," she said, laughing and taking a step back, "he never looked like *this* in high school!" With that, she reached out, took his face in her hands, and planted a kiss on his puckered lips.

Justin was sure his face was going to turn a brighter shade of red than even Frank's, but his embarrassment was cut short by the unwelcome arrival of Guy DeBussey and his entourage of one, the menacing and dangerous-looking bodyguard Justin remembered from the dinner a few nights ago.

"What the fuck are *you* doing here?" DeBussey said indignantly, his heavily accented English sounding harsh and haughty. He planted himself squarely in front of Justin, leaned very closely into his personal space, and reaching up, stuck his stubby index finger into Justin's chest.

"I said, in case you didn't hear me, *what... the fuck... are you... doing here?*" he exclaimed loudly, this time tapping his finger with increasing intensity into Justin's chest with each word.

"Ah...I...ah...," was all Justin could get out before DeBussey splashed his champagne all over him and Lala stepped in between them, pushing her husband away.

"Get your hands off of him, Guy!" she said with a snarl that immediately turned into a forced smile. "Justin and his friends are my guests tonight, so get over it." Still *faux*-smiling, she glanced to Bruno and he took over. The burly bodyguard quickly escorted the enraged DeBussey to the other side of the grand dining hall and appeared to be trying to calm him down.

"Boss, please look around," Bruno said in a low voice after they'd crossed the room. "This is the biggest night of your life, and everyone is watching you and what you do." DeBussey took a curt glance at the famous and well-known faces in the crowd. Many of them looked away as his eyes met theirs. "Don't let this shit American's presence ruin your triumph by making more of a scene... just let it go, my friend...let it go." In the next instant, and he didn't know why, Guy DeBussey suddenly felt his blood stop boiling and his level of anger drop by at least half.

"Those Americans have big balls, coming to my home, but for once, Bruno, I am going to take your advice," he said, quickly adding, "but I want you to keep your eye on that asshole and his friends, and if they do anything further to embarrass me, I want you to make them disappear!"

Bruno nodded in agreement and steered Guy DeBussey out of the room and toward the big tents. Dinner was about to be served.

## CHAPTER SIXTY-NINE

The guys were still shaking their heads in shocked disbelief as Lala dabbed at Justin's damp face and Hugo Boss blazer with a cloth *serviette*. After she told them where they should look for dinner seats—in the far end of the second tent, well away from her husband's table in tent one, they followed the rest of the guests filing out of the grand dining hall through the large etched glass and wood doors and out into the gala night air.

But Lala had insisted Justin remain with her for a few minutes so she could help him freshen up, and he followed her through an arch that led into the château's large, modern kitchen.

"Justin, I—" she started, her voice full of concern, but he stopped her in mid-sentence.

"Lala, please, there's no need to apologize for your husband again," he said as she removed his blazer and laid it out on the wide granite countertop of the kitchen's center island to try and press the champagne out of the lapels. He looked around the luxurious kitchen and into her eyes and then gave her a warm, disarming smile.

"You know, other than the fact that you're married to a complete dick, I'd say your life is pretty damn good! Now, where's the bathroom?"

When he returned a few minutes later, Lala had his jacket ready to go, and she also had two glasses of her favorite rose champagne ready on the counter. After Justin had his coat back on and properly adjusted, she handed a glass to him and proposed a special toast.

"To Justin James, my hero!" she said, and they both drank their glasses down to the dregs. She then pointed him back out towards the grand dining hall, and with his back turned, nonchalantly dropped a now-empty little pale green and yellow capsule into the trash.

René had been lying prone on the roof and watching for over an hour, when through his small, ultra lightweight tactical binoculars, he finally spotted Guy DeBussey coming out of the château. He and his flunky Bruno were slowly walking amid a group of guests, past a colorful, gauzy-looking ice sculpture and toward the main tent. If he had been a much better marksman, he could have finalized this mission right now and been on his merry way. But, unfortunately, that wasn't his forte. René was more about finesse than flash.

Dinner service had just begun, so he settled in for what he was sure was going to be a very long wait. He didn't know what was on the menu, but he could smell the delicious food all the way up on the roof of the winery, and its aroma was so enticing that it started his mouth watering.

He was reaching into his utility belt for a protein energy bar when something else caught his attention, something so large and instantly identifiable, that he knew exactly who or what it was without the benefit of his binoculars. It was Frank *the Tank* Murphy, and when the disbelieving René checked through his field glasses, to his dismay he saw that Frank was surrounded by the rest of the Orlando crew, minus Justin.

*Merde, merde, merde!* First Sister Marie Agnes and the other nuns and now Frank and the Florida boys. René's hand automatically smacked into his balaclava-covered forehead, and he started massaging his now-throbbing temples. How could they possibly have gotten into this party, the super-exclusive Celébration de Vin, and how much more complicated and chaotic could this mission possibly get?

He was tempted to light up a Gitane right here on the roof and call the whole thing off, until he looked back into the binoculars and saw something else that caught his eye. Although he knew he was still missing *something,* this new development answered at least one question.

There was Justin, arm in arm with DeBussey's stunning wife, on their way out of the château, lightly canoodling like two lovers on their way to a secret rendezvous. When they reached the fork between the two big tents, she embraced him and gave him an amorous and unabashedly deep kiss. She then pointed towards the winery and to her watch, and then bid him farewell as she headed into tent one.

*Justin, Justin, Justin,* he thought, his growing smile concealed by the black balaclava, *I am going to fuck DeBussey up, and you, my friend, are going to fuck DeBussey's wife!*

As she walked in his direction, she had her phone out and appeared to be sending a text, and René took the opportunity to take a much closer look at the delicious and dangerous Lala DeBussey. *Hmm...nice girl....bad girl!*

While the band played on, Justin entered the amazingly elegant second tent, and after dodging servers and navigating his way through the tight, crowded aisles, he located the guys sitting on the opposite end, sharing a table with a friendly, but non-English-speaking couple from somewhere in Italy.

A chair had been pulled out for him, and as he sat down between Brad and Mike, he found that he was feeling a little woozy and flushed. He took a minute to catch his breath and even dabbed his linen napkin into his water glass and then onto his face for some relief. That helped. A little.

"You all right?" Brad asked after Justin had finished refreshing himself. "I mean, you've had a pretty eventful evening so far."

"I thought that ugly little midget was going to bite your head off," Mike said.

"Yeah, if he could've reached it!" Frank added, and he and Mike collapsed into a fit of laughter. The Italians across the table were smiling and laughing along, too. Justin wasn't sure why.

"Gentlemen, gentlemen," Steve admonished his cackling cohorts, "decorum, please!"

"You know, I think I've already had too much to drink," Justin said as he drank the rest of his water down, "or maybe I just need to eat something."

"Maybe it's all the attention from Lala that's going to your head," Brad said, nodding and grinning. "The question is, 'which head'?" That got all of them laughing.

By the time the starters arrived at their table, Justin had worked his way through three dinner rolls and was buttering a fourth and feeling a bit less shaky, so he took his chances and allowed himself alternating glasses of water and the fantastic Celébration de Vin Commemorative Cuvée, made from one hundred percent merlot, that was being poured nonstop by the very attentive wait staff.

Between the wine, the food, the festive atmosphere and the music—and Lala's frisky, forward behavior—he found himself feeling more alive and liberated than he had ever felt before.

Of course, he'd been surprised and slightly alarmed by Lala's over-the-top attention... at first. But by the time they'd walked out arm in arm onto the grounds and under the party lights, it was like he was living in a fantasy. And that last kiss she had given him had really lit his fuse!

He felt no weight on his shoulders or guilt in his heart, and he found himself eager to join Lala for the "private tour" of the château and grounds she had promised him. Now...what time had she said they would meet...?

# CHAPTER SEVENTY

*10:30.* That was the text message Bruno received as he and
DeBussey stepped up and took their places at the head table on
the dais in the center of the expansive tent and greeted their
distinguished guests. They had one more champagne toast with
Richard Fox, his wife, and some very important business
people from around the world, and then the service staff was
hovering and buzzing around them like worker drones
attending the queen bee.

Bruno's queen, however, was missing in action and her
chair vacant. He was starting to get really nervous because
DeBussey didn't seem to notice or care that his wife was
absent, and Bruno was worried the little troll was already too
far out of it for the final phase of their plan to be put into
motion.

When Lala finally appeared midway through the first
course and made her way around the table to greet the guests,
many of whom had witnessed the altercation in the grand
dining hall, Guy DeBussey reacted by standing and proposing a
boozy-sounding salute.

"Attention, everyone, please welcome my *wife,* who just
loves to make her husband look like a fool. *Santé,*" he said, his
words angry and slightly slurred, and plopped back down into
his chair. That momentarily silenced the guests at the head
table, until Lala raised her glass and answered.

'I'll drink to that!" she replied with a hearty laugh, and the
others at the table joined in with smiles and nervous laughter of
their own.

And Bruno laughed, too, albeit with relief. DeBussey's little outburst indicated to him that he was indeed lucid enough to still be a complete asshole, a key part of their strategy, and that meant the time was near. He wondered what tomorrow's newspaper headlines would say, and he looked forward to cutting one or two of them out them out and pasting them into DeBussey's treasured, leather-bound scrapbook. On its final page.

Marie Agnes tried, but she couldn't keep up with the demands of her dishwashing duties, and Sister Ralph, God bless her, had told her to take a rest in the chair she had left for her just outside the kitchen service truck.

So while the party-goers reveled loudly on the other side of the enchanted forest screen, she relaxed and saved up her strength for the opportunity and the moment she just knew He would provide tonight.

*A few more minutes of rest,* she thought, *and I'll take another look around the partition to locate that evil little bastard.*

When she felt ready, she willed herself up and haltingly traversed the short distance to the big dividing screen, once again peering around the edge and out into festively-lit, side-by-side tents, hoping to spot him somewhere close by.

The tents were full of loud, merry guests, and the aisles and walkways were congested with servers and runners bringing food in and taking dirty dishes and glassware out, so it took her a few long minutes to finally find Guy DeBussey, sitting at a slightly elevated table in the center of the dining area of one of the tents, raising his glass in an obvious toast.

Feeling the energy draining from her sick, tired body, she slowly shuffled back to her chair, gingerly sat down, and made her decision. *If I wait until after dessert is served, I just might have enough strength to reach him.* She closed her eyes and prayed for a miracle.

# CHAPTER SEVENTY-ONE

From his vantage point atop the winery building, René was able to keep tabs on the entire venue, and although he couldn't view the full interior of either tent, he could see enough to know exactly where DeBussey and Justin were sitting. He kept his focus on both locations while sweeping the area for any more interesting or complicating developments.

The gala's dinner service was well under way, and as the aroma of foods wafting up to him increased in intensity, René found himself wishing it was his father sitting at the head table on the dais, and that he and the rest of his family were all there with him for tonight's special occasion.

He could almost taste the saucy *steak au poivre* he'd be enjoying right about now, but the chemically, cardboard flavor of the protein bar he was munching on brought him harshly back to reality…maybe next time *he* would be the one sitting at the head table, instead of that undeserving runt, Guy DeBussey.

The band had been on break for a while, and important people and dignitaries from this company or that agency trickled up to the stage to address the crowd, make announcements or sing the praises of their hosts and thank them for putting on such a wonderful affair.

In the middle of a particularly tedious speech by a nasal-sounding, stuttering old gentleman from the Bordeaux office of tourism and marketing, René saw Bruno Bastian leave the main tent and head quickly toward the château and the toilette trailers. Nothing unusual there.

But five minutes later, he did see something strange. Justin left his tent and also headed to the porta-potty trailers, but upon his exit, instead of heading back to rejoin the guys, he very slowly and almost drunkenly walked past both dining tents and then along the service path that lead to the edge of the enchanted forest partition. And the winery. Something was going down, and he was betting it would be Lala.

During dinner, Lala had kept her phone on her lap, and no one noticed as she discreetly reached under her serviette and pressed the numbers six and nine, the speed dial combination for Bruno's number. Seconds later, he answered the non-call and went through the fiction of discussing a problem with the concierge in front of the château.

"Boss," he whispered quietly into DeBussey's ear after he'd "ended" the call. "I have got to go deal with something, and I'll be back as soon as possible." DeBussey's eyes were glassy, but he was still in control, and as Bruno turned to head off, he grabbed his arm and pulled him back.

"Just make sure you keep your eyes open...you know what I mean...yes?"

*Yes*, Bruno thought, *I'll be keeping my eyes open, but for entirely different reasons.*

With Bruno gone and DeBussey busy occupied by the endless stream of guests that came to the main table seeking a word or giving him their compliments, Lala waited for a few more minutes and then excused herself.

The band had just resumed its spirited renditions of favorites young and old, so she headed in the direction of the stage and lost herself in the crowd now dancing under the party lights strung overhead in front of the bandstand. After she had pretended to enjoy the music and dancing just long enough, she did her best to fade into the background and slip around to the far side of the tents and the unlit gravel path that led directly to the front door of the winery.

When she reached the end of the second tent and turned the corner, she saw Justin standing unsteadily in the glow of the dim lights from the building's entrance, slowly rubbing his eyes with both hands and gently swaying back and forth like he was on the deck of a cruise ship in a moderately choppy sea. Lala picked up her pace: the last thing she needed was for poor Justin to pass out prematurely!

The moment he'd stood up and excused himself to hit the men's room, Justin realized he was in bad shape. Standing at the urinal and trying to focus his eyes on the spot directly in front of him had proved nearly impossible, and the walk back seemed to have taken much more time and effort than it should have. He was completely wasted.

Waiting in front of the winery for Lala, he noticed that the sounds of the band and the partying crowd had coalesced into a buzzing drone that seemed to be centered in the middle of his brain, and he suddenly felt as though the slightest breeze would knock him over... and out. What he needed was a nap, and soon.

He tried to rub his eyes awake, but that didn't work. He then heard a voice calling out his name and lost his balance as it echoed and bounced around inside his head. And then she was standing at his side, helping him down the steps and into the building. She was saying something about a nice place to take a rest and a glass of water, and...whatever...it sounded good to him.

Everything in his shrinking field of vision was cloaked in darkening shadows, and he felt even more lightheaded, like his body was slowly rising through the air. Then, the sensation abruptly ended, and he was lying on his back on a fantastically soft, luxuriant bed, his clothes seeming to have magically melted away and disappeared.

He felt her close to him, touching him, the sound of her heavy breathing adding one hundred decibels to the buzzing in his skull. As he forced his eyes open for the last time, all he saw was her long black hair falling down over her beautifully bare breasts. But, when he tried to reach out and touch them, they were suddenly gone. And so was he.

# CHAPTER SEVENTY-TWO

René was humming the tune of an old '80s Hall and Oates hit song as he scooted back from the edge of the roof and fired up the display on his phone to check the feed from the MiniCam.

Moments after he'd seen Justin stumbling up to the winery, Lala had appeared on the darkened pathway that ran in back of the tents, and when she saw him swaying back and forth, she had quickly rushed to his side and helped him down the steps and into the building.

René could tell from the slight vibration on the roof that the service elevator was on its way up to the tank top level for their tryst, but based on Justin's apparent condition, he was pretty sure that it would be the only thing rising in the winery tonight.

The MiniCam had been positioned to afford him a view of the open tank seven in the background and the chinchilla blanket in the foreground, and sure enough, within moments, two figures appeared in the poorly-lit, grainy black and white video image. He plugged in the headset and popped one of the little buds into his left ear.

He watched as Lala carefully helped Justin down onto the blanket and uncorked the chilled bottle of Billecart-Salmon champagne, pouring them each a glass and gently helping him to take a long drink. That was obviously the last thing the kid needed, especially if her goal was to have a quick toss or two with him during her husband's big affair.

But then she was all business, and she began to quickly and almost aggressively remove his clothing; first his jacket and tie, and then his shoes and shirt. The whole time Justin was nearly silent, and whatever he did manage to say had been completely unintelligible.

She unbuckled his trousers, but before pulling them down and forcibly tugging them off, she suddenly stopped and reached for her mobile phone...to send a text! *Something is definitely not right.* Wouldn't they be heading back to the party after they had done their dance? So why hadn't she even taken a short second to fold his clothes for later or hang them neatly over a chair? Instead, she threw them off to the side, where they had presumably wound up in a crumpled heap.

But he did feel a little better about the almost comical situation when Lala stripped off her sequined evening gown and panties, added them to the pile, and did her best to revive her nearly comatose friend.

*My, my,* he thought as he watched her flawless, well-practiced technique, *she really IS a Maneater!*

Guy DeBussey couldn't remember a more wonderful night in his entire life, and he felt supremely at peace and self-satisfied. What an evening it had been, and what a huge success to add to his long string of business accomplishments!

Now, he *really* couldn't wait until next week to spring his big surprise on his absent rival and many of these unsuspecting idiots. If half of the people coming up to the table to kiss his ass had any idea what he was going to do to them, they'd be spitting in his eye instead of shaking his hand.

He savored another sip of his delicious Celébration de Vin Cuvée and exulted in its opulent, sexy bouquet, its full ripe fruit flavor, and its exquisitely balanced structure; it tasted like triumph and victory in a glass. Its flavor was full of ethereal sweetness and perfection, just like this evening, and there was absolutely nothing that could spoil it for him.

The sudden vibration of his mobile phone startled him, and after fumbling for a moment, he slowly pulled it out of his jacket. It was Bruno calling.

"Boss!" his henchman shouted on the other end of the line. "I just saw Lala with that American, and they were hanging all over each other like two teenagers in heat!"

"What?" DeBussey exploded into his phone. "Where are they now?" he demanded while pushing himself slowly out of his chair.

"I am pretty sure they are heading into the winery. But I am still dealing with a problem here...I need a few more minutes..." Bruno's voice trailed off.

"I don't need to wait for you," DeBussey said thickly. "I'm on my way to break up their little class reunion right now, and I think this is going to be the highlight of my entire night! Join me as soon as you can." He was laughing as he hit End and walked unsteadily out of the tent.

# CHAPTER SEVENTY-THREE

For almost ten minutes, René looked on with great interest as Lala tried in vain to bring Justin up and around. When she finally gave up, instead of standing and getting dressed, she poured more champagne for herself and sat back down, straddling the unresponsive and now totally silent Justin.

And she waited. *But for what?* René didn't understand and knew that he was totally missing something of real importance here.

Now that their show was over, he moved back to the edge of the roof to locate DeBussey at his table, but he wasn't there. And neither was Bruno. That put his internal mission radar on high alert, and he silently admonished himself for being so easily distracted from his main purpose here tonight.

When he did spot Bruno, he found him swiftly and surreptitiously approaching the winery using the same path Lala had taken. He was in an obvious hurry, but just before leaving the relative cover and darkness of the pathway and arriving at the building's dimly lit entrance, he paused to reach into his jacket pocket and remove a pair of gloves, which he quickly slipped onto his big hands and flexed his long fingers, as if to say… 'ready.' *Ready for what?*

*God! I could really use another cigarette right now,* he thought as he watched Bruno's image appear in the grainy video transmission and, not-so-surprisingly, kiss the still-naked Lala, who had sprung up and embraced him as he entered the frame. He struggled to make out their words over the ambient noise from the party and the low hum of the tanks, and when he raised the audio output from the MiniCam, he could clearly hear their conversation. In that exact moment, it all became alarmingly clear.

In his mind's eye, all of the seemingly unrelated fragments of information click into place like a bizarre, life-sized jigsaw puzzle, and René instantly knew what he must do. He needed to get back down into the winery immediately, and he didn't have much time.

He'd just spotted the last piece of the puzzle walking through the crowd and past one of the melting ice sculptures, and he was on his way directly toward Justin, Lala, Bruno, the winery, and total chaos!

Sister Marie Agnes didn't know how long she'd been resting, and as she opened her eyes and felt for the flashlight dangling around her neck, it only took her short a moment to remember where she was and why she was here.

This was it, and the old nun quickly prayed for God to send all of His strength into her feeble, ailing body. She was going to need every ounce of it to will herself up and out of this chair, around the big partition and across the considerable distance to Guy DeBussey's table in the center of the main tent.

She closed her eyes, once more begging the Lord to send her the miracle that would enable her to do His will and carry out her plan for retribution and salvation. And when she reopened her eyes, *hallelujah*, an extraordinary vision appeared before her, not more than ten meters away!

There was the *Bastard of Bordeaux*, waddling along in his expensive suit, between the enchanted forest screen and the large building next to the row of service trucks. And, he was all alone as he walked beyond her and into the building's wide-open door.

*Thank you, thank you, thank you!* her heart sang out in gratitude, and she felt a supernatural surge of energy lift her out of her chair and propel her towards the winery. It was as if her legs could barely keep up with her desire as she rapidly covered the short distance. Nearing the entrance, she pulled her flashlight over her head, and in the process, its tether knocked off her lightweight summer head covering.

*No time to pick it up now*, she thought, as she held the small innocuous-looking unit in front of her and pointed it into the open doorway. She pushed the 'on' button and as power surged into its contact prongs, the device hummed and crackled to life as it morphed into the very potent and dangerous Rattlesnake Terminator XXX.

She quickly pointed its intensely bright beam down toward the ground—there was no need to give that evil bastard any early warning—and put her hand through the tether's loop to secure it tightly around her fragile wrist.

Walking into the building's murky light, she heard DeBussey's harsh voice filtering down from up above, so she stepped into the waiting service elevator to ride up and find her wicked, hateful prey at the top of the large stainless steel tanks. Praise God—retribution was nearly at hand!

# CHAPTER SEVENTY-FOUR

*"What do you mean you gave him the whole pill?"*

As Monsieur René crept back unnoticed into the winery and stealthily placed himself in the darkly shadowed nook diagonally across from its counterpart between tanks seven and eight, he listened as the two partners in crime argued about what should happen next.

"You told me to give him the whole thing!" Lala answered defensively. She pushed Bruno away, folded her arms, and began nervously pacing up and down next to Justin's naked, unconscious form.

"I said to only give him half!" Bruno answered, throwing his hands up in exasperation. "How are we going to make it look like the American killed the troll if he can't even open his eyes to see this?" Bruno held up his telescopic truncheon and flicked it open to its full length. It made a small *clack* as it locked into place. "*Shit*...what are we going to do now?"

Lala immediately stopped her pacing and turned to face her co-conspirator.

"It's simple, Bruno. We'll have to kill both of them," she said coldly. She was so matter-of-fact about it that it sent a shiver up René's spine.

"Oh… right…*we'll* have to kill both of them."

"Don't worry my big French oak," Lala exclaimed lustfully as she grabbed Bruno by his crotch and started to unzip his fly, "I am here to help."

As he listened and watched, René simply couldn't believe what an outrageous nympho Lala DeBussey had turned out to be. *I told you to stay away from her, Justin,* he thought, as he withdrew his own baton from his utility belt and extended it slowly and silently by hand.

"Quiet! I think I hear him coming up the back stairs," he whispered. Bruno pushed Lala back, telling her to get back on top of Justin and give her soon- to-be-dead husband a loud, distracting show.

"If you want to be a rich widow by the end of tonight, make it look good!" were his final instructions as he left her straddling the sleeping Justin while he ducked down around the side of tank eight.

He could hear them on the top floor—his little Chinese whore and that shit *Americain.* He needed to get up there now, but after repeated presses of the call button, the service elevator still hadn't returned to the bottom floor, and Guy DeBussey couldn't wait one more second to catch his wife and her bastard American boy-toy screwing in his winery! He shuffled across the concrete floor to the rear stairs and, as quietly as he could, made his way up.

And he wasn't scared or nervous about getting into a scuffle, either. As a matter of fact, he had this wonderful feeling of omnipotence and invincibility—it was fantastic, and he just couldn't get the smile off of his face! In any case, if he did need assistance, Bruno would be here any minute to help him put the finishing touches on the greatest night of his life.

As he made the top of the stairs, he could hear her urging him on...*come on...come on... oh... harder...oh...* and it made him laugh almost uncontrollably, until he heard her shout...*oh Justin, my husband never did it like that!*

That brought his anger instantly up and his blood back to a low boil, and he almost ran down the narrow walkway past each of the big tanks until he arrived at the space between seven and eight, almost tripping over the edge of a chinchilla blanket. And there he found his wife on top of the American, humping away with wild abandon and loudly cursing in Chinese.

*"Well, well, I knew it!"* he yelled at the top of his shrill voice. "It's Lala, *Pussy DeBussey Galore!* Get up, you cheating bi…"

As soon as DeBussey began ranting like a madman, René pulled himself back further into the shadows while Bruno jumped into action, bolted around tank eight, and came up behind his soon to be ex-boss. When Bruno spun him around and forcefully smacked DeBussey full across the face with his baton, the little man fell hard at his feet. A thudding nudge to the prone man's ribcage verified that he was out cold.

"Hit him again, Bruno! Kill him now!" Lala said in an agitated, almost out of control voice.

"Not yet," the big man answered breathlessly. "First, we have to take care of your sleeping friend, and then we'll kill the troll."

"Just hurry…do it fast." She turned her back to him and slipped into her panties and dress. Just as Bruno was about to step over DeBussey and move towards Justin, who was now loudly snoring like an overweight old man with a bad case of sleep apnea, René flashed out of the shadows and swung his baton at Bruno's right knee, collapsing it with a sickening *crunch.* Then, a black-booted foot violently connected with his solar plexus, knocking every last breath of air from his lungs and breaking a few ribs. The masked René then stood over him and poked his baton into Bruno's pain-stricken face as he gasped loudly for air.

"If you move one centimeter," René said quietly as Lala jumped back in surprise and tried to press her body into the wall as far as it would go, "I will break your other knee."

"Who the hell are you, and what do you think you're doing here?" she demanded boldly.

"Let's just say that I am a concerned citizen here to do a very good deed," René answered. He approached her and stuck his baton into the center of her chest and forced her to the floor. "Now, sit down and shut up."

"I will do no such thing!" she said as she moved to get to her feet. The pressure from his boot on her shoulder easily kept her down.

"You are on my property, and I will have you arrested for trying to kill my husband!" Lala yelled defiantly. "It is my word against yours, and no one will believe a man dressed in a ridiculously phony black ninja outfit!"

"Oh, I think someone will," René answered as he removed his boot from Lala's shoulder and stepped back. He reached into his belt and removed his IPhone, holding it out so she and Bruno, who was on the floor wheezing and writhing in pain, could both see themselves in its display.

"Look, you two are movie stars!" he said with a laugh. He pointed his baton towards the top of tank eight and continued, "And you see that little red light? That's the camera that has been recording everything you have said and done here tonight. I might even post it on YouTube!"

That absolutely startling revelation left Lala speechless and made Bruno start to whimper and moan. Putting the phone back into his belt and keeping his eyes glued on the two them, René carefully backed up and retrieved the MiniCam and carefully placed it into his backpack. He then took out a Gitane and lit up. He needed to think this through before doing anything else that might send this mission into even into deeper disarray and total pandemonium.

As René was stubbing out his first cigarette and preparing to light another, Guy DeBussey began to stir and managed to get up on one knee. He had a big purple-ish knot on his forehead and his already wide, flat nose was even wider and flatter than it had been before. But other than that, he had survived Bruno's initial assault.

"What the fuck happened...how did I get here? I can't remember anything," he said in a dazed, strained voice as he gingerly rubbed his head and took in the surreal scene. "And who the fuck are you?" DeBussey demanded as he pointed to René.

"Do you see that tank, Monsieur?" René said, motioning to number seven's dark opening and ignoring his question. "These two were going to kill you, throw your body in there, and blame it all on the poor unconscious naked guy on the floor. And I think they meant to kill him, too."

"No! That can't be true," he said in disbelief. "Why would they…" DeBussey's voice trailed off as he rubbed his eyes and slowly shook his head.

"Yes, it is most certainly true," René answered. "Try to remember, Monsieur. Try."

"No… I…can't …I…uh…No…" Guy DeBussey sounded bewildered and almost sad, and René nearly found himself feeling sorry for him. Nearly.

In the silence, the wheels of Guy DeBussey's drug-addled brain must have started to spin a little faster. He took a loud, sharp breath, and his demeanor totally changed.

"*Yes! I do remember,*" he yelled angrily and pulled himself unsteadily to his feet.

"You smacked me in the head with something," he continued, as he pointed accusingly at Bruno, who had now rolled on to his side and was holding his shattered knee. "And I guess you must have hit me here, too." He pawed at the spot where Bruno had kicked him. "So, it's true!" DeBussey shakily made his way over to the edge of the open tank and peered into the dark chasm. "How long has this tank been open? Maybe we can save the juice."

René was astounded. Here the man had just been presented with a plot against his life by his wife and his right-hand man, and all he could think about was the fact that he might lose money on the deal!

He was about to tell him how truly pathetic he was and give him another smack across the face when, at the end of the row of tanks, the door to the service elevator suddenly opened, and as it's dull yellow light spilled into the loft, a dry, hoarse voice called out from within.

# CHAPTER SEVENTY-FIVE

*Guy DeBussey, the Bastard of Bordeaux,* the voice said, *God has sent me here to make you repent for your multitude of sins and beg his forgiveness.*

René instantly recognized the ancient, ghostly-sounding voice, and out of the elevator walked Sister Marie Agnes. She looked exceedingly worn, weary, and haggard, and even in the dim light, he could see that her cadaverous face had lost all of its color and that she probably wasn't long for this world. She lifted her arm and shined a very intense beam of light through the stale, dense air of the winery, illuminating Guy DeBussey in its glare and casting his giant shadow on the back wall.

As the old nun slowly walked by and around Justin's naked form, all the while keeping DeBussey framed in the flashlight's bright beam, René got a closer look at the device she was holding in her hand and recognized it for what it really was. But instead of stopping her or obstructing her in any way, he did nothing.

"You've got to be kidding me." DeBussey sneered with cruel contempt as he held up his hand to shield his eyes from the beam. "You crazy old bitch, what are you going to do with your little flashlight, *blind me to death?*" The reality of the attempt on his life and the effects of the blow to his head must have put him into a state of shock, because he then started laughing, almost maniacally.

"Do you deny all of the evil deeds you have done in this world and especially to my poor children and the Sisters at the orphanage?" the old nun spat. "Well, Monsieur DeBussey, let us see how hard you laugh when you feel the Lord's retribution and face his judgment!"

She rapidly closed the distance between them, and as she jammed the prongs of the Rattlesnake Terminator XXX into DeBussey's outstretched hand, she pressed the white button. The unit was fully charged, and its entire ten million volts of surging, agony-inducing power blasted out of the stun gun and into Guy DeBussey's body with a single flash of blue-ish lightning.

The tuxedo-clad tyrant collapsed onto the floor and began to twitch and shake violently, with his mouth open wide in a silent scream that left his tongue ricocheting from one side to the other and his eyes bulging like they were about to explode in their straining sockets.

Sister Marie Agnes stepped back and covered her mouth with her free hand, but it wasn't done in shock or alarm. The old nun was laughing blissfully and there were tears freely streaming from her rheumy eyes and down her wrinkled, translucent cheeks.

"Thank you Jesus and hallelujah!" she proclaimed, still pointing the Rattlesnake at DeBussey. "I think he's seen the light!"

*Amen to that,* René thought as the effects of the charge wore off and he watched the frazzled DeBussey slowly get to his feet.

"Somebody, take that thing away from her!" he gasped pleadingly and then hunched over and threw up all of the *hors d'oeuvres* and dinner he had wolfed down throughout the party. No one moved to help him.

He sloppily smeared his tuxedo-covered forearm over his mouth to wipe away any residue and suddenly lunged at the unsuspecting old nun, tackling her and trying to wrestle the stun gun out of her hand.

René wanted to whack him with his baton and help poor Sister Marie Agnes, and he thought that if DeBussey gained the upper hand, he might have a shot. He got as close as he dared, but they were locked so tightly together and rolling from the floor of the loft and onto the blanket and back, that he just couldn't take the a chance of doing anything that might bring him into contact with the prongs of the stunner. It was still fully-charged, and the air was humming and crackling with static electricity.

DeBussey tried, but couldn't get the gun out of her hand; its tether was too tight and her will too strong. When they rolled back onto the floor just in front of the gaping tank, he suddenly found himself on top of the unbelievably resilient woman and in good position to take her out with a blow to the head. But to do that, he'd have to release one of his hands from the stun gun, and as he did, Marie Agnes saw her opportunity to administer the Lord's final justice.

As he pulled his hand back to launch his fist at the ferocious nun struggling beneath him, with her last bit of strength the old Sister forced herself up and stabbed the prongs of the Rattlesnake Terminator XXX into Guy DeBussey's vomit covered neck while she pressed its little red button.

As the gun discharged in a never-ending high voltage stream of electric current and they both began to scream and shake from the power and the pain, Sister Marie Agnes said a last prayer of thanks to God Almighty and used her remaining momentum to roll them over and forward, plunging them both into the commodious, murky darkness of tank seven.

When they splashed into the fermenting wine, the air inside the tank exploded in a huge blue white flash and a fog of grey smoke wafted up and out. It had a peculiar, burnt electrical odor, and smelled of something else, too. The power in the entire winery then went completely offline, and for a moment, aside from the sound of Justin sawing wood on the floor, it was completely dark and silent.

René Gascogne then did the only thing he possibly could— he lit up another cigarette.

# CHAPTER SEVENTY-SIX

It had been a long, demanding service, but now that dessert was being served and most of the dinner dishes had been washed and stacked, Sister Ralph could finally take a moment to relax and take a break to check on Marie Agnes. The last time she'd had a chance to stick her head out the door, her old friend had been peacefully asleep in her chair. But that had been well over an hour ago, and she hoped she was still all right.

After she cleaned and dried her hands, she left the confines of the service truck only to find the chair empty and Sister Marie Agnes nowhere to be seen. She turned around to ask the other Sisters if they had seen her, and then very quickly checked in with workers in the other kitchen trucks. No one had seen her.

Ralph then thought that perhaps the missing nun had taken a short walk around the partition and out onto the party grounds...and that might mean she could come into contact with Guy DeBussey! She had to stop her before it was too late.

She walked back down the line of trucks and was about to turn the corner of the enchanted forest screen, when out of the corner of her eye, she caught sight of a familiar object lying on the ground. It was a nun's summer head covering, and she and the other nuns were all still wearing theirs.

Sister Ralph walked to the fallen garment, which was sitting almost directly in front of the wide open door of the winery building, and picked it up. She wasn't sure what to do, but something told her to go inside.

"You're going to let us go now?" Lala said as she waved the smoke away from her face. It was more of a demand than a question. She kneeled down to check on Bruno, who was still whimpering, groaning and having difficulty breathing. "Oh, my big French oak, I am so sorry," she said, surprising René with her show of concern and affection.

"Perhaps," was the only answer she got from René, who was peering into the tank with his penlight and checking on the two bodies floating below. He felt badly for Sister Marie Agnes, but she had given her life for something she truly believed in, and in René's mind, there was no higher calling or honor.

And he knew the children of Our Lady of Mercy would remain in good hands. He would do his best to see to it, because it was the very least he could do for the woman who had prevented him from taking a man's life on French soil and becoming a real murderer.

But René wasn't sure what to do next. His anonymity was still intact, and the mission had been successfully completed for him, but he still had these two rotten apples and an unconscious friend to deal with. Somewhere, an emergency generator kicked over, and the power flickered back on.

He pointed his baton at Lala and instructed her to go to the loft's kitchen and fetch a pair of winery coveralls and a white coat, and then to come immediately back and clothe the naked guy with them.

"And if you don't do exactly as I tell you," he said menacingly, "any chance of working out a deal with me will be finished. Then, I will very painfully break your friend's other knee…and, when I catch you, one of yours, too."

Lala quickly complied, and as she was pulling Justin's underwear up and wrestling the coveralls onto his uncooperative body, René gathered up Justin's crumpled suit, shirt, and tie and stuffed them into his backpack. He then gathered the butts of his smoked Gitanes from the loft floor and lit one last cigarette as he weighed his options, considered his leverage, and suddenly saw the unique set of incredible possibilities laid out in front of him like a winning hand in a high-stakes poker game.

"Okay, you two," René said, pointing his baton at his captives, "if you want to live out the rest of your miserable lives in freedom, this is how it will be."

# CHAPTER SEVENTY-SEVEN

*"Allo...Allo?* Is anyone up there?" Sister Ralph heard indistinct voices from upstairs and wondered if the old nun had found her way to the upper floor of the building. She called out again, "Sister Marie Agnes, is that you?"

"Who is there?" a much younger woman's distressed voice cried out from above. "Please, take the elevator and come up to help us. Please hurry...it's an emergency!"

Sister Ralph rode up in the elevator and when its door opened, she was greeted with a cloud of swirling white smoke filled with the smell of burnt electrical equipment and something that was reminiscent of the bacon and onion-flavored chips she had been snacking on before she'd left the orphanage.

She walked by the big stainless steel tanks and came out onto the loft, where she found a man and a woman, whom she instantly recognized as Guy DeBussey's bodyguard and his wife. As she got closer, broken glass crunched under her big feet and she saw the glint of large pieces and shards of what looked like some sort of glassware, scattered all around.

The man was lying on his side on a large black and silver blanket and writhing in obvious pain, and DeBussey's wife was crying hysterically. It looked like they had been up to no good here in the loft, with the blanket, the broken glass, and the bottle of champagne standing in an empty ice bucket, and they certainly needed help. But in truth, and she hoped God would forgive her, she couldn't care less about these two.

"Have you seen Sister Marie Agnes? I think you know who she is," Sister Ralph said firmly. That made DeBussey's wife visibly tremble and cry even more intensely. "Well, have you seen her?" Sister Ralph demanded loudly. DeBussey's wife nodded and cocked her head towards the big, smoking tank to her right.

Sister Ralph bolted to the edge of the open tank and shrieked in surprise at the sight of her friend and the evil bastard Guy DeBussey, floating lifelessly in the vat of foul-smelling wine, locked for all eternity in a death embrace. She fell back in revulsion, made the sign of the cross, and tried to wipe the image from her mind.

"The old Sister saved our lives," the dead man's wife said between intense sobs and racking shivers. "My husband caught us here fooling around and was going to kill us, but she appeared like an avenging angel and sent him to hell."

The last of Lala's anguished words faded into the distance as Ralph ran back into the service elevator and hurried downstairs to tell the other Sisters about the unbelievable tragedy that had occurred in the winery.

"How long has it been?" Brad asked with concern. He pushed his empty dessert plate away, sipped on his second glass of the other-worldly, amber-gold 1990 Château d'Yquem, and then drummed his fingers on the table. Justin should have returned from his pit stop long before now.

Steve, working on his second glass of the 1977 Dow's Porto and a flourless dark chocolate torte, reached into his jacket pocket and pulled out his phone.

"It's easily been over an hour," he said, setting the phone down on the table and finishing off the rest of his wine.

"He was pretty wasted when he left," Mike added. "Do you think maybe we should go look for him?"

"Don't worry, I know right where he is!" Frank said, and bounced his eyebrows for the amusement of the Italian couple across the table. "I'll bet he's up in the château with that hot number Lala, doing what they never did under the bleachers in high school."

"Right..." Brad said sardonically as he grabbed a chocolate-covered profiterole from Frank's heaping plate and popped it into his mouth. "We'll give him five more minutes, and then we'll split up and start looking for him."

Steve's phone buzzed and lit up. It was a text from Monsieur René, and he passed it around so they could each read the perplexing message: *Guys, please leave now and meet me at the house. No worries. Justin is with me. But do not delay—this is very important—do it now!*

The Gypsy band was cranking on a classic Stéphane Grappelli/Django Reinhardt *Le Jazz Hot* number and the party was in full swing, but you could have heard a pin drop at the table full of vino-tourists from Orlando.

Ten tense minutes later, after he'd tracked it down with the help of one of the valets, Brad pulled the van out of Château La Tour Noir's gaily lit drive and headed toward home. Within sixty seconds, half a dozen police cars, with their blue lights flashing and their Euro-sirens screaming, sped by in the opposite direction and disappeared into the night.

And then, you could have heard a pin drop in the big Mercedes as they drove in silence all the way back to St. Quentin de Baron.

After René placed Justin into his small car's front seat, he popped the trunk, stowed his gloves, gear, and balaclava and then did his best to stretch the pain out of his aching body.

He hadn't carried a comrade on his back and out of danger in many years, and it had taken a lot effort to lug Justin through the underbrush and back to the small farmhouse. But at least tonight, he didn't have to worry about taking weapons fire or being hit in the ass by an RPG.

He'd dumped cold water from the ice bucket onto his sleeping friend's head and roused him enough to get him into the elevator and down from the top floor of the winery, but as soon as they'd made it into the trees, Justin was out again, and he'd had to hoist him over his shoulder.

Now, to avoid any more complications this evening, he needed to contact the guys and get them off the premises before all hell broke loose, and the fastest way to reach them was by text message. Sure, it was traceable, but with the two bodies in the tank and Lala and Bruno playing their parts, no one was going to be looking to tie him, Justin, or anyone else to what had happened at Château La Tour Noir tonight.

He'd made it clear to the two would-be killers that if they didn't follow his improvised, virtual script to the letter, an anonymously submitted copy of the video he had made would quickly find its way to the Bordeaux police commissioner's desk. At the very least, it would implicate them as co-conspirators in the murder of Guy DeBussey, and they would be sent away for a very long time. Not a good option for the partners in crime.

So, the odds were definitely in his favor, and he took his chances, hit send, and pulled out onto the dark back road. Now, if he could just find an open fast food place to get something to eat, this mission would have a perfect ending. And he really liked perfect endings, especially this one.

Not long after Brad had pulled the Mercedes van into the driveway of the rental in St. Quentin de Baron, the gate chime rang, and he rushed outside to witness Monsieur René pulling up in his little sports car. René waved him over, and Brad, now joined by Steve and Frank, helped lift Justin out of the front seat and carry him into the house.

René had Mike search for as many extra sheets as he could find and lay them across Justin's bed, and by the time they'd brought the unconscious kid into the room, the bed had been covered with four or five extra layers of protective padding. They laid him down and René placed a bottle of water on his night stand and the rest of the box of greasy French-style "Kentucky" chicken he'd picked up on the pillow next to his head—just in case he woke up and needed some food, which wasn't likely.

"Why are you both wearing those strange clothes," Brad asked, pointing at Justin's winery coveralls and René's black assault suit.

"And why *the hell* do you guys smell...*so bad?*" Mike said, waving his hand in front of his face as if it would help to clear the air.

"Ah, apropos." René laughed. "It's a very long story, and I am going to tell it to you, but first I had you put the extra sheets down to protect the bed, and your damage deposit, from... eh... let's say...from the scent of our little *adventure* tonight." Although René was trying to put them all at ease, no one was smiling. Then they started asking him rapid-fire questions, all at the same time.

"Guys, please, relax" the Frenchman continued as he pulled his shoes off and started to get undressed. "Let Justin sleep as he is for now—he's probably not going to wake up anytime soon—and give me a few minutes to take a hot shower and change into clean clothes. Then, over some wine, I will tell you everything."

# CHAPTER SEVENTY-EIGHTY

The sound of air loudly rushing over and into his ears was his first clue that he was once again in Dreamland. He could feel his hair whipping about his face and head. The cool damp of the thick fog felt reassuringly familiar and almost welcoming.

Justin wanted to take a look and see who was at the wheel of the old convertible this time, but no matter how hard he tried, he couldn't get his eyes to open against the strength and power of the rushing wind.

A deep-seated anxiety that was totally alien to this recurrent dream crept into his consciousness and nearly overwhelmed him, but it quickly passed as he became aware of a distinct and highly recognizable scent wafting through the air. It smelled like...like...he took another deep breath, and then he knew...it smelled like a cigarette...like a *Gitane!*

His eyes opened quickly and he saw that he was, indeed, on the misty mountain road heading down to the coast highway, somewhere on the other side of this dangerous bank of dense fog.

And everything else seemed as it normally did in his familiar dream: there were nebulous, unidentifiable objects floating weightlessly in the gauzy distance, and the thick haze that surrounded him was once again blocking out most of the light from the sun he could sense was hovering just above his cloudy universe.

From his position in the back, he looked first to the driver's seat and then to the front passenger's, expecting to see the faces of the man with the black hair and the intelligent blue eyes, and the warm, comforting woman who always accompanied him on their journey into misfortune. But they weren't there.

Instead, at the wheel of the old convertible, he found a defensive lineman-sized nun with a funny little moustache, carefully driving the car down the steep mountain road. She looked around and gave a him little wave and a smile.

Her passenger was an old, scary-looking nun with a deeply wrinkled, severe face. But when she turned to look at him and smile, her watery grey eyes told Justin that her soul was full of only goodness and love, and that he had nothing to fear. She reached out a spotted, blue-veined hand and took his in hers.

"Justin, I have a message for you," the old nun said to him in French. Miraculously, he understood every word, but the noise from the wind was almost overpowering, and he had to struggle to hear her.

"A message? I don't understand ," he replied, also in French. His accent was perfect!

"Yes. A message from your Aunt Annette. She says that she had always intended to tell you when the time was right," the old Sister went on, "but, well, for her, the time was never right."

"Please tell, me," he pleaded, "what's her message?" He tried to lean forward to catch every word against the roaring wind, but as always in his foggy dream, he was somehow restrained and could hardly move.

"It's a very simple one. First, she loves and misses you very much, but I am sure you already knew that. But here's something you don't know—once you return home, you must look on the top of her closet and find a large box. Inside it, you will find the answers to all of the questions you have been asking your whole life, the questions your aunt could never bring herself to discuss. She says she is sorry, but it was too painful for her. Once you learn what is inside," the old nun continued, as her voice became fainter and more distant, "you will be free and will never travel down this mountain road again." She turned away and the old convertible came sharply around the final curve, the last twisting turn that always signaled the calamitous conclusion of his disastrous dream.

He was totally prepared for what always came next, but this time, there was no large tanker truck blocking the roadway, and the man in uniform, instead of waving his arms in warning, was standing on the road's narrow shoulder and directing them past a row of glowing red emergency flares.

When Justin realized the truck must have already been towed away and there would be no violent crash through the guardrail or headlong plunge into the abyss, the heavy fog suddenly evaporated, and the sun was shining directly overhead from a cloudless, deep blue sky. It was unbelievable.

He twisted his body around and looked back at the man in uniform, who was still directing traffic around the flares. Justin had never seen him this clearly before, and he noticed he was silver-haired and slim, and that he looked oddly familiar.

When their eyes met, the man gave Justin an enigmatic smile and a two-fingered, military-like salute. Then, he stubbed out his Gitane on the pavement and simply disappeared into the ether.

# CHAPTER SEVENTY-NINE

When the magic carpet he'd been flying on finally touched down and he gradually regained consciousness, Justin found himself lying on his back and thinking he had died and gone to hell.

He tried to sit up, but the throbbing in his temples and the buzzing in his brain quickly forced him back down onto his pillow, and both of his hands reflexively shot up to his pounding head as he tried to massage away the gnawing pain and droning discomfort. Hmmm…that wasn't working. Not by a long shot.

He listened for the sounds of his buddies snoring their brains out or moving about outside or in the kitchen, but strangely, he heard… nothing. Slowly opening his nearly glued shut eyes, he saw that the lace curtains had been pulled all the way back and the patio doors thrown open wide. Brilliant yellow-gold sunshine was streaming into his room, but that shed no light on the question of how he had gotten back to the house and wound up in his bed. He simply couldn't remember.

Squinting and peering around his sun-drenched quarters was even more painful, and as he turned away, he came face to face with an open box of greasy, half-eaten "Kentucky" chicken fingers, the sight and smell of which immediately caused him to hurl himself out of bed and into the bathroom. He made it to the toilet just in time, and after *that* room stopped spinning, he was able to throw some cold water on his face and look at himself in the mirror.

As his blurry image came into focus, the first alarming thing he noticed was that he was wearing what looked like a white lab coat over an ill-fitting jumpsuit. He'd never seen either garment before and had no recollection of changing into them. He couldn't remember!

The second and even more alarming thing he noticed was that he smelled like a nauseating combination of vomit, electrical smoke, and burnt bacon, and that sent him back over the toilet for a second, gut-wrenching round of gagging and heaving that left him spinning and spent on the cold bathroom floor.

After picking himself up and catching his breath, he peeled off the gross-smelling clothing and got himself into the shower for a nice long soak. When he emerged, clean and almost sober, he threw on his board shorts and a T-shirt and stumbled out onto the pool deck.

There he was surprised to find Monsieur René, sitting at the umbrella-shaded table in his neon-green speedos, reading a newspaper, drinking coffee and, *naturellement,* smoking up a storm.

"Allo, Joosteen," he said in bright greeting. "So good to have you back in the world of the living. I heard you in the bathroom, so I made some fresh coffee for us."

As Justin wandered over, René put his paper down and poured them each a cup.

"How long have I been asleep?" Justin asked as he yawned and stretched. "Where are the guys...and do you know how I wound up in those disgusting-smelling clothes?"

"Oh, my friend, you have so many questions today," René responded with a smile as he checked his watch. "You have been out for about eleven hours, and the guys have all gone to day three of the Vin Expo. Now, I have a little question for you; do you remember anything at all about last night?"

"Sure! What do you mean?" he answered quickly, and then, "of course, I remember... I..." His voice trailed off as he looked skyward and did his best to recall the elegant, extravagant Célébration de Vin last night at Château La Tour Noir, and although he didn't draw a complete blank, he realized that after a certain point, it was as if someone had hit the 'erase' button on the videotape of his memory. After sitting down with the guys for dinner, there was nothing but static and white noise.

"Hmm, that's what I thought." René picked up his newspaper and laid it in front of Justin.

There, on the front page of the *Aquitane Presse* were two large side-by side full-color photos, one of Guy DeBussey and one of the wrinkled old nun Justin thought he recognized from the protest outside of the dinner they'd attended a few nights back. René explained it to him, but the meaning of the headline was perfectly clear: *Tragedy, Death and Scandal in St. Émilion!*

Checking his watch again, he motioned for Justin to follow him inside the house, and he flipped the TV on just in time to catch the beginning of the local midday newscast. As René once again translated, Justin watched as the hectic scene from last night played out.

There were shots of police cars with their blue lights flashing, video of EMS crews rolling two blanket-covered gurneys out and into waiting ambulances, and multiple interviews with stunned party-goers, many of whom said they would never be able to forget this incredible night and its now infamous ending.

Richard Fox was also interviewed and expressed his deep sorrow at the startling loss of his partner and friend, Guy DeBussey. They would be suspending all company activities for the remainder of the week, and he offered his apologies to all of the guests that had their gala evening ruined by the terrible turn of events.

But by far, for Justin, the most mind-blowing exchange was with DeBussey's bereaved widow, Lala. He watched with detached amazement and listened as she gave her tortured, sobbing account of what had happened in the winery, and René translated her choked, twisted fairy tale—the story that all, including the police inspectors, would come to regard as gospel truth:

*I tell you, the old Sister appeared like an angel and saved our lives...Bruno and I...we wanted to have our own private Célébration together, but Guy...I think he suspected something for a long time....he must have followed us...* She broke down and sobbed as the flashbulbs popped all around and the reporters tastelessly shouted their questions.

*He had some kind of a metal stick, and he used it to smash my poor Bruno in the leg...he couldn't fight back...I thought I was next...and then...then...I don't know how she got into the party, but it is well-known what Guy did to her and the poor children at the orphanage...* Lala again paused for another round of tears...*she said it was God's judgment and then there was a flash and smoke...no...I can't ..no more please...*

After René switched off the report, Justin contemplatively stroked his chin and gently shook his head. On an almost subconscious level, he knew something didn't add up, but he didn't understand *what* it was and *why* he knew it.

"Now, my friend," the Frenchman began, "and this must never leave this room, I will tell you what *really* happened."

# CHAPTER EIGHTY

Brad thought that the mood would be somber and subdued for day three of the Vin Expo, but had been wrong. He had driven the guys, minus Justin, to the Exposition Parc and arrived at Hall Two along with thousands of other attendees, all exuberant and ready for another long, difficult day of tastings, seminars, and other assorted forms of hardship and cruelty.

It was definitely business as usual, and no one seemed to be talking about the deadly events at last night's Celébration de Vin or mourning the untimely demise of one Monsieur Guy DeBussey—although a makeshift tribute had been quickly erected in front of the closed and shuttered Fox/DeBussey pavilion. One thoughtful soul had actually left a single flower—such was the outpouring of love and respect for the man.

Posted at the main entrances to Hall One, there were hastily made "In Memoriam" signs featuring DeBussey's mug shot-like picture and the years of his birth and death, as well as stacks of a one-page, multi-language bulletin outlining the details of his stature in the business, his various accomplishments, and his tragic end during the Celébration de Vin.

Not many appeared to be paying attention to the posters or the flyers, but each of the guys took a copy to familiarize themselves with the information that had been made public about the unbelievable situation.

When they arrived at the Cosmo display, Destiny was just finishing a presentation to a small group of tasters at one of the hi-top tables, and she immediately came over to the pavilion's entrance to greet them.

"So, were you guys still at the party when the police arrived?" she said excitedly, as she held up her copy of the Guy DeBussey bulletin. "What a terrible, totally insane thing to happen at such an elegant affair, especially considering you and Justin were all there. Where is he by the way…off getting coffee or something?"

"The last time we saw Justin, he was lying in bed and out like a light," Brad said playfully. René had told him that the most effective misinformation or outright deception usually came wrapped in a partial truth, and Brad was certainly being truthful about Justin's condition this morning.

"Is he all right?" she asked, with a look of concern clouding her beautiful features.

Brad then did his best to stick to the storyline they had all promised René they would follow, and he recounted the partially fabricated sequence of events to Destiny and Cosmo, who had just joined them.

No, they had already left the party by the time the crime had been discovered, and they had been surprised and stunned when they'd heard about it this morning; yes, it had been a phenomenal event with all sorts of famous, rich, and beautiful people; the food was extravagant and plentiful, and the line-up for the pre-dinner tasting was beyond belief; they'd all had a wonderful time, especially Justin, but he wound up having far too much wine, far too much food, and way too much fun; at dinner they could all see that he was getting really hammered; when he'd stumbled off to the restroom just before dessert and didn't return for quite a while, Brad went and found him, sick in one of the stalls; at that point, they'd decided to leave the party and get him taken care of.

There were no good-byes or farewells to Lala or anyone else, just a quiet exit and a trip back to St. Quentin de Baron with Justin fast asleep in the front seat. They'd carried him into bed and checked in on him throughout the night, and this morning, he was so groggy they'd decided to leave him at the house to totally recuperate.

"We're sure he'll be up and around long before we get back to the house," Mike added with a smile and nods of assent from Steve and Frank.

Brad tried to keep it light and his description of events as matter-of-fact as possible, and by the end of his narrative, both Cosmo and Destiny were laughing and shaking their heads at the mischievous, out of control antics of Justin James, Babe in the Woods.

After they made plans to meet again at the Cosmo pavilion at the end of the Vin Expo tomorrow afternoon, to have one last tasting and then dinner out together in Bordeaux City, the guys headed towards their last scheduled seminar at the opposite end of Hall One; Vega Sicilia Unico, a Retrospective.

Brad was especially glad to have gotten the discussion behind them, and he hoped his hung over friend wouldn't feel as uncomfortable stretching and bending the truth to Destiny and Cosmo as he just had.

But like René had said over a few bottles of wine very late last night, *brothers in arms take care of their own.* Juice Brothers, too.

# CHAPTER EIGHTY-ONE

*Somewhere over the Atlantic*

He had tried, but he just couldn't sleep, so Justin reached for the control panel and raised the fully reclined flat bed of his business class slumber-seat to an upright position. But looking out the window at the Atlantic far below was no different than lying down and closing his eyes, and no matter what he did, his mind kept quickly flashing over every last unsettling detail of the past forty-eight hours and the end of his unforgettable journey to France and the Vin Expo.

Of course, he *had* forgotten some of the most noteworthy aspects of his trip, and now he found he was almost sorry that Monsieur René had robbed him of his ignorance and filled him in on all of the dirty details. Well, like the man said, he had a right to know.

René had started by telling Justin that, for their mutual protection, he had sworn the guys to secrecy, and that no matter what, they must all sing the same song and have the same story about the end of their night at the Célébration de Vin.

Then Justin had listened in disbelief as René had revealed the events of Tuesday evening and what had nearly happened to him: why they had actually been invited to the party in the first place; how Justin had been targeted and unknowingly involved in a conspiracy by Lala and Bruno—the deceased's right hand man—to murder Guy DeBussey; the lies, the deceit, the drugs, and the contrived scenario to lure both Justin and DeBussey into the winery, commit the crime, and pin the killing of the jealous husband on the unsuspecting American.

Of course, after Justin learned the truth, all of Lala's flirting, over-the-top attention and affection made perfect sense. She was quite the actress, and it had totally pissed him off. Even here at 35,000 feet, as he thought about what might have been, his stomach started to once again churn with uneasiness.

He still had difficulty believing sweet Lala Chang, his adorable high school friend and French language drill partner, could conceive of such a dark, wicked plan or be so cavalier in her willingness to murder her husband or cast his own life aside like an empty, used-up bottle of Billecart-Salmon Brut Rosé But she had!

René then told Justin how the guys had kept interrupting him and asking him how he knew this, or how he knew that, and finally, what the hell was he actually doing inside the winery at Château La Tour Noir on that particular night, dressed like a ninja?

His answer to them had been a long, studied silence, and he let each of them draw their own conclusions about his presence and intentions that night. A cover story and timeline was then agreed to, one that would be told by all to any interested parties.

"Of course," he'd told them, in closing. "I was *never* there... and we *never* had this conversation."

And then, René relayed to Justin all of the details he'd withheld from the others— why he was personally there that night and how he had prevented Bruno from putting out Justin's lights for good; how after he'd passed out from the effects of the drugs and the wine, Lala had stripped him down and waited for her accomplice to do his part and bring the other sheep in for slaughter; and finally, after the unforeseen intervention of the poor old nun, how he'd gotten Justin dressed in whatever was available, scooped him up, and gotten him the hell out of there.

Justin could still feel the cold sweat that had broken out all over his body after René had finished his story, but as the Air France Air Bus A330 continued farther on its westward voyage, he found himself able to slowly let go of the anxiety he'd felt ever since that unnerving moment of revelation.

Instead, he focused his thoughts on the last day of his remarkable trip and his final evening in France with Destiny, the brightest spot and highest point in his entire life. She was a truly amazing gift, and he felt so lucky and blessed on so many different levels to have her in his life…he'd just have to work around his feelings of guilt over the fact that he would have to continue to twist the truth every time there was talk of that "notorious night." But, somehow, he'd learn to deal with it. He would keep Monsieur's René Gascogne's dark secret, and his own, safely under lock and key.

After all, that's what a brother did. Especially a Juice Brother.

# EPILOGUE

In the weeks that followed his return to Orlando, Justin happily got back into the familiar rhythm of his resident math-wiz job at FedEx but the rest of his formerly boring, almost empty existence had radically changed forever.

It seemed that he and Destiny were now joined at the hip and everything they did, they did together. She had been traveling on business here and there, and there had been one boy's night at the Twisted Cork since their return, but those were the only evenings Justin had spent without his significant other by his side.

That night at the Cork with the boys, Barry Love had taken him aside to let him know that René, his old brother-in-arms, had taken him into his confidence and shared their secret with him. "I told you he was one bad-ass dude!" was the last thing that Barry or anyone else had to say on the subject of their adventure at the Célébration de Vin.

Cosmo Koulouris had come to town twice, and each time had insisted the young couple join him for dinner as his expense—he wouldn't take no for an answer! He spent most of their time together talking wine and praising what he called Justin's 'Golden Palate.' He was funny, friendly, and even fatherly, and Justin was looking forward to spending more time with him and getting to know him better.

Monsieur René had emailed to let everyone know that he would be staying in France for the foreseeable future, and Phyllis Braunstein would look after his Orlando high-fashion women's shop during his extended absence. Separately, he had also emailed Justin a link to the online English version of the

*Aquitaine Presse* and encouraged him to watch for "interesting developments."

He'd checked every day, and in mid-August, Justin was interested to find a surprising front page story about the fallout from Guy DeBussey's tragic death earlier in the summer.

The article stated that his widow, Lala Chang DeBussey, had made arrangements to sell off all of his holdings throughout France, with his company, Beverage DeBussey, being split up and deals worked out to return some of its parts to their former owners at the same bargain-basement selling prices the dead mogul had forced the former owners to accept.

Most notable among these transactions was the sale of the flagship property, Château La Tour Noir, back to Madame Florence Gascogne, for the grand sum of One Euro. *Oh, that René,* Justin had thought, *I knew he hadn't told me everything!*

A day later, he received one last email link, this time to a story about an orphanage in St. Émilion called Our Lady of Mercy. There in the photo were Lala and Bruno, standing amid a group of smiling nuns and shaking hands with a very large Sister sporting a patchy little moustache. The caption read:

*Sister Rafaela accepts a generous donation of land and money from Lala DeBussey.*

The article went on to say Lala had signed over ownership of the land and presented a check for 150,000 Euros to get started on the rebuilding of a new, improved orphanage on its former site. Justin again briefly wondered just what René *hadn't* told him, but it didn't matter. He didn't want or need to know.

Toward the end of the summer, Justin decided to officially move out of his tiny room and into Aunt Annette's much larger space. Destiny helped him pick out a stylish new bedroom set, and he donated the old furniture to a local Catholic charity.

The day they came to collect the donation, the older nun riding along with the driver was very friendly, and she warmly thanked Justin for his generosity. As soon as they drove away and Justin turned back towards the house, he was suddenly struck by a thought that had been hovering at the edge of his memory, shrouded in grey mist like an object obscured by a dense fog. He momentarily stopped in his tracks when he remembered exactly what he had nearly forgotten and then rushed into his new bedroom at full speed and tore open the closet door. There on the top shelf was an old Robert Mondavi Vineyards box, and Justin carefully brought it down and placed it on the floor.

Inside, lying on top of the stack of dusty papers, photo albums, and framed plaques were a few old, frayed and yellowed newspaper clippings preserved in a clear plastic folder. Justin opened the folder and picked up the largest one. The headline made his heart stop:

*Local couple killed in mountainside crash. Toddler survives.*

He dropped the faded newsprint on the floor as he was overcome by a wave of emotion that left him with a feeling of swirling, hollow angst in the pit of his stomach and a tight, air-constricting sensation in his throat.

Justin removed the two smaller clippings from the folder and immediately understood that he was about to get the answers to the questions he'd been asking his whole life— answers his beloved aunt would never and, for some reason, could never give him. He had always trusted her advice— to look only to the future and never delve into the past. But that was over. Right now.

The clippings were a pair of obituaries and the faces in the grainy black and white photographs were shockingly and instantly familiar. Without a doubt, this was the young couple that usually occupied the front seat of the doomed convertible in his disastrous, recurrent dream. As he sank slowly down to the floor, Justin picked up the news report and continued to read:

*California Highway Patrol officers reported that Palo Alto residents, Jason and Alicia James, were killed in a tragic accident on a fogged-in mountain road just off of State Road 84 near San Gregorio late Sunday afternoon. Miraculously, their two-year-old son, Justin, survived the crash unharmed.*

*Witnesses said visibility was exceptionally poor, and as their car came around a sharp bend, it swerved to avoid an overturned tanker truck blocking the road, broke through a guardrail, and plunged into the adjacent ravine. Rescuers pronounced the couple dead at the scene. The child was found unharmed in the back in his car seat.*

Justin placed the old article back into the clear folder and then looked over each of the smaller clippings. He gently touched the images of his parents' faces as he read their obituaries and could only assume that Aunt Annette had written them.

His mother, a pleasant looking young woman of twenty-eight, had been a professor of advanced mathematics at Stanford University at the time of her death and had recently completed her PHD studies. *Well,* Justin thought pensively, *no huge surprise there...I guess I've always been my mother's son.* It felt comforting. It felt good.

But when he read about his father, who in his obit photo looked very much like Justin's own mirror image, chills ran from the bottom of his soul to the tips of his fingers and toes.

Jason James, director of wine and head sommelier at the notable *La Folie* restaurant in San Francisco, had been the youngest person ever to receive the title of 'Master Sommelier' and the accompanying diploma from the Court of Master Sommeliers!

Justin's heart took off like a rocket. He stared blankly into space for a few moments, struggling to catch his breath. A tingly, cold sweat broke out on his skin, and when he recovered from the shock and wiped the sheen from his forehead and face, he carefully sorted through the contents of the box and gingerly removed what looked like a cheesy old bowling or sports trophy. But it wasn't. When he dusted it off, the meaning and importance of what he held in his hands became dramatically clear.

Tears welled in his eyes as he held the golden goblet statue and read its inscription: *Presented to Jason James, Golden Palate Par Excellence.*

And for the first time in his life, Justin James knew exactly who he was—he was his father's son! He couldn't wait to tell Destiny and his Juice Brothers what he planned to do next.

# AUTHOR BIO

First-time author, full-time wine enthusiast, and cancer survivor Howard K is a composer and producer of music for television, film and advertising.

He lives with his wife and family in the Tampa Bay, Florida area.

You can find Howard at:

WEBSITE
www.dialmformerlot.com

EMAIL
HowardKbooks@gmail.com

DIAL M FOR MERLOT ON FACEBOOK
https://www.facebook.com/#!/dialmformerlot